Brexit Demise of Great Britain

Rulers of One of the World's Great Powers Go Haywire

Ernie Hasler

authorHOUSE®

AuthorHouse™ UK
1663 Liberty Drive
Bloomington, IN 47403 USA
www.authorhouse.co.uk
Phone: 0800.197.4150

Scripture taken from the New King James Version®. Copyright © 1982 by Thomas Nelson. Used by permission. All rights reserved.

Published by AuthorHouse 11/30/2018

ISBN: 978-1-7283-8055-1 (sc)
ISBN: 978-1-7283-8054-4 (e)

Library of Congress Control Number: 2018913309

I wish to thank all my family members for their generous love and support, which seems to me to have been largely one-way. I now realise I was selfish in the extreme.

Thanks to the skilled tradesmen who patiently taught me their skills and gave me a keen sense of solidarity with working people everywhere.

To all those footballers who gave me so much enjoyment, and my belated apologies for being a clumsy spoiler, who only had the skills to get in the way, but I enjoyed playing.

Emmaus Glasgow and all the good people I have met there.

Thanks to my dear friends, who put up with my idiosyncratic ideas and ways on my search for Bible truth, resulting in this book.

I know many of you will recognise this well-known portion of scripture. Oh, how much hidden meaning it contains.

Psalm 118 verses 20 to 24 Amplified Translation (AMP)

This is the gate of the Lord;
The righteous will enter through it.

I will give thanks to You, for You have heard and answered me;
And You have become my salvation [my Rescuer, my Saviour].

The stone which the builders rejected
Has become the chief corner stone.

This is from the Lord and is His doing;
It is marvellous in our eyes.

This [day in which God has saved me] is the day which the Lord has made; Let us rejoice and be glad in it.

Table of Contents

Introduction

Imagine an all-powerful group that knows no national boundaries and has set itself above the laws of most countries. It endeavors to control every aspect of politics, religion, military, police, energy, food, water, commerce, industry, banking, insurance, mining, and the underworld. It's a group answerable to only its own members.

It is the revered capitalist system based on greed and competition where ruthless self-interest is the central criteria.

The Roman Gladiatorial Games were a costly show by a government who wanted to keep the idle masses entertained because they knew that a large group of poor people was a major threat to their empire. Therefore, the Romans enjoyed many different forms of entertainment, most of which were free. If you think carefully, could all the above possibly describe the world's political and religious order today, masked and obscured by popular diversions such as the religion, sport, media, art and entertainment. In the manipulation of the masses. "There is nothing new under the sun". A phrase adapted from the Book of Ecclesiastes;

You need to think about your own experiences as you read this book. Take your dark glasses off and read on … if you dare!

Chapter One

Total and Humiliating Failure

Felicity and Kelly, wearing backpacks with essential provisions and waterproof clothing, rushed out of the Faslane Peace Camp and boarded the bus going into Helensburgh, Scotland. After hiding in bushes on the periphery of the camp, they had left their departure to the last minute to try to avoid the attention of the Ministry of Defence (MOD) security police.

They were pretty sure they had not been observed, at least by any means obvious to them, and they relaxed a little. With a cynical laugh while pushing her long red hair back from her face, Kelly said, "Ministry of Defence police. How absurd is that description when they are guarding offensive, illegal weapons of mass destruction?"

Felicity nodded, frowned with an appropriately serious face, and added, "It's all part of the great deception. The PR department of the war machine employs the best talent from our universities and confuses and controls the voters with deliberately chosen descriptions to cause desired misperceptions in their thinking about big moral issues."

Kelly laughed loudly. "Wow, that was a mouthful! Oh, this is our stop."

The women nervously lingered in a café until 4.30, looked out the window facing the Firth of Clyde, and were silent in their own unspoken thoughts and fears. Felicity, who continually checked her watch, suddenly said, "It is time." The women quickly donned their waterproof clothing and backpacks, left the café, crossed the road, and stood near the entrance to the big seafront car park.

Just before five o'clock, a large white van slowly turned into the car park. Felicity waved to the driver. "Good. It's Jacques." The van stopped beside them, and the women divested themselves of their backpacks and waterproof outer clothing, climbed into the cab, and closed the door.

The driver nervously looked left, right, left, and right again. He stalled the engine as he let out the clutch too quickly with too few engine revolutions. He stammered, "S'excuser, s'excuser. I mean sorry." He slowly turned the van back into in the car park, approached the exit again, and turned left onto the main road. "I was trying not to be noticed, but this is a petrol engine with less torque than a diesel. So the opposite happened."

Felicity replied a little harshly, displaying her tension. "Yes, Jacques, I know". She paused then added, "I know you were trying your best, but don't dwell on it. Just concentrate on the task ahead."

They descended into silence as they approached the Faslane nuclear submarine base. Felicity gave each of them a piece of very thin black gauze and said, "Drape this over your head to cover your face." They could easily see through the gauze, but it prevented the security cameras from seeing their features. They drove past the peace camp without glancing at it. Soon they were past the military establishment and approaching the town of Garelochhead.

Felicity asked, "Jacques, do you think anyone is following us?"

He replied, "Non."

Felicity instructed, "Turn off the road and park over there." They quietly watched the road, the sky, and the loch for about fifteen minutes until Felicity was satisfied no one was following.

Jacques turned onto the road again. They drove through Garelochhead and round the top of the sea loch. Then they drove down the Rosneath Road on the other side of the loch.

When they were opposite and beyond the base, Kelly pointed and exclaimed, "Over there, where the shore is shielded by trees."

Jacques stopped the van. He helped the women unload the tandem sea kayak and hide it in bushes near the shore. He quickly returned to the van, reversed it, and drove back the way he came.

Working silently, Felicity and Kelly erected the tiny, two-person tent in the middle of a big, hollow rhododendron bush, which completely hid the tent. They immediately crawled inside, zipped up the tent, and lay quietly side by side.

After sharing some sandwiches, Felicity passed Kelly a bottle of water and motioned to her to drink. Kelly drank about half its contents and passed the bottle back to Felicity, who finished it. They kept strict silence to avoid being heard by some passer-by. Each woman's mind raced as she imagined and visualised the possible encounter to come.

Kelly was wakened by Felicity, who held up her luminous watch, indicating 2.30 a.m. She whispered, "Get up, have a pee, and dress in the waterproofs. Don't forget the life jacket. Oh, and watch out for nettles. You don't want to crouch down with your bare fanny on top of a stingy nettle."

Kelly burst into giggles as she visualised the unexpected scenario.

After unzipping the tent, they crawled out and relieved their bladders. They checked each other to ensure they were properly dressed in the waterproofs and life jackets. Then with hearts beating quickly, they found the tandem sea kayak and quietly placed it in the water.

A sea mist had engulfed the loch with its wet drizzle, and coupled with the darkness of the night, it was impossible to see more than about twenty metres. They carefully climbed into the two cockpits and pushed themselves away from the shore. They slowly paddled into the seemingly impenetrable darkness, but the sounds coming over the water warned them they were not alone.

Kelly's heart beat so loudly that she thought the police patrols in their boats must surely hear it. They could hear boat engines, sometimes nearby and sometimes faintly in the distance. In the darkness and sea mist, their minds amplified every sound, increasing their fear.

Suddenly there was a very noisy helicopter above them. Then there was the blinding glare of searchlights. The noise of the helicopter became unbearable. The great black hull of a submarine towered high above them. There was a hard jolt as the kayak was bumped hard and pushed sideways through the water as a high-speed police patrol boat forced it away from submarine.

The kayak capsized with the force of the impact, and the women found themselves violently ejected into the freezing water. In the darkness, it was utter confusion and panic as they thrashed about, trying to keep afloat and stay together as they were engulfed by the strong displacement currents surrounding the huge vessel. They soon became aware of rubber-suited divers in the water beside them, and they were firmly forced to the side of the big MOD police patrol boat, where they were both roughly hauled aboard.

The police patrol boat had stopped its engines. There was now no sign of the submarine, which had silently disappeared into the sea mist and darkness.

After being stripped naked by two of the divers to ensure they were not carrying weapons, they suffered an invasive search by a female MOD police officer in full view of the crowded central cabin. The police kept Kelly and Felicity separated as far as possible in the small cabin.

The journey to the Faslane base was a blur of misery.

At the base's MOD police detention centre, they were made to strip again and shower. Wearing only big, damp bath towels precariously wrapped around them, the women were taken to separate rooms and intensively interrogated by MOD police officers for about ten hours. The interrogation techniques were a colossal mental, physical, and emotional ordeal.

When they thought they couldn't take anymore, Kelly and Felicity were suddenly reunited and told to dress in their still-damp clothing. They were taken to the main gate and roughly put out on to the road.

Felicity tried to comfort the shivering and sobbing Kelly by saying, "I should have told you about the strip search. I remember how bad I felt the first time it happened to me."

Kelly stayed at the camp for two more days in a state of shock, regretting how she had ended up in this situation. Eventually, Kelly felt a little bit better and announced she wanted to go home.

Felicity accompanied her to the bus stop and whispered as Kelly was about to board the bus, "Thank you, Kelly. You were great. It was a good try, and we will do it better next time." She hugged Kelly tightly and then let her board the bus, handing up her rucksack.

The bus drove away before Kelly could process the implications of Felicity's words and exclaim, "What do you mean, next time?" But her words were lost in the noise of the accelerating bus engine.

Chapter Two

Debating Club

As she travelled home, Kelly thought about how she'd ended up in this extreme situation. At the beginning of the fourth year at high school, Kelly and Douglas, her boyfriend, were made school prefects. They joined the school debating club and spent many enjoyable sessions expressing their opinions on a vast range of topics.

By the end of the fifth year, Kelly seemed to return to the debate of nuclear arms more often than other topics. Her viewpoint started from concerns about nuclear contamination and its possible effects on the procreation of all life species. Douglas began to support her arguments in these hotly contested events by arguing from a Christian perspective, repeatedly saying, "If we are truly a Christian country, why do we deny our God by putting our faith in the destructive force of a nuclear missile as if to confirm, 'The glory of God has departed us'?"

By the end of the sixth year at school, Kelly found herself entered in an international speaking competition promoting the position that nuclear arms were morally and legally wrong. She got a lot of help from the Scottish Campaign for Nuclear Disarmament, particularly on the international legal position, which provided the central core of her argument.

She rehearsed her argument, repeatedly saying, "Over thirty years ago, the nuclear weapon states undertook to disarm all their nuclear weapons in the Nuclear Non-Proliferation Treaty."

She was confident in her argument, but she narrowly lost the judgement, and so she comforted herself with the view that the result was heavily influenced by the largely male audience and their embedded caveman perceptions of conflict resolution.

After getting over the disappointment of losing the debate, she said to Douglas, "I would like to spend some time at the Faslane Peace Camp."

He answered, "Are you serious?"

"Yes. I want to go there to discuss and listen to the peace campaigners. You know that I would like to eventually specialise in international law, and there is so much to discuss about nuclear weapons and international law, but the peace camp is the only place where you can hear the truth."

By the end of the fifth year at school, both Kelly and Douglas had accumulated the five A grades necessary, and in the sixth year they had also supplemented these with advanced highers in arts and social sciences and passed the National Admission Test for Law. They were both offered places at Glasgow University's Faculty of Law, Business, and Social Sciences, studying for a law honours degree.

Kelly's father already suffered the symptoms of miner's disease when he lost his job with the closure of Polmaise Colliery. He did not qualify for the prescribed industrial disease compensation because regardless of his chronic individual symptoms, the authorities had imposed a working time, and he did not have the twenty years' qualifying exposure required.

However, through the National Union of Mineworkers, he applied for, and was granted, a place in a charity-run care home for miners with advanced respiratory diseases.

Although they were only nineteen years of age and about to become full-time students, Kelly and Douglas decided to get married. They argued that two could live cheaper than one, and two in a bed do not need to have the heating on.

Kelly asked Douglas, "Are you worried that my strong commitment to nuclear disarmament might change the outcome of our lives? Instead of nice, comfortable careers as lawyers, we might end up on the outside."

Douglas was in a light-hearted mood and replied with a big smile, "I don't mind, Kelly, as long as I am sharing your bed with you."

Kelly responded with a worried frown and an involuntary shiver as she thought about Faslane and its sinister black submarines, which Douglas didn't even notice as he pushed her towards the bedroom.

Despite expectations from family members about traditional church weddings, they quickly married using an ancient Scottish wedding ceremony with minimum formalities and expenses over a blacksmith's anvil, conducted by their local blacksmith friend.

After their honeymoon, when Kelly's father was settled in the care home, he said to them both, "I will not be coming out of here until they take me out in a coffin. I want you to sell my house and use the money as a fund to get you both through university." Although they both protested, he was adamant. "Seeing you two get off to a good start is my way of passing on the baton in the race of life. You won't deny me that last pleasure."

Before starting the first university semester, Kelly made her second visit to the Faslane Peace Camp outside the HM Naval Base Clyde, at Faslane on the Gareloch, a River Clyde estuary sea loch. It was some twenty-five miles northwest of Glasgow, which was home to the United Kingdom's strategic nuclear deterrent and the headquarters of the Royal Navy in Scotland.

As she waited for Felicity, a peace camper who had arranged to meet her at the entrance of the peace camp, a MOD Land Rover vehicle slowly drove by.

Too late, Kelly realised that the passenger was pointing a camera at her. She shivered from a sense of evil that pervaded the dark, deep sea loch, with its grey naval installations surrounded by a high fence and rings of razor wire installed along the top.

Felicity laughed as she greeted Kelly with a big hug. "I hope you got over the shock of the last visit, when there was no time to familiarise you with the camp. I remember how you'd just arrived in time to go on the mission."

Kelly nodded and said quietly, "Yes, I don't think I will ever forget."

"This time let me explain property. Faslane Peace Camp has been outside the submarine base since June 1982. The camp's primary purpose is to oppose nuclear weapons, and its residents live in an alternative way to the society that produced such evil weapons of indiscriminate destruction."

As they entered the camp, Kelly observed that it was a colourful but well-weathered collection of caravans, a bus, a tepee, a bender, a tree house, and various sheds and self-built structures.

Felicity explained, "It is deliberately visible to all traffic coming towards the base from the direction of Helensburgh, and it is much resented by many of the rich, big-house owners in the area. The camp is under surveillance twenty-four hours a day by the Ministry of Defence police. They drive past the camp to the bus stop at the south end of the camp, where they turn around and go back towards the base again."

Kelly considered the information she had been given and then said, "The Ministry of Defence police drove past me, taking my photograph. Should I worry about that?"

Felicity replied with a laugh, "Not unless you want a government job. The pigs drive past every fifteen minutes and try to identify all visitors. All cars that park at the camp get checked out via their registration plates, and they are given an identification number that is held on the national intelligence database. Many of the workers at the base don't morally agree with nuclear weapons. Although they are uneasy about it, they justify their situation with their need for jobs to pay mortgages and support families. But unlike me, they are not happy. Regarding worrying about it, the meaning of my name, Felicity, is 'happy'. My motto is, 'Do what is right, and sleep at night.'"

Felicity continued, "However, living at the peace camp is not a holiday. Every dry day, lots of wood needs to be chopped. Most of the caravans and other dwellings are minimally heated with wood-burning stoves, so every day the campers must get some more fallen wood from the forests. There is always cooking, tidying, washing up, sweeping, cleaning, and more to be done. In wet weather, there is mud everywhere, particularly in winter—it being Scotland with all that rain.

"Shopping for typically a dozen people must be done every day. The peace campers are continually engaged in maintenance and get on with what needs doing: fixing roofs, gardening, painting caravans inside and out, raking leaves for the compost loo, changing the barrel in the compost loos.

"Then there are the strategic activities, making banners, planning actions, canoeing the Gareloch to see which submarines are in the base camp, writing letters to the local newspaper, keeping the mailing list up to date, replying to letters people send us, and keeping the food kitty.

"Every once in a while, a nuclear-warhead-carrying convoy is spotted heading to Scotland. Often someone tracks the convoy to see which route and how long it's taking, and can then we can also let the ambushers know when to expect it.

"The peace campers rush around phoning people on their convoy stop list, arranging a time and a place to ambush the convoy, crawl under it or climb onto it, and do what we can to disrupt their evil intentions. In fact, we have a canoe expedition in the early hours of Wednesday morning. We have heard on the jungle drums that a submarine is preparing to sneak out."

Kelly asked, "Can I take part again?"

Felicity replied, "That's great. I was hoping you would come back. We have a tandem sea kayak being delivered to a point opposite the base on the other side of the loch on Tuesday evening. We will meet the van in Helensburgh at 5 p.m., and the driver will deliver us to some woods on the edge of the loch opposite the base. We will take a small tent and lay up until about three o'clock in the morning, when the submarine is due to leave. Then we will launch the kayak and try to intercept the evil monster."

Kelly shuddered as she thought, *how did I get involved in this big, massive thing? What am I doing?* She couldn't think of how better to describe such an overwhelming life commitment that froze her frail body to the marrow with an all-pervading sense of fear.

But she forced an outward smile.

Chapter Three

University

When Kelly went to bed, she thought again about how she had arrived here. Using a little of her father's gift of the proceeds from the sale of his house, Douglas and Kelly had rented and moved into a small flat near the university.

She smiled as she remembered the Emmaus Glasgow charity shop, where over several weeks they'd selected and purchased excellent quality furniture at bargain prices and soon had their flat furnished to their liking.

Douglas and Kelly took to Glasgow University like ducks to water.

Kelly found herself playing for one of the university's women's hockey teams, and Douglas made his way into one of the university's rugby teams. They both continued their interest in debating, which was intellectually challenging at the university. Douglas also joined the university pipe band. What with their studies and all their social interests, their time had to be well managed.

The fact that they were both taking the same law degree was powerfully beneficial, and they continually discussed points of law with each other. Both of their fathers had been staunch trade unionists and

Labour Party members, and so Douglas and she joined the university's Labour Party branch.

She remembered with sadness the previous year when John Smith, the new Labour leader, had raised high hopes amongst the party faithful, but he'd suddenly died of a massive heart attack on the morning of 12 May 1994. Kelly vividly remembered that she and Douglas were in the university library when the news quickly spread, leaving many Labour Party supporters deeply shocked.

The ensuing leadership contest following John Smith's death saw the election of the youngest-ever leader of the Labour Party. He was widely known to be a moderniser, and his leadership election statement was clear that the Labour Party must be reformed radically if it was to win office again. "New Labour, New Life for Britain" was a political manifesto published in 1996 by the British Labour Party. While opposed by some traditionalists, especially Arthur Scargill, the coal miner's union leader, the proposed changes won overwhelming support at a special conference in April 1995.

The Socialist Labour Party was launched at its first congress on 1 May 1996. It was initiated by leading trade unionists and campaign activists led by Arthur Scargill following the final abandonment by Tony Blair's New Labour of any commitment to progressive change for socialism in Britain.

The following year in 1996, unconnected to New Labour and much to Kelly's delight, the International Court of Justice reaffirmed the Nuclear Non-Proliferation Treaty, adding that this promise was a legally binding obligation. This opinion also confirmed that nuclear weapons, like all weapons, were subject to the constraints imposed by international humanitarian law. These prohibited the use of weapons that could not discriminate between military targets and civilians. Based on test data and other evidence, it was scarcely imaginable that any nuclear weapon, including the British Trident system deployed from Faslane, could comply with these restrictions.

Kelly incorporated these new judgements into her debating arguments. She was convinced and secure in her knowledge, and on every occasion she could, she said, "The UK government has presented no reasoned argument to show that Trident could ever be threatened or used lawfully."

The 1997 election campaign saw the Tories in decline over sleaze, tax rises, and division. Labour's campaign, by contrast, was smooth and efficiently run like a national sales campaign, with no commitment to nuclear disarmament.

A Labour prime minister gave new direction to the country with the introduction of a national minimum wage, one million more jobs, smaller class sizes in primary schools, and the biggest-ever sustained investment in the NHS. Like most of the Labour Party members, Douglas and Kelly supported Labour, but both had a festering discomfort that this New Labour Party had lost its soul and, like the Tories, continued to hide behind the threat of a nuclear holocaust.

Chapter Four

Iona Retreat

His Boy Scouts background had embedded a moral compass in Douglas's mind, and Kelly had similar standards well established in her character from the Girl Guides, most of which were based on Old Testament standards for decent family and community living.

As the second year at university ended successfully, she asked Douglas, "How do you feel about spending a week on the island of Iona? I would like to think about Saint Columba and how he brought Christianity to Scotland. I want to take time to consider the biblical perspective of nuclear weapons in such a peaceful setting."

Douglas immediately replied, "Yes. I have never explored Iona and its history, and I like the idea very much. We can see where John Smith, our late Labour leader, was buried."

They planned and booked a week in a modest bed-and-breakfast guest house near the ferry terminal on the island. When the time came, they travelled by an early bus from Glasgow to Oban, and then they caught the Caledonian MacBrayne ferry, MV *Isle of Mull*, to the main ferry terminal on Mull, at Craignuir. The sail was very pleasant, giving nice views of Oban as they sailed out into the Sound of Kerrerra.

They got into conversation on the ferry with a Messianic Jew, who explained, "I am a university historian visiting Iona to see where the early Celtic church had been established. I am trying to research if any of its old truths remain since the Romanisation of the Western gospels and the suppression and obliteration of the Celtic church following the Synod at Whitby in 664."

Douglas was immediately intrigued and asked, "What do you mean, suppressed and obliterated?"

The Messianic Jew explained, "Prior to this conference in Northumbria, the missionary influences were largely early Irish and Scottish, having come first through Ninian, where he established his See at Whithorn. There, in about 397, he built a whitewashed stone church—hence Whithorn, or White House, a notable departure from the customary wooden churches of the Britons.

"These missionaries were followed by Patrick a generation later, and Columba a century and a half later. Ninian was a principal agent in preserving the tradition of the early Church and forming the character of the Celtic church. Although not Roman Catholic, these missionaries were much later claimed by the Roman Catholic Church and said to be saints of that foreign and imposed church.

"In important matters of discipline, the Roman and Celtic traditions did not agree. The Celtic church was based on strict Torah beliefs and practices, particularly the Passover, with a revealed messianic witness added. Thus, when the Northumbrian King Oswy and his household were keeping the Eve of Passover memorial to Yeshua Messiah and observing the holy days during the Passover season, his queen, who had been brought up in the south under the Roman system, could be still fasting for Lent prior to the Roman Easter. She really caused a rumpus about it with the king, and a debate was arranged where, not surprisingly, the Roman arguments and his wife's insistence won the day."

During subsequent centuries, all traces of the Hebrew influences were removed and replaced with Christian practices.

Nazarene Judaism

Yeshua, the Nazarene Rabbi - Teacher of Torah –

Pentateuch - the first five books of the Bible. These books are Genesis, Exodus, Leviticus, Numbers, and Deuteronomy. The word Pentateuch comes from two Greek words that mean "five books" or "five scrolls".

The explanation was too complicated for Douglas, and this fact about St Ninian being first to bring Nazarene Judaism and not Christianity instead of St Columba was a bit sudden for him. He quickly changed the conversation to anticipating disembarking as the ship tied up to the pier at Craignuir. They boarded a waiting bus destined for Fionnphort, the ferry terminal for the island of Iona.

The weather was bright sunshine, and it was a gorgeous drive through the western part of the Isle of Mull, with deer seen in the distance.

They passed along Ben More, the island's largest mountain, looming large and dominant at 966 metres. Douglas said, "Looking at that mountainside gives me a strong urge to climb it."

Kelly replied with a big smile, "Not today, we won't."

The bus driver occasionally gave interesting observations on features of the beautiful wilderness as they passed, including once stopping the bus to let the passengers watch a white-tailed sea eagle soar gracefully on the wind. "It is Britain's largest bird, with a wingspan of over eight feet."

However, his main theme and pride of his knowledge was the story of Saint Columba, adding forcefully, "His name is properly pronounced 'Saint Columkille'. He was born in the year of our Lord 521 and died in 597. He was an Irish missionary to Scotland, was called the Apostle of

Caledonia, was a prince of the O'Donnells of Donegal, and was educated at Moville and Clonard.

"Columkille and several companions sailed to Scotland. They landed at Iona, where they established their monastery and went about preaching in the Highlands and North Lowlands. Before Columkille's death, the north of Scotland was almost entirely evangelised."

The bus driver took great pleasure in pronouncing the *kille* part of the name *ceely* in his strong and exaggerated West Highland accent, which Kelly found funny.

After about an hour, the bus arrived at Fionnphort, and the passengers disembarked at the ferry slipway. They stood and watched the small ferry approach, lost in their own thoughts.

When they disembarked, Kelly and Douglas quickly found their way to the small boarding house, where they were welcomed as if they were extended members of family. After settling into their well-appointed room, they decided to explore the island. Douglas picked up a free tourist leaflet about the island of Iona as they left the boarding house to help them find their way around.

The main street led up from the jetty, past the post office and grocer's shop. They walked slowly, trying to absorb the peace of the place, and reached the entrance to the ruins of the nunnery dating from the early thirteenth century. Many old tombs could still be seen, including that of the last prioress, Anna, who'd died in 1453.

Kelly said, "It's amazing that her memorial is still here after more than five hundred years." Then after a moment's thinking, she added, "I wonder if Anna was anything like me? I don't suppose her problems would be any different from any other woman. Despite all the politician' promises, gender equality is still a long way off."

They lapsed into thoughtful silence in the warm sunshine as they sat on one of the modern benches set inside the rectangular stone walls, gazing at a row of three arches edged with pale stones. The ancient stone ruins were a mix of colours ranging from pink to grey, forming an oblong enclosure which had once been a roofed building of human habitation and shelter from the Atlantic storms.

After sitting quietly for a long while with their own thoughts, drinking in the atmosphere and imagining what it must have been like occupied in its prime, Kelly finally stood up and said, "Let's go to the abbey."

The grey-stoned abbey rose in front of them above the fields. As they began to walk towards the abbey, they heard a shout behind them. They turned and saw the Messianic Jew woman walking quickly to catch them. As she reached them, she said, "Are you going to the abbey?"

Kelly smiled and replied, "Yes. Join us, and we will go together."

As they walked along the road, their Messianic companion pointed and said, "MacLean's Cross, a Celtic sun cross from the fifteenth century, now retrospectively stamping the island with a Roman mark. The circle depicts Sol Invictus, the Unconquered Sun, from pagan Baalism."

She continued without a pause. "It acts like a sentinel watching through the centuries a stream of loyal pilgrims travelling to the extremity of the Roman Empire, each making a long journey often on foot in search of moral significance or seeking the real meaning of their distorted religion."

A bit lost with the references to the sun, Douglas said, "Yes, sounds about right. According to the tourist leaflet, it's a marker predicting the end of the journey for centuries of Christian believers."

They bought their entry tickets, and a volunteer in the reception hut handed them a leaflet in exchange for small change dropped into the donation box for the Iona Cathedral Trust.

While reading from the leaflet, Douglas said, "It wasn't until the start of the twentieth century that the church itself was restored, when the Duke of Argyll made it over to the Iona Cathedral Trust. In 1938, Macleod, a minister in Glasgow, founded the Iona community and initiated the long process of reconstructing the monastic buildings."

In front of the west door stood another carved cross. Once they were inside the nave, the church was surprisingly bright and crowded with tourists and pilgrims. They passed through to the other side of the abbey and found themselves in the cloisters. Warm sunlight caressed the sheltered open area of grass surrounded by spectacular rows of stone arches.

Standing in the middle of the grassy quadrangle was *The Descent of the Spirit*. It was a strange and inspired work of art by Jacques Lipchitz, a Holocaust refugee. Their companion became silent, knelt, and began a wailing form of prayer that went on and on.

Kelly was transfixed with the agelessness of the space, almost as if time was suspended. She said quietly, "It's almost if all history's painful experience and exuberant hope is in this place." Douglas and Kelly stood for several minutes before leaving the praying Messianic Jew, the cloisters, and the abbey. Regularly consulting the leaflet, they continued along the road in the warm sunshine to the northern tip of the island.

After a mile or so past the odd farmhouse, they reached a track leading through sandy fields to hidden dunes. Standing on the highest point, they could see a golden stretch of sand to their left. In the distance, the island of Staffa was illuminated by the bright sunshine, clearly showing the shadowy mouths of the famous Fingal's Cave and the Boat Cave.

To the north-west, the lumps and bumps of the Treshnish Isles were clearly visible, with the outlines of the islands of Coll, Tiree, Rum, and Eigg in the background. Looking back down Iona's coast, they could see the ferry crossing over to Fionnphort. In the distance, they could make out the Paps of Jura some thirty-five miles south.

Kelly said, "This must be as near as we can be to heaven."

Douglas nodded and breathed in the fresh sea air laden with the pleasant smell of decaying seaweed. Reading from the leaflet again, he said, "The geology of Iona is as special as the island itself. Amongst the oldest rocks known on earth, Lewisian Gneiss outcrops on Iona date to 2,700 million years old. Also found on Iona, in the south-central region of the island, is an outcrop of white rock called anorthosite. Perhaps almost as old as the gneiss, anorthosite is also found on the moon. Legend has it, that when the rest of the world sinks below the waves, Iona will remain."

Kelly responded to the reading. "Fascinating that the oldest rock on earth is here and also on the moon. This place really is special."

The weather was kind to them all week. They joined in the daily worship services at the abbey, went on several boat excursions (including Fingal's Cave), and even had a game of golf. Most evenings they went to the nunnery ruins and sat for an hour or two discussing their marriage, their personal goals, their Christian beliefs, and their political doubts about New Labour and its clear lack of democracy.

They met the Messianic Jew several times during their wanderings, and her pronouncements shook their shallow Christian beliefs to the core. The first day that they met again, the woman told them, "I have come to Iona as a historian to try to find the basis of early Irish Messianic belief, which in St Columba's day was pure and followed the example of Rabbi Yeshua Messiah in keeping Torah commands. The Christians seem to have obliterated these in favour of their own pagan traditions."

Kelly started to question her but quickly thought better of it because it was too academic for her to quickly absorb.

The Messianic Jew continued. "There existed fundamental and far-reaching differences between the Celtic Christians and the Roman Church, which held them as schematics and heretics and which led to the total suppression and obliteration of Celtic Messianic Judaism after the Synod of Whitby in 664."

They met her most days, and she finally explained her belief. "I believe in Messiah Yeshua, the resurrected Son of Yahweh, and the ancient Way of Torah that he proclaimed and followed. Yeshua repeatedly demonstrated his affinity with the excluded and deprived and was critical of the Sadducees, who rejected resurrection, angels, and other scriptural truths. Yeshua Messiah taught obedience to the scriptural laws but condemned the Pharisees for adding to and changing scriptural requirements, as do modern Orthodox Jews."

She continued. "He, and subsequently his disciples, taught that there was only one Yahweh and that a special Passover Lamb, the anointed human son of Yahweh, was the only door through which ordinary, sinful, repenting people could come to the Father. Finally, Yeshua willingly gave his life as the sacrificial Passover Lamb of Yahweh in fulfilment of Yahweh's blood covenant with Abraham and his descendants, Israel, thus beginning the spiritual harvest phase of the plan of Yahweh. He was crucified on a living tree (reputed to be an almond tree), buried in a rock tomb, and rose from the dead three full days and nights later as he himself predicted. Over five hundred witnesses on twelve separate occasions confirmed with their own eyes and ears his resurrection and final commission then he spiritually ascended to heaven to sit figuratively speaking at the right hand of the Father Yahweh, fulfilling the meaning of his Hebrew name, 'Yahweh's Salvation'."

The great shock came when on the third day, the Messianic Jew exclaimed, "What the Christian Church doesn't want you to know is that the earliest of the extant manuscripts of the Western Greek to English translations of the New Testament, although largely based on the earlier writings of the Sect of the Nazarene, do not date back beyond the middle of the fourth century AD."

On the fourth day she explained, "It was British-born Emperor Constantine (AD 272–337) who authorised the compilation of the writings now called the New Testament. Most modern-day Christian writers suppress the truth about the development of their religion. Constantine's intention at Nicaea was to create an entirely new god for his empire who would unite all religious factions and beliefs under one deity and a universal church."

On the fifth day, she told them, "Fortunately some of the early Eastern scattered churches preserved the original writings, but these are in Aramaic, and so you need to find an Aramaic to English translation from the earliest versions to be sure.

"To fully understand the Way of the Nazarene, the best place to learn is within the pages of scripture itself. Eyewitnesses of the Messianic advent—Matthew, Simon Peter, James, John, and Jude—were all Torah-keeping Nazarenes. Read their writings from the Aramaic English translations predating Constantine in the context of the Torah and the Prophets, and the Way of the Nazarene will become clear. I also recommend Revelations for a focused study of his clear instructions to the called-out ones, but I don't want to burden you with too much at one time."

As something of a relief, they did not see the Messianic Jew again, but the encounters led them to ask each other questions. Every evening the conversation always came to the same quandary: New Labour's continued reliance on the nuclear deterrent.

By the end of the week, they both agreed with the Messianic Jew. From their limited knowledge of the gospels, the Bible clearly taught that keeping the Ten Commandments was required, and therefore from an Old Covenant perspective, hiding behind a nuclear missile was idolatry of the worst kind.

They further agreed that the basic Christian commandments to love God and your neighbour as oneself could hardly be fulfilled by building and deploying nuclear weapons.

Douglas and Kelly very reluctantly left Iona, grieving about the Old Labour Party that their fathers had supported. Now they were both firmly alienated from New Labour and its charismatic leader, and they were determined to change.

Chapter Five

Democracy Questioned

In 1997, Douglas and Kelly both had their twenty-first birthdays. Their new feeling of maturity prompted them to face their feelings of unease about the New Labour Party's attitude towards nuclear weapons. However, an unusual set of circumstances came together with the election of New Labour that same year which accelerated their decisions. This brought into office a fundamentally different administration from any seen since the early twentieth century.

Labour had been out of office for so long that none of the senior cabinet posts was occupied by anyone with experience of governing. Furthermore, New Labour came to power with a deep suspicion of the nation's institutions and a determination to smash them. New Labour set about undermining another bulwark of the system, the Civil Service.

This involved the introduction on a huge scale of management consultants to provide advice once given by civil servants. A consequence of this was the imposition of a target culture that stifled local decision-making and suffocated common sense.

Douglas and Kelly reacted to this dismal prospect by resigning from the Labour Party and joining the Socialist Labour Party, led by the former trade union leader Arthur Scargill. They were convinced that he could see the clear danger signs of something worse than Maggie Thatcher emerging in New Labour.

Their choice of their new party was also partly a nostalgic impulse based on their two fathers' histories and allegiances to their mining communities.

Kelly put forward an argument at the university debating chamber that Blair was the new Thatcher. She started by saying, "New Labour accepts the Thatcherite ground by saying, 'There is no turning back to the pre-Thatcher days of Old Labour.'"

She went on. "New Labour rejects the rights-claiming culture fought so hard for by the Old Labour heroes and heroines. The prime minister and his modernisers believe that much of what Thatcher did was good and that they need to be more Thatcherite in favouring the financial institutions and the cult of celebrity."

That was as far as she got with her argument. The audience was predominantly student members of New Labour, and they loudly and continually barracked her until she was finally forced to leave the rostrum.

Although defeated by the New Labour bullies, she was exhilarated by the clarity of her thinking and her public condemnation of New Labour. She excitedly told Douglas about her experience and her joy. "Douglas, although I was drowned out by the boo boys, the fact that I loudly declared my beliefs in the face of such opposition embedded my beliefs and commitment even more firmly."

As they completed their second year at the university, Douglas went on a two-week tour of rugby matches with the team, and so Kelly arranged to spend the same two weeks at the Faslane Peace Camp, where she met an Old Labour Party member who remembered with great affection ex-Prime Minister Michael Foot, who had been very active in the Campaign for Nuclear Disarmament movement. After the camp members had eaten, they settled in the evening sun with various large bottles of cider around several tables and chairs supporting planks joined together to form an inward-looking square.

Kelly started the discussion with her statement previously rehearsed at the university debating chamber. Her distinguished friend applauded her and said in a loud voice, "Dear Michael Foot made this famous quote away back in 1954, and it is truer today than it was then. 'Is the Labour Party to remain a democratic party in which the right of free criticism and free debate is not merely tolerated but encouraged? Or are the rank and file of the party to be bludgeoned or cowed into an uncritical subservience towards the leadership?'"

That began one of the most stimulating discussions Kelly had ever experienced. However, it slowly deteriorated in quality as the evening passed and the cider bottles emptied.

Kelly enjoyed the two weeks and renewing her friendship with Felicity. When the time came to leave, as the Glasgow bus approached, Felicity pushed a piece of paper into Kelly's hand and said, "Read and then eat the paper."

Grasping the paper tightly, Kelly quickly boarded the almost empty bus and found an isolated seat near the back. She carefully unfolded the paper and read the message, which said, "Evil monster is sneaking out of lair on the sixth of September. Help me like the last time, and I will try to board the beast. P.S., Felicity means happy."

It was as if an electric shock hit Kelly in the stomach. She froze for a moment, then opened the paper again, double-checked the date, put the paper in her mouth, and chewed as her stomach slowly thawed.

Then she thought about the MOD police officers, the invasive strip search, and prolonged interrogation; her mouth seemed to dry up.

She smiled again as she remembered the words "Felicity means happy." The paper had almost dissolved, and she swallowed it all and concluded that Felicity must have used rice paper. She did not notice the rest of the journey because in her new-found commitment, she had decided to help Felicity. The seriousness of her decision weighed heavily upon her with a strong sense of foreboding.

Chapter Six

Strange Encounter

Kelly met Douglas coming off the bus at Buchanan Street bus station, and they hugged on their reunion. When they got to the flat, they showered together and then spent a couple of hours in bed.

Soon they got up, showered again, and dressed. Douglas produced a wad of banknotes and said, "We are dining out tonight."

Kelly asked, "Where did you get the money?"

He replied, "I will tell you over dinner."

Douglas had phoned ahead and booked a table for two at a chic Italian restaurant on Byres Road. They both ordered pizza Siciliana, and Kelly chose a bottle of white Soave.

Douglas told Kelly about his rugby trip. "The rugby trip came about through one of our players, Neil Campbell, with a brother at Cambridge University who plays in one of their rugby teams. During a home visit by the older brother, a challenge was made, and subsequently a match was arranged between our rugby team and theirs on the morning of their end-of-year graduation day. One thing led to another, and as part of the gamesmanship, I was asked to bring my bagpipes and full piper's outfit to pipe the team into the ground and into the dressing room. When we arrived, we stopped the team bus on the road outside the ground, and with me leading and playing the slow tune 'Rowan Tree' on the pipes, the team marched slowly and deliberately into the ground with the bus following behind."

Kelly asked, "What did you do that for?"

"For effect," said Douglas. "Anyway, it looked good and worked well. The ground was already full of spectators, mainly parents enjoying the sunshine and expecting to see Cambridge beat Glasgow, but at the end, we beat them with a late penalty goal.

"Later, while we were having some after-match food and refreshments, and one of the Cambridge team's father, Mr Ian Campbell, came over and spoke in the poshest voice you have ever heard. 'Young man, I have a special request to make of you. I am singing the song Rowan Tree at a big function in London tonight. Will you come immediately in my car and accompany me on your bagpipes at this function?'"

Kelly asked, "And is that all he said?"

Douglas looked at Kelly with a big smile. "When he mentioned the very large fee, Mr Brodie, my old Boy Scout leader and mentor, came into my mind. Although it meant missing the rugby team celebrations, I immediately accepted. Mr Brodie would not approve if I missed such an opportunity to make money."

Kelly laughed and said, "Mr Brodie still has a substantial influence on you. Did it go okay?"

"Yes, but it was unbelievable, like something out of another world."

"What do you mean?"

"The function was in the main auditorium in Freemasons' Hall in London, and you would need to see the inside of this building to understand what I mean. It is the most opulent place I have ever seen and there was over one thousand people seated in the audience."

Kelly asked, "But did your piping go okay?"

Douglas said, "Yes, much better than I thought possible. I played right at the back of the huge stage so as not to drown out the singer and the pianist, who were using microphones and the public-address system at the front of the stage. The overall sound balance was controlled brilliantly by a sound engineer. The audience responded with a standing ovation, and then I was immediately escorted out of the hall to the entrance foyer and told to wait.

"I went into a toilet, changed out of my piper's clothes, and packed them in my rucksack with my bagpipes. I dressed in my casuals, ready for travelling, and then I returned to the entrance foyer to wait for my fee. After about twenty-five minutes, a man in a dinner suit came out of the hall carrying a silver tray with a letter on it."

Douglas gave Kelly the hand-written letter to read.

> Thank you for your exceptional performance. It was even better than what I had envisioned. Find enclosed your fee of 150 pounds as agreed, plus 25 pounds to cover your tube and train tickets back to Cambridge; you will have time to get back tonight. I include a card with my secretary's phone number. Please phone her and give her your contact details, as I will want to repeat this occasionally in the future.
>
> With best regards,
>
> Ian Campbell

Kelly said, "Well, that's nice work if you can get it."

Douglas replied, "Yes. When I got home, I phoned his secretary and gave her my contact details. However, a strange thing happened while I was waiting in the entrance foyer for my fee. A strange and sinister incident occurred."

As Douglas paused, Kelly prompted him. "Tell me—don't stop now."

"A very well-dressed and distinguished-looking gentleman was led out of the hall by two attendants He'd obviously had too much to drink and was trying to resist them. One of the attendants got his coat and white silk scarf from the cloakroom, helped him to put them on, and sat him in a chair despite his protests. They took his car keys out of his jacket pocket and said to him, 'You just wait there for about twenty minutes, sir, until we run around to the car park and get your car and our car. One of us will drive you home in your car, and one of us will follow in our car to bring your driver back. Now, sit there. You don't want to embarrass yourself further tonight.'

"One of the men shouted to me, making a sign with his hand as if drinking from a glass. *'Keep your eye on him while we get his car.'* The two men hurried out of the main entrance.

"When they left, the distinguished-looking gentleman got up and staggered over to me and said in a very cultured but slurred voice, 'Young man, this country is in grave danger. The Americans and the Europeans are pushing their noses into everything. Do you know? They got rid of Margaret Thatcher because she opposed the European super state designed by the Bilderbergers?'

"I asked him, 'Sir, who are the Bilderbergers?'

"He said, 'The annual Bilderberg Group conference is the most important meeting in the world. Now held at Davos Switzerland, it is attended annually by more world leaders, more top politicians, more royalty, and more business leaders than any other gathering of any kind. No other meeting is attended by the leaders of all the major international institutions, such as the World Bank, the IMF, the UN, and the EU. Collectively, these are the people who control the world, and their decisions therefore affect every human being on the planet, now and in the future. But it really is an extension of the Committee of Three Hundred, which has been controlling the world since the eighteenth century.'

"He took out two pages of A4 paper printed on both sides. After opening the list, he pointed to a name and blurted out, 'I know what I am talking about. That's my name on the list of the three hundred. I have been a member since 1975, the year before we forced Prime Minister Harold Wilson to resign because we thought he was a Russian spy. Unfortunately, I have badly blotted my copybook here tonight—too much to drink, I am afraid.'

"His shoulders and his head slumped momentarily as though beaten, but then he straightened up like a military man coming to attention. 'They immediately informed me that they have taken my name off the list and ejected me from the meeting, and I now fear for my life. Take this list, which up until tonight was the three hundred names, including mine, making up the Committee of Three Hundred. Guard it carefully because you will forfeit your life if they find out you have it.'

"I quickly hid the papers inside the front of my shirt as the man continued. 'The people who are exclusively invited to the Bilderberg Group are an extension of the Committee of Three Hundred, and the topics discussed are official secrets which the media is forbidden from reporting. Bilderberg is effectively an elite secret society ruling the world from behind closed doors and outside the democratic framework. Yet Bilderberg Group meetings receive no publicity and are not reported in the news.'

"At that moment, the two attendants returned and firmly assisted the elderly gentleman, leading him out of the main entrance. He shouted back at me, 'Do not forget what I have told you!'"

Kelly demanded, "What did you do?"

"I thought that this was a case of a distinguished member drinking too much and the exclusive organisation looking after him by seeing him safely home. I waited for about five minutes after he had been taken out, and my escort returned from the hall carrying the silver tray with the letter and my fee on it. I took the letter from the escort and stuffed it into the front of my shirt. My escort immediately took me to the main entrance and opened the door for me to leave. I asked, 'Where is the nearest Underground station?'

"He answered, 'Turn left along Great Queen Street and then continue straight along Long Acre. You will get to Covent Garden Tube station in about five minutes.'

"I found Covent Garden Tube station just as the escort had instructed. I looked at the clock and was relieved to see that it was only ten past eight. I arrived back at the halls of residence at in Cambridge just before eleven.

"On the Saturday morning, we played our last rugby match against a Southampton University team. After the Saturday night celebrations, on Sunday morning it was obvious that most of the players were struggling to get up. After I had my breakfast, I walked down to the local shop and bought some Sunday papers. By the time I got back, they were herding the last of the players onto the bus.

"As the bus started the journey back to Glasgow, I picked up a paper and started to read. Suddenly a headline caught my eye: 'Member of Aristocracy's Body Found in River Thames.' The article didn't enlarge much, except to provide the name of the person and the fact that it was thought he had been to a late-night social function. It added that the police did not think there were any suspicious circumstances leading to his death. Standing up, I found the list of the Committee of Three Hundred in my bag; I quickly scanned the list and found the same name on the list."

Kelly asked, "What did you do?"

"I wasn't sure whether there was any connection between the two names. The whole episode had been surreal—the invitation to perform, the opulent location, the huge audience, and the story told by the distinguished gentleman all seemed dreamlike. Do you understand what I mean?"

Kelly nodded with a serious frown and said, "Yes, Douglas, I do."

"I looked at some of the other names and was staggered to find the names of some the world's most prominent people on the list. Shocked, I quietly returned the list to my bag and sat down to think until I got home. It is better that you don't know the murdered man's name. I don't want you implicated in this."

He gave Kelly the list, which she scrutinised, but she did not know what to think or say.

Finally Douglas said, "I think I should go to the police and tell them about the well-dressed man being taken out of Freemasons' Hall, but I will keep quiet about what he said and the secret list of the Committee of Three Hundred people who rule the world."

Kelly said, "Yes, I agree."

Douglas went to the local police station, and after being shuffled about between several officers who made notes, he was thanked and told that the information would be passed to the Metropolitan Police. However, Douglas could not get the dead man out of his mind; it was as if he was haunting him from beyond the grave, and Douglas knew that he would not be easily exorcised.

Chapter Seven

Retribution

While trying to put the strange and sinister incident to the back of their minds, Douglas and Kelly resolved to enjoy the summer break from the university. They visited old friends in their hometown and played lots of sports, keeping their fitness levels high.

One day at breakfast, Douglas said, "Kelly, I was thinking back to before my father died. I remember my mother and I helping him to hide a secret list in the graveyard of the church. I have this nagging recollection that it was a secret list of those who ruled the world; I cannot get it out of my mind. I must compare the two lists to see if they are the same or whether any of the names changed.

Kelly looked at him incredulously and asked, "How can they be? You are not even sure if they are the same, are you?"

He admitted, "No, I was only a small boy, but my father was deeply involved in the miners' strike, and he told me it was a list of the bad people who ruled the world."

Kelly replied, "Oh! Well, you won't be happy until you do, will you?"

Douglas smiled. "Let's phone and see if we can stay with my mum tonight." Kelly agreed.

Douglas phoned his mother, and she was agreeable. He retrieved the secret list from his university locker where he had hidden it, but he realised that it was not really the safest place to keep it. When he returned to their flat, he said, "Kelly, let's visit your father while we are in that area."

They popped into the supermarket and bought some food for Douglas's mum, as well as some fruit and other necessities for Kelly's father in the care home. They travelled by bus.

First, they visited Kelly's father at the National Union of Mineworkers' sponsored care home. It was a sad visit because her father was now dependent on drugs and oxygen to help his much-laboured breathing.

When they left and were outside the building, Kelly released her anger and frustration by shouting, "These politicians and fat-cat mine managers who decided he didn't qualify for compensation don't come to see the once strong coal miner gasping his last breaths." She then had a cry, saying, "It's not fair, it's not fair."

Douglas said, "That's why you are studying to become a lawyer."

She recovered her composure and said, "Come on. Let's get over to your mother's."

They arrived at Douglas's mother's house around tea time. They were surprised when his mother showed them into the front room and said, "This is David. He has moved in with me as a lodger."

Douglas thought to himself, *He is not much older than me,* and he held out his hand. "I am pleased to meet you." But David did not respond to the offer, causing an embarrassing silence.

Kelly intervened by asking, "Have you eaten yet? We have brought some food with us."

David went into the hall, put on his shoes and his anorak, and shouted aggressively, "I am away to Edinburgh, and I won't be back tonight. I will come back on Saturday morning, hopefully when the house is less busy." He stomped out, banging the front door.

Douglas's mother said, "Oh, dear. He's gone off in the huff for a few days. He threw a tantrum earlier when I told him you were staying overnight."

Kelly asked, "Can I use the kitchen to cook a meal?"

Douglas's mother replied, "Yes, please. It will let me talk to Douglas."

Kelly went into the kitchen closing the door behind her.

Douglas's mother said, "Sit down, Douglas. I want to explain the situation about David."

Douglas quickly interjected, "No, Mum, you don't have to explain to me."

She held up her hand to cut him off. "I want to explain because it is very important. David was a young police officer who was involved in the battles with the striking miners. He was present when your father died of the heart attack. Since experiencing regrets about his involvement in the traumatic events over the year of conflict, he subsequently suffered a nervous breakdown, turned to drink, lost his job, and became homeless. He eventually came to my house driven by guilt to apologise for the death of your father. I took him in as a non-paying lodger and have been slowly gleaning a complete picture of what happened to your father."

Douglas said frantically, "Tell me. Please tell me."

His mother replied, "It is fairly simple. The police targeted your father because MI5 wanted to interrogate him about a rumour they had heard: that he had possession of the secret list of the Committee of Three Hundred, allegedly given him by Arthur Scargill, the coal miner's union leader, for safe keeping.

"The police arrested your father when he was picketing a coal mine. They took him to a nearby police station and put him in a cell. David was one of the arresting officers, and they quickly noticed his breathlessness. Two MI5 officers, Mr Smith and Mr James, arrived and took him into their custody. David was told to provide transport for them. They instructed David to drive them to a remote river, where they forced him into the deep water and kept pushing him under, trying to force him to answer their questions. It seems that they stressed and questioned him for about quarter of an hour until he was not just gasping but rasping for breath. Then he suffered a massif heart attack and despite frantic efforts to revive him.

"David told me, 'His death caused much annoyance to the two MI5 officers because he refused to say a word about the location of the secret list. They warned me to never say anything about what I witnessed.'

"So, there you have it. An induced heart attack with no signs of violence, although it is clear they did not intend his death. It was vital information about the location of the secret list that they were seeking, but without regards to his suffering or his human rights."

Douglas felt his anger boil up. "I want to batter your lodger for his part in what they did to Dad."

His mother replied with tears in her eyes, "I don't want him staying here anymore, but I don't want you to ruin your life by getting into trouble with the police through him. You must understand, Douglas. Your father went down fighting for a cause which he believed in, instead of slowly spluttering and gasping to a slow death of complete dependency. Although we didn't realise it, it was a much better way for him to go."

Kelly knocked the door, waited for a moment, and entered the front room. "Dinner's ready. I have made macaroni and cheese. Come through to the kitchen and get it." They moved through to the kitchen and sat at the small table, eating Kelly's satisfying meal.

When they finished eating, Douglas said, "Mum, I have a second copy of the secret list, and I want to compare it with the first one. Do you remember the night we hid the list in the church graveyard?"

Douglas's mother replied, "I am surprised you can remember that. You were very young, probably only about eight or nine."

Douglas said, "It's one of my earliest memories. I think it's etched on my mind because I was scared of that spooky graveyard and its dark shadows."

His mother laughed. "I was scared of the dark graveyard too."

He continued. "I have the second copy with me, and I have brought two torches, four slab lifter tools, and a couple of screwdrivers in a bag. My friend at university does slabbing at weekends, and I asked him if he had any tools to make it easier. He loaned me these four special hand tools for lifting slabs. They are American and made of hardened tool steel, so thin that they are easy to insert in the gaps between the slabs."

His mother replied, "It's unlikely that anyone will be at the church or in the graveyard this evening. If we all go, you can work while it is still light, and I can keep a lookout near the gate."

The three of them left the house and made their way to the church. Their three pairs of eyes scrutinised every feature in the failing light. It appeared to be deserted, and so they walked round the back of the church to the old walled graveyard. They entered the graveyard, each of them taking different paths and checking for signs of other people. Satisfied that they were alone, they met back at the gate.

Douglas's mother whispered, "I know where the slab is. Follow me." She led them to the slab in front of the angel-shaped memorial stone and stood on the slab. "This is it. I will go back to near the gate and keep lookout."

Douglas quickly emptied the tools out of the bag. He grabbed his thin screwdriver and quickly scraped the loose debris from between the slabs at one corner. Then he inserted the thin L-shaped foot of the slab lifter under the bottom of the slab and whispered, "Kelly, hold the slab lifter in place while I get another one located."

He repeated the process until he had four slab lifters in place. He stood up, held two of the slab lifters, and whispered to Kelly, "Nice and steady. You lift your two slab lifters in time with me and lay the slab over there." The slab came up, and they laid it to the side, revealing the waterproof package in the bottom of the hole.

Douglas quickly opened the outer wrappings and took out the two laminated pages. He took out his copies obtained at the Freemasons' Hall and sat on a stone bench to compare the two versions in the now dim light, glad that he had brought torches.

He found many new names on his list and whispered to Kelly, "Just as I thought. It is the same basic list, but some of the names have changed. It means that this list is regularly updated, proving that this committee is active."

He quickly wrapped up the old list and laid it back in its place. Then he and Kelly used the four slab lifters to put the big slab back in place. They stood on it to make sure it was bedded down. When he was satisfied, Kelly helped him to carefully fill in the gaps with earth and moss.

Douglas packed the tools and his copy of the list into the tool bag, and he and Kelly quietly retreated to the gate, where they re-joined Douglas's mother. They made their way to his mother's house where they stayed overnight.

The following morning, Douglas and Kelly returned to Glasgow. In the afternoon, he visited his usual library and went into the reference section. He acknowledged the two librarians with a wave and a smile.

He browsed for a while and then took down a very large and thick reference book, *The British Yearbook of International Law*. Douglas carried it over to a table and sat down. He opened the front two pages and secreted the two pages of the secret list inside the protective book cover, which the librarians had enclosed the original book in to protect it. Satisfied that it was unlikely to be discovered, he returned the big book to its position on the shelves.

As he passed the librarians, one of them said, "That didn't take long today."

Douglas replied, "No, I was just checking a small reference point."

Early Friday morning, he phoned his mother from a public phone box and asked her, "Has David returned yet?"

She replied, "No, but he phoned to ask if you had gone. When I told him that you had, he said, 'I can get a lift back on Saturday morning. By the way, could you lend me some money for the weekend?' I have drawn out fifty pounds for him, but I am not looking forward to him coming back to stay."

Douglas replied, "Mum, you don't have to worry about me getting into trouble; I will stay with you overnight. I will be there when he arrives, and we will negotiate a deal he can't refuse. Remember that I am studying to be a lawyer."

"Would you do that? It would be great relief to get rid of him."

Douglas said, "Listen, I have just had an idea. If you meet me at Livingston bus station at three o'clock, we could take in a movie, have a meal afterwards, and then come back to your home, where I will stay with you until David arrives on Saturday morning. Put the fifty pounds in an envelope addressed to your brother in London."

His mother gasped in puzzlement. "Why send it to my brother?"

Douglas said, "I will explain when we meet. Do you still want to go to the pictures?"

"Oh, yes, please. That will be great, see you at three o'clock.

He met his mother at the bus station, and they took in a movie and had a nice meal. He explained his plan, and they posted the letter to her brother with a note enclosed by Douglas. Then they returned to her house to await David's arrival in the morning.

The ex-policeman arrived looking worse for wear at eleven o'clock on Saturday morning. Douglas met him at the door. David began to panic at the unexpected sight of Douglas and tried to turn away. Douglas remembered that as an ex-policeman, David would know about close combat. Still, Douglas grabbed his hair with both hands and pulled him roughly into the house, holding his head down about waist level. He shouted at him. "You are a murdering bastard! I know what you did to my father, so your life is in great danger right now."

David fell to the floor and whined, "Don't hurt me. Please don't hurt me!"

Douglas stood over him until he stopped whimpering. He eventually said, "Get up. Here is a bag—pack your all things in it. Don't leave a single item of yours in this house."

David skulked away to his room carrying the bag, closely followed by Douglas, who was keeping the initiative by hurrying him along. Eventually David packed all his things in the bag to Douglas's satisfaction.

Douglas pushed him roughly into the hall and shouted, "Into the kitchen. You are a murdering bastard, so sit at the table." He turned to his mother and said. "Do you have a writing pad and a pen?"

His mother found them and handed them to Douglas.

Douglas laid them in front of David, sat in the chair opposite, and looked intently at David. "We know my father was interrogated and murdered in the countryside. We know Mr Smith and Mr James of MI5 oversaw the interrogation."

David pleaded, "No, no, they did not mean him to die. It was just that he was so stubborn, and I was only a junior constable carrying out orders to drive them." The ex-policeman was clearly shaken and very frightened.

Douglas stood up, leaned across the table, placed his face close to David's, and shouted, "I know all that! But that leaves you carrying the can for a murder unless Mr Smith and Mr James are implicated, and now we have no hard evidence that they were there. They are experts at being shadows and staying in the background." He sat down again to let the implications sink in.

It didn't take long. David clicked on right away and asked, "Can I turn Queen's evidence and get immunity from prosecution for telling the truth? What if I agree to give the information that Mr Smith and Mr James were in charge of the interrogation?"

Douglas replied, "Yes, that is possible. Write a statement on that writing pad about what happened to my father and the names of everyone involved, including yourself, and what roles each person played. Keep it simple and factual like a police report—after all, that's what you are trained to do. Remember to sign it and date it."

Douglas retreated to the kitchen doorway to give David a bit of space to think and write.

When David finished writing, he signed it with a flourish and pushed the writing pad across the table. Douglas immediately walked over and lifted it. He read the statement several times and then said, "Yes, that seems okay. Mum, do you have a camera in the house?"

She replied, "Yes, I will get it."

She returned with the camera, and Douglas said, "Take several photographs of David so that we can find him again and take a close-up of this statement."

His mother shot several photographs of David and said, "Douglas, I will get these developed and send you copies."

Douglas shouted at David, "Get up and go into the hall. Pick up your bag, open the front door, and get out." Douglas followed him out and pushed him along the path. He said in a faint voice so as not to draw the attention of neighbours, "My mother has sent fifty pounds to her brother in London, who will meet you off the first overnight bus from Edinburgh in the morning. He will give you the money."

He kept pushing David along the road until they came to a bus stop. Douglas handed him a red neck scarf and said, "Tie this red scarf round your neck so that the man meeting you in London will recognise you. Remember, he also knows that you were involved in the murder of his brother-in-law, Sandy Hamilton, so don't give him any more reason to dislike you. Now, get this message loud and clear: if you come anywhere my mother again, I will find you and break both your legs and both your arms. I am coming to Edinburgh with you to see you onto the London bus.

As he pushed David onto the overnight London bus, Douglas whispered in David's ear, "Remember this well. There are four people who know you were involved in the murder of an innocent man, and now we have your signed statement confirming it."

Douglas watched the large bus drive away from the bus station, satisfied that it contained a very frightened man.

Chapter Eight

Mysterious Break-in

About a month before they had to start thinking of heading back at university, Kelly realised that the incident of the murdered man in London still weighed heavily on Douglas. She said, "I wish we could go back to Iona for a week and try for a baby, but I suppose we need to think about the cost."

Douglas asked, "What, the cost of a baby?"

Kelly said, "No, stupid. The cost of taking a holiday."

Douglas thought for a moment and said, "We could camp at the Fidden Farm Campsite, about two kilometres south of Fionnphort on Mull, in the most perfect location you could imagine. It has stunning beaches of white sand and pink granite, overlooking Iona and the Atlantic Ocean. Mr Brodie will lend me all the equipment that we need from the Boy Scouts store, and that way it will cost very little."

They agreed and within two days were on the bus with a large personal rucksack each and two additional rucksacks containing the tent, sleeping bags, food, and cooking equipment.

When they reached Fionnphort, they carried the rucksacks containing the equipment to Fidden Farm Campsite. They returned to the ferry terminal and carried their personal rucksacks back to the campsite. It wasn't too busy, and so they chose a pitch away from the other campers for privacy, erected their tent, and organised their stores, bedding, and equipment.

Much to Kelly's annoyance, Douglas was still a bit preoccupied with thoughts about his father's death, and he was very subdued. She said, "Come on. Let's explore." As they explored the beaches, they were eventually out of sight of other campers. Kelly quickly stripped off all her clothes and ran into the clear but cold water.

She was in a very frisky mood, and after posing provocatively and splashing for a few minutes, she ran naked in the shallow water, all the way back to their tent. Douglas picked up her clothes and shoes and walked back to the tent to find her lying on her back, waiting for him. His mood quickly lifted, and they spent a glorious week at Fidden Farm Campsite, visiting Iona most days but also relaxing in this natural paradise and each other's company.

They returned to Glasgow completely refreshed, but when they returned to their flat, Kelly said immediately, "Someone's been in here."

Douglas replied, "What makes you say that?"

She whispered, "Those two pictures are in the wrong place. They have been swapped." She went into the kitchen and opened a cupboard. "Someone's taken all the contents out but has put them back higgledy-piggledy."

Kelly visited location after location and found further evidence of disturbance. She finally picked up a book she had been reading before they left and said, "Even the bookmark is in the wrong place." She cried for about five minutes.

When she finally composed herself, Douglas said, "Come on. We will go down to the police station."

It was the same police sergeant who had been on duty the day Douglas had reported the incident he witnessed at Freemasons' Hall.

When the sergeant looked up, he appeared to be startled when he saw Douglas. He quickly recovered his composure and asked, "Yes, sir, how can I help you?"

Douglas said, "Our flat has been broken into while we were away."

Kelly intervened by shouting hysterically, "Everything in the flat has been disturbed!"

The sergeant replied equally loudly, "Is there any evidence of an actual break-in? Is there a broken lock or a broken window?"

Kelly said, "No, but everything in the flat has been moved about. Even the bookmarker in the book I was reading was in the wrong place."

The sergeant smiled and said, "That's not substantial evidence, miss. I think you are mistaken. You look like you've been in the sun too long."

Kelly lost her temper and started shouting. "Don't mess me, you are just a typical patronising male chauvinist!"

Douglas physically pushed her out of the door, saying, "Calm down, calm down."

The sergeant followed them out. "By the way, sir, two detectives from London were looking for you last week. They tried ringing your doorbell several times, but no one answered. They left this card with their phone number for you to call them as soon as possible."

Douglas took the card, put it in his wallet, and said, "Thank you, Sergeant. I will call them in the morning."

He led Kelly away, but she shouted at the sergeant. "Are you not going to investigate our complaint?"

Douglas pulled her firmly away, and they left the police station with Kelly still protesting loudly. When they were outside, he said, "Come on. Let's get a coffee."

Kelly was angry and upset about the reaction of the sergeant, and she kept complaining to Douglas about their treatment.

Douglas said, "There is more to this than meets the eye. That sergeant knew our flat had been searched."

Kelly still seemed dispirited but asked, "How do you know?"

Douglas replied, "Did you not notice a momentary look of panic when the sergeant first looked up and recognised me? Then, what was his initial reaction to our reported break-in?

Kelly exclaimed, "The sergeant asked, 'Are you sure? I don't think so. How can you know?'"

Douglas asked, "Exactly. Is that not a strange thing to say unless he believed the break-in would not be discovered? What was his next statement?"

Kelly excitedly exclaimed, "'Is there any evidence of an actual break-in? Is there a broken lock or a broken window?' It was as if he knew that there was no evidence of forced entry. Then when we were leaving, he said, 'By the way, sir, two detectives from London were looking for you last week. They tried ringing your door-bell several times, but no one answered.' It's so obvious it was these London police who were in our flat."

Douglas smiled and said, "Well done. However, there is a lesson in this experience for both of us, if we are to become good lawyers. We find it difficult to think rationally because we are personally and emotionally involved. We must both learn to remain objective if we are to defeat our clever enemies."

They finished their coffee deep in thought, and finally Kelly said, "These are no ordinary policemen. Ordinary policemen do not sneak in, leaving little trace of their presence."

The following day, Douglas phoned James Smith, Information Consultant, at the telephone number given on the business card. He introduced himself when James Smith answered. The voice at the other end hesitated before saying, "Yes, yes, ah! Mr Hamilton, I was trying to locate you."

Douglas replied quickly, "So we noticed."

"Eh!" There was a distinct pause. James Smith, now fully composed, said in his deepest voice, "I would like to interview you regarding the statement you made at your local police station. I can fly up tomorrow and meet you at the police station at eleven o'clock."

Douglas said, "Yes, that's fine. I'll see you at eleven o'clock." Without waiting for a reply, Douglas put the phone down. He said to Kelly, "Let's go for a coffee." When they were outside the flat and walking down the road, Douglas said, "Even though it sounds fanciful, we have to assume the worst. At least our telephone will be tapped; the flat may also be bugged. I think these people are from MI5, so we need to be very careful."

Kelly replied, "If they are MI5, what do they want?"

Douglas said, "I don't really know, but I think they are following up on the missing secret list the dead man had, and I think they want to know what I know about the dead man.

I think they were in our flat looking for the list of names of the Committee of Three Hundred. The fact that the man who gave the list to me was murdered indicates how secret and important the list is to them.

They will also have concerns about our connection to the Miner's strike of 1984, and Arthur Scargill's copy of the secret list given for safe keeping to my father."

Kelly asked, "Where is the Arthur Scargill's copy now?"

Douglas said, "No offence, but I feel so bad about bringing this grief to you. For your own safety, it is better that you don't know. I hope you understand."

Kelly nodded. "Yes, I do."

The following day, Douglas entered the police station at five minutes to eleven. He was shown into an interview room by the sergeant. Two men in plain clothes were sitting at the other side of a table set in the centre of the room. One of the men said with a big smile, "Ah! Mr Hamilton, it so good of you to come to see us. My name is James Smith, and this is my colleague, Mr James. We just want to have a friendly chat with you about the statement you made regarding an incident you claim you witnessed in Freemasons' Hall on Wednesday, the second of July 1997."

Douglas's memory flashed back to a time during his first year in the big high school, when the school prefects got the better of his friend Curly and him, when they took their eyes off them to help their other friend, Ginger, get up from a beating he was receiving from the prefects. He also recognised the well-practiced "put your victim at ease" techniques being used by alias James Smith, and he began to warm to the challenge with his entire faculties alert.

Douglas suddenly asked loudly, "Who are you?"

This momentarily put the detective on the back foot. "Oh, you are asking for identification. Yes, yes, here is my badge." He flashed open a wallet, briefly showing an identity badge. Mr James did the same.

Douglas looked him straight in the eye and asked, "Can I have a proper look at your credentials?" They reluctantly brought out the wallets again and handed them to Douglas. He carefully studied them. "It does not say who you actually work for."

Smith quickly said with a forced laugh, "We are part of the intelligence services and don't like to advertise the fact."

Douglas snapped very quickly, "How do I know that? Although you will already know, I remind you that I am about to go into the third year of my law degree, so I know my rights. Or do you want me to lodge a formal complaint?"

Smith said, "Look, there is no need for that. There is no hassle. We just want to check out the statement you made regarding an incident you claim you witnessed in Freemasons' Hall on Wednesday, the second of July 1997."

Douglas said, "I still don't know who you are."

Mr James intervened softly, clearly controlling his temper. "What do you suggest?"

Douglas asked, "What is the name and phone number of your manager?"

Mr James looked at Mr Smith and said, "Give him Whiteside's name and telephone number." Smith wrote the name and telephone number on a piece of notepaper and handed it to Douglas.

Douglas said, "I need access to a telephone with an outside line."

Mr James said, "Come on out to the sergeant's desk." They all went to the sergeant's desk, and Mr James asked, "Can he use an outside telephone?" The tone he used made it clear that it was not a question.

The sergeant said, "Be my guest. It's nine for an outside line."

Douglas picked up the handset, held it to his head, dialled nine, and then entered the telephone number. It was answered by a Mr Whiteside, the name written on the piece of notepaper. Douglas said, "I have two operatives, Smith and James, claiming that they work for you."

Mr Whiteside cautiously said, "Yes."

Douglas asked very quickly, "I need to verify their authenticity. Can you do that by telling me where they should be right now?"

Mr Whiteside said, "Yes, they should be interviewing a Mr Hamilton in Glasgow."

He replied very quickly, "Thank you, Mr Whiteside. Just as definite positive confirmation, what organisation do they claim to work for?"

The way he posed the question, Mr Whiteside had no option, and after a pause he reluctantly said, "MI5." Then he dropped the phone onto its cradle, knowing he had been cleverly put in a corner.

Douglas said, "Okay, that's fine. Let's go back to the interview room."

They entered the interview room, and Mr James said, "We need to take a break." The two operatives left the room, closing the door behind them. Douglas knew that they were trying to regroup, and in order to break his grip on the situation, they would come back much more assertive.

They came back into the room and sat down, and Mr James started by stating loudly, "Right, let's put a stop to all this bloody nonsense. We want to know if the man at Freemasons' Hall told you anything or gave you anything."

Douglas caught them off guard by asking a direct, piercing question. "Is that why you broke into my flat?"

Mr James exploded and stood up, pointing his finger at Douglas. "Listen, smart-arse, we are conducting this investigation—not you."

Smith quickly jumped up and enclosed Mr James in a tight hug. He forced him back and resettled him in his seat, with his face pressed against Mr James's face, until Mr James stopped struggling. James Smith turned to face Douglas and sat back in his seat, forcing a slightly embarrassed smile to his face. "We are not used to being questioned; it is usually the other way around. We ask all the questions."

Adrenaline drove Douglas to snap loudly, "Yes, a one-way process, like the time you interrogated Sandy Hamilton. You didn't let him ask for a break—you just interrogated him to death."

Mr James and Mr Smith looked at each other for several moments. Finally, Mr Smith stood up and said, "End of interview for now. We will definitely continue this at another time."

Douglas walked out of the police station and into the freedom of Glasgow's West End, knowing that this was just the beginning of the nightmare.

Chapter Nine

Kelly's Surprise

When the postman delivered the mail, there was a blue quality envelope amongst the usual assortment of unwanted mail shots. Douglas carefully opened the envelope and extracted a bundle of Bank of England twenty-pound notes and a card. It was a blue-coloured card with a picture of a teddy bear wearing an apron with "Just a Note" printed on it.

The handwritten a message read:

> I am singing "Rowan Tree" again on Saturday, the sixth of September, at the same place at the same time, seven thirty. Please be at the entrance to Freemasons' Hall at seven o'clock prompt, where you will be allowed to tune your pipes in the basement room as before.

> I enclose train tickets from Glasgow and a paid booking confirmation for the Saturday night for a room in my favourite hotel just south of Russell Square Gardens,

which is near to the venue. Please confirm with my secretary.

With best regards,

Ian Campbell

He found Kelly and took her out for a coffee in case their flat was bugged. When they were seated at the table, he told her fully about his encounter with the two MI5 agents and then said, "I know that you love our little flat, but I am worried that our flat is bugged. Would you mind very much if we moved?"

Kelly said, "I feel the same, and since the break-in, I feel that the flat is contaminated."

Douglas replied, "Good. Let's go down to the charity shop and see if they will move our furniture and other belongings for us. We must move quickly and keep MI5 on the wrong foot."

Kelly nodded. "Let's go to my hockey friend Betty, the estate agent, first."

As they walked along Byres Road, Kelly continued. "Douglas, I want you to understand about Betty. When she was at school, she met a boy, and they started going out together. They went together through the last two years of high school, and like us, they planned to marry before they went to university. She arrived at the church for her wedding to find the groom had not turned up. It later came to light that he had run away to another girl friend in London.

"The shock was so devastating on Betty that she spent three months in a psychiatric hospital and a further six months housebound at home. Since recovering sufficiently and borrowing just enough money to buy an estate agent franchise, she has dedicated herself solely to her business and her hockey team. She is still hurting very badly."

Kelly didn't tell Douglas, that she occasionally comforted Betty by sleeping overnight in her bed, which including kissing, cuddling and touching, but it was better he didn't know, as he would never understand.

They arrived at the estate agent's shop, and Kelly greeted Betty using the high five slapping routine which had become a feature amongst the hockey team members. She immediately said, "Betty, I am sorry to trouble you, but we are being troubled by aggressive and sinister men whom Douglas accidently came in contact with in London."

Betty replied, "What kind of trouble?"

Kelly put her off, saying, "It is too complicated to explain in a few words, but we are frightened of these men and need to move into a new flat very fast."

Betty gave a loud laugh. "Right. I am just your girl to confound these rotten men, and I will do so with pleasure."

They were shown several possible flats just off Byres Road, and they visited the most appealing one. It was in very good condition and had been completely redecorated, so they agreed and completed the deal in Kelly's middle and maiden name there and then, with the agreement that there would be no link in the records to their old address, which was in Douglas's name.

They walked along Dumbarton Road to the big charity shop and went in with the intriguing hoarding message "From Solitude to Solidarity". Cecelia, the shop manager, gave them her usual very friendly greeting, and they arranged for the van boys to move their belongings into the new flat the following day.

With the help of the charity shop boys, and with Douglas inspecting every item of furniture and fittings for electronic bugs, it was with some relief that he did not find any surveillance devices. Douglas now wondered when the MI5 operatives would discover they were gone. It had transpired that the flat didn't seem to be bugged, and so it may well be a few days, or even weeks, before the security police noticed the lack of occupancy.

Internally, Douglas questioned himself if he was becoming too paranoid.

They loaded the two vans, thoroughly cleaned and locked the flat, and then delivered all the household goods, clothing, and bedding to the new flat. With Kelly directing operations, they got the place arranged to her liking.

Although suffering some self-doubt, Douglas now felt more secure knowing that there were no surveillance devices overhearing them.

As September approached, Kelly noticed small changes in her metabolism and made an appointment to see her doctor. She waited for Douglas to come home and said, "Douglas, I have been to the doctor, and she says that I am pregnant."

He was delighted and said, "That's great news! If we work together, we can look after the baby and still keep up with university course work."

Kelly threw her arms around him and hugged him hard for a long time, tears of joy running down her face.

They were only in the flat for a few days before Kelly noticed that the date was the fourth of September, and she realised that she had put the Faslane mission to the back of her mind.

She told Douglas that she had to go to Faslane for a few days, and then she travelled by bus to the peace camp, full of apprehension about what was to come.

Chapter Ten

Freemasons' Hall and Westminster Abbey

Douglas travelled to London, catching a train at 6 a.m. and arriving at London Euston just after 12.30 p.m. Using an A to Z Map of London Streets he'd bought in the station newsagents, he walked the straight half mile to the hotel pre-paid by Ian Campbell and booked in. He asked if he could iron his dress shirt, and the receptionist said that the hotel could provide him with an iron and an ironing board because laundering services were not available during the weekend. He was given a key to a room on the first floor by the stairs and made his way to it. It was a nice room with an en-suite toilet and shower.

After carefully removing his chanter, bagpipes, kilt, belt, sporran, jacket, skein du, and kilt shoes from his rucksack, he hung some up on coat hangers and laid others out on suitable flat surfaces. He laid out his shirt, underpants, and socks, which he would wear with his piper's outfit. A porter knocked his room door and handed him an ironing board and an electric iron. He ironed his shirt and his jacket and then carefully hung them up.

He cleaned and brushed his highly polished evening buckle brogue shoes and his kilt belt; using black leather polish, he wiped clean all the leather parts. Finally he gave the silver-plated buckles an extra shine using toilet tissue paper.

Satisfied that everything was ready, he looked at his watch and saw that it was only 2.30 p.m. He looked out of the window and could see that the sun was shining. After putting his room key in his pocket, he left the hotel and used his map to explore his route to the venue.

Freemasons' Hall was less than half a mile from his hotel, and he carefully embedded notable landmarks in his mind as he walked towards it. Heading down the Kingsway, he turned into Great Queen Street. Memories from his previous visit triggered the knowledge it was the building he was seeking as he approached it. However, as he walked along the side of the building, its conservative architecture disguised the reality of the enormous internal dimensions of the interior.

When he arrived in front of the building, he tried to analyse his feelings induced by the austere facade. Adorned with two great columns, the sheer squareness of the entrance, with the building tapering wider as it grew in length and with the apparent bell tower adorned with symbolism. created a desire to come inside. He retreated across the road to view it from a distance and to put these feeling into perspective.

After contemplating the uniqueness of this building, he noticed that he was standing on a street called Drury Lane. and the well-known children's poem came into his head making him smile.

"Do you know the Muffin Man, who lives in Drury Lane."

The spell of Freemasons' Hall broken, he took out his A to Z Street Map and plotted a route to the Waterloo Bridge over the River Thames by making his way down Drury Lane. He found himself singing the children's poem as he walked through the warm afternoon.

He came out into the bright sunshine on to the Victoria Embankment and stood for a few minutes surveying the riverside in both directions. He recognised many famous landmarks from television and film memories, but it was the Palace of Westminster, also known as the Houses of Parliament, with its many towers and ornate elevations that had the greatest impact. The familiarity of these well-known images made him feel good, as though he was somehow in the centre of the universe.

He walked slowly over Waterloo Bridge, stopping often to feast his eyes on the famous London skylines. When he reached the other side of the river, he walked south-west towards the Houses of Parliament and went back over Westminster Bridge. He walked around the famous landmark until he came to Westminster Abbey. Without thinking about it, he paid the entrance fee and entered.

According to the information displayed, Westminster Abbey was steeped in more than a thousand years of history, from when Benedictine monks had first come to the site in the middle of the tenth century.

As a church, it was the most splendid and spectacular, multifaceted monument Douglas had ever seen. He was left wondering, *to what is the reverence directed?* It seemed to his simple mind to be a celebration and statement of England's powerfulness.

He was still pondering this when he chanced to enter a side room that he could have easily missed. It was a curious octagonal room called the Chapter House, dating from 1250, where the first English Parliament used to meet. In fact, in the vestibule of the Chapter House was a door claiming to be the oldest door in Britain, dated to the 1050s. Although faded, he recognised ancient wall panel paintings of scenes from the book of Revelation, and a chilling thought went through his mind—cold decisions made by the ruthless monarchs about the life and death of individuals regularly took place in this room. An inscription underneath stained-glass windows recalled the work of the original masons: "In the handiwork of their craft is their prayer."

That brought his mind back to the reality and purpose of his London visit, tonight's gig in Freemasons' Hall, prompting him to backtrack and get ready.

Chapter Eleven

Another Gig

Douglas still had time to spare, and he wandered into Leister Square, where he bought a slice of pizza from a street cafe and sat on a seat in the square while he ate it. Thinking about dehydration, he went back to the counter, bought a cup of tea, returned to his seat, and indulged in some people watching for a while.

He slowly made his way back to his hotel, showered, shaved, and dressed in his Highland piper's outfit. Then checked his bagpipes and put them back in their bag. Douglas went down to reception and told the receptionist that he was going out to an appointment but would not be late.

Douglas walked to Freemasons' Hall and felt a build-up of nervous pre-performance tension. Has met by a doorman, and after verifying who he was, he was shown in and confronted by a reception desk.

The male receptionist didn't smile and said in a very condescending manner, "Yes, Mr Hamilton, you are expected. Just wait here."

At exactly seven o'clock, a man approached and said, "Mr Hamilton, my name is Gerry, and I am the sound engineer. We briefly met the last time, although we were too rushed to prepare properly. Come with me down to the basement, where you can tune your bagpipes and I can take some sound measurements."

After they finished the technical measurements and adjustments, Gerry said, "That's perfect. I can balance the unamplified sound of your pipes with the outputs from the piano and the singer. Just remember to keep the maximum distance from their microphones. Come with me to the Grand Temple, and we will go to the back of the stage. It's about fifteen minutes before you play."

The performance went very well, and the audience of over one thousand rose to their feet, applauding enthusiastically and calling for more. However, the master of ceremonies was not to be diverted from his programme. Gerry led Douglas away from the back of the stage and back to the front of the building by a way of corridors and unoccupied side rooms.

Douglas walked back to the hotel and then cleaned and packed his bagpipes and piper's clothes. Now dressed in casual clothes and trainers, he went out to do a little sightseeing. Douglas made his way onto the Underground Circle Line and caught a tube to Tower Hill tube station. He walked along the river past the Tower of London, thinking again about individuals who were tortured in the basement dungeons of the great building while the rulers wined and dined in the floors above.

When he finally came back to his hotel, he decided to go into the bar for a beer before going to bed. Mr Ian Campbell was sitting at the bar on a bar stool. He saw Douglas and shouted, "Come over. What would you like to drink?"

"Can I have a half pint of lager, please?"

Ian said in his loud, very cultured voice, "I don't do half pints. Barmaid, a pint of lager for my friend, and another glass of Glenmorangie for myself—and get yourself one. Come here, Douglas, and sit beside me." This was followed by a loud laugh.

Douglas sat on the high bar stool and took a sip of the lager. He said, "Thank you. That's nice and cool." Ian was still dressed in his expensive full Highland kilt and accessories, and so Douglas asked, "Would you not be better putting your good clothes away in case they get stained?"

Ian laughed loudly and said, "No, I like to fly the flag down here." Douglas noticed that his voice had a distinct slur. "Give me another glass of Glenmorangie, dear," Ian continued without a pause. "My song went down a treat tonight. A brilliant idea of mine to back it with the bagpipes playing in the background. That's what you call vision, and that's what makes us Olympians stand out from the rest."

Douglas didn't have a clue what he was talking about, and so to make conversation he asked, "Do you sing professionally? Is that what you do for a living?"

Ian almost fell off his stool, laughing loudly. "No, no. I am sales director of one of the biggest arms manufacturers in the world. Hush, hush—I can't tell you too much. Let's change the subject. Are you a boxing fan? I am a fan. I am friendly with a boxing promoter down in the East End."

There was a pregnant pause for a moment following the forced interruption and change of subject. Douglas tried another tack. "Olympians? Did you compete in the Olympics?"

"No," replied Ian with a laugh. "Another glass of Glenmorangie, please, barmaid. The twelve great gods of the Greeks were known as the Olympians. Together they presided over every aspect of human life. As we enter this new age of Aquarius, the Olympians are now three hundred world individuals picked in a few cases for their bloodline, but mainly individuals whose intellect is in the genius class and who are in positions of power. This world is spiralling into degeneration, and we Olympians will resurrect and establish a new world order."

He took a sip of his whisky, theatrically swilled it round his mouth, and said, "Beautiful, beautiful, Glenmorangie. Truly the Vale of Tranquillity." He smacked his lips as though he was kissing the air.

Ian Campbell looked straight at Douglas and said with a definite slur, "The Olympians will save this doomed world through the globalisation of everything. It will take time, because national identity and national pride are very deeply ingrained. You only must look at Scots and Irish history to see extreme examples, but it is true of all nationalities. They will all die for their flags if challenged. Then you have the added complication of religion. Again, people will withstand torture, even to death, for their tribal religious beliefs."

He paused as though deep in thought with a glazed look in his eyes.

Douglas eventually said with a laugh, "I don't think you will see the elimination of these core human loyalties in your lifetime."

Ian snapped out of his daydream and shouted, "We will! We will. Once we have good people like the News Corporation chairman in full control of the media, we will apply the latest methods of mind control on the ordinary people."

Douglas felt his working-class hackles rise and asked aggressively, "What do you mean, 'the ordinary people'?"

Ian reacted quickly, stating, "In every age, there is small elite of gifted people whose intellect sets them apart from the masses writhing about and fulfilling their bodily needs and functions."

Douglas responded angrily, "Who do you think you are?"

Ian interjected quickly and loudly. "Sorry, sorry. I have drunk too much and said too much. Enough drink for one night." He lurched to his feet and marched away, two steps forward and one to the side.

Well after he was gone and out of earshot, the barmaid approached and quietly said to Douglas, "Be careful not to upset Mr Campbell. He has connections with very serious people." She quickly moved away, as though frightened someone would see her speaking to Douglas. Douglas sat quietly thinking as he finished his pint.

The following morning, Douglas showered, shaved, and dressed in his casual clothes before going down for breakfast. He read two newspapers because there was plenty of time in hand to catch his train. Feeling satisfied, he collected his rucksack from his room and reported to the reception desk to check out. The receptionist handed him an envelope and said, "Mr Campbell left this envelope with instructions to give it to you."

He put it in his rucksack, paid his bill, and left the hotel, and then walked the short distance to Euston station. The indicator board told him the Glasgow train was boarding, and he found the coach and his seat number specified on his ticket. There was no reserved ticket on the seat next to his, and so he assumed that if he was lucky, he might have the double seat to himself. He took out the letter and put his rucksack on the empty seat.

The train slowly pulled out of the station, and Douglas opened the letter. He took out the contents. There was 150 pounds in fifty-pound notes, Mr Ian Campbell's business card, and a letter written on the same light blue paper as before.

> Thank you again for your high-quality accompaniment. I know that I have already paid you, but this is a measure of my added appreciation.
>
> I will not repeat the same entertainment next year, or it will become commonplace and less appreciated, but maybe again in three or so years?
>
> Remember to inform my secretary of future changes in your contact details.

My advice to you is qualify in international law because as globalisation increases, so will the demand for international lawyers, and I have contacts in News Corporation.

With best regards,

Ian Campbell

Douglas carefully secreted the money in a secure pocket and sat back to think about the enormity of what Mr Campbell had inadvertently revealed through drink.

Chapter Twelve

Dangerous Mission

At the Faslane Peace camp, Kelly found Felicity, who was hyper with excitement and contemplating the coming adventure.

Felicity and Kelly each wore a small backpack containing essential provisions and waterproof clothing. They caught the bus into Helensburgh and met Jacques with his large white van. The trio repeated the previous journey to a wood across from the Faslane nuclear base. This time, just in case security checked the old campsite, they chose a location farther down the road near Rosneath.

The two women lay still until the appointed time and then went into action. This time, although it was dark, it was a clear night and they could see the activity across and farther up the loch. They were camped opposite the Rhu Narrows, and it was a particularly high tide, with the water lapping inches from their tent. However, the nuclear submarine would have to pass near the wooded shore where they would launch their kayak.

The women were tensed like two springs when Felicity suddenly said, "Let's go." They pushed the kayak into the water and waded after it, quickly climbing into their respective cockpits. They were paddling furiously within seconds.

They had intended to cross the bow to try to bring the nuclear submarine to a halt, but Felicity had misjudged the speed of the submarine, and their impact point was now going to be near the rear of the huge vessel, which was running with its deck just above the water, giving them new hope that they could clamber aboard.

A security patrol boat spotted them and raced towards them. They paddled furiously, but just before they reached their target, the patrol boat intentionally struck the rear of the kayak, forcing their bow into the huge, fanlike propeller of the submarine. The very sophisticated propeller, designed for silent running, was more like a giant version of a multi-bladed kitchen blender.

The submarine did not slow down but continued its way into the night, leaving a shimmering wake behind it.

The patrol boat circled behind the submarine. It then chased after a shadowy shape in the water, which proved to be a school of porpoises.

Deciding that there was no trace of the protesters and conscious of their primary task, the patrol boat raced after the submarine, reformed into their standard escort position, and continued to shepherd the evil monster towards the ocean deeps.

The waters of the deep loch slowly returned to stillness with no sign of the kayak and its occupants, almost as though nothing had disturbed them.

However, Felicity was floating on her back, using the buoyancy of the life jackets. She cradled the unconscious Kelly in her arms and kept her head just above the water. When the porpoises had diverted the patrol boat away in the opposite direction, the tidal current had carried them away from the scene of the incident.

Eventually they washed ashore near a gypsy encampment, and their presence attracted the attention of the camp dogs. Fortunately, the dogs were tethered, but they set off an onslaught of barking that brought several gypsies running to investigate.

Chapter Thirteen

Questioned on Suspicion of Murder

Douglas arrived back in Glasgow from his gig, went to the Underground Tube, and caught a Clockwork Orange train. He got off at Hillhead station and walked to the flat.

With his heart beating wildly, he made his way up the stairs and opened the door. He gingerly made his way in and checked all the rooms, but it was just as he'd left it, with all the carefully set traps to detect intruders in place. He tried to phone Kelly's mobile phone but got a message that the number was unobtainable.

Two days passed. Then on the third morning, at 5.30 a.m., police dressed in combat gear broke open his door and rushed into his bedroom. One of the officers pulled the duvet off him, and another officer pulled away the pillows, leaving Douglas completely naked and lying on the fitted bed sheet.

With the two police officers in their combat gear standing menacingly over him, a female police officer stepped between them and asked, "I am Inspector Mackenzie. Are you Douglas Hamilton?"

Douglas said, "Yes."

"I am making enquiries about the whereabouts of your wife, Kelly Hamilton. We have good reason to believe that she has come to harm. Do you know where she is?"

Douglas did not know what to say. He did not want to betray Kelly's last known whereabouts to the police. He tried to sit up, but one of the police officers pushed him back down hard with the point of his baton.

She repeated the question. "Do you know where your wife is?"

Douglas remained silent. His nakedness made him feel vulnerable, and he knew the police were exploiting it. He tried to swing his legs over the edge of the bed, and the other police officer hit him hard on the shin with his metal baton. The pain was excruciating, and Douglas lay writhing in agony for several minutes until the pain eventually subsided to an ache.

Eventually the inspector said, "I am asking you for the third and last time. Do you know where Kelly Hamilton, your wife, is?" Douglas remained silent. She said, "Let him dress and bring him to the police station for further questioning."

As they left the building, Douglas caught the briefest glimpse of Mr James and Mr Smith from MI5 sitting in the backseat of one of the police cars parked at the pavement.

They held him at the police station, making sure he did not sleep. A succession of police officers questioned him for about twenty-four hours, but he remained silent, except for whistling and drumming his fingers on the table to the tune "Rowan Tree" until they realised it was futile.

As they discharged him, they warned him to not leave the area because he would be required for further questioning.

It was a week since he'd returned from London, and still no word from Kelly, Douglas was concerned. After all, he remembered her saying that she was going for only a few days. He got a bus to Helensburgh and went into a local café for lunch. After enquiring how to get to the Faslane nuclear base and being informed he should catch the bas at the bus stop across the road, he travelled to the peace camp.

It was a lovely day, and the peacc campers were sitting at a table in the open air, eating their lunch.

Douglas approached and said, "My name is Douglas Hamilton."

He stopped speaking as he saw one of the women make an expression with her mouth like a silent *Oh!* She gathered herself and said, "Sit down." The others rose and quietly left. The woman said, "My name is Megan. I don't know how to make this easy." She paused.

Douglas quickly said, "Go on. Please tell me what you have to."

Megan looked at him in the eye and said, "On the sixth of September, Kelly and Felicity went out in a kayak to intercept a nuclear submarine leaving the base. They did not return. We tried to make enquiries, but we were told that the base did not know anything about them. That was just over a week ago."

Douglas's mind was racing. "Tell me all you know."

Megan said, "For security reasons, the two women organised the mission themselves and were completely on their own. You must understand that the security forces infiltrate the camp with one of their own people from time to time; in this game, you cannot trust anyone. However, I knew about the rumour that one of the submarines was preparing to leave the base, and so Andy and I cycled down to Rhu and, using binoculars, watched the narrows from the beach. We watched the submarine approach. Then we saw two people on the other side of the loch, who we assumed to be Felicity and Kelly.

"They launched the tandem kayak and started paddling furiously towards the submarine.

One of the police patrol boats spotted them and raced to stop the kayak from getting to the submarine. The submarine came between our line of sight and the boats, so we could not see what was happening.

After the submarine passed, the police patrol boat reappeared behind the submarine. The patrol boat circled the area in the wake of the submarine for about five minutes. Then it raced back to cruise in formation alongside the submarine. There was no sign of the kayak. It had disappeared."

Douglas was confused. "What about the police? They must know something."

Megan replied, "We tried asking them, but they claim they don't know anything about it. However, we registered Kelly and Felicity as missing with the police at Dumbarton, and we have reported the incident as two suspected fatalities to the Health and Safety Executive in Glasgow, but they don't want to know. I will make you a cup of tea."

Douglas said, "No, I will go to the submarine base."

Chapter Fourteen

Going into the Dragon's Den

Two Ministry of Defence police officers confronted Douglas as he approached the entrance to Faslane Submarine Base.

He introduced himself, "My name is Douglas Hamilton. I am here trying to find my wife, Kelly."

He caught a sense of panic as each of the police officers glanced nervously at each other. One of them, wearing sergeant's stripes, eventually asked, "What makes you think she is here?"

Douglas said, "Because this is where she was last seen."

The other police officer aggressively blurted out, "No, she wasn't here. She was on the loch."

The sergeant glared at him and shouted, "Shut up! I'm the senior here, so let me do all the talking. Keep your stupid mouth shut."

Douglas asked, "I wish to see the most senior officer at this base. Will you arrange it, or do I go get a court injunction?"

As he waited for them to get instructions, Douglas mentally noted their police numbers displayed on the shoulder epaulettes of their uniforms by repeating them in his mind.

After a seemingly long hour waiting outside the main gate, a car arrived from somewhere inside the base and stopped just inside the gate. A woman dressed in civilian clothes got out of the rear seat of the car and came towards them.

One of the police officers opened the gate, and she walked through, holding out her hand to Douglas and saying with a big, sparkling smile, "Hello, I am Gloria Pentangle, public relations. Come in, and I will take you to my office after you sign in and get a visitor's badge."

Following a thorough frisk search by the MOD police officer, who smelled of whisky, and then receiving a short visitor's induction, Gloria ushered Douglas into the backseat of the car and then walked round and got into the other side. The car took them to an office block, and she inserted her identity card in the door entry system to gain entry to the building.

As she passed through the central office, she said to a man, "Stuart, will you join us, please?" It was clearly not meant as a question. She led Douglas to her office with Stuart following. They entered the bright office, and she gestured to Douglas to sit at a table with four seats.

Gloria said with a big smile, "This is Stuart. He will make notes of our meeting, just to make sure that we understand your concerns if we are to help you with your enquiry." She finished by looking at Douglas with a big smile, showing an almost perfect set of sparkling white teeth.

He had a momentary flashback to his schooldays, reminding him of the way the sly prefects presented themselves when they were lying to the school management team.

Gloria took the initiative by asking Douglas, "What do you think we can help you with?"

Douglas was highly stressed and shouted, "You know perfectly well why I am here! The police sergeant told you why I am here! This is not some kind of game I am playing!"

A man opened the office door, stuck his head in, and asked, "Is everything all right?"

By this time Douglas was hyperventilating, and he tried to stand but felt light-headed. He fainted, falling to the floor.

Douglas woke lying fully clothed on a bed in a small room with a nurse standing beside the bed. She said, "Ah! You are awake now. Everything is all right. You fainted. I am Nurse McIntosh, and I will make you a cup of tea."

He got off the bed and sat on a chair. His mind was in turmoil, and he could not think straight, but he had this heavy feeling in his heart and stomach and a thought at the forefront of his mind: *I have to find* Kelly.

The nurse came back with a mug of tea and a small plate of cheese sandwiches, saying, "I have a feeling you need something to eat. When did you last eat?"

Douglas was so distraught by losing Kelly that he could not think when he had last eaten, and so he shook his head.

The nurse picked up a sandwich and proffered it to his mouth. Douglas accepted the food like a small baby and ate it. The nurse continued until he had eaten all the sandwiches. Then she held the cup to his mouth until all the tea was finished.

She asked, "Is that enough?" Douglas nodded. "What's wrong? You are very shocked."

Douglas said, "I have lost Kelly." Then he began to cry. The nurse went out and closed the door.

After a while, Douglas stood up and walked over to the wash basin. He washed his face and wetted and combed his hair. After looking in the mirror, he dried his face. He opened the door and found the nurse. He said, "Thank you. I am okay now. Could you please get in touch with that PR woman, Gloria?"

Stuart arrived at the medical centre after about ten minutes.

Douglas asked, "Can we carry on with the meeting?"

Stuart was hesitant. "I don't know. I think we thought the meeting was over."

Douglas snapped, "Well, it's not over. Contact your boss, Gloria, and tell her I want to finish the meeting."

Stuart left the medical centre to report Douglas's demand to Gloria Pentangle.

Chapter Fifteen

Enemy Confronted

The nurse asked, "Douglas, do you really think it is a clever idea to have an important meeting when you are in a state of shock? These people are professionals."

Douglas smiled for the first time and said, "I know, but I appreciate your concern. I can tell that it is genuine. If you really want to help me find out what happened to my wife, you could check your logbook for the sixth to seventh of September to see if any emergency was recorded."

The nurse opened a drawer and lifted out a large book with "Shift Logbook" printed on it. She opened the pages, found 6 September, and laid it on her desk. She pointed to the photocopier and then she exclaimed, "Excuse me, I have to go to the loo. I have terrible constipation."

Duncan grabbed the book, strode to the photocopier, placed the page he wanted on the glass, and closed the lid. He pressed the copy button, but the warming-up message appeared. It seemed to take an eternity, but eventually the copier acted, and a copy of the page was delivered out. He quickly closed the logbook and returned it to its drawer and closed the drawer.

He checked the photocopy of the page, which told him that the medical staff were put on alert and instructed to prepare to possibly receive two badly injured or dead bodies from the loch, thought to have impacted with the submarine's terrible propeller.

Douglas carefully folded the photocopy so as not to damage the important message and inserted it down the side of his sock.

The nurse returned and said, "What a relief, constipation is no fun. Let me take your pulse."

While she was doing that, Stuart returned and said, "You are lucky Gloria is still here and can give you a few minutes."

The nurse asked, "Are you sure this is wise? Your pulse is racing."

Douglas said, "It's okay, and thanks for the tea and sandwiches."

Gloria was sitting at the table and facing the door when they entered her office. She said immediately and aggressively, "Sit down. I hope you realise I am past my finish time."

Douglas looked her straight in the eye and said, "I want to know what happened to my wife on the night of sixth of September in an accident with your submarine and its patrol boats."

Gloria looked him in the eye and said, "We didn't find any evidence of an accident that night."

Douglas quickly replied, "So you *did* have an incident that night."

The speed of his reaction caught even this experienced liar off-balance. She stammered, "There was no trace of them."

Douglas shouted very loudly, "Them? So, there was more than one!"

She hesitated to look towards Stuart, but he averted his eyes and made a gesture that seemed to say, *I told you so.* it was clear that he did not want to be implicated, and she seemed to be undermined "No, two. We think there were two, didn't we?" Again she looked at Stuart, but his eyes were clearly looking at the desktop. She tried to compose herself, and then she tried to backtrack. "We did all we could, but the patrol boat couldn't find anything that night. Whoever it was must have been shredded by the propeller, and there were no traces of people or clothing.

Only a little debris from the broken kayak could be found the following morning." She showed signs of some internal emotional conflict. "Anyway, our priority is to protect the submarines, not protesters."

She got up from her seat with tears streaming from her eyes and almost ran to the office door. She turned and shouted, "Stuart, call security and tell them to put Mr Hamilton off the base. I must leave. It's away past my time. People don't appreciate how many hours I work, and I am so overtired." She ran out of the office and pushed roughly past the two MOD police officers who were coming in the main door.

Douglas was escorted to the police patrol van by the same two officers who had initially met him at the gate. The sergeant said, "Get him in the van."

Douglas moaned, "I feel faint," and he slumped onto his knees on the road beside the van.

The junior police officer shouted to the police sergeant, "Ronald, he's fainted!"

The sergeant came running around, exclaiming, "Bastard! Larry, open the rear doors, and we will get him in the back. We don't want left with him on our hands."

Douglas pretended to be unconscious and tried to be a dead weight. The two MOD Police Officers struggled to lift him, and so they dragged him to the back of the van and roughly bundled him in, closing the double doors behind him. The junior police officer started the engine, and the van began to move slowly away from the administration block.

He pulled himself into a sitting position and said, "Well, it's been a fruitful day."

The sergeant snapped, "What do you mean by that?" Douglas remained silent. The sergeant repeated aggressively, "What did you mean by that last remark?"

Douglas replied quietly, "Oh! Nothing, really. Just, that the PR lady was very helpful."

The sergeant asked quickly, "How do you mean very helpful? Tell me."

He looked at the sergeant and saw that the man was quite agitated. He paused to prolong the suspense and then said, "The PR lady confirmed to me that there had been an accident involving your patrol boat and two peace protesters as a submarine left the base on patrol. She said, 'The officers who let me into the base, Ronald and Larry, were on the patrol boat that night and knew most about it.' She said I should to ask them to account for their actions, not her."

The driver suddenly braked, stalled the engine, and shouted, "No! She wouldn't say that, not Gloria! She wouldn't hang us out to dry!"

"Shut up, Larry," snapped the sergeant. "Don't say any more. Get this guy out of here and don't say another word."

The two police officers silently led Douglas to the main gate and rushed him through, closing and locking the big gate behind him. Douglas shouted through the bars, "See you soon, Ronald!"

Megan was watching for him. She ran to meet him and escorted him across the road to the peace camp. She made him a big mug of tea, which he drank slowly. Megan reappeared with a bowl of soup and two slices of bread. She sat watching him as he slowly supped the soup.

When he was finished, he said, "Thank you, Megan. Do you have a pad of writing paper and a pen?" She took the cup, bowl, plate, and cutlery away and came back with a small reporter's notebook and a pen. Douglas wrote on the top sheet of paper. "What was Felicity's surname?"

She replied, "Gray."

When he finished, he tore the sheet out of the note book and handed it to Megan. Megan took the sheet and started to read.

> On 6 September 1997, a nuclear-missile–carrying submarine left the base on patrol. Two peace protesters, Felicity Gray and Kelly Hamilton, tried to intercept the submarine using a tandem kayak.

A police patrol boat with at least two police officers, one a sergeant named Ronald and one an officer named Larry, tried to force the kayak away from the submarine but instead forced it into the submarine's propeller.

The accident happened in darkness, and no bodies or wreckage was found. Only debris of the broken kayak was found, no trace of the two protestors, or their clothing was found.

The two police officers have first-hand knowledge of the accident, and Public Relations Officer Gloria Pentangle knows all about it.

He looked at Megan and said quietly, "They think Kelly's dead, but I don't think so. They did not find any human remains or clothing. Keep that paper safe in case anything bad happens to me. I would appreciate if you would make photocopies. Keep one yourself, send one to the Health and Safety Executive, send one to the police, and give me the original back, please."

He briefly told Megan about the police raid on his flat and being interrogated at the police station. He finished by saying, "Megan, I think they are trying to fabricate a charge that I murdered my Kelly."

Megan said, "Come into my caravan. There is a spare bedroom; you can sleep there. I have a big bottle of cider, if that helps to kill the pain."

Chapter Sixteen

Strategic Decision

Megan knocked on Douglas's bedroom door and entered carrying a mug of coffee. "Drink this to liven you up, and then come through for breakfast." She put the mug on the little bedside table and left the small bedroom.

Douglas threw back the duvet, sat up on the side of the bed, and slowly drank his coffee. He was wearing his underpants and noticed that the bottle of cider was empty. He felt terrible, but he could not work out whether it was the effect of drinking all that cider or his worry and grief.

He went through to the bathroom and then came back to the bedroom and dressed. He found Megan in the little kitchen-cum-diner and sat at the small table. He said, "Megan, I feel terrible. I miss Kelly, and for the first time in my life, I don't know what to do."

Megan placed a plate of bacon, sausage, and eggs on the small table and said, "Eat this. It will make you feel a bit better." As Douglas picked slowly at his food, she said, "Kelly told me about the man found in the River Thames, the break-in at your flat, and your interview with the MI5 agents trying to find out if you had the secret list of names. Following your visit to the base and the mistakes they made in answering your questions, now you tell me that the police are trying to frame you for Kelly's murder. All taken together, this puts you in danger. If this is as big as it seems, with worldwide implications, the police are not going to seriously investigate the alleged incident involving protesters at a nuclear submarine base, especially if they can use it to discredit your reputation in case you reveal their secret list.

"In your grief, you are not in a fit state to deal with these professional killers, and it won't be long before they come here looking for you. The bin men are due any time to empty our wheelie bins, and they are peace camp sympathisers. Here is the name of a street newspaper seller at Queen Street station in Glasgow. Go to him, and he will help you disappear."

She handed him a piece of paper with the name Carroty Charlie written on it and said, "You will know why he is called Carroty when you see his red hair. Tell him Megan says, 'Don't put your faith in nuclear idols.' Douglas, take this notebook. I have written my peace camp phone number. Remember that the pigs monitor all the phone calls, so I have put some code words and numbers in the book for you to use, if you phone me—but keep your message short. If we must meet, make it the bar in Queen Street Station in Glasgow, but do not mention the meeting place on the phone; so far it remains a safe venue. Come now. The refuse lorry is here."

They ran from the caravan screened from the road by the side of the big refuse lorry. Megan opened the cab door on the passenger side and said, "Quick, get into the cab and lie on the floor so that the pigs won't see you."

The driver didn't even look at him, and the bin loader climbed into the lorry and sat on the passenger seat as if he didn't see Douglas either. The lorry moved off along the road without anyone asking Douglas who he was. After a few minutes had passed, the driver said, "We will drop you at Garelochhead railway station. There is a train due for Glasgow in less than an hour."

As an afterthought, he asked, "Do you have enough money to buy a ticket?"

Douglas, who was still lying on the floor of the lorry cab, said, "Yes."

After a while, the lorry slowed down, the driver selected a lower gear, and the lorry climbed up what seemed to be a long incline. The lorry stopped, and the bin handler opened his door and jumped down, saying, "This is it." He helped Douglas down and pointed to the station further up the hill. "Good luck."

Douglas made his way to the station and waited. There was no one else waiting, however he felt very noticeable and he stood against the fence trying to be small. The train soon arrived, and he boarded. He saw the ticket collector and approached him, saying, "Can I have a single to Glasgow, please?" He paid, put his ticket in his pocket, and took an empty seat.

Douglas was very confused, and his grief from knowing that his pregnant Kelly was missing overwhelmed him. The train arrived at Queen Street Station, and he got off. He decided to have a cup of coffee to try to straighten out his thinking. The more he tried to think, the more confused he became. He fingered the keys to his flat, but icicles of fear entered his heart because Kelly would not be there—and the bogeymen from MI5 might be waiting.

After taking out his wallet, he looked at his personal bank card. He knew he had 2,500 pounds in his own personal account. He thought the MI5 agents would get around to closing his and Kelly's accounts to deny them money. If he wanted to draw out the bulk of his personal account, he would need proof of identity.

He decided that he was being paranoid. He would chance it and go to their flat.

Douglas walked to the Underground station at Buchanan Street and bought a return ticket. Not feeling very confident, he got off at the Hillhead station and slowly walked towards the flat, carefully scanning the area with his eyes. He could not see anything unusual on the street.

With his heart beating wildly, Douglas made his way up the stairs and opened the door. He gingerly made his way in and checked all the rooms, but it was just as he had left it, with all the carefully set traps to detect intruders still in place.

Rushing now, he found his passport, his birth certificate, his last employment P45 form, a recent electricity bill, and his last bank statement. He carefully put them in a small briefcase. Then Douglas remembered his piper's kit, which was still packed in the rucksack with his toilet kit. He opened the rucksack and packed as many pairs of underpants, socks, and T-shirts as it would take.

He changed into his trekking boots that he had bought for the West Highland Way and tied a relatively new pair of trainers to the outside of the rucksack. After belting his Gore-Tex hill-walking jacket to the top of his rucksack, he put on his best fleece jacket as a way of taking two jackets with him.

He said out loud, "If I am on the run, I need to travel light. That's all I can take."

Douglas quelled a terrible feeling of panic. He then went through every piece of clothing and furniture that would be left in the flat, removing every piece of paper or plastic containing any kind of personal information. He cut these into many small pieces before putting them into a polythene carrier bag, surprised at how much there was; he had to part fill a second carrier bag to complete the job.

He carried out a final check, picked up his now bulging rucksack and two carrier bags, and left the flat, locking the door behind him. Douglas spotted a wheelie bin outside a shop and deposited the two carrier bags under some of the contents of the bin.

Satisfied with his disposal of possible leads to the agents of MI5, he went to his usual bank and waited in the small queue. When it was his turn, he approached the bank teller. He handed her his bank card and said, "My wife has …" His voice broke, and tears streamed into his eyes.

He gathered himself and said, "I need to draw my money out of my personal account to cover the costs of a funeral. You, see my wife has been killed in a dreadful boating accident at the Faslane Peace Camp." With his eyes still streaming, he pushed the evidence of his identity towards the teller, who knew him well as a regular customer.

Embarrassed by his distress, she quickly checked the papers, photocopied them, and passed them back to him, saying, "How much do you want?"

Douglas croaked, "Two thousand four hundred."

She counted out 140 twenty-pound notes into fourteen separate piles of ten. Then after checking each pile again, she rolled them into cylindrical bundles and looped an elastic band round each bundle. She put them together in a cardboard folder, which she secured with two strong elastic bands. The bank teller processed the paperwork and bank card through her machine, which produced a receipt that she passed to Douglas to sign. He passed it back to her, and she separated it into two copies, put one in the bank folder, and passed it and his bank card to Douglas.

She said quietly, "I am really sorry about your wife."

Douglas barely managed to say, "Thank you," and walked away.

Once outside the bank, he went into a café and ordered a cup of coffee. He asked where the toilet was and went into the small cubicle, locking the door. He opened the bank folder and spread the fourteen bundles of notes into seven zipped pockets in his trousers, anorak, and rucksack.

He went to the estate agent and sought out Betty, his wife's friend. He said, "Kelly is missing. They think she was killed in a tragic accident at the Faslane Peace Camp, but there was no trace of humans, just debris from the kayak." He broke down again.

The estate agent said, "Come into the staff room, and I will make you a cup of tea." They went to the staff room where Betty made a cup of tea. They sat at a small table with two chairs. "Please tell me what happened."

Douglas took out his wallet, extracted the piece of paper he had written at the Faslane Peace Camp, and handed to Betty. Betty read the note twice and then handed it back to him. She sat back, not knowing what to say. Finally, she said, "I am so sorry. Can I help you in any way?"

Douglas gathered himself and said, "Thank you, I'm okay. But I need to cancel the lease on the flat. We furnished it very nicely, and I am happy to leave the furnishings in place."

Betty said, "That is very good of you. Let's walk over and have a look." They got up from the table and went into the shop. She said. "Janice, look after the shop for half an hour." She inspected the furniture, carpets, and curtains with an expert eye and said, "It's really nice stuff. Your furniture is all solid hardwood. The carpets and curtains are new. The flat won't need redecorating, and that alone will save me at least a thousand quid. I think the furnishings are worth at least fifteen hundred pounds cash to me, and I can let it as a quality furnished flat almost immediately." Smiling, she asked, "What do you say to two thousand smackers, cash in hand?"

Douglas was flabbergasted. He had not expected this generosity, and he had planned to get the charity shop to clear the flat, but he had not expected anything in return. He replied quietly, "That's very kind. Kelly would be pleased if she was here …" His voice broke at the mention of her.

Betty coughed to cover her embarrassment and said, "Let's go back to the office." She went into the staff room for a few moments and then returned. She counted out twenty hundred-pound notes and said, "Swap your keys for these. I really liked Kelly."

He handed the estate agent his house keys, saying, "I am sorry, I haven't got Kelly's keys. They must be still at the Faslane Peace Camp."

Betty said, "It doesn't matter; we change the locks as standard practice. Give me your forwarding address."

Douglas said, "I don't have one. I don't know what I am going to do now. Remember that Kelly told you nasty men were bothering us? They are secret service agents and because I have important information that could rock the political establishment. They are trying to frame me for the murder of Kelly, but you have just read what happened."

The estate agent said, "In that case, I will get Janice, my assistant, to notify all the utilities, services, and the post office that your residency at this address is now ceased."

Douglas said. "Just in case Kelly contacts you, please tell her that Douglas has gone to ground, but he is still looking for her."

He thanked the estate agent and left her as she noted the electricity meter readings and closed off the water supply. He hid the two thousand pounds at the bottom of his rucksack because there was no room left in zipped pockets.

He made his way to the local library, where he previously had hidden the list of the names of the committee of three hundred. Douglas nodded to the librarians, who knew his face quite well, and went over to the reference section. He took down a very large and thick reference book, *The British Yearbook of International Law*, and opened the front two pages, where he had secreted the list inside the protective book cover. He knew the first page would not be of interest to readers.

He extracted the three sheets of paper containing the list of names of the Committee of Three Hundred, and again he hid the folded papers in the small briefcase and placed it at the bottom of his rucksack.

He carefully replaced the book and walked past the librarians. One said, "You are the only one who looks at that book."

Surprised by the comment, he responded as best he could with the reply, "Yes, I have to check it occasionally, because I can't remember it all."

The librarian a laughed. "If you could, you would get the job as the Memory Man."

Relieved that he had done all that he could, Douglas caught the Clockwork Orange underground train back to Buchanan Street station. He walked to the Queen Street main railway station to begin a journey into the unknown.

Chapter Seventeen

Disappearing

It didn't take Douglas long to find Carroty Charlie, the street newspaper seller, because he had a big head of curly red hair and periodically shouted, "Read all about it. How did Diana die?"

Douglas approached him, and he automatically held out a copy of the evening newspaper. As he searched out some loose change and paid him, Douglas whispered, "Are you Carroty Charlie?"

The newspaper vendor replied in a hoarse whisper, "Who's asking?"

Douglas, looking straight into Carroty Charlie's piercing eyes, replied, "Megan gave me your name and description and said you would help me to disappear. She said tell him Megan says, 'Don't put your faith in nuclear idols.'"

Carroty Charlie looked at him until Douglas felt uncomfortable under the intense scrutiny. Then Charlie suddenly said, "I still have about twenty papers to sell. Go into the station bar, and I will join you there later."

Douglas found the station bar and ordered a coffee. He paid for it and carried the cup and saucer over to an empty table to wait on Carroty Charlie. He read the newspaper, but in his grief, the stories seemed to be in a different dimension, as though he was reading though the wrong end of a telescope.

He tried to focus and make sense of the lead story about Princess Diana, which was reporting on claims that her death was the work of MI5 on behalf of the royal family. This revelation startled him, and in his stressed state, it caused his adrenalin to flow like an electrical current. He now read the article intently, examining every word as though magnified through the right end of a telescope.

Eventually Carroty Charlie appeared carrying two glasses of whisky and two half pints of beer. He placed one glass of whisky and one-half pint of beer in front of Douglas. He sat down and threw back his glass of whisky in a single gulp. He screwed up his face as if in severe pain, swallowed nosily, licked his lips, took a sip of his beer, and said, "Oh! My, that was beautiful." He said this placing a heavy emphasis on the *u*. He looked at Douglas and said, "Oh! I need another. It's a hauf of the Famous Grouse, with water and nae ice."

Douglas went to the bar and bought one whisky, topped it up with water, and brought it back to the table. He sat opposite Carroty Charlie, who scrutinised him intently. Eventually the news vendor asked, "So you want to disappear, do you?" He looked at Douglas for a long time. "If Megan sent you, you must be all right. What did you say Megan told you to tell me?"

Douglas replied, "Don't put your faith in nuclear idols."

Carroty Charlie's face broke into a big grin, revealing his heavily nicotine-stained teeth. He lifted his whisky glass and threw it back in a single gulp. He again screwed up his face as if in severe pain, swallowed nosily, licked his lips, took a sip of his beer, and said, "Oh! My, that was beautiful, so it was." He held up his glass. "Here's to Megan. Och! Son, my glass is empty again."

Douglas got up and bought him another at the bar, returned to the table, and gave Carroty Charlie the whisky. This time Charlie laid the glass on the table and said quietly to Douglas so that no one could overhear, "Son, do you realise that disappearing is very hard? You will not be able to trust anyone, you will need to leave town, and you can't stay in Glasgow where so many people know you. The loneliness will be so intense that it will be worse than a continual toothache."

He threw back the glass of whisky and gave the empty glass to Douglas, this time without any comment. Douglas replenished the whisky and sat back down.

Carroty Charlie said, "Go to WH Smith's and get a pen and the smallest notepad that they have."

Douglas went to the station bookseller and bought a small notebook and ballpoint pen. He returned, getting another whisky as he passed the bar.

He laid the items on the table in front of Carroty Charlie, who took the pen and began writing in the notebook.

Disappearing without Identity Papers

1. You need to be aware how tough disappearing is. One slip-up, and they will find you.
2. You will need to change your appearance.
3. You will need to use a new name.
4. You will need to connect with the criminal underworld, or you will end up rough sleeping.
5. You will go to a town or city where you are unlikely to meet anyone you know.
6. You cannot apply for anything where you need to supply personal information.
7. You can't claim government benefits, pay National Insurance, or pay income tax.
8. You cannot get medical or dental treatment unless you use a private practice that asks no questions.

9. You cannot own or use anything electronic that can be traced to you.

10. You cannot trust anyone.

Carroty Charlie picked up his empty glass and handed it to Douglas. "Get yourself one as well; you are going to need it. This is going to be a hard lesson for you." Douglas went to the bar and bought two haufs of the Famous Grouse topped up with water. He sat opposite Carroty Charlie and tried a sip of his whisky; it was so horrible that he screwed up his face just like Carroty Charlie, and then he said with a grimace, "Lovely."

Carroty Charlie laughed and said, "You're learning, son." He pushed the notebook in front of Douglas, turning it the right way around. "Read the ten commandments."

Carroty Charlie sipped his whisky as he waited for a reaction. Douglas read the ten commandments of disappearing without identity papers several times over, and then he looked at Carroty Charlie. "I am an ex-Boy Scout, and I am also studying to be a lawyer. I can't keep commandment four."

Carroty Charlie got up and went to the bar; he came back with two more whiskies and said quietly, "If you are on the run from the police, you have three choices. One, you hand yourself in. Two, you disappear, keeping to the Ten Commandments I have given you. Three, you very quickly run out of money and end up sleeping rough, with all the misery that comes with it. Take it from me, son. I've been there several times over, and when you are rough sleeping, you just go down and down and down. You regularly see the Grim Reaper come, and you hope he will take you away in his mercy, but he passes you by, leaving you to suffer your misery as he takes someone else. Believe me, it is that bad. How long do you think your money will last? Look how much you have already spent tonight."

Carroty Charlie got up with a hearty laugh, went to the bar, and bought two more drinks. When he came back, Douglas asked, "Is there no way to do this without becoming a criminal?"

Carroty Charlie thought hard for a few minutes and finally said, "Yes, there is. I have a good feel about you. You must forget your own name. I am giving you the new name Desperate Dan, and you are now one of us. Take this ring and wear it. Other street newspaper vendors wearing a similar ring are members of our network. I will spread the news and add your new nickname to the list, which is passed on hand to hand to all street newspaper vendors in our national network. If you meet a street news vendor wearing a similar ring, you will introduce yourself, and when asked to confirm it, you will reply, 'Scotch Mist.' That's your identity tag. Desperate Dan. Scotch Mist." Carroty Charlie laughed loudly. "Do you get it? When the Scotch mist comes down, it hides Desperate Dan? Write that down in your book, you will get the hang of the anonymous code words in a short time."

He didn't wait for an answer but eventually stopped laughing and said, "Find Sammy Seal, a newspaper seller at Oxford Circus Underground station in London, and tell him Carroty Charlie sent you and has named you Desperate Dan. He will ask you what I said to tell him. Tell him Carroty Charlie says, 'The Famous Grouse is beautiful.' He will reply, 'Flap flipper flap.' You reply, 'Desperate Dan hopes the Scotch mist will come down to hide in.'

"Then tell him that you need a street newspaper vendor's job in London's East End and a drum to live in where no questions are asked. That way you are not really a criminal, except that as a non-person, you can't pay tax. Remember, if you think anyone is watching you, don't hesitate to disappear again."

Carroty Charlie wrote the name "Sammy Seal" and "flap flipper flap" in the notebook and handed it to Douglas, saying, "You need to remember these names and passwords, and look for the special ring on his finger."

Douglas realised that Carroty Charlie was right, and changing his name was his only option now. "Thanks, Carroty Charlie. Would you like another drink? Desperate Dan is buying."

Carroty Charlie replied abruptly, "No. Do you think I am an alcoholic? You need to be focused and very careful. There is an overnight train leaving Central Station at 11.30 every night. Get a ticket for tonight's train. Speak to the steward and tell him Carroty Charlie says a spare sleeper berth is worth a fiver for a friend. Go now. I don't want to see you in Glasgow again, and I certainly don't want to read about you in the newspapers."

Without drinking his whisky, Charlie got up, turned around, and walked away. However, he stopped, turned, and shouted with a smile. "Desperate Dan, it's good to see you have adopted your new name already." He turned and walked away.

The two haufs of whisky were still full, and so Desperate Dan swallowed them one after the other, screwing up his face in a terrible grimace each time. He thought, *just like Carroty Charlie, I could easily get used to these.*

Desperate Dan picked up his bulging rucksack and carried it out to the main station concourse before hitching it onto his back. He looked at the station destination board and saw that it was only half past eight. He left Queen Street station and made his way to Glasgow Central station. Desperate Dan worried badly about Kelly, and his mood swung from the task in hand to serious depression.

He bought himself a single ticket to London Euston, which fortunately automatically allocated him a coach and seat number, or he wouldn't have thought to book a seat. Upon looking up at the destinations board, he saw that it was too early for his train to be displayed, and so he walked through the station looking for somewhere to eat, but the good food outlets seemed to have closed.

Desperate Dan walked out of the station, found a chip shop, and bought a portion of potato chips.

He finished eating the chips and threw the wrappings into a street waste bin. It began to rain, and he passed the open door of a public house. He went in and stood at the bar, wedging his big rucksack between his feet where he could feel it if anyone tried to lift it.

He looked at the curious black ring on his finger. His eyes were naturally drawn to the two skull-and-crossbones motifs engraved in the bright, stainless-steel metal. The rest of the ring had been coated with fired black enamel, providing the starkest possible contrast between it and the exposed stainless steel. It made the unusual double image easily visible to a searching eye.

He ordered a hauf of the Famous Grouse, paid for it, topped up the glass with water, and began to sip it with an occasional involuntary tear falling onto the bar as he contemplated a lonely future without Kelly.

Chapter Eighteen

Journey to London

Desperate Dan boarded the overnight train to London Euston at eleven o'clock. He found his seat and stowed his rucksack on the large luggage racks at the nearest end of the coach, and he was comforted by the fact he could see his rucksack from where he sat.

Upon returning to the door of the train, he stepped down onto the platform. He saw a uniformed steward with a big moustache swaggering along the train towards him, and Desperate Dan asked, "Excuse me, are you the sleeping coach steward?"

He replied, "Yes, how can I help you?"

Desperate Dan noticed that the steward was wearing a similar ring on his pinkie. "Carroty Charlie says a spare sleeper berth is worth a fiver for a friend."

The steward looked intently at him and asked, "What else did he say?" Desperate Dan replied quickly, making sure his ring was in clear view. "The Famous Grouse is beautiful."

The steward smiled and cautiously replied, "A fiver to a friend is a pleasure. By the way, my handle is Sleepy Stuart. Do you get it? Sleeping coach steward. My authentication passwords are, 'A spare sleeper berth is worth a fiver for a friend.' What's your handle?"

He answered, "Desperate Dan, and my confirmation phrase is, 'The Scotch mist will come down.'"

Sleepy Stuart replied, "I will come and find you after the train is rolling." Desperate Dan deftly slipped him a fiver, which he'd been holding in his clenched fist, and Sleepy Stuart quickly concealed it in his own hand.

Dan went back to his seat. A man dressed in a business suit had occupied the seat beside his and had placed his hand luggage in Desperate Dan's seat. He said quietly, "Excuse me, this is my seat."

The businessman made a snorting sound that could only be interpreted as extreme annoyance. He then made a lot of fuss standing up and placing his hand luggage in the overhead rack. After moving his luggage from one position to another as though it was an inconvenience, he finally plumped himself down in his seat and stared out of the window.

Desperate Dan said, "Thank you." After the safety announcements, the train slowly moved off. The public-address system then announced that the buffet bar was open and situated in coach three. Desperate Dan felt uncomfortable beside the other passenger, who was taking as much of the space as he could. He remembered his grief and quickly made his way to the bar.

He ordered a miniature of the Famous Grouse, a small bottle of Highland Spring water, and a glass. He slowly sipped the whisky, standing in the space in front of the buffet bar and bracing himself against the swaying of the high-speed train. He bought another miniature of the whisky to finish the water left in the bottle. He then bought four cans of beer, two quarter bottles of the Famous Grouse whisky, a bottle of water, and two plastic glasses. The barman put these in two paper carrier bags.

He made his way back towards his seat carrying the two paper bags, but before he reached it, he saw Sleepy Stuart coming towards him. As he approached, the steward said, "Follow me, and I will show you where your cabin is, sir."

Desperate Dan replied, "I need to get my rucksack."

Sleepy Stuart said, "Show me where it is, and I will get it, sir." He showed him the rucksack, and the Steward picked it up. "Follow me, sir." He led him to the sleeping car and opened a cabin. "You can have this one. There are hardly any berths booked tonight."

Desperate Dan asked, "How can you account for the use of this cabin if it has not been booked through the system? I don't want to get you into trouble."

The sleeping coach steward looked suspiciously at Desperate Dan and said, "That's none of your business. Why are you asking?" Desperate Dan blushed scarlet for a few moments of oppressive silence, and then Sleepy Stuart let out a genuine laugh and said, "Don't you worry about that, Desperate Dan. I just put it down as a complaining customer who wanted to be moved. It happens all the time."

With that explanation, Desperate Dan felt better about the reprimand, but a thought crossed his mind. You could get used to dishonesty, just like you could get used to the Famous Grouse whisky.

Sleepy Stuart quickly showed him the features of the sleeping cabin and then asked, "What time do you wish to be wakened? The train arrives in London Euston about half past six in the morning."

Desperate Dan thought for a minute and then replied, "Quarter to six will be fine."

Sleepy Stuart pointed to his paper carrier bags, laughed loudly, and said, "Have a good sleep, Desperate Dan. I hope the Scotch mist comes down."

It was warm in the cabin, and so Desperate Dan stripped off and sat down on a seat. He hinged down the little table and opened one of the paper bags. Then he took out a can of beer and poured some of it into the plastic drinking glass, thinking to himself, *It's not a glass; it's a plastic. It's time someone gave the plastic ones their proper name.*

He took out a quarter bottle of the Famous Grouse, poured himself a measure, and topped it up with water. *I am beginning to argue with myself about the name of a plastic glass. What did Carroty Charlie say? The loneliness will be so intense that it will be like continual toothache.* He threw back the whisky to try to kill the pain. He was in such a state of grief, despair, and confusion that he continued drinking the alcohol until it was all gone.

Finally, he curled into the bunk, pulling the duvet over himself. He instantly fell into an inebriated sleep. He was wakened by Sleepy Stuart with a hot cup of coffee and a bacon roll. Desperate Dan really enjoyed the bacon roll and the coffee. He then brushed his teeth, shaved, had a good wash in the small basin, and dressed.

He visited the toilet and said to himself, "It's a good job you had a sleeping cabin to yourself so that no one heard you arguing with yourself and your demons." He returned to his sleeping cabin. He packed his toilet things in his toilet bag and placed it in a rucksack pocket, put the empties in the waste bin, put on his fleece jacket, picked up his rucksack, stiffened his resolve, and went out to face his dangerous new world.

Chapter Nineteen

Arriving in London

Upon leaving the train, Desperate Dan followed the signs and made his way to the Underground. He studied the large map of the Underground system displayed on the wall and saw that he needed to find the Victoria line to go to Oxford Circus.

He bought a day ticket, and because of his depressed state and lack of confidence, he asked the way to the Victoria line. The attendant, looking at him as if he was daft, said, "Just follow the signs to the Victoria line. That's what the signs are for."

That mild criticism snapped him into reality, and he soon got the hang of it again. He found himself on the platform going in the direction of Oxford Circus. He arrived at the busy station and started to look for a newspaper vendor. It didn't take long to find one. Dan approached him and said, "A *Daily Mirror*, please."

As the newspaper vendor stretched out his hand to reach the newspaper, Desperate Dan noticed he was wearing a double skulls-and-crossbones black ring. He asked, "Are you Sammy Seal?"

The newspaper vendor gripped Desperate Dan's wrist and held up his hand, displaying the two rings. "Who's asking?"

"Carroty Charlie sent me, and he has named me Desperate Dan," he stammered, surprised by the intensity of the stare being applied by the paper seller.

The newspaper vendor asked aggressively, "What did Carroty Charlie tell you to tell me?"

Desperate Dan replied, "Carroty Charlie says, 'The Famous Grouse is beautiful.'"

The newspaper vendor said, "Flap flipper flap. I am Sammy Seal."

"Desperate Dan hopes the Scotch mist will come down to hide in," he blurted, hoping it would clear the air.

Sammy Seal laughed loudly.

Encouraged by the reaction, Dan added quickly, "I need to disappear with an untraceable job in London and a drum to live in, where no questions are asked."

Sammy Seal laughed even louder and then eventually asked, "That's a big order. Do you think these important things grow on trees? Okay, do you think you can take over my pitch here while I go and make some phone calls to my contacts? Some people will try to cheat you, and if you let them, they will wipe out your whole day's profit. Don't give them the paper until you have checked the money and check that the money is genuine. They will regularly try to slip worthless foreign coins to you. Don't give them change without holding the large note they gave you in your hand, until they agree that they are happy with the change you are about to give them. Don't submit to retrospective claims of wrong change. You are surrounded by predators down here. They will steal the sugar out of your tea if you don't watch them. This is a test to see if you are worth recommending."

Heeding Sammy Seal's warning, Desperate Dan secured his rucksack containing all his worldly possessions by tying it tightly under the portable newspaper vendor's stand, and he began selling newspapers. While concentrating hard on the money exchanges, he soon got the hang of it, and business was brisk.

Several people tried to pay him short, and one tried to claim he had given him a twenty-pound note when it was only a fiver, but he adopted a very aggressive attitude. It quickly hardened him up to life on the streets.

When Sammy Seal came back, he was pleased to see that almost all the newspapers were gone. He said, "Finish selling the last of the papers while I make another phone call. I have useful information about a special job that will suit you fine."

Desperate Dan sold the last newspaper, took off the rain canopy, and dismantled the folding newspaper stand. Sammy Seal returned, took the bag of money from Desperate Dan, and said, "Follow me, and bring the newspaper stand." Desperate Dan carefully untied his rucksack, hoisted it onto his back, and followed Sammy Seal to some cleaner's store just off the entrance to the station.

Sammy Seal opened the locked door with a key and carefully stacked his folded newspaper vendor's stand high up on top of a rack of shelves. "It doesn't bother anyone up there. That's the secret: If you are not a problem, you don't draw attention to yourself. Now, the money is a different matter. I must put it somewhere safe. We need to go to my safe depository. Here is a day ticket for the Underground. Quite a few of my customers give me them when they have finished travelling for the day."

They caught two Underground trains, and Sammy Seal said very quietly, "It is good that I have to change lines, because I can easily check if anyone is following me. Desperate Dan, you must learn quickly that you can't trust anyone if you are to disappear successfully. I keep my money in a safe-deposit box on the outskirts of London; it's near the Underground station at the end of the line. What I like about them is that they are open until eight o'clock weekdays and five o'clock on Saturdays and Sundays. It's much better than any bank, and of course there are no records for the taxman. Most of the London gangsters, business people, politicians, and celebrities use this facility."

Sammy Seal seemed to value Desperate Dan's company and began to tell him about himself. "I am an orphan since as long as I can remember, and because I am small, I was in orphanages all my life. No one picked me for adoption—they always picked the tall, pretty ones. I was an awkward child and was always getting into trouble, so when I was fourteen, I ran away from my last home and caught a bus to London.

"I soon met the man who previously did this job. He was old and in bad health, and he could hardly lift the bundles of papers, so I began to help him. We worked together for a couple of years, and then one morning he did not turn up, so I carried on myself and began to put some money away every day."

When they arrived at the end of the line, they made their way out of the station and walked to the safe depository. Sammy Seal said, "You wait outside. My business inside is private. This is another good lesson for you when you are on your own: never keep much money on you, and keep it somewhere safe. Listen to me, don't learn the hard way."

Chapter Twenty

The Live-in Job

Sammy Seal came out of the safe-deposit box centre and said, "Right, that's me sorted." They walked back to the station and caught a tube train back to London Moorgate station. "Let's catch a Circle Line tube train to Liverpool Street station."

Sammy led the way to the main line railway station and said, "I'm really hungry. Let's get something to eat." When they finished eating, Sammy looked across the table. "I have got you a job as a night-watchman at a scrap metal yard. Thieves recently stole a whole skip-load of copper, and so the owner needs a reliable night watchman. I have told him you are the right man for the job. It's only one pound fifty per hour, but the hours are twelve hours a day, seven days a week, which adds up to about 126 pounds a week cash in hand, tax free.

"The Boss, as he likes to be called even by his family, is the father of four sons who were all professional boxers like him. The father runs a scrap metal business, and the oldest son runs a security company that specialises in providing door stewards for bars and night clubs. The second oldest son runs a boxing and martial arts gymnasium and is a local boxing promoter. The third oldest son is a travelling racecourse

105

bookmaker, and the youngest son, Samson, works with his father in the scrap metal business.

"This man you are going to work for is a big man in the East End. When he was at his peak as a professional boxer, he was odds-on favourite and supposed to lie down in a title fight, but his testosterone took over, and he almost killed the bookies' long-odds contender that they had backed.

Before the bookies' minders got to him, his boxing trainer set fire to the circus tent that the fight was staged in, and they escaped in the confusion. That night before the bookies had time to organise themselves, the fight promoter and the bookies died in a casino fire that they jointly owned, although they also had unexplained serious injuries not likely caused by the fire.

"The Boss, as he is now known, quickly filled the vacuum left by the deaths and took over fight promotion in the East End. His four sons had short professional boxing careers; however, the four strands of his family business are now apparently trading legally.

"In truth, they are all a nice mix of legitimate business and illegal underworld operations, which are difficult to distinguish between, especially when key officers in the police are kept sweet. But it is dog eat dog in these games, and maintaining his reputation is so important for his continued dominance of the territory. That is why he has installed a brand-new caravan on the site, which will be your home. For you and for him, it's a very neat package with no records. The reason he wants a strange face is that he does not know whether he has a traitor at his scrapyard.

"Be very careful not to upset him or cheat him. Give him perfect timekeeping and obey orders without questions. He is ruthless, and the reason he is employing you is that he hopes the thieves will come back again so he can catch them. Word is out across London that he took a big hit, and he needs to find the thieves to recover his reputation. Enough said?"

Desperate Dan nodded with a serious expression on his young face.

Sammy Seal continued, "You need to buy some essentials like bread, milk, cheese, soap, toiletries, et cetera."

Desperate Dan visited a couple of the station shops and came out with two carrier bags of supplies. Sammy Seal said, "Give me the carrier bags; you have enough to carry with that giant rucksack. Follow me. There is a train to Dagenham leaving in fifteen minutes."

They caught the train to Dagenham, disembarked, and had to wait until the train cleared the level crossing and the barrier was raised, giving them access to a road leading down to the River Thames and a complicated congestion of well-fenced yards and sheds surrounding the wharfs and their various cargo ships.

As they walked along the road, Sammy Seal said, "The people you are going to work for are not part of the paper seller's fraternity; they don't know our secret names and our authentication passwords. They won't recognise our rings. Keep these secrets and do not divulge them to outsiders. You will just be known as Dan. You are not on any books, and that will be enough. If anyone asks you, just say that you prefer to use only your first name."

Sammy Seal approached a large gate and pressed a bell set in the gatepost. A loud, gravelly voice asked, "Hello, who is it?"

Sammy Seal replied, "Sammy. I am bringing Dan, the new night watchman."

The voice said, "You will need to wait until I come and unpadlock the gate."

A big man approached slowly and looked them over for what seemed a long time before he unlocked the padlock on the chain looped around the two centre posts of the double gates. He wore only a vest on his upper body, and the huge development of his chest, shoulders, neck, and upper arms marked him as a serious weightlifter.

He grunted with a gravelly London East End accent. "Come in." He re-padlocked the chain in place. "Come on, follow me."

The three of them approached a Portakabin office with lights showing through the windows. The big man ushered them into the office, where they found themselves facing a man sitting at a desk. Sammy said immediately, "I have brought you Dan, the night watchman. He is a good man."

The big man behind the desk said in a thin, steely voice, "I certainly hope so, Sammy. For your sake, I certainly hope so." Then he looked at Dan very intently. "You will call me Boss, and this is Samson, my youngest son. That's all you need to know about us. Be careful not to stick your nose in where it might get cut off."

Desperate Dan could see a strong resemblance between the Boss and Samson; the Boss was older with a similar physique, though his muscles were not as pumped up as Samson's.

The Boss stated, "A couple of weeks ago, thieves broke into my yard with a lorry and a skip. They hand-loaded the skip with about ten tonnes of scrap copper worth about twenty-five grand and disappeared into the night. From our internal records, we have been aware that insignificant amounts of copper have steadily been disappearing for months now. I should have done something about it sooner."

He paused for a few moments as though considering carefully what he was about to say. "This latest heist on one single night is a big-time robbery, showing that they are getting confident about my complacence. They are getting greedy, and I know that, no matter how long I must wait they will come back for more, and this time I will be ready for them. In my position, I cannot be seen to be soft, and I need to make an example of these thieves. This way I will get them all at the one time.

"To show you how serious I am to get a reliable night watchman who will stay for possibly months, I have bought a new caravan for you to live in, and we have installed it in a corner of the yard. We have also installed four CCTV cameras with movement detectors which cover the whole yard, including the entrance gate, with individual monitor screens dedicated to each camera located in your caravan. They are night-capable cameras which include the infra-red spectrum, so you don't need to put the yard lights on to use them in the dark. That way we will also give the robbers an extra sense of security.

"You will work all the silent hours, from 6 p.m. to 6 a.m., seven nights a week, when the yard is locked. You will not remain in the yard during the day in case one of the yard workers gets friendly and learns about our security. Obviously, you need to get some sleep, and the movement detectors will alert you with a local alarm should you doze off, provided you are not in a drunken sleep. Do you understand me? I hope for your sake that you do.

"I have cut the fence behind the caravan to give you an escape route. If the thieves arrive, you will be alerted when they stop at the locked gates to cut the padlock and chain off, giving you enough time to get away without being seen. When you are clear of the yard, you will phone this preloaded number on this mobile phone, which will alert us that the thieves have arrived.

"Even if they have a team of four men, it will take most of the night to separate, sort, and hand-load up to twenty tonnes of small copper scrap. Here, take this mobile phone. Oh! Have you seen one of these before? Will you know how to use it?"

Dan replied, "Yes, I used to have a mobile phone of my own. Just show me the preloaded number. I don't want to use it except once, because police can trace mobiles."

The Boss showed Dan the preloaded number and said, "You are a smart boy, Dan. When the thieves come, get out and go. Don't return to the yard in case it all goes wrong. Once you are clear of the yard, phone the preloaded number. Make your way to Central London and contact Sammy. We will get word to you through Sammy when it is safe to return. Here is one of the spare keys to the padlock on the main gate. Come, and I will show you the caravan."

He showed Dan the essential features in the caravan, especially the security cameras. Then he asked Dan to demonstrate that he could work the system in all its capacities. This Boss didn't leave anything to chance.

When he was satisfied, he and Samson left Sammy and Dan to settle in. They watched Samson on the CCTV carefully chaining and padlocking the double gates as he left the yard to join the Boss in his car outside the main gates.

Sammy Seal stayed with Desperate Dan for ten minutes to let the Boss and Samson get clear of the area before he said, "Well, I am off now. You know where to find me. Come on, let me out and then lock the gates again behind me."

As he did so, Desperate Dan said, "Sammy Seal, thanks for all your help."

The newspaper man walked away without looking back. Desperate Dan watched him until he was out of sight, with the feeling that he was now completely alone.

Desperate Dan went back to the caravan and played with the CCTV controls, panning and zooming on specific objects until he was satisfied with the system. He zoomed out each of the cameras and centred them to give complete coverage of the whole yard.

He settled into a routine, staying in the caravan during the twelve-hour night shift but leaving the yard every morning after the Boss arrived; he rushed out to open the gates to let in the Boss's car. He was happy about the instructions of the Boss; because of the movement detector alarms, if he too was alert to the alarms, he could catnap during the silent hours.

The Boss continually insisted that he leave the yard during the day shift so as not to get known or become friendly with any of the yard workers or office staff. Dan would travel into London and spend the day travelling on the Underground and visiting various places of interest. He got to know London quite well, but it was very lonely, and he often felt homesick and wondered how Kelly was doing. He visualised her with a growing bump.

He often recalled Carroty Charlie's words: *The loneliness will be so intense that it will be worse than continual toothache.*

Just over seven months passed quietly, until one night at the beginning of April. Dan was dozing on top of his bed, dressed and ready in a tracksuit, underwear, and socks. The alarm started to bleep, immediately waking him, and he also saw that the alarm light on the CCTV display was flashing.

He jumped up from the bed and looked at the CCTV monitors. He could see a lorry approaching outside the gates. He quickly slipped on his training shoes without tying the laces and grabbed his anorak. He took one last look at the CCTV monitors, which displayed a man crowbarring the padlock off the chains on the gates. He switched off the CCTV system, leaving the caravan in total darkness. Without further hesitation, he slipped out of the door, which was hidden from view from the main gate.

Desperate Dan was fully awake now, and he quickly uncovered the gap in the fence, squeezed through, and entered a big yard with its giant piles of aggregate. After quickly closing the fence, he moved behind a big pile of sand, where he laced up his trainers. Then he ran through the yard and found himself on a deserted road.

He had scouted out the route before and knew it ran past large ponds, which had willow trees around the edges.

Desperate Dan ran to the ponds and found a nice, thick drooping willow tree. He hid in its spacious confines. After removing the mobile phone from his pocket, he switched it on. When the screen showed that it was ready for use, he located the preloaded number and activated it. Desperate Dan listened intently to it ringing the number, and then Samson gruffly answered, "Is that you, Dan?"

He replied, "Yes. The robbers have arrived. There are four of them, and I switched off the CCTV and got out undiscovered."

Samson barked loudly, "Good man. Leave this to us. You lie low and contact Sammy first thing tomorrow morning. If it's safe to come back, we will phone you. I have your mobile phone number, and Sammy's just in case. We will probably need you tomorrow."

The phone went dead.

It wasn't too cold, and so Dan decided to stay where he was until morning and join the early morning rush hour commuters on the train at the railway station. That way he would not be noticed in the crowds. He wondered with trepidation what was about to happen in the darkness of the night back at the scrapyard.

Chapter Twenty-one

Rough Retribution

It was just after midnight when the robbers jemmied the padlock off the chain holding the double gates to the scrapyard. Two of the four robbers opened the double gates, and the lorry with its skip reversed into the yard. The two robbers closed the gates behind the reversing lorry. One of them wrapped the chain round the closed gates, giving the impression that it was fastened.

They ran over to the caravan, entered, and found it empty. They did a search of the yard and concluded that the yard was unoccupied. One of the robbers said, "I thought they had a night watchman. I guess he's probably got a fancy woman living somewhere nearby."

The other robber laughed and said, "If you pay peanuts, you get monkeys, and you know that monkeys are always chasing their nuts."

The lorry continued reversing until it was close to a huge pile of copper scrap. It then dropped the skip onto the yard very close to the work area. The two robbers joined the other two and reported, "The yard is deserted, and the caravan's empty. The night watchman must be playing away tonight." They couldn't resist repeating the joke. "If you pay peanuts, you get monkeys, and you know that monkeys are always chasing their nuts." The four robbers laughed loudly at this release from the tension of possibly having to confront the night watchman and having him raise the alarm.

Now feeling confident and wearing industrial leather gloves, they began to select pieces of copper scrap, cut them into manageable bits, and throw them into the skip. They worked hard at the mammoth task, only breaking occasionally to drink from bottles of beer that they had brought with them.

About one o'clock, two large cars slowly approached the aggregate yard behind the scrapyard along the deserted road. The cars parked opposite the aggregate yard, with the drivers remaining in the cars, ready for a fast getaway if it was needed.

Eight men—the Boss, his four sons, and three trusted gang members—quietly assembled, each carrying their preferred weapons ranging from vicious knuckledusters, to baseball bats and steel crowbars.

The men wore luminous, brightly coloured armbands so that they could identify each other in the dark during the expected battle.

The Boss quietly instructed them. "We have all the time in the world. Walk quietly and slowly through the aggregate yard so as not to make any noise and climb through the gap in the fence behind the caravan. I will go into the caravan and use the CCTV to spot if anyone else is hiding in the darkness. Split into two groups, and when I switch on the yard lights, the two groups will run down each side of the lorry and attack the robbing bastards at the back of the skip. Be ruthless. These guys will pay for their treachery with their lives. I want dead bodies fast. Don't give them any time to escape. This will be the perfect revenge with no evidence left behind."

The seven men split into two groups of three and four and crouched at the front of the lorry with their deadly weapons ready for the battle. The Boss switched on the CCTV and scanned the whole yard. When he was satisfied, he switched on the yard lights.

The two groups rushed along the sides of the lorry and skip. They caught the four robbers completely by surprise, and within seconds, they had beaten them to the ground.

The two men with the heavy steel crowbars quickly dispatched each of the restrained robbers to the afterlife with a massive blow to the side of the head.

The Boss came around and checked the four bodies. "Yes, I know one of them. The grapevine has been warning about this lot for the last year. They are a new, young Lambeth team. I heard that they were getting ambitious and elbowing out the small gangs around them. Recently, they put the owner of a family scrap business in the West End in the hospital. If they were experienced boys, they would know better than to stray into the East End. Clearly, they didn't know the pecking order. They certainly learned the hard way, but it's a bit late for them now."

A wave of hysterical laughter erupted amongst the men at the final joke, which acted as a trigger for the relief needed from the intense, adrenalin-driven conflict.

When the laughter eventually subsided, the Boss shouted, "Right, men. There is a stack of concrete-reinforcing steel mesh in the far right-hand corner of the yard. Cut a piece or pieces to fit into the skip to form an elevated platform about halfway up the depth of the skip. Wire the four bodies securely to it, cover the bodies with a tarpaulin, and make sure you tie the tarpaulin down to the mesh all the way round. Then load the skip back onto the lorry."

The drivers brought the two cars into the yard.

The Boss continued, "When you have done that, post a guard of two men on the lorry and two men on the main gate until we get a delivery of concrete to fill the skip in the morning. The spare men will stay in the canteen hut and relieve the guards every two hours. Stay alert. Samson and I will be in the office if you need us."

At 7 a.m., the Boss woke up in his office chair, where he had dozed off. His brain clicked into gear, and he said, "Samson, phone Fast-Setting Pumped Concrete Deliveries and get them to deliver sixteen cubic metres of fast-setting concrete."

Samson woke with a start and sleepily replied, "Can you write it down, Boss? I can't remember all that."

The Boss said with some feeling, "Oh, give me the Yellow Pages, and I will do it myself. What do I pay you for?" He ordered the concrete delivery for around ten o'clock.

He then phoned a small south coast workboat company and arranged to hire a self-propelled barge capable of taking the skip lorry on its deck. Explaining that he had a River Thames barge that he regularly used for bulk scrap, and that Samson had a barge master's ticket, was enough to satisfy the owner.

Fortunately, the barge was unemployed, tied up to a wharf, and available cheap because the owner had cash flow problems.

The Boss turned to Samson and said, "Pat has a heavy goods vehicle licence and can drive the skip lorry down to the south coast. Load it on to the work barge, and when you get out to deep water, he can drive the lorry loaded with the skip off the ramp and sink it and its load in deep water. Get Dan back here before you go.

Chapter Twenty-two

Hide the Evidence

The lorry with the concrete arrived just before ten o'clock in the morning. The guards on the gate directed it into the yard to a position right behind the skip on the skip lorry. They explained to the driver that they needed to completely fill the skip on the lorry. He connected a suitable length of hose to the concrete pump and passed the free end up to one of the men standing in the skip.

The driver started the pump and began as if to climb onto the skip lorry, but one of the men held him back with his hand on his shoulder, saying, "Health and safety. Only our men are trained to climb onto our lorries. You know how strict regulations these days are."

The lorry driver was a little taken aback but replied, "Oh. Right."

The man moved up and down the skip with the hose, making sure the liquid concrete was fully filling the void under the steel mesh platform. When it reached the level of the mesh, he handed the hose to another man standing on the back of the lorry, outside the skip.

His turn done, he climbed out of the skip, saying, "I am going to the canteen for a rest; it's been a really hard night, and I feel exhausted. You take over." The second man took about two hours to laboriously fill the skip to the top with the heavy hose, and he eventually shouted to the concrete delivery driver to stop the pump.

The Boss saw that they were wilting and realised that the killings had taken a lot out of his men. He believed in leading by example to maintain his authority, and he came out and shouted, "Get some of the men, and bring a railway sleeper over to the middle of the yard. Bump the skip lorry over the sleeper a few times to make sure that the concrete is well settled down."

He watched Pat, driving the skip lorry, bump over the railway sleeper a few times. Sure enough, the concrete settled a good bit lower than the top of the skip edge. He said to the men, "Get another two of those railway sleepers and tie the three of them together, making a bridge along the top of the skip, so that I can safely walk along above the concrete. I don't want to be encased in concrete like those dummies who thought they could steel my copper."

After laughing at his joke, the men quickly found two more timber railway sleepers and some lengths of two-by-two square section timber. They cut the timber into six cross batons. They nailed and lashed the three heavy railway sleepers strongly together.

Despite being a heavy man and now advancing into old age, the Boss climbed up on top of the three sleepers firmly lashed together with cross batons, and he carefully walked along the length of the skip, pushing a long brush handle down into the wet concrete. Then he shouted, "Start the pump."

The delivery driver started the pump again. Carefully aiming the hose, he progressively topped the level of the liquid concrete back up flush with the top of the skip. Finally satisfied, he said, "That's better. There are no air voids in the concrete block. You can disconnect the hose now."

The driver of the concrete delivery lorry dismantled the hose and washed out the system before stowing the all the accessories on the back of the lorry. One of the men signed the delivery driver's paperwork, and he drove the concrete delivery lorry away.

The Boss asked the driver of the skip lorry, "Pat, how much fuel is in the tank?"

Pat, answered, "The tank is almost full, Boss."

He took out an envelope and handed it to the driver. "This is the address of the wharf where the workboat is moored. We need to wait for another passenger, and then you will drive there with the skip lorry. When you get there, you will drive onto the flat deck of the workboat. When you have sailed well out into the English Channel and over deep water, you will put the lorry into low gear, start it moving forward, and jump out just before it goes over the stern landing ramp."

Pat panicked and whined, "Boss, I can't swim."

The Boss ignored the plea and said, "There are two thousand pounds for tonight and today's work, and another thousand for dumping the lorry and skip in the English Channel. Don't let the others see how much you are getting."

Pat said, "Thanks for the pay, Boss. Much appreciated."

The Boss handed each of the other men envelopes with their two thousand pounds and counselled them to put it in a safe place, keep quiet, and not draw attention to themselves by spending it recklessly. The Boss and Samson returned to the office while the men went into their canteen to get some food and rest after the very stressful battle.

Samson, who was an experienced river barge master, planned for the sea voyage with some apprehension because it was something he had never done before.

Chapter Twenty-three

No Rest for the Wicked

At about six o'clock, Desperate Dan left the confines of the thick, drooping willow tree and made his way to Dagenham Dock railway station. He caught the first train to Liverpool Street station. He met Sammy Seal, who was at his newspaper pitch.

Sammy Seal said, "No time for breakfast this morning. Samson has phoned me to say that you must go back to the yard immediately. They have successfully dealt with the robbers, but they need you to accompany a lorry to the south coast." He added, "Take care, Desperate Dan. These are hard and ruthless men, and your job for them is done. Remember, you can't trust anybody in the world, especially the underworld."

Desperate Dan arrived back at the scrap metal yard around 10.30. The man guarding the gate said, "The Boss said to look out for you and have you report to the office."

Dan knocked on the office door, and it was opened by Samson, who said gruffly, "Come in."

The Boss asked him, "Can you drive, Dan?"

Desperate Dan said, "Yes."

The Boss said, "That's good. I need you to follow the skip lorry down to Brighton with a car. You will be leaving about twelve o'clock, so get yourself something to eat. Oh, and you will need something warm and waterproof to wear, because you will be going on a sea voyage."

Desperate Dan went to his caravan, stripped, showered, and dressed in fresh clothes. He made himself a cheese sandwich and a cup of tea. When he finished eating and drinking, he lay down on his bed. He set the alarm clock for 11.45, closed his eyes, and immediately fell asleep.

The alarm woke him, but he felt refreshed with the short nap. Then a sobering thought relating to the last thing Sammy Seal had said flashed through his mind. Was he needed now that the robbers seemed to have been dealt with? What about his night watchman's job? What about his caravan? Was he a risk to the gang now that his purpose was no longer needed?

He went back out to the yard to see what was going on. As he approached the lorry loaded with the skip, his fears were confirmed. He overheard the Boss saying to Samson in his loud, gravelly voice: "When you have dumped the lorry and the skip, get rid of Dan. He probably knows too much about us and what happened last night."

Dan hesitated for a few moments, stunned by what he had just heard. Then he coughed loudly, rounded the back of the lorry, and came into full view.

Samson called him over and acted as if everything was continuing as it had before the ruthless murders. "Here are the keys to the black Mondeo. We will be leaving for the south coast in about fifteen minutes. You follow close to the skip lorry, and don't lose us. Just in case, I have your mobile number. Here is the business card with the address of the wharf we are heading for, as an added safety measure."

Desperate Dan slipped the business card with the address into the back pocket of his jeans and began to check the car he was to drive. It was a Ford Mondeo. He put the keys in the ignition and turned on the engine. It fired the first time, and the dashboard lights quickly settled down with no warning lights.

He looked at the fuel gauge and noted with satisfaction that it indicated a nearly full tank. Finally, he checked the tyres, including the spare.

Once satisfied that all was okay, a worried Desperate Dan quickly went back to his caravan and packed all his belongings into the big rucksack. He brought it to the Ford Mondeo. He knew that he would not be coming back, and so he opened the boot and put all his worldly possessions in before carefully locking it.

A few minutes later, Samson came over and asked, "Are you ready to go?" Desperate Dan nodded. "We are not in a hurry. We are leaving now to miss the worst of the rush hour traffic later. Just follow us." Samson climbed into the skip lorry passenger seat and closed the door, and the lorry approached the scrap metal yard gates. The gateman opened the gates and let the lorry and Desperate Dan's Ford Mondeo through before closing the gates behind them.

Desperate Dan found the Mondeo easy to drive. Pat, the lorry driver, was sticking to the Highway Code to make sure that they did not draw the attention of the traffic police.

The drive to the south coast was uneventful, and they arrived at the small boat repair yard and marina in just over an hour and thirty minutes after leaving Dagenham. They parked up in a vacant space at one end of the boatyard.

Samson went alone to the central office. Pat asked Desperate Dan, "Can I lock this envelope in the glove compartment of the car? I don't want to get it wet; it would be daft to take it out on a boat."

Desperate Dan gave him the car keys, and the skip driver locked his envelope in the glove compartment. He locked the car and checked all the doors, and then he handed Desperate Dan the car keys. "I hope you have a safe pocket for these keys. There is a lot of money in there."

Desperate Dan put the keys in one of the pockets of his Gore-Tex hill-walking jacket, tapped his pocket, and said, "It will be safe in here with this strong zip."

Samson reappeared after about twenty minutes and signalled them to join him. Pat and Desperate Dan walked over and joined him. Samson said, "Follow me. We will eat in the café." Without asking the others, he ordered three full breakfasts and three mugs of tea. They sat at a table in the otherwise empty cafe, and Samson said, "It's midweek, and the marina is very quiet. The few people here are the yard workers. We are going to load the lorry onto the barge after dark. The crane driver will come back to the yard at ten o'clock, and we will load it when no one is about. The crane driver is keen to earn an unofficial backhander and won't tell anyone about it. In the meantime, we can doss down in the changing rooms until ten o'clock; no one is using them today."

The waitress came with two of the breakfasts and then returned to fetch the other one on a tray with three mugs of tea. Samson said to the waitress, "The three of us are out at sea on the barge all night. Can you please make us three packages of mixed sandwiches and a crate of bottled drinking water?"

Without further words, the three men tucked into the food until all three plates were almost clean. They finished the mugs of tea, and Samson paid the waitress, who handed him two carrier bags, one filled with sandwiches and one filled with bottled water. With Samson carrying the bags, they left the café to find the changing rooms.

Pat was trying to hide his panic attacks caused by his fear of water.

Chapter Twenty-four

Out of the Frying Pan and into the Sea

The facilities were just like sports pavilions, with multiple changing rooms, bench seats, toilets, and showers. Samson immediately spotted some life jackets on the shelves. He lifted one down and laid it on one of the benches as a pillow for his head, and then he lay down and closed his eyes. Pat and Desperate Dan copied his example, and soon all three were sleeping.

Desperate Dan woke about seven o'clock. He got up and went through for a wash. When he came back to the changing room, the other two were getting to their feet. Desperate Dan said, "It's only half past seven. We have plenty of time."

At nine o'clock, Samson said, "Let's eat now in case we don't get a chance during the night." They ate all the sandwiches and drank one litre of water each.

A car drove into the boatyard exactly at ten o'clock, and the crane driver got out. Samson said with a laugh, "I hope you are not a union health and safety rep, because I want you to work with no lights. I don't want to draw the taxman's attention to your extra earnings." The crane driver was not sure what he meant, but he didn't ask. The four men walked over to the skip lorry and had a look.

The crane driver asked, "Is the skip full of concrete?"

Samson nodded and said, "Yes, it is less than sixteen cubic metres. We ordered sixteen, but there was plenty left when the skip filled."

The crane driver said, "Then we will need to lift the skip off and split the load into two lifts. Sixteen cubic metres will be about thirty-eight tonnes, and my boat lift is only fifty-tonne capacity. We will lift the lorry onto the barge, then the skip."

Samson said, "Okay, let's get on with it."

The four men worked in harmony and lifted the skip off the lorry. Then they fitted the chains to the lorry and lifted it onto the barge, positioning it facing the hydraulic end ramp. They removed the chains and fastened them to the skip, and the crane lifted the skip back onto the lorry.

The crane driver asked, "Do you want these sleepers on top of the skip? We can always use sleepers in the boatyard."

Samson immediately panicked at the thought that these sleepers had been part of the murder scene, and said in his gravelly East London voice, "No! Leave them on the top of the skip."

The crane driver shied back, obviously alarmed by the aggressive tone. He looked timidly at Samson over the top of his glasses.

Samson said, "Sorry, no offence intended. It's just that we are running late and should be out to sea by now. Thanks very much. You have done your job well. Here is your payment. You get off home now, and we can take it from here." The crane driver accepted the payment, locked up his boat lift crane, and walked to his car.

Samson watched him drive away from the boatyard, and then he said, "Okay, let's see if we can get this barge to work. I used to work on the riverboats, so I will soon get the hang of it." Samson spent about twenty minutes checking the barge controls, the engines, the steering, the fuel tanks, and the bilges. He started the engines and then went to the stern to examine the loading ramp. He operated the ramp down and back up again to check that it was working.

He returned to the wheelhouse and announced, "Everything is okay, and we are ready to go. I want you two to loosen the mooring ropes one at a time while I manoeuvre the barge to get you some slack. Jump back onto the barge before it gets too far away. Then take a fending pole each in case you have to push it off the wharf. It's been a while since I've handled a big barge."

Desperate Dan and Pat did as they were instructed, both pushing the barge off the wharf. When it was clear, they returned to the wheelhouse. Samson instructed them go back out as lookouts on each side of the boat and to warn him of any obstacles. With the engine revs very low, Samson engaged the gearbox and slowly moved the barge forward. He continued slowly steering the barge past moored boats and towards the main channel out of the boatyard.

After what seemed to be a very long time in the extreme tension of manoeuvring this big barge, by rudder and altering the revolutions propeller (including sometimes reversing), they were suddenly clear of the harbour mouth and in the English Channel. There was a sea mist, and it was very dark, but fortunately it was also calm. Samson increased the engine revs and selected high gear.

He watched the compass and headed roughly south-west. "I was always a river man, and I have not used a compass since taking my ticket. I want to get out of sight of land, but with no radar, it is dangerous in these conditions. A big ship could come out of the mist at any time, so you two keep your eyes and ears peeled."

Petrified and in a state of high tension, they continued running at this speed for fifteen minutes.

Then Samson, who was visibly panicking and reacting to every apparent shadow in the clinging mist, put the gearbox into neutral and slowed the engine revs. He was sweating profusely and said, "That's far enough."

Samson left the wheelhouse and made his way to the stern ramp. He lowered the ramp until the end was in the sea and said to Pat, "Start the lorry, put it into first gear, get it moving forward onto the ramp, and then jump out."

Pat climbed reluctantly into the lorry and started the engine. He stopped the engine and jumped out of the cab, saying, "I can't do it. I can't do it! We are in the middle of the English Channel. It's deep water, and I am frightened of deep water." He ran back to the wheelhouse and went inside.

Samson said, "Dan, put the handbrake off. I will get the barge moving again, and the lorry might roll off with the swell." Desperate Dan jumped up into the lorry cab and let off the hand brake. Samson put the barge into gear and increased the revs. The lorry didn't move. Samson came back out to the lorry and asked, "Have you got the ignition keys?"

Desperate Dan looked down and saw that Pat had left the ignition keys in place. "Yes, they are in the steering column lock."

Samson asked, "Can you swim?" Desperate Dan replied, "Yes."

He said, "Drive the lorry right off the barge. We can't risk it getting stuck halfway off the ramp. You can jump out of the cab just before it goes over."

Desperate Dan pressed down on the clutch pedal and started the engine. He selected a gear and pressed the accelerator pedal, slipping the clutch at the same time. Slowly the lorry began to roll forward onto the ramp, but Dan's foot slipped off the strange clutch pedal, and the lorry suddenly shot forward and off the end of the ramp.

The buoyancy of the cab and the weight of the concrete-filled skip turned the lorry tail first in the water. The water quickly filled the cab through the open driver's door.

Desperate Dan forced himself out of the open cab door before the lorry sank. He grabbed the end of the ramp of the barge and hauled himself back on board. He saw Samson coming towards him, and he held up one hand for a helping pull, but Samson stamped on his other hand. Dan fell back into the water. He looked round as he swam but it was so dark, he could not see anything.

He heard the barge engines starting, and he heard the sound increase as they were revved up. The barge searchlights came on, but they faded away as the barge sped away into the misty darkness, leaving him behind.

Suddenly his hand struck against something solid, and after exploring it, he recognised it as the three railway sleepers still firmly lashed together. Dan secured his fingers on the top of the edge of one of the sleepers. He managed to get a good grip on one of the cross batons and pulled himself up onto the top of the floating raft.

He carefully spread his body along the sleepers, trying to not capsize his precarious platform, and he found himself just clear of the chilly water.

He zipped up his Gore-Tex hill-walking jacket and lay out on the raft. At least he was out of the water; it was cold, but not critically so.

The long, chilly night passed with him regularly turning on each of his sides to ease the ache caused by the hard sleepers. The morning light slowly crept up, and Desperate Dan felt a new optimism. His eyes pierced the rapidly increasing horizon, searching for land.

Chapter Twenty-five

Perseverance

Samson initially celebrated when he saw the lorry go off the ramp so quickly, but as he watched, he was dismayed to see that Dan had managed to get his hands on the edge of the barge's ramp and had begun to pull himself back on board.

He went towards him, and as he approached, Dan reached out towards him with one hand. Samson did not hesitate. He kicked at Dan's other hand, displacing its grip on the ramp. Then he ran to the bridge and revved up the work barge engines to move away from the scene of the sinking lorry.

Keeping the revs high, he surged backwards to get away from Dan. Suddenly a very loud foghorn startled him, and he listened intently, imagining a huge ship bearing down on them in the darkness and mist. In the dark, his panic increased, and he became disorientated. He eventually put the gearbox in neutral and slowed the engine down to give himself time to think.

Sweat ran off Samson's forehead and down his face. His colleague, Pat, was still cowering in the corner of the wheelhouse and was no help to him.

Samson was a man of action, and he shouted loudly to himself, "Take the initiative, man! Don't wait for things to happen to you!"

After revving up the engine and selecting high gear, he switched on the rear-facing lights and could see the propeller wash cab and a dark shape on the surface of the water—or was it his imagination? It was difficult to tell in the mist and darkness, but whatever it was, it made him shiver.

He switched on all the running lights on the barge so that other ships could see them. Then he looked at the compass and spoke to himself again. "I'm not sure where we are, but I don't want to run aground. The safest direction is farther out in the channel. I will head west-south-west until daylight."

Having made up his mind, Samson was happy in himself. He was an ex-professional boxer of the type who kept going forward into the storm no matter how fierce. The newspaper boxing hacks used to write about him, "Samson's so thick, to knock him down, you would have to hit him with a sledgehammer."

***

Meanwhile, as the morning light increased, Desperate Dan could see white cliffs and was pleased to see that they were quite close. The tide was carrying him on the raft of sleepers along the shoreline, but also towards the shore.

He watched impatiently as a promontory point came closer and closer. It seemed to take a long time, but eventually the sleeper raft washed against the limestone debris, and Desperate Dan jumped onto land. He carefully made his way along the narrow promontory and towards a walkway. Following steps up from the walkway, he found himself in a South Downs coastal village.

A bus was approaching in the distance, and he stood at the bus stop, quickly combing his disheveled hair. The bus stopped, and he stepped on, pulling out the wet business card for the ship repair wharf. He asked,

"Do you go anywhere near this place? "The bus driver said, "Yes, we go right past it. That will be seventy pence. Yes, mate. Sit somewhere near me, and I will give you a shout." Desperate Dan found a damp five-pound note tucked into the little cash pocket near his belt buckle, and he paid the fare with it. "I am sorry it is a bit damp." The bus driver laughed and replied, "Don't worry, mate. You wouldn't believe the sights I see coming onto my bus around here."

The bus travelled along the main coast road, making small detours into local communities and then re-joining the coast road. Desperate Dan didn't notice the scenery because he was deep in thought. *I can't risk going back to Dagenham. Sammy Seal said I can't trust anyone, and Samson has just proved that to be true. The gang might even be watching him, thinking I might try to contact him. What about Megan? I can trust her. I wonder if she has any news. How can I talk to her? The pigs tap the peace camp phones, but what if I was very careful and clever using the code words, she gave me?*

After about forty minutes, the bus driver shouted, "Right, mate, this is your stop."

Desperate Dan looked down to the boat repair yard and could see the Ford Mondeo where he had left it. He scanned the whole marina and boat repair yard, but he could not see any sign of the work barge, he relaxed as this meant that he was well ahead of Sampson.

Desperate Dan noticed the public phone kiosk in the café, and so he went to the car and opened the boot, looking for Megan's little notebook in one of the rucksack pockets.

He lifted the rucksack out, locked the car boot, and made his way to the café, carefully looking in the windows. There were no customers to be seen.

He realised that he was very hungry, and so he went in and ordered a full breakfast and a mug of tea. The waitress asked, "Just the one today?"

He replied, "Yes, my friends are still at sea. They should be in later."

She said, "Take a seat at a table, and I will bring it to you when it is ready."

While he waited for his breakfast, he found some pound coins in a rucksack pocket. Desperate Dan phoned Megan. Using code words and normal words very sparingly, he identified himself to her and asked if she had any news. She said she had, but they would need to meet. Again, using code words and numbers, he arranged to meet her at noon in two days' time. Although he knew Megan would know, he had to resist a powerful desire to confirm the place in normal language as the bar in the Queen Street railway station. Desperate Dan felt good about the phone call. It seemed she had something positive to tell him, and it was great to hear her well-known and trusted voice.

He sat back at the table just as the waitress appeared carrying a tray with his breakfast and mug of tea. The breakfast and tea did wonders for his morale. He debated with himself about using the car, but his Boy Scout background came to the fore. Mr Brodie, his Boy Scout leader, had taught that although most of the Christian churches had abandoned the Ten Commandments, they were still required.

He put up a short prayer and analysed his plan, considering his understanding of the commandments. First, he did not have insurance for the car. Second, the car was not his. Third, Pat's money was in the glove compartment.

Having worked out his plan and feeling that it was ethical to Mr Brodie's standards of honesty.

Desperate Dan placed his Gore-Tex hill-walking jacket under the top flap on the rucksack and fastened it down. He put one arm in a shoulder strap and swung the heavy rucksack onto his back, and then he pushed his other arm though the other shoulder strap.

He walked over to the waitress and paid for his breakfast. "Can I leave the car keys with you to give to my friends when they eventually come back from sea with the work barge?"

The waitress took the car keys with a smile. "Yes, I will watch out for them."

Desperate Dan left the café and walked over to the changing rooms. He stripped off all his wet clothing, quickly showered, and changed into dry underwear and a tracksuit.

He felt very tired from the stress and exposure of the previous night, but he made his way from the boat repair yard to the main road. The rucksack now seemed very heavy, and so he stopped at a bus stop and looked at the timetables. He found the bus was scheduled to stop at Brighton railway station and sat in the warm sun to wait for it.

The bus finally arrived at Brighton railway station, and he bought a single train ticket to London Victoria. Upon boarding the London train, he found an empty seat and promptly fell asleep.

Amazingly, the ticket collector waited until they arrived at London Victoria railway station before wakening him out of a deep sleep and asking to see his ticket. Without thinking, he slowly made his way to the Underground and made his way to Euston station. He was so tired that he made his way to the hotel where he'd previously stayed when he'd played his last gig for Mr Ian Campbell.

Desperate Dan entered the hotel and asked the receptionist, "Do you have a single room available for tonight with toilet and shower facilities?"

The receptionist consulted her computer and said with a smile, "Yes, we have a room."

He replied, "Good, I will take it."

The receptionist pushed a form and a pen towards him and said, "Please fill in your details."

He felt panic rise in him as he remembered that he had disappeared and could not leave any trace. To play for a little time, he said, "How much is the room?"

The receptionist replied, "It's forty-five pounds per night, sir."

Desperate Dan had recovered his calm and filled in the hotel booking form with the name and address of a live-in publican in Glasgow whom he knew of, although he did not know the postcode. The receptionist handed him his room key and said, "Your room is on the second floor, and it is on the left when you leave the lift."

He took forty-five pounds out of his wallet and said, "I will pay now, and I will pay for any extras as I get them." The receptionist appeared not to notice the missing postcode, accepted the money, and gave him a receipt with a big smile.

It was only three o'clock in the afternoon, but Desperate Dan was very tired. He closed the curtains, stripped off, and had a shower. He towelled himself dry and went into the bedroom. There was a hairdryer provided, which he used to dry his hair. Finally, he got into bed and promptly fell asleep.

Desperate Dan woke in a darkened room because he had closed the curtains. Initially he not sure where he was, but he knew he was hungry. The room telephone had a time-and-date display, and he noticed it showed 8.15 p.m. He got out of bed and opened his big rucksack, finding his toilet bag. He brushed his teeth and shaved. He pulled out dry clothing and dressed in underwear, tracksuit bottoms, T-shirt, socks, and trainers.

He opened the curtains, noticed it was still light, put a twenty-pound note in his pocket, combed his hair, and picked up his room key. He went downstairs, found the dining room, and ordered a steak-and-ale pie and a pot of tea.

While he waited for his meal, a conjurer with a jacket with the name "Tommy Tricks" emblazoned on it approached his table and began to astonish him with close-up magic tricks. Then he said suddenly, "Take a card. Turn it over." He jumped back with his hand on his forehead, saying. "Oh! It's the Joker. When it appears in a reading, it means that something unexpected and uncontrolled can occur. Good luck, sir." He picked up the joker and quickly went to another table to showing the people his tricks, occasionally looking back at Desperate Dan.

Dan really enjoyed the meat pie, potatoes, and peas. He washed it down with two cups of tea while watching the conjurer in the distance, wondering why the man kept looking back at him.

It was still early, and so Dan decided to go out for a walk. He had become familiar with the area of London around Euston railway station and that part of London north of the river. He strolled in the mild evening air, moving past now-familiar buildings.

Suddenly he realised that he was on the other side of the road opposite Freemasons' Hall, and he was shocked when he recognised two figures in dinner suits leaving the building: James Smith and his colleague Mr James from MI5.

Desperate Dan walked slowly with his head bowed down and his back hunched, hoping to look like an aged man. He hoped they would not recognise him. They crossed the road and began to overtake him; however, the two men were in deep conservation, more than slightly inebriated, and not aware of their surroundings.

They walked past him, and as they did so, James Smith was saying angrily, "We have to find that list. Whiteside has threatened me with transfer to MI6 and a posting to Bulgaria, in a very exposed position—and you know what he means by that. If I go to Bulgaria, you will certainly be coming with me. We've got to find that Hamilton. He is only a student, damn it. It shouldn't be this difficult."

Desperate Dan waited until Mr Smith and Mr James were a good distance away. Significantly shocked by the near discovery, he turned and walked in the opposite direction, back to his hotel.

Needing a drink, he arrived at the hotel and went in, immediately making his way towards the bar. Mr Ian Campbell was the only customer, sitting at the bar on a bar stool and facing him, still dressed in his expensive Highland dress featuring the Campbell tartan kilt.

He said in a loud, drunken voice, "It's Douglas! You may have changed your appearance, but I recognise your distinctive posture. What are you drinking, my man?"

Desperate Dan replied, "Can I please have a half pint of lager?"

Ian said in his loud, slurred, but still cultured voice, "I don't do half pints. Barmaid give me a pint of lager for my friend, and another glass of Glenmorangie for me. Come here, Douglas, and sit beside me."

Desperate Dan thought to himself, *I seem to remember this conversation from the past.* He sat on the high bar stool and took a sip of the lager. "Thank you. That's nice and cool."

Ian looked intently at Desperate Dan for what seemed a long time and asked, "Do you know that you have been causing a lot of people a lot of worry? They have been searching the whole of Scotland looking for you." He tried to push his finger at Desperate Dan's chest as he finished the word *you*, but in his drunken condition, he missed completely and fell off his high bar stool, ending up lying on his back on the floor.

Desperate Dan immediately jumped down and, with the help of the barmaid, assisted Ian to regain his feet. It was clear that he was too drunk to get to his room unaided. The barmaid picked up a telephone and summoned the night porter, who arrived within a couple of minutes. The barmaid said, "Mr Campbell, room 104."

Desperate Dan and the night porter managed to support him to his room, and the night porter opened the room door with his master key.

They got him to the bed, and the night porter said, "Let him fall forward onto the bed with his face downward so that if he is sick, he won't choke." The night porter then lifted his legs onto the bed, shaping them in the recovery position. They retreated from the room, leaving Ian Campbell to sleep it off.

Desperate Dan immediately went to his room and packed his rucksack. He looked at the time displayed on the telephone: 10.45 p.m. He knew the last train to Glasgow Central was 11.50. He checked his room to make sure he had left nothing behind. Then he closed the room door behind him and made his way down by the stairs. As he passed the entrance to the bar, he saw that the night porter was talking intently to the barmaid, but fortunately they were not looking in his direction. He quietly opened the main door of the hotel and let himself out into the night without them seeing him.

Desperate Dan got to Euston train station at eleven thirty, and although it was expensive, he bought a single-berth sleeper to Glasgow Central. He made his way to the train and found the sleeping coach attendant. Unfortunately, he was a stranger and not wearing the double skull-and-crossbones ring. Desperate Dan did not want to risk drawing attention to himself by asking peculiar questions. He installed himself in the security of his single berth and began to assess his situation.

The police were after him as a murderer because of the disappearance of his wife. MI5 were after him because they thought he had a list of the three hundred secret rulers of the world, as well as knowledge of the murder of the man who had given him the list. The Boss and his East End London gangsters could be after him in case he knew too much about the murders they had committed.

He went to sleep thinking; *can it get any worse?*

Chapter Twenty-six

A Place to Rest

The sleeping coach attendant woke Desperate Dan in the morning with a knock on the door, followed by handing in a mug of tea and a bacon roll. He said, "We are forty-five minutes off of Glasgow, giving you time for a wash and a shave."

Desperate Dan enjoyed his hot bacon roll and washed it down with the mug of tea. He then visited the toilet, brushed his teeth, and had a good wash. *I wonder if that was a negative comment about my beard?* Checking carefully that he had not left anything, he waited until the train came to rest in the station.

Desperate Dan left the train knowing police would be watching at the ticket barriers. He merged into a group of passengers and immediately noticed an electric maintenance truck full of dust sheets parked beside another train at the next platform. Upon sidling up to it, he saw there was a safety helmet and a yellow high-visibility jacket on the driver's seat. His luck was in, and he could hardly believe it: the keys were in the lock on the vehicle's steering wheel.

After putting his rucksack in the back of the vehicle and covering it with a dust sheet, he put on the yellow jacket and the safety helmet, slipped into the driver's seat, turned the key, and slowly moved the truck forward. With his heart pounding and expecting a shout of discovery, he kept slowly driving towards the ticket barriers. He spotted two police officers carefully watching the disembarking passengers.

As he approached the barriers, a ticket collector opened a wide gate section of the barrier and directed him through. The police officers didn't give him a glance. Dan kept driving slowly across the huge station concourse and away towards the far corner. He targeted a natural parking space behind a fast food outlet and parked the electric vehicle. He removed the safety helmet and yellow jacket and left them on the driver's seat.

He lifted out his rucksack and carried it towards an exit stairway. Dan came out into Argyle Street, turned right onto Hope Street, and crossed over to a bus stop. Without waiting, he got on the first bus that stopped, pretended to not speak English, and held out his hand with coins in his palm. The driver selected a few coins and handed him a ticket.

Desperate Dan waited until they were well clear of Central Station. Then he got off the bus at the top of Hope Street with a big sigh of relief. He watched carefully to see that no one else got off the bus, and he quickly walked to the Queen Street railway station. He approached slowly looking to see whether police were watching but he could not identify anyone suspicious. He looked at the train destination board. None of the present destinations appealed to him.

Remembering the advice of his old Boy Scout leader to analyse the situation, Desperate Dan forced himself to slow down and buy a cup of coffee. He sat at one of the tables to do some thinking, first repeating the conclusions he had come to the night before. The police were after him as a murderer because of the disappearance of his wife. MI5 were after him because they thought he had a list of the three hundred secret rulers of the world and knowledge of the murder of the man who had given him the list. The Boss and his East End London gangsters could be after him in case he knew too much about the murders that they had committed.

He involuntarily let out the words buried in his subconscious from William Shakespeare's *Hamlet*. "Oh! Woe is me. To have seen what I have seen, see what I see!" Several people looked curiously at him as they passed by.

Dan remembered the old soldier Mr Brodie had brought to the Boy Scouts to tell them about his experiences of surviving as a prisoner of war on the Burma railway. He remembered the advice on how to calm panic, and Dan started to breathe slowly and deeply. The image of Oban and the hillside campsite on Gallananch Road, where as a Boy Scout he had camped with his patrol for a week one summer holiday, came to mind.

Inspired by his memory, he made his way to the ticket office and asked, "Can you tell me the time of the next train to Oban?"

The ticket clerk replied, "Twelve twenty-one and 18.21."

Desperate Dan said, "Give me a return to Oban, please, travelling there today and coming back tomorrow." After he paid for the ticket, he asked, "Is there a left-luggage store at this station?"

The ticket clerk pointed with his finger. "Over there, out by the taxi rank."

Desperate Dan decided that there was little risk of anyone searching his rucksack. He relieved himself of the weight of the load packed with his Highland piper's outfit, bagpipes, and other essential worldly possessions by depositing it in the left-luggage store. He looked at the time on the destinations board and noted that it was just half past ten.

He made his way to the Millets outdoor specialist shop on Sauchiehall Street and bought himself a nice two-man tent, a blow-up mattress, a sleeping bag, a lightweight ex-army rucksack, two tracksuits, two T-shirts, three pairs of socks, a pair of light trekker shoes, five pairs of underpants, a towel, a toilet bag, and a couple of rolls of toilet paper.

He removed labels and packaging, packed all the new items in the new rucksack, and tried it on his back. After adjusting some of the buckles and straps, he put on the rucksack and walked out of the shop.

He arrived at Queen Street station at ten minutes to twelve. He bought a cup of coffee and a ploughman's sandwich and sat down at one of the tables. When the platform number seven for the Oban train was shown on the departures display, he got up and with his rucksack, put his ticket through the automatic ticket machine, and walked along the side of the train on platform seven.

He passed a notice board which said, "Front two coaches only for Oban." He walked to the front of the train, entered the first coach, selected a seat, placed his rucksack above it, and sat down. The internal public-address system repeated the message.

The train started on time and made its way out of the station. It soon cleared the outskirts of Glasgow and ran along the edge of the River Clyde. He felt free and at home for the first time in seven months.

The train climbed up the side of the mountains with a long, narrow sea loch far below on the train's left-hand side.

Shortly after this, the public-address system in the train said, "We are approaching Crianlarich, and the two front coaches will go to Oban. The rear coaches will go on to Fort William and Mallaig."

The train soon started again after further warnings to passengers to make sure that they were on the right part of the now-separated train. They passed the beautiful approaches to Connel Ferry, and soon the train was spiralling down the hillside and into the town of Oban.

Desperate Dan sat in his seat and watched the few passengers as they walked along the station platform. He did not recognise any of them, and when he was sure that they were all off, he disembarked and followed at a distance. When he came out of the railway station, he turned left, made his way onto Gallananch Road, and walked the two miles to the campsite.

He went up to the farmhouse and knocked on the door. A woman opened it and looked at him enquiringly. He said, "I would like to pitch my tent here for a few days."

She pointed to an area overlooking a steep slope, "Yes, you can pick your position anywhere over there."

Desperate Dan said, "Good. I will pay for a week in advance." He handed her a twenty-pound note. She took the banknote and said, "Just a minute while I get your change."

He walked over to the area she had indicated and noted that the grass was fresh, with no faded areas visible. It overlooked the sea. He separated the tent bag from his rucksack and laid out all the components on the grass. The tent was one of the new flexible dome tents suspended from external flexible poles. Desperate Dan found it easy to erect and had it complete in less than ten minutes. After blowing up the inflatable mattress, he installed it in the tent.

Then he spread out his sleeping bag on top of the mattress and realised that he was hungry.

Chapter Twenty-seven

Taking Risks

After placing his rucksack inside the tent, Dan zipped up the entrance flap from the outside. He looked at the tent with a feeling of satisfaction and then walked down the drive to the road, where he walked back to Oban to get something to eat.

It was a pleasant spring afternoon, and he enjoyed walking along the road and looking at the sea. Desperate Dan stood mesmerised for a while. Then he spotted what looked like porpoises or dolphins playing in the water about two hundred metres off the shore.

He arrived in town at 5.15, made his way to a small fish-and-chip shop, and ordered fish and chips and a mug of tea. Another diner engaged him in conversation but fortunately wanted to talk about himself rather than ask Desperate Dan any questions.

The waitress delivered his big plate and said, "It's fresh off the fishing boat this morning." He carefully peeled off the batter to expose the fish, squeezed the lemon juice onto it, and tasted it. It was delicious. He somehow felt full of zing.

Leaving the fish-and-chip shop and feeling bored, he walked west along George Street. He looked at the cinema to see what was on but did not fancy the film, instead walking down William Street to the seafront and east along the Corran Esplanade. He pottered about the North Pier, looking down into the boats tied up alongside. He still felt restless, lonely, and a bit bored.

Desperate Dan sat on a bench seat at the corner of the pier to do some people watching, looking across the harbour at the busy railway pier and George Street. He found his eyes drawn upwards to McCaig's Folly, a Colosseum lookalike sitting on top of the town like a crown. For a few moments in the warm evening sun, Desperate Dan's grief and troubles seemed a lifetime away. His mind switched back to tomorrow's meeting with Megan at noon at Queen Street station.

He looked at the clock near the South Pier and saw that it was seven o'clock. He thought. *It is too early to go back the campsite just to sleep. I will go for a pint and a hauf of the Famous Grouse.* He rose from the bench and walked round the harbour twice.

After evaluating the outside of several public houses, he eventually selected one and entered. It was a real old-world bar with lots of wood. As he entered the poorly lit barroom, the noisy conversations immediately died He approached the bar, aware that all eyes were on him. He sat on a stool at the far end of the bar, where he could see all the other customers.

The barman approached and asked, "Do you want a drink?"

Desperate Dan replied, "A hauf of Grouse and a pint of lager."

He watched the barman pour the whisky from the bottle into a measure and then pour the whisky into a glass. He caught sight of the barman winking at the other customers as he turned around, and he walked over with a kind of swagger and placed the drinks on the bar in front of him. Now alert for every sign, Desperate Dan took a ten-pound note out of his tracksuit pocket and handed it to the barman.

The barman held up the English ten-pound note for everyone to see and asked, "Do you come from around here?" The silence in the barroom was oppressive, and Desperate Dan realised that this was some game locals played on tourists. His mind flashed back to the school prefects and how they'd distressed younger pupils by asking them personal questions. His anger became aroused.

The barman went to the till, still holding up the English ten-pound note in full view of the bar customers, looking at it against the dull lighting as if it might be a forgery. "I think it is probably genuine." He eventually put it in the till. He selected some coins and returned to Desperate Dan, handing him his change and saying loudly, "I asked you if you come from around here."

Desperate Dan carefully placed the change in his tracksuit pocket and then looked the barman straight in the eye for a long moment. "And I asked you for a hauf of Grouse."

The barman, taken aback, stuttered, "What do you mean?"

Desperate Dan, still looking straight into the barman's face, pushed the glass of whisky towards him and said, "I gave you the full price, but what you gave me is not a full measure."

The barman shouted, "It is a full measure!"

Desperate Dan replied very quietly, making everyone in the bar strain their ears. "Then you pay for it and drink it and give me my money back before I call the police."

The barman said, "Okay, I don't want an unhappy customer. I'll drink it and give you another on the house." He poured another hauf, made sure to overfill the glass, and placed it in front of Desperate Dan. Then he lifted the offending hauf and drank the evidence.

The silence in the bar was slowly replaced by an increasing babble as the customers realised that the stranger was no pushover and that the show was over for the moment. He slowly drank his drinks, but no one approached him or even risked eye contact.

It was nine o'clock when he finished his drinks. He quickly got off his bar stool and left the public house quickly, doubling back along a couple of side streets until he was sure no one was following him.

He joined Gallanach Road at its very end due to his dodging up side streets and doubling back. It was a lovely summer night, and Desperate Dan enjoyed the walk, however he carefully looked back as he turned each bend in the road. He now felt a bit guilty at drawing attention to himself as he had in the barroom. But the confrontation had also released some of tension in him as a result of trying to be anonymous for all these months.

He reached the campsite and walked up the drive towards his tent, noticing that another tent was pitched about twenty feet away from his. From the animal-like sounds emanating from the tent, it was obvious that it belonged to a vigorous young couple, then he realised that the voices and laughter were both female and the language they were using was very descriptive and left him in no doubt in what they were doing to each other.

Desperate Dan visited the toilet block and then returned, looking at the other tent he imagined two naked female bodies writhing together. He quietly opened his tent and crawled inside. He opened his sleeping bag, stripped off all his clothes, and got in, zipping the sleeping bag closed. The sounds coming from the other tent caused a deep yearning for Kelly in his heart and stomach, but he eventually fell asleep despite his aroused condition.

He woke suddenly from a deep sleep, dreaming that he was being crushed into the ground and being suffocated. Now he was conscious that someone or something was lying beside him and on him. He was petrified, lying without moving and feeling the breathing of the strange apparition. He slowly slipped the zip down the side of his sleeping bag until it was open all the way down the side away from the stranger.

He quickly rolled out of the sleeping bag and unzipped the inner fly screen, and then he unzipped the tent door flap and burst out of the tent like a sprinter coming off the starting blocks. He about turned to face the stranger, only to see a startled sheep struggle to get to its feet and lumber away. Desperate Dan immediately concluded that the sheep must have been lying against the tent and was using it as a wind break.

Releasing the tension, he began to laugh loudly. Then he realised that he was standing completely naked in the bright moonlight and quickly crawled back into his tent in case the females in the other tent investigated the noise.

Chapter Twenty-eight

Megan

Desperate Dan woke to the early light coming through the tent fabric. Remembering his panic in the night, he smiled at the thought of the sheep. It suited him to be up before 6 a.m. because he had to catch the 8.11 train to Glasgow.

He put on his tracksuit and trainers, picked out his towel and toilet bag from his rucksack, unzipped the tent, and headed for the toilet block. It was empty at that time in the morning. He used the toilet, had a shower, towelled himself dry, and wished he could shave but decided not to. He knew police would have photographs of him, and perhaps the beard would confuse them.

Now refreshed, he put his track suit and trainers back on, returned to the tent, and dressed in fresh underwear and socks. Desperate Dan took fifty pounds out of his rucksack, which was all the money he had brought with him, the rest being hidden in the left luggage at Queen Street railway station. After closing the tent, he began his walk back to Oban.

He arrived early at the railway station with more than an hour to spare and so continued up the main street, where he found a café and bought a bacon roll and a coffee. He made his way back to the train station, bought a newspaper, boarded the waiting train, settled into a seat, and began to read. As he turned over to page three, his eye was caught by a photograph of Kelly and him with the headline 'Police Search for Husband of Missing Wife'. Dan read the article intently and was dismayed to find it included the names Douglas Hamilton and Kelly Hamilton, including a profile of each of them. He instinctively sank deeper into his seat.

The ticket collector came, gave a good impression that he was still half asleep by cursorily checked his return ticket, and went on his way. The train arrived at Queen Street railway station at 11.30.

Desperate Dan disembarked and quickly made his way to the Millets outdoor shop, where he bought a lightweight fisherman's hat designed as protection against midges which gave good face cover. After putting on the hat, he made his way back to Queen Street railway station and entered the bar. He ordered a coffee and sat at a dark corner table to wait for his appointment.

***

Megan had started off from the Faslane Peace Camp at 7.45 a.m. and flagged down the bus as it approached. Smiling at the driver, she said, "A single journey ticket to Helensburgh, please."

She sat in the back of the bus and carefully watched the traffic behind the bus to ensure the bus was not being followed. After disembarking from the bus two stops before the pier, she went into a newspaper shop and bought a *Daily Record* newspaper. She hesitated in the doorway as she left the shop to enable her to survey the street. Then she quickly walked to the pier and boarded the ferry going to Gourock on the south side of the River Clyde.

Pretending to read her newspaper, Megan watched the other passengers on the small ferry. She cast glances at the spectacular backdrop of mountains on the north shore of the River Clyde and felt anger at how these beautiful mountains had been used to provide stores for vile and evil nuclear weapons.

When the small ferry docked at the Gourock pier, she waited until all the other passengers made their way up the gangway and hurried away to catch the Glasgow train at the adjoining train station. However, she didn't board the train. She walked through the railway station and out on to the main road. Then she stood at a bus stop where she could see the station exit. A few minutes later, a Glasgow-bound bus stopped. She boarded the bus and purchased a single journey ticket to the main Glasgow bus terminus at Buchanan Street.

Assured that her convoluted journey and scrutiny of possible followers made it almost impossible for anyone to follow her, she relaxed and thought about how she had ended up where she was in her life.

After qualifying as a nurse, Megan had volunteered to serve for a year near Bhopal, India, when she heard about the horrific industrial pollution incident on 3 December 1984, when more than forty tonnes of methyl isocyanate gas leaked from a pesticide plant in Bhopal, immediately killing several thousand people and causing significant morbidity and premature deaths for many thousands more. As usual, the American company profiting from the business had measures in place to dissociate itself directly from legal responsibility and liabilities.

It took her nearly a year to find financial support to secure a one-year placement with a small charity with a clinic in Sehore, where she worked long hours for all that time, treating victims of the exposures of the chemical gas cloud. However, she quickly found that there was no treatment protocol for the complex conditions that the people exhibited, and so the doctors prescribed large quantities of painkillers, antibiotics, or steroids, all of which compounded the problem with their side effects. At least she could give the poor patients lots of nursing care. She returned home without seeing much of India, except the clinic and the journey to and from Sehore.

After a short rest before starting work again in a hospital, Megan found that she could not get the same job satisfaction from the National Health Service's bureaucratic approach to nursing management. To compound her dissatisfaction, she was still incensed and angry at the injustice of what had happened to the people of Bhopal.

To help her to deal with these strong emotions, she began to attend Campaign for Nuclear Disarmament meetings and demonstrations, which only increased her outrage at such monumental evil as nuclear weapons.

She moved to agency supply nursing in order to be able to earn money and to allow her increasing periods of time to stay at the Faslane Peace Camp. Megan concluded her short meditation by saying out loud, "Even though I am not like most women, I am happy doing what I do."

Chapter Twenty-nine

Good News

Megan arrived at Queen Street railway station and entered the bar at ten past twelve. Without greeting Desperate Dan, she said sharply, "Follow me." Walking quickly, she led him out of the station's main entrance and onto the pavement. Megan pushed him against the wall of a building and gave him a tight hug. Above the noise of two passing buses, he heard her say, "I have good news about Kelly. Now, get on this bus."

They boarded the bus, and Megan handed the bus driver two pounds and demanded, "Two returns to the Saint Mungo's Cathedral." After a short journey, she said, "Come on. This is our stop." They got off the bus, and Megan said, "It's a lovely day. Let's go up to the Necropolis."

Desperate Dan looked at her skeptically and said, "It's a cemetery."

Megan laughed and said, "Yes, but what a cemetery."

They approached the main entrance over a bridge and walked through the gates and onto a paved road lined with trees, most of which were still not in leaf.

Megan stopped, turned to look at Desperate Dan, and said, "I think we are safe from prying ears here. It is strange that I bring you to the resting place of the dead to tell you the good news that Kelly is alive, safe, and well."

Desperate Dan was completely stunned. Then he grabbed Megan in a tight hug and danced her round and round, exclaiming, "Ah! Ah! Ha! Ha!"

After a few moments, he settled down, and they sat down on a small, paved-in shot to the flower beds. They sat in silence for about two minutes, and then Megan told him the story. "Attempting to board the nuclear submarine was a disaster. The MOD police patrol boat rammed the kayak at high speed, forcing the bow of the kayak down into the flailing propeller, which threw the kayak and its occupants up into the air. Overshooting the position because of their high speed, the patrol boat had to do a long circle to return to the scene. However, a school of porpoises following the submarine diverted the attention of the police in the patrol boat into investigating their splashing movements in the water, which was enough to confuse them as to exactly where the impact had been. The police were torn between their main job of protecting the nuclear submarine or finding the protesters' bodies. They had to break away and return to their primary purpose of protecting the submarine.

"Meanwhile, Felicity was floating on her back, using the buoyancy of the life jackets, cradling the unconscious Kelly in her arms, and keeping her head above the water. A tidal current was now running, and eventually carried them to the shore. They beached just beside a gypsy encampment. They were long-time friends of Felicity and the peace campers, so the gypsies made a bender tent and furnished it with the basics to make it habitable for the two women.

Douglas interjected, "So she's safe."

"Yes. After a month of lying low until the incident faded into history, and when she was satisfied Kelly had reasonably recovered, Felicity came back to the peace camp and told me the good news. Through contact with a MOD police officer who drinks too much, the gypsies knew that you had gone to the base looking for her and that you were now on the run, suspected of her murder. They decided that it was best for Kelly to stay with them in the meantime, and she accepted their offer. The hunt for you has just been given national press publicity."

Douglas said quietly, "Yes, I know."

Desperate Dan and Megan sat in silence for a long time in the warm sunshine. Eventually, Desperate Dan turned to look at Megan, and he said with a big grin, "Megan, that's the best news I have ever had. Where are the gypsies now?"

Megan replied in almost a whisper, "Somewhere up the west coast. They go up the west coast during the early spring cockle picking. Then they come back down the east coast during the summer to work at the berry picking around Blairgowrie. They told Felicity that they were going to try to spend the spring at the forest on the west side of Kentra Bay, on the north coast of Ardnamurchan, above the village of Salen. It's very remote, and it is a long way out there. I think you would need a mountain bike to find them. They camp in the forest, where they hope they won't be noticed, so they will be very hard to find."

She became less serious and said with a big smile, "Anyway, it's good to be the bearer of good news. But I need to get back to the peace camp, so I will leave you here. Wait for at least half an hour. We don't want to make it too easy for the pigs."

She stood up and then bent down to kiss Desperate Dan on the forehead. "May Yahweh bless and keep the three of you and may his countenance shine upon you."

Desperate Dan said simply, "Thanks, Megan. And God bless you too."

Megan quickly walked away, leaving Desperate Dan pondering what to do next, but he was so happy.

Chapter Thirty

But It Only Gets Worse

Desperate Dan watched Megan walk out through the splendid gates of the Victorian cemetery, and he heard a church clock bell strike two peals. He sat in the warm spring sunlight fretting to get on his way, but Megan had said to wait for half an hour. Desperate Dan's mind almost exploded with the desire to go find Kelly.

His memory suddenly returned to an old soldier Mr Brodie had brought to talk to the senior section of the Boy Scouts one evening. Desperate Dan could not remember his name, but he could remember his face, with its broken nose and scarred face; the man had walked tall as a proud warrior.

The old soldier had told them of the cruel treatment given by the Japanese on the Burmese railway of death to the British and other prisoners of war who were forced to build it. He remembered him saying that about ten thousand British and Commonwealth prisoners of war had died from the cruelty on the Burma railway. He also remembered the basics of what the old soldier had taught them.

"When you get angry or feel panic, concentrate on your breathing.

Try to eliminate everything else from your mind and just concentrate on your breathing."

Apparently, a Zen Buddhist monk who was also a prisoner was attached to their work party because he could speak both Japanese and English. He acted as a translator and taught the prisoners of war meditation techniques.

While sitting in the sunshine, Desperate Dan began to calm his mind of all thoughts and concentrated on deep, slow breathing. Every time thoughts invaded his mind, he eliminated them by concentrating harder on his breathing. Before he realised, he became aware of a church clock chiming three times, and he said out loud, "Three o'clock. That meditation certainly works."

Desperate Dan knew of a cycle shop in the Salt market area, which was nearby. He came out of the cemetery, walked down High Street, and then made his way along George Street to Queen Street railway station. Dan retrieved his rucksack from the left luggage and took it out to George Square. He found an empty, isolated bench and checked the contents of the rucksack. He extracted four bundles of ten twenty-pound notes and put them in different pockets of his anorak.

Satisfied that he had enough money in his pocket to buy a bike, he secured all the pockets on the rucksack, put it on his back, and walked the short distance to the Saltmarket. He found the cycle shop and entered.

The salesman immediately greeted him with a smile and said, "Good afternoon, sir. How can I help you?"

Desperate Dan took his rucksack off and replied, "I am going to do some cycle touring and camping in the Highlands, and I need a good, robust bike to carry me and my two rucksacks."

The salesman said, "You are in luck. I have a second-hand Raleigh Tourer in the shop, and it is in nearly new condition. It's a bargain at only ninety-nine pounds. It comes already fitted with front pannier bags, a rear luggage rack, and rear pannier bags." He went into the back shop and wheeled out the bike.

Desperate Dan looked it over and said, "Yes, that's just what I want. If you throw in eight bungee elastic cord bike fasteners, it's a deal."

The salesman went behind the counter and picked four double packets, each containing two pairs of bungee cord bike fasteners. He handed them to Desperate Dan and said with a smile, "Done."

Dan handed the salesman one roll of banknotes. "I think you will find one hundred pounds in the roll."

The salesman secured the money in his till, gave Desperate Dan one pound in change, and helped him to fasten his rucksack to the luggage rack on the bike.

Desperate Dan took the bike outside. Because the roads and pavements were busy, he pushed the bike back to Queen Street Station and installed it in the left-luggage store. He knew that the Oban train was due to leave at 6.21 p.m., and he had time to have something to eat, but he thought it better to avoid using the station bar.

After walking across George Square, he eventually found a café on one of the adjacent streets and ordered a baked potato with cheese-and-onion filling and a mug of tea. When he finished eating, he thought, *I wonder if Carroty Charlie is still at his usual newspaper pitch?*

He wandered over to the pitch outside Queen Street Station's main entrance. It was a strange person wearing a hooded top on the pitch, but it was certainly not the distinctive figure of Carroty Charlie. Desperate Dan walked over and asked for an *Evening Times*.

He noticed that the man was not wearing the double skulls ring. He took the paper with one hand and paid the seller with the other, making sure his own ring was in view.

The newspaper seller suddenly grabbed his wrist in a vicelike grip, saying in a Cockney accent, "Got you at last, you troublesome bastard."

Desperate Dan suddenly recognised Pat, the driver from the scrap metal yard. Pat pulled him toward the rear of a van parked in a coned-off area and banged on the rear door. The door opened, and Samson leaned out and yanked Desperate Dan up and into the van using one of his mighty arms. Pat got into the driver's seat, and with the van tyres screaming, he drove off, knocking over the traffic cones.

Samson shouted, "You certainly gave us a challenging time finding you!" Desperate Dan asked, "How did you find me?"

Samson laughed loudly and said, "Once we started torturing Sammy, it didn't take long to get him to talk. However, Carroty Charlie died before he talked."

Suddenly there was a loud impact. Samson and Desperate Dan were thrown hard into the bulkhead separating the back of the van from the driver's cabin.

Desperate Dan looked at Samson and saw that he was unconscious. Fortunately, his giant body had cushioned Desperate Dan's impact. Dan quickly got to his feet and he tried the back door, which opened easily.

He jumped out and saw that the van driver had tried to go up the one-way Cochrane Street against the traffic flow and had crashed into an oncoming lorry.

People ran towards the crashed vehicles, and so Desperate Dan concluded that Samson and Pat would get plenty of help. He slipped away unnoticed through the courtyard in the centre of the City Chambers.

Now out of sight of the traffic incident, he walked quickly back to Queen Street railway station, bought a single ticket to Oban, collected his bike and rucksack, and caught the train with a few minutes to spare. After he stowed his bike, he watched out of the window to see that he was not followed by the van driver or Samson. He thought that was unlikely given the violence of the impact.

As the train moved away from the station and into the dark tunnel, Desperate Dan slipped the ring off his finger and dropped it through the open window, onto the railway track. Being surprised by Pat and

Samson had shocked Desperate Dan, and he worried about it all the way to Oban. He thought, *they tortured Sammy Seal, and he must have cracked and told them about Carroty Charlie. They must have come to Glasgow to find out what he knew. They must have hurt him so much that he died on them.*

His heart ached terribly as he thought deeply about his two strange friends, and he wondered whether he would be next.

Chapter Thirty-one

By Sea and Island

Before Dan realised it, the train was stopping at Oban railway station. He sat in his seat and watched all the passengers leave the train. It gave him a sense of relief when he did not recognise any of them.

He collected his bike and pushed it out of the station. He mounted his bike, looked around in case anyone was watching him, and slowly rode along Queens Park Place round the harbour, towards the North Pier. Without indicating, he suddenly turned right into George Street, made a quick left turn, and drove the bike hard up Stevenson Street. He pedalled hard right into Combie Street and then left, forcing the pedals with all the strength in his thighs. Dan moved fast along Albany Street and finally on to Gallanach Road.

Confident that no one could have followed him round that mazy route at such a high speed, he slowed to a modest pace and soon reached the campsite. He was pleased to see that his tent was on its own at that part of the campsite. He unzipped the flaps and checked the black thread he had suspended across the entrance. Relieved to see that it was still undisturbed, he checked his rucksack and found it to be as he had left it.

He concealed his bike behind his tent and brought his big rucksack into the tent. After lying on his sleeping bag, he fell asleep for about half an hour. Upon waking, he looked at his watch and saw that it was eleven o'clock. He crawled out of the tent and sat behind it, looking across the Sound of Kerrera in the relatively bright light of a full moon shining on the water and the land. When he finally tired, he used the campsite toilets, entered his tent, stripped off, and got into his sleeping bag.

Dan gently woke and felt the warm, early morning sun coming through the tent fabric. He finally extracted himself from the sleeping bag. After visiting the toilet block, which again was empty at this early time in the morning, he showered, came back to his tent, dressed, dismantled his tent, packed everything in the bike pannier bags, mounted his bike, and made his way to the road.

It was only seven o'clock, and the Mull ferry was due to sail at quarter to eight. Dan slowly cycled along the road to the ferry terminus. As he approached, he carefully scanned the pier. A thought crossed his mind: *Am I becoming paranoid?* He did not see police or anyone he recognised, and so he entered the ticket office and bought a single ticket to Craignure.

Desperate Dan boarded the Mull ferry with his bike; he now knew he was becoming a bit paranoid but remembered the advice Sammy Seal had given him. He decided to stay close to his bike, with its array of pannier bags containing all his worldly possessions, including a considerable sum of money.

When the ticket collector came to check his ticket, Desperate Dan asked him, "I believe there is another ferry to and from Mull?"

The ticket collector smiled and said, "No, there are several other ferries. Fionnphort to Iona is a busy ferry, which is about thirty-six miles west of Craignure. Another ferry runs from Fishnish to Lochaline in Morvern on the east coast of Mull, and it's about six miles north of Craignure. There is the Tobermory to Kilchoan ferry, as well as several smaller private ferries."

Desperate Dan was happy to get the information without explaining where he was going. Probably the ticket collector would assume that he was making for Iona like most other visitors to Mull.

Realising that he was hungry, Dan suppressed his paranoia with an effort and left his bike to go to the ship's cafeteria. He bought a full breakfast and a mug of tea. Desperate Dan remembered something that Megan had said about the Ardnamurchan peninsula being very remote and almost unpopulated. He decided to buy some extra food rations. His choice was very limited, and so he bought three sealed packs of filled sandwiches and five one-and-a-half-litre bottles of still water. He bought a map of the west of Scotland and returned to his bike.

After studying the map, he decided to head for the Tobermory to Kilchoan ferry. Amazed that he still found storage space, he carefully packed the bottled water and sandwiches into the various pannier bags. He gave a bit of a frown as he thought about the weight of the large bottles of water.

Desperate Dan waited at the ferry terminal until all the disembarked passengers had gone on their various ways. Then he mounted his bike, turned right onto the coast road, and started peddling north. The heavily loaded bike forced him to pedal slowly, and the nature of the road required him to stop periodically to let vehicles pass.

Desperate Dan worried about how he could find Kelly somewhere on the hundreds of miles of coast. So preoccupied was he that he hardly noticed the lovely coastal scenery. "Plod on. Plod on," he kept repeating as he peddled the heavily loaded bike along the twenty-mile journey. It took about three hours, but he hardly noticed the passage of time. Before he knew it, he was freewheeling down the East Brae and into the beautiful island town of Tobermory. The colourful view and perfect setting momentarily lifted him out of his obsessive worry about finding Kelly.

However, his uplifted mood was short-lived because he saw the ferry begin to sail away from the slipway. He cycled to the ferry terminal and found out that the ferry he had just missed was the one o'clock ferry; the next one would leave at 2.30. He noticed the terminal building and saw a sign for Café Fish Tobermory. *Well, I have an hour and a half. This might be the best chance to get something to eat for a while.*

He went in and had a look at the menu. It was a bit pricey by his normal standards, but he justified it by saying to himself, *I might be in the wilderness for the next few days. It's time to load up with some protein.*

The waitress came over with a big smile and asked, "Lovely day, sir. Would you like to order?"

Desperate Dan replied, "Yes, I would like some fish on its own. I am touring by bike, and after the last part of the journey, I feel the need for some quality protein."

The woman looked at him for a moment, and then she said, "We have some nice, fresh monkfish, just landed this morning. I can give you a good portion lightly boiled in milk for four pounds. It will be delicious and filling on its own, with some lemon juice garnish to give it some zing."

Desperate Dan smiled for the first time in days and replied, "How can I refuse a sales pitch like that?"

The waitress laughed as she walked away and said, "It will take me about twenty minutes."

Desperate Dan said as an afterthought, "Oh, and some tea, please." Then he went out to his bike, found the map, and brought it in to his table.

He studied the map, found Tobermory, and then followed the dotted line of the ferry route to Kilchoan. With his eye, he followed the road marked on the map from the Kilchoan ferry terminal, turning east and going through Ardslignish. His eye moved on to Glenborrodale, and then he noticed a stream coming off the hillside at Laga. The map showed woodland around the stream, which would give him cover if he decided to camp. Desperate Dan put in the back of his mind that he could camp above Laga, where he could get fresh water.

The woman appeared with his large plate of fish and a half lemon. Desperate Dan squeezed the lemon juice over the fish and picked up his fork and knife. He tasted his first mouthful and let out an audible, "Oh." He had not tasted monkfish before and had been a bit dubious. It was a white fish that melted in his mouth in a tasty way. He ate slowly to saviour the large portion. He slowly drank the tea and then refilled the cup from the teapot.

When he finished, he rose from the table and paid the waitress, giving her a pound tip. "That's the best fish I have tasted for a long while."

The waitress replied with a smile, "That's what we are here for, sir. You don't by any chance want to buy some of our smoked fish? It's sealed in plastic packaging and will keep for weeks if it is not opened."

Desperate Dan's face lit up as he visualised smoked fish sealed in plastic. "What is your cheapest smoked fish?"

The waitress answered, "The smoked mackerel is very good value and full of healthy fish oil."

He bought five sealed packs, left the café, packed the mackerel and the map in the pannier bags, and pushed his bike to the ferry terminal, his mind now deep in thought. He watched until the ferry came into view round the headland. With his paranoia heightened, he watched everyone with suspicion. He wheeled his bike down the slip and onto the ramp and parked the bike exactly where the boatman pointed. He remained with the bike, and when the boatman came for his ticket, he completed the exchange, avoiding conversation and concluding by saying, "Danke."

With a kind of blank look, the boatman mumbled something like, "Can you not learn English?"

The voyage took about thirty-five minutes, and Desperate Dan had to wait until the cars had disembarked. Then the boatman signalled him to move onto the ramp.

Chapter Thirty-two

Search and Find

Dan pushed the bike up the slipway pier at Kilchoan, mounted slowly, and cycled to the end of the short road leading from the ferry terminal. He stopped, dismounted, and looked for a moment at the scattering of mostly white houses snuggled under the rugged hillside. He took out his map, studied it intently, and then turned right as he remounted his bike and started pedalling east.

Dan conserved his energy by using low gears to power his heavily loaded bike. He pedalled steadily but very slowly. The first few miles took him inland. Then the road came back down to Loch Sunart at Ardslignish. At one good viewpoint across the loch, he stopped, dismounted, and sat in the sunshine, looking at the spectacular view. The chasing packs of crooks, MI5, and the police seemed so far away in this beautiful wilderness, and he dozed off in the warm sunshine.

Desperate Dan woke with a start. He had been dreaming that he was being chased by wolves—or worse, a large conspiracy of wolves who were behind him and on each of his flanks. No matter how fast he ran, they kept up with him. The sweat ran off his forehead as he woke in the direct sunshine on the edge of Loch Sunart.

He frantically looked around expecting to see wolves, but the only things he could detect were the songs of the birds and the movement of butterflies, insects, and a colony of rabbits grazing in the sunshine.

Suddenly some baby rabbits scuttled into their burrows at the edge of the trees. The mother rabbit crouched expectantly in front of the entrances to the burrows as though on guard. Desperate Dan caught the rapid movement of the weasel out the side of his eye as it darted towards the mother rabbit.

At the last moment, the mother rabbit about-turned. Facing away from the approaching predator, she kicked out with both hind legs, a perfectly timed and powerful impact, throwing the weasel high up into the air before it landed heavily winded on the ground, squealing as though complaining about the unexpected violence. It skulked away into the undergrowth. Desperate Dan thought he saw a fleeting smile of satisfaction on the mother rabbit's face as the baby rabbits quickly reappeared in the sunshine.

He sat thinking about what he had just witnessed. *Those meek species that are preyed upon by predators have to hide, but the courage of the mother rabbit in the face of her offspring's danger overcame her natural fear, and she won the day. There is a lesson somewhere in what I have just witnessed, meant for just for me.*

He returned his thoughts to Kelly and the gypsies. *The gypsies are not liked, especially here in this rich man's paradise, and so they are going to be hidden. It's going to make my job of finding them much harder.*

He got out his map, studied it carefully, and said out loud to himself, "They told Felicity that they were going to try to stay concealed through the spring at the forest on the west side of Kentra Bay, on the north coast of Ardnamurchan, above the village of Salen." He looked at the position of the sun in the sky and estimated that it was about five o'clock. "It's about twenty miles to Kentra Bay. I could easily make it before dark.

Right, Desperate Dan, concentrate on the job. Get going and keep going until you get there."

He realised that he was talking to himself, but he wasn't bothered. Speaking out loud helped reinforce his resolve, and in his isolation, he needed support from wherever he could get it.

Chapter Thirty-three

Sweet Reunion

Dan fastened the bags, mounted his bike, and started to slowly pedal towards Glenborrodale. He no longer noticed the scenery, and his mind was now set on getting to the forest. Eventually he reached Salen, where the road turned inland, but he didn't stop. He had made his plan and was single-minded to reach the forest on the west side of Kentra Bay before stopping.

Desperate Dan was getting a bit weary and hungry when he arrived at the small settlement at Acharacle, but he did not stop. He kept going, looking for the old drove road to Arivegaig going off to the left from the B8044. He found the minor road turn-off on the outskirts of the settlement and turned his bike onto it, heading west. Soon his spirits greatly lifted when he realised that he was on the southern edge of Kentra Bay and could see the mature forest plantation in front of him.

Desperate Dan noticed a south-west-facing spot just off the road. It was sheltered from view behind a neatly stacked pile of newly felled and trimmed logs. He dismounted from his bike, opened his pannier bags, and extracted a bottle of water and one of the packs of sandwiches. He looked at the sun and observed that it was getting low in the sky;

it would soon be dark. He sat secure from view behind the logs, slowly drank the bottle of water, and ate the sandwiches.

He studied the landscape around him as it rose up onto a rocky escarpment above the road, where there were lines of trees growing along geological fault lines filled with eroded soil. He pushed his bike up to one of these and found a perfect spot to pitch his tent beside a natural spring trickling out of a large crack in the rock. He concluded that the water would be very clean coming off the rocky hillside in such a remote location, and he washed his hands, cupped them together to collect some water, and tasted the crystal-clear wonder that sustained life.

The ground was very rocky, but where the trees had established themselves, there were quite deep pockets of eroded soil and scree.

Desperate Dan congratulated himself on his choice of tent as he once again experienced how easy it was to erect. He noticed the midges swarming, and so he rushed and had the tent complete in less than ten minutes. He quickly blew up the inflatable mattress and installed it in the tent. Then he spread out his sleeping bag on top of the mattress, placed his rucksack inside the tent, crawled in, zipped up the entrance flap from the inside, and zipped up the insect screen.

He stripped off and lay on his back on top of his sleeping bag. After closing his eyes, he focused on each part of his body for any midge itching sensation, but he could not detect any.

He then recalled the meditation technique he'd learned from the old soldier. Desperate Dan relaxed all his limbs in turn, right down to his toes. He let his eyes rest in their sockets and let his tongue relax in his mouth, and then he concentrated on his breathing, fully emptying his lungs each time he breathed out using his diaphragm. He did this for twenty-five minutes, chasing away any thoughts as they entered his mind by returning constantly to deep, slow breathing. He rolled onto his side and dozed off.

When he woke, he was cold. The tent was in darkness. He unzipped the insect screen and the tent entrance flap and looked out. He quickly pulled on his tracksuit and trainers and crawled out of the tent.

It was night, but in this light pollution–free wilderness, the sky was arrayed with a myriad of stars. He scrambled up to the highest point of the rocky escarpment, which he had thoroughly surveyed earlier, and looked out over the forest. Out of the side of his eye, he caught sight of moving lights contrasted against the deep blackness of the forest. They were intermittent and random, Desperate Dan guessed that they were handheld torches being used amongst trees, and he estimated their distance to be about two miles away. He guessed that their location would be close to the road running through the forest.

It was now very dark, and Desperate Dan carefully scrambled down from the rocky escarpment without mishap. He had new hope in his heart.

Before going back to the tent, he located the spring, cupped his hands, and tasted clean and cool water. He crawled back into the tent, stripped off again, and crawled into his sleeping bag.

Waking refreshed in the morning, Desperate Dan washed in the painfully cold spring water. He waited naked for the wetness to dry in the air, and he looked towards the forest and thought he could see the faintest wisps of smoke. Excited by the possibility that it might be the gypsy camp, he dressed, ate another pack of sandwiches, and drank two cups of spring water. Then he dismantled and packed his camping equipment, packing all his equipment in the pannier bags and leaving the campsite almost undisturbed. He pushed his bike down the rough hillside. It was six o'clock when he reached the road and mounted his bike.

He cycled along the road into the forest, carefully examining the right-hand side of the road for any sign of a track leading into the forest close to where he thought he saw the lights. About two miles in, he spotted a track; it had been carefully camouflaged with some large rocks blocking it from the road.

Desperate Dan's heartbeat rose as he anticipated finding Kelly, but he was more fearful that he wouldn't, causing his extreme tension. He dismounted and pushed his bike with some difficulty through the heavy growth of ferns to get around the large rocks blocking the track. Once he was through, the track opened and was clearly two tracks kept clear by vehicle wheels. He pushed his bike slowly along the track for about two miles and came to the edge of a clearing.

Suddenly dogs barked furiously, and then the sky fell in.

He woke lying on the ground with Kelly washing his face with a wet flannel. He raised his arms up and hugged her tight, shouting hysterically, "I have found you! I have found you, I have found you!"

Kelly kept saying his name. "Douglas, Douglas, Douglas." Eventually they calmed down.

Kelly helped Douglas onto his feet, and he realised his head was sore. He felt the side of his head and was shocked to feel a definite swelling. He looked at Kelly and laughed. "You are really going to have a baby. The size of your bump could mean twins." He suddenly became aware of others standing in a circle around them.

Kelly said loudly, "This is Douglas, my husband."

A big man stepped forward and held out his hand to Douglas. "Welcome, Douglas. My name is Harman. Sorry about the bump on the head, but we didn't know you were Kelly's husband. We were still sleeping when the dogs started barking. When you are Romanies in a hostile world, you act first and ask questions later." The circle of Gypsies burst into laughter, and Douglas shook the big man's hand, laughing along with them. The big man said, "You and Kelly go to Kelly's bender tent and catch up on your love life, and I will talk to you later today."

Before entering the bender tent, Douglas took the food and water out of the pannier bags. He took one packet of sandwiches and one bottle of water and gave them to Kelly. He took the rest of the sandwiches and packets of smoked mackerel and handed them to the oldest gypsy woman. Then he made his way back to Kelly's bender tent.

Douglas held her tightly and asked her. "How are you? Is the baby all right? When is it due? People told me you were dead. Oh, it's been a nightmare! Please tell me that you and the baby are all right."

Kelly kissed him for a long time, and then she said. "Yes, we are all right. We have been looked after by the gypsies all these months, and the baby is due in a couple of weeks. So far everything is fine. Now, tell me about you."

Douglas said with a smile, "Apart from being chased by the police, MI5, and some murderous gangsters, I am fine now that I have found you."

Eventually they went to bed and lay on their backs. Kelly said, "Look at the bender tent above your head. I helped to make this one, and I am very proud of it. They are made from easy-to-find materials and are quick and simple to construct. By building them within the forest, they did not draw attention to the fact gypsies were in the area." She smiled, pointing at the elements of construction. "To make a bender tent, we cut a dozen lengths of supple tree branches about ten feet long. The ends of ten of the branches were stuck into the ground in two rows of five, at two-foot intervals. We made the ridgepole about eight feet long out of two poles tied together with gap. The tops of the side poles were bent over, pushed into the ridgepole gap, and tied tightly. The other two long poles were placed at the closed end of the bender and bent over and lodged through the first two side poles. Then we threw tarps over this framework to cover it and joined the tarps to the end poles."

Douglas said, "Clever girl. Now, shut up and give me a kiss. And take your clothes off—I want to look at you and your big bump."

Chapter Thirty-four

All the World Is a Pecking Order

Kelly and Douglas spent the entire day in the bender tent cuddling each other, during which they also ate Douglas's sandwiches and drank a bottle of water. They dressed and emerged to join the others gathering at the communal evening dinner.

Kelly introduced Douglas to each of the gypsies individually and in a formal manner. At each introduction, he was given a blessing in the name of Yahweh.

Several tables had been constructed out of suitable thin, straight branches cut from trees, grouped together and covered with a large carpet, which was then covered with waxed paper cut from a large roll. The table places were set with plates and cutlery, and then the women brought large bowls of food from their bender tents and placed them in the centre of the table.

The leader of the travelling community, the big man who had welcomed Douglas, said a formal grace. The cling film was removed from the bowls of food. Everyone waited for Douglas and Kelly to help themselves, and then they took their turns.

After eating the food, the table was quickly cleared, the waxed paper tablecloth was wiped down, and wine was served. A man picked up a guitar, and a woman began to sing a Romany song full of melancholy pain. The entertainment didn't last long before the Scottish midges intervened, and everyone rushed to the security of their bender tents.

Harman, the gypsy leader, said to Douglas and Kelly, "Come to my bender tent." Douglas and Kelly followed him. The inside of Harman's bender tent was striking in its decoration. All the main furnishings were constructed from thin, flexible branches cut from forest trees and lashed together in a form to suit their function.

However, Harman's young wife had draped everything in brightly coloured fabrics, and there was a seven-branch menorah lamp stand prominently displayed.

Harman indicated a chair to Douglas and one to Kelly. "Please sit down." He positioned another chair directly opposite and sat facing them. "While you were unconscious and Kelly was attending to you, one of the men searched the bags on your bicycle, and he found this." He held up a document while carrying on speaking. "This list is the current names making up the Committee of Three Hundred."

They were both startled by the frank simplicity of the revelation. Douglas's complexion turned pale, and then he blushed.

Harman laughed and said, "You are surprised that I know what this list is." He stood up, took down a bottle of wine from a shelf, opened the bottle, and selected three glasses from a shelf.

Kelly said, "No, thanks. I have the baby to think about."

He put one glass back on the shelf and filled the remaining two glasses with wine. Harman handed over one glass to Douglas. "You will see from the ornaments adorning our tent that we are Messianic Jews. The old Romany legend is that it was Romany gypsies who gave hospitality to Yeshua, Mary, and Joseph when they fled into Egypt to escape Herod's murdering soldiers. Let me give you some background of the Romany people. Where shall I start?

"Linguistic and genetic evidence indicates the Romanies originated from the Indian subcontinent, emigrating from India towards the north-west no earlier than the eleventh century. The traditional Romanies place a high value on the extended family. Romany social behaviour is strictly regulated by Hindu purity laws, still respected by most Romany people. What most people don't know is that these purity laws are the same as those in the Old Testament of the Bible.

"These regulations affect many aspects of life and are applied to actions, people, and things. Parts of the human body are considered impure and vulgar. Virginity is essential in unmarried women. Men and women often marry young, when hormonal levels become significant. This has caused controversy in several countries over the Romanies' practice of child marriage.

"The married woman is part of the husband's family, and her main job is to tend to her husband's and her children's needs, as well as to take care of her in-laws. The power structure in the traditional Romany household has at its top the oldest man or grandfather, and men in general have more authority than women. Women gain respect and authority as they get older. Young wives begin gaining authority once they have children.

"As our people travelled in Europe, we were subject to ethnic cleansing, abduction of our children, and forced labour. In England, Romanies were sometimes hanged or expelled from small communities. As a result, large groups of the Romanies moved to the east towards Poland, which was more tolerant, and Russia, where the Romanies were treated more fairly as long as they paid the annual taxes.

"During World War Two, the Nazis embarked on a systematic attempt at genocide of the Romanies, and they were marked for extermination and sentenced to forced labour and imprisonment in concentration camps."

Harmon stood up from his chair and shouted, "It shouldn't surprise you if I, a leader of a Romany community, know about the Committee of Three Hundred. After all, they have been responsible for spilling a lot of Romany blood!"

He gathered himself, took another bottle, refilled the wine glasses, and said to Kelly, "When we dragged you from the sea, you were in a bad way. My mother is a good nurse and tended you for days. You were delirious with fever for two or three days, and she overheard your nightmares. We learned about your involvement at the peace camp and your attempt to board a submarine. We also learned about a murder of a Freemason in London, the secret list of names, and the police and MI5. In conclusion, I think you must be the most sought-after persons on the planet, and for that reason, I am willing to let you join our community."

Harman sat back in his chair, looked at Douglas and Kelly, and sipped slowly from his wine glass as though he was relieved to have exercised such a big decision.

Douglas sat for what seemed a long time and then said, "Thank you, but you need to know it's not just MI5 and the police that are after us. Serious London gangsters are even more dangerous than the others."

Harman laughed loudly and replied, "What does it matter who kills you? It's all the same in the end; you can only die once." He reached out with the bottle and refilled the wine glasses.

Douglas added, "I don't think they managed to follow me. The gangsters were involved in a vehicle accident, and they were both unconscious when I escaped from them. I have been using a false name. I don't have a mobile phone or any state benefits that they can track, and I have started to grow my hair and a beard."

Harman noted, "You are nearly as good as Romany already." The three of them laughed long and loudly, as if relieving a build-up of nervous pressure.

Harman became serious again and looked intently at Douglas. "You may have noticed that the community sees me as leader, as well as my elderly mother, Esmeralda, to whom I noticed you gave a gift of food and water. That act of respect immediately said something about you. She is our gypsy queen, and she advises all the young women, including my wife, who are very young and nubile. Their husbands are all my sons, but they are still just youths who need a lot of direction and sometimes physical correction. You are slightly older than all my sons, and you could become my second in command. But you will need to be willing to give me your absolute loyalty and support, which may include physical violence from time to time. If you are being pursued by packs of wolves working in conspiracy, you won't find a better ally than this old Romany bear."

Douglas held out his hand, and Harman enclosed it in his mighty paw, issuing a loud laugh. Harman said, "We need to give you a new name. Romanies are superstitious about using their real names in case some enemy curses them."

Douglas said, "Desperate Dan will be my name."

Harman said with a big grin, "And Kelly's name will be Kizzy. Finish your drink, Desperate Dan, and get an early night. You will have to win your position as second in command over the next few weeks."

Chapter Thirty-five

Acceptance into the Gypsy Community

Desperate Dan and Kizzy, as they were now called, returned to their bender tent. Dan said, "Harman has offered to let us stay with the community, and he said I could try to establish myself as his depute. What do you feel about that, especially the implications of bringing up our baby? You know how intolerant and prejudiced people are towards gypsies."

Kizzy replied, "I like it because I have you again. I feel safer here from the evil people who are still after you, and we know the gangsters will kill you if they find you. But it won't be easy for you. The young men will see you as an outsider, and you will be excluded when you are trying to work with them. Do we really have another option?"

He replied, "In that case, let's get to bed. I will need my sleep. Oh! Remember, my new name is Desperate Dan."

Kizzy laughed and said, "If your name is Desperate Dan, you will need to be gentler in bed, because there are three of us now, and one of us is very small and delicate."

They woke early in the morning; Kizzy made some breakfast and some sandwiches, which she wrapped up. She produced a large bottle of water, a roll of toilet paper, and a small first aid kit from a cupboard and placed them in a small backpack. She kissed him and said, "You will be working in the forest all day. Always keep this safe beside you. Your young rivals could accidently lose it if you are not watching. God bless you and keep you, at least until tonight, Desperate Dan."

He put the backpack on and left the bender tent. The young men were beginning to gather at the centre of the site. Harman appeared, looked around, and then shouted, "Where is Pesha, that lazy offspring of a Russian peasant?" He walked over to a bender tent and banged on the side of a water barrel.

Pesha darted out of the bender tent, just dodging the pretend kick aimed belatedly at his backside.

The young men laughed loudly at this common ritual. Harman let the laughter die away and then announced loudly, "I rename this new family member as Desperate Dan. He is Romany in all but parentage. Believe me, he qualifies for his inclusion in our family by his recent history better than most of you, simply because of your youth. You will accept him as one of us as he begins his induction into our traditions. His wife will be known from now on as Kizzy. Their marriage is sacred. Let no member of this family defile their marriage, on pain of death. Let it be so now, for thus it is fitting for us to fulfil all righteousness to Yahweh."

Each of the young men shook hands with Desperate Dan in turn, saying, "Welcome to the family, brother Desperate Dan, and may Yahweh bless you."

Harman resumed loudly. "Today we will search for and kill a deer; the forest is full of them. Pesha has had more sleep than the rest of us, so he will lie in wait downwind of the deer with the crossbow. The rest of you will go to the west side of the forest and drive the deer towards Pesha. Do not go near the road, take your time, and stay on the small animal tracks deep in the forest so that you are not seen by travellers. Once you are on the west side, spread out and begin your drive at five o'clock. At that time, gamekeepers will be home having their tea. Be extra careful to not be seen or heard. Take the two pointer dogs. They have been trained to not bark and to listen and smell for gamekeepers."

One of the youths walked over to Desperate Dan and said, "I am known as Ferka. Come with me, and I will keep you right."

Three of the young men, Desperate Dan, and two dogs walked slowly along a small path that meandered through the trees.

Ferka said, "The deer that made this path don't keep to straight lines, and because it winds so much, it takes ages to get anywhere. Follow the winding path, but generally keep the sun to your left." The forest was at most two miles wide, but the winding path covered about four miles. Eventually they emerged onto sandy beaches and the sea.

Ferka said, "We will spread out in a line about two hundred metres apart and slowly walk back towards our camp. The two others will take each flank with the dogs. You and I will take the middle. Try to keep me in sight, and I will try to keep you in sight. Remember we are returning in the opposite direction, so you will try to keep the sun on your right and slightly behind you."

The four men and two dogs waited together until just about five o'clock. Then Ferka said, "Right, time to go." The two men with the dogs moved to the right and the left. Desperate Dan and Ferka separated by about one hundred metres. When they were at about the correct spacing, Ferka raised his arm and gestured to move forward.

Desperate Dan found a small path and followed it. Like the previous path, it was very narrow and often split into two paths, but by following Ferka's advice to keep the sun to his right and slightly behind, he was confident he was heading in the right direction. Occasionally he heard and got the briefest of glimpses of startled deer darting away from him. When this happened, he heard birds giving alarm calls to their friends.

After about two hours, he began to worry that he may be lost, but suddenly one of the dogs was beside him, wagging its tail while running down a path, stopping, and looking back at him. He decided that the dog was trying to lead him, and so he followed it. After about fifteen minutes, they emerged into the gypsy camp. The men had slung a deer carcass up from a branch on a tree and were busy gutting and skinning it.

Harman was pleased with the result of the hunt, and he said with a laugh, "Ah, there's Desperate Dan. We thought you had run away."

After a wash-up, Desperate Dan returned to the centre of the camp, where the women had the evening meal ready to serve. As before, the table places were set with plates and cutlery, and then the women brought large bowls of food from their bender tents and placed them in the centre of the table.

Harman again said a formal grace. The food served was fish and mashed potatoes, and like the previous night, after eating the food, the table was quickly cleared, the waxed paper tablecloth was wiped down, and wine was served. A man picked up a guitar, a woman began to sing a Romany song, and all the extended family members swayed in time to the music.

However, this evening a breeze had blown up, which kept the midges away. The tempo of the music changed, and one of the women kicked off her shoes and began to dance. Others took it in turn to dance, depicting various ancient stories with great artistic expression. Eventually Kizzy, as she was now known, was persuaded to dance, and even though she was heavy with a child, she danced a gentle interpretation of the Highland Gaelic dancing at which she was once a champion.

Harman brought the festivities to a close by saying, "Tomorrow it's out to work at three o'clock in the morning to catch the low tide. We have lobster creels and fishing lines with baited hooks pegged along the seabed, and we need to harvest them and rebait them at low tide, while the women gather cockles until the tide comes back in."

Desperate Dan and Kizzy retired to their bender tent at ten o'clock, but he said to her, "Straight to sleep tonight. Three o'clock is a tough test."

Kizzy replied, "Ah! Well, I guess we will just need to rename you Tired Old Dan."

Chapter Thirty-six

Surrounded by Blessings

It seemed that they had only just gotten to sleep when the alarm clock went off at 2.30 a.m. Desperate Dan had to fight hard to stay awake and finally roll out of bed. Kizzy resumed a rhythmical snoring as he pulled on his clothing and training shoes. He unfastened the bender tent flap and stumbled outside, still half asleep.

Harman's mother was stirring a big pot of simmering porridge on a charcoal fire constrained in a ring of large stones, beside a large kettle simmering on the same fire. She smiled a toothless smile and said, "Pour yourself a mug of tea, and I will ladle you a plate of gypsy porridge."

Desperate Dan replied, "What's gypsy porridge, Esmeralda?"

The old lady laughed loudly and said, "Ah! You are trying to pry my secrets out of me. These are the secrets handed down from mothers to daughters to give them power over their men. We include some forest medicines to make our husbands more virile."

She continued to cackle to herself as though enjoying some deeper meaning than was obvious to Desperate Dan. He began to gingerly sip the porridge, but it was a bit hot, and so hc let the spoonful cool in the air before trying another taste. It was surprisingly tasty, with a strong cinnamon flavour. It had fruit through it, and he guessed that it was a mixture of chopped apple and whole raisins. It was the best porridge he had ever tasted.

Harman came out, went to three of the bender tents, and banged hard on the side of the water drums that were at the side of each tent. The tarpaulins were folded at the sides to form two gutters, which directed rainwater from the large tents into two water drums at the side of each. He walked over to Desperate Dan, who was pouring himself a mug of tea, and said, "What size of shoes do you take? We will need to try to get you a pair of waders."

Desperate Dan replied, "Size nine."

Harman said, "Good, I think Ferka takes size nine, and last month he bought three pair of fisherman's waders at Wilson's Auction Market at Dalry in Ayrshire. It was unbelievable, the bargains that went for less than a song at the auction."

Ferka and two other men approached the breakfast table and accepted plates of porridge from Esmeralda. Harman asked, "Ferka do you have a spare pair of size nine fisherman's waders?"

Ferka replied, "Yes, I have two spare pairs."

Harman asked, "Would you sell a pair to Desperate Dan?"

Ferka replied with a big smile, "Yes, they were a bargain. I got three pairs for twelve pounds at the auction, and I will be happy with a tenner for one pair."

He returned to his bender tent and came out with two pairs of fisherman's waders. Desperate Dan went to his bender tent and came back a few minutes later with a ten-pound note, and they made the agreed exchange. Desperate Dan tried them on and confirmed that they were a good fit.

Harman then goaded everyone into action by saying, "Come on, come on. It will be light before we get to work." He picked up a long metal rod, which was bent into a hook at one end and had a T-handle welded on the other end. Then he led the other four men, carrying net bags, into the forest; obviously he knew the path well because he only occasionally used a small torch.

The women followed behind, and Harman led them all out of the forest and onto a sandy beach. The tide was still going out, and they followed him down to the edge of the water. He waded over to a rock that was protruding above the surface. He dipped the metal hook into the water on the seaward side of the rock and hauled up a lobster creel. Two of the men took the creel and laid it on the sand. They opened the creel and began to take out the assortment of fish, lobsters, and crabs.

The women walked out to the water line of the receding ebb tide, and Desperate Dan marvelled the sight of cocklers, many clad in waders, bent double over the small rakes used to drag back the mud and expose cockles. Then they shook riddles, or sieves, to separate the small cockles and pack the harvest into onion sacks.

Harman broke the spell by saying, "Come here." Using the hook, he followed a rope that was tied to the creel, lifting it out of the water as he walked along. "Look, we have a fish. There is a short fishing line with a baited hook tied to the rope at intervals between the creels. We use some of the poorer quality of fish to renew the bait in the creels."

He took the dead fish off the hook, took out his knife, sliced off a piece of flesh and skin, threaded it onto the hook, and threw the rest of the fish to the men on the beach, who were working at the creel. Then he moved along the rope to the next fish hook.

With Desperate Dan watching, learning, and helping where he could, they worked away for about two hours and serviced twenty-five creels. The lobsters were examined; females with eggs and young ones were put back in the water. The others had their claws closed and restrained with very strong rubber bands, and they were placed in net bags and submerged in the sea to keep them alive. As they worked their way along the creels, they renewed the bait in each and returned the creel to the security of its underwater location.

By the end of the short shift, they had filled one net bag with five good-sized lobsters and nine big crabs, and two net bags with good-sized filleted fish. They carried the bags to a natural harbour in the rocks and submerged them, tied to a four-metre-long rope with a bright orange float tied to the other end. The men then collected and carried eight bags of big cockles to the natural harbour.

Harman explained, "At high tide, a friend in a fishing boat will come in, pick up the float, lift the bag of lobsters and fish, and take them with his own catch to Mallaig, where they will be sold in the fish market. The beauty of this little bit of the coast is its many rocks, which the fishing boats tend to avoid. If we are careful, we don't get noticed."

Carrying a bag of filleted but less marketable fish, they made their way back to the camp through the increasing dawn light and birdsong.

Harman said to Desperate Dan, "Romanies listen to nature. They are children of nature and are at one with all the flora and fauna. Togetherness of the family is important. In a balanced family, the man and the woman do not compete against one another. The man is the head of the family, and the woman is the heart of it. They both are equally important for the well-being of the family."

They got back to the camp at seven o'clock in the morning and immediately handed the fish to Esmeralda, who cut them into strips, coated them in butter and herbs, wrapped each piece in aluminium foil, and placed them on a high grill above the charcoal fire to cook them slowly.

The rest of the camp appeared out of their bender tents, bringing tables and chairs with them, which they soon set up as the breakfast table was covered with the carpet and waxed paper. Everyone made themselves mugs of hot tea, and those who hadn't already eaten sat down to Esmeralda's special porridge.

There was a lot of happy banter at the breakfast table, and after the porridge was eaten, Esmeralda served the baked fish, still wrapped in aluminium baking foil, to each person. The baked fish was a special treat, buoying everyone up for the day's work.

After everyone had a second mug of tea, Harman said, "The fishing team are allowed to go back to bed until lunchtime, although I would appreciate if Desperate Dan and Kizzy spent the morning with me to learn about the traditions and values of Romany people." He then read out a list of tasks allocated to individuals for them to achieve before lunchtime.

When the members of the extended family had left to complete their tasks, Harman, Esmeralda, Kizzy, and Desperate Dan refilled their mugs of tea and sat facing each other around the table.

Harmon started speaking. "To truly understand why gypsies, seem to have mysterious powers, you have to understand how we live. We roam freely and live very close to nature. It heightens our senses about the ways of nature, and we become very observant in other ways as well."

Esmeralda intervened. "We know about nature's cures freely found in woods and hedgerows. All of this is not just myth—it's fact, passed from adult to child and through living so close to Mother Nature. But the foundation of health is a sensible mixed diet, just enough but not too much." She smiled, pleased with her contribution, and gestured to Harman to continue.

He added, "If gypsies seem to have more sixth sense than others, it is because we acutely understand how much we are part of nature." He took a drink of his tea.

Esmeralda, seeing her opportunity, was quick to add, "The birth of a baby into a family is also a highly celebrated affair because it signifies the growth of the family line." She paused for a moment and then said loudly, "The Romany people have witnessed terrible plagues affecting many countries through the early Dark Ages, and as a result our standards of hygiene are high. Cleanliness is an important issue in our culture. In fact, it is embedded in our religion. The Romany term *mokkad* refers to a code of cleanliness, with rules for dealing with infectious disease, personal hygiene, housekeeping, washing clothes, and food preparation. Kizzy, I will give you a copy of the code of cleanliness later today. It is not difficult to understand."

Harman finished off the lesson by saying, "The welfare of the family is very important to us. Strict quarantine to prevent infection is practiced when certain diseases are suspected. Moving the deathbed out of the bender tent can save the rest of the family. Touching the body of the deceased is discouraged, for fear of contamination. Because of this, he or she is washed and dressed in the finest clothes, where possible, immediately before death. If death has been unexpected and this has not been possible, a non-Romany, such as an undertaker, is usually called in to perform these tasks."

Esmeralda excused herself and left the table because she wanted to begin preparations for the evening Shabbat meal.

Harman waited until she was out of hearing and said quietly, "The reason I am telling you these important things is …" He paused for a moment and visibly swallowed. "I have cancer of the oesophagus." He paused this time to let the impact of what he had said wear off. "I left it very late to go and see about it, and now the outlook is very poor."

He paused longer this time to gather his composure. "The important thing is the survival of this ancient Romany gypsy family. My sons are mere boys and not yet able to take leadership. You two have managed to disappear from your pursuers, so it is advantageous to you to stay in this secure situation, but it also proves to me that you have survival skills that will help my family. When I pass on—which will be very soon—if you two take leadership and support Esmeralda, between the three of you, the family will survive."

The three of them sat in stunned silence. Eventually Kizzy looked at Desperate Dan and nodded solemnly. She stood up and held out one hand to Harman and one hand to Desperate Dan. She shouted, "Esmeralda, come and join us!"

Esmeralda walked over, and all four linked hands, standing in a circle. Kizzy asked a blessing on the continuance of the Romany gypsy family.

Harman said. "Great Yahweh Elohim, we come in the name of Yeshua to ask your continued blessing on our family now extended by three more members. In Yeshua's name, we ask this."

Chapter Thirty-seven

Whatever Is True

The family gathered for the sunset meal, marking the start of the seventh day Sabbath in accordance with the ancient Hebrew calendar. The women brought out the pre-prepared Sabbath meal and laid the covered food out on the makeshift table in the open air because it was a nice mild spring night.

Harman started the evening off explaining for the benefit of the new members of the family. "All believers of our creator Yahweh should acknowledge His holy days, whether you believe in Yeshua the Nazarene as the Messiah or not! Sometime in the future, there will be a day when you are standing in line, and upon nervously looking up, you receive a majestic nod to step forward and give account. Never let it be said, 'You couldn't do the least you could do.'

"The term *worship* means a show of respect or esteem to our Creator's higher authority. The simplest art of the observance of the holy days can be accomplished by simply lifting your head, looking to the heavens at the beginning of the holy day in the evening sky, preferably facing towards Jerusalem, and saying, 'Hear O Israel, Yahweh our Creator is one and He is the only Elohim.'

"All the holy days together picture Yahweh's grand, majestic design of the unfolding spiritual events affecting all humanity. That is why it is so meaningful to pass on His teachings to others."

Esmeralda lit a taper and then used it to light the seven candles fitted to the seven candle holders at the top of each branch of the menorah.

Harmond resumed his teaching, "The first disciples were believers in Messiah Yeshua the Nazarene and therefore already saved. The observance is a sign of our love and respect for our Creator and His Covenant with us, as you can read in 1 John 5:3. 'For this is the love of Yahweh, that we keep His commandments; and His commandments are not a burden to us.'

"Perhaps I need to explain Yahweh and Yeshua. YHVH, pronounced Yahweh, is the Hebraic name of Almighty God, always expressed in scriptural usage 'I AM'. Yeshua is the Hebraic name of the Son of God, which literally translates as 'the salvation of Yahweh'. This conveys the sense that, in Yeshua, Yahweh has revealed Himself to us as a human being in response to the cry of His people for salvation.

"Thus, He is *'I AM revealed'* or *'I AM with us'* or *'Immanuel'*, in fulfilment of Isaiah 7:14. 'Therefore Yahweh himself will give you a sign. Look, the virgin (young maiden) shall conceive and bear a son, and she shall call his name Immanuel.'

"The name Yeshua a derivative of the name Yahweh, and this direct connection is unique in the Bible. Therefore, it is so important to maintain the proper names because Yeshua has Yahweh's name in him and serves Him even to the point of sacrifice for the sake of many.

"Let me read Exodus 23:20 from this Hebraic Roots Bible. 'Behold, I am about to send a messenger before you, to guard you in the way, and to bring you to the place that I have prepared for you.' Yeshua followed the Way of Torah, the ancient path of scripture, and as His followers we should too. After Adam's fall from grace and long before Moses was even born, Yahweh laid down rules, the Way, for his people to follow.

"Cain was the first of many to stumble when he slew Abel (Genesis 4:1–8. Despite that, the laws were successfully passed from generation through the faithful line of Seth, Enoch, Methuselah, Noah, Shem, Heber, Abraham, Isaac, and Jacob. They were expanded and recorded in the Torah by Moses with instructions to the tribes of Israel to obey them, but they did not. So, Israel fell, and Yahweh was forced to intervene.

"Thus, approximately two thousand years ago, in accordance with the ancient scriptures Yeshua, our Messiah was born of an Israelite mother in Bethlehem of Judaea, grew up in Nazareth, and became a highly respected teacher of Israel. He was a fully Torah Observant rabbi who gathered an unusually large band of followers around him. The inner core of this group numbered at least five hundred men and women, who were led by twelve apostles. So important was the message of Yeshua, and so gentle his ways, that people flocked to hear him in their thousands, some travelling great distances within Israel and from other countries both near and far.

"It became apparent to his followers that he was no ordinary rabbi. They came to realise that he was indeed the Son of Yahweh, the manifestation of the Most High, living the Spirit of Torah. He was critical of the Sadducees, who rejected resurrection, angels, and other scriptural truths.

He taught obedience to the scriptural laws but condemned the Pharisees for adding to scriptural requirements. He taught that there was only one Elohim, Yahweh and that he, Yeshua, the son of Yahweh, was the only door through which ordinary, sinful people could come to the Father (John 14:6).

"Finally, he gave his life as the sacrificial Lamb of Yahweh in fulfilment of Yahweh's blood covenant with Abraham and his descendants, Israel. He was crucified, was buried, and rose from the dead three full days and nights later before the end of the Weekly Sabbath. More than five hundred witnesses testified to his resurrection, and then he ascended to heaven to sit at the right hand of the Father Yahweh. His Apostles and Disciples quickly taught Yeshua's teachings throughout Israel and to the ends of the earth. They were known as Nazarenes, and their doctrine was called the Way. They had no New Testament. The Holy Scriptures from which they taught were to be found only in the temple and synagogue scrolls.

"There were no special requirements for salvation. Proselytes, of any nationality or prior faith, simply accepted Yeshua as their Saviour, were born again, and were baptised in water. They attended the local synagogues each Sabbath to learn his commandments contained in the Torah, and they tried to live by them. Their witnesses to both his manifestation in fulfilment of prophesy and his Torah-centred teaching was their testimony. This good news (gospel) was soon committed to writing in the common Israelite languages of Hebrew and Aramaic and thankfully preserved by a few of the Eastern churches. Later, it was translated into Greek and included with the writings of Paul and writings of some of his disciples, however with the sacred names changed.

"Finally, this new covenant gospel, a substantially different gospel to that taught by Yeshua, was further Romanised during in its adoption by Constantine, the Roman emperor, and designed to be the universal religion by incorporating the gods and superstitions of the many religions of the Roman Empire.

Constantine's intention at Nicaea was to create an entirely new god for his empire who would unite all religious factions under one deity, incorporating their entire god's and superstitions in one universal religion."

Harman paused and then said, "Perhaps a conspiracy of deceit greater than any other in history." He gathered himself again and continued.

"To fully understand the Way, the best place to learn is within the pages of scripture itself. Eyewitnesses of the Messianic events—Matthew,

Simon Peter, James, John, and Jude—were all Nazarenes. Read their writings in the context of the Torah, the Prophets, and the Way will become clear.

"That means you must read over the year, at each Shabbat meal, a balance of the first five books of the Old Testament, the prophecies in the Old Testament regarding Yeshua, and in the New Testament Matthew, Peter, James, John, Jude. You should also understand Revelation. Do not use the Greek to English translations—use the pre-Constantine Aramaic or Hebraic to English translations.

"Maintain and proclaim the names of Yahweh and his son Yeshua every week at your Shabbat evening meal. They sung a psalm, broke and shared the bread and the wine, and then sat down to the meal followed by songs and gypsy dancing."

Desperate Dan asked Harman, "Although we have already been baptised when we were babies, can Kizzy and I be baptised by choice as adults?"

Harman's face lit up. "Delighted, if you would like to be baptised. I will give you a copy of that sermonette I have just taught for you to live by and to teach to the family when I am gone. We will baptise you both tomorrow morning when it is light. You will need a change of clothing and a towel because we baptise people fully clothed."

Chapter Thirty-eight

Time to Move

I n the morning, the whole gypsy family made their way through the forest to the beach, and Kizzy and Desperate Dan were baptised much to the delight of everyone assembled.

Two weeks later, Esmeralda took care of Kizzy's delivery of a baby boy, and with Desperate Dan driving them, Esmeralda took her in to Bedford Hospital Fort William for a medical check at the midwifery unit, where mother and baby were found to be well.

When they returned to camp, Kizzy and Desperate Dan announced to the whole family at the evening meal, "We name our new baby boy Harman." The mighty Harman laid his huge hand on the baby's head and asked Yahweh's blessing on him.

The family had lived very well in the forest for most of the spring and early summer, but the time came for them to move on to Blairgowrie for the berry picking, and Harman began to make plans to break camp.

Harman took Desperate Dan for a walk in the forest, where no one could overhear their conversations. They sat down until the birds resumed their normal birdsong. Harman observed, "In the forest, you know when you are not alone by listening to the birds. Listen to them just now. You can only hear a general babble and no harsh alarm screeches."

They sat in silence for a minute, and then Harman said, "Although I have only known you a few weeks, I know I can trust you. Remember I told you that gypsies seem to have more sixth sense than others? Well, my sixth sense is very warm when I am with you."

Harman stood up and walked over to a foxglove which was in flower. He picked a single bell flower off and walked back to Desperate Dan. "Hold out your left hand." Desperate Dan held out his left hand. Harman placed the bright pink foxglove flower bell over the end of his index finger and said, "Fairies supposedly play within the flowers of foxglove bells, and each spot inside marks the spot where a fairy has touched the surface. Placed in front of the house, foxglove is believed to protect the occupants from evil influences. Picking foxglove from the garden and bringing it inside is believed to anger the fairies. Placed in a charm or talisman, a piece of foxglove flower is believed to keep one inside protective fairy light.

"With this foxglove bell, I pass on to you the well-being of my Romany gypsy family. Remember this day you wore the foxglove bell on your finger to remind you nature is reality, not the television."

The shafts of sunlight beamed brightly through gaps in the trees, and Desperate Dan experienced a warm glow. The forest itself seemed to be more alive with birdsong and insect flight.

"You know these stories about the foxglove are just superstition, but the sermonette I delivered last night is the core truth that keeps this family together and apart from the world, which hates Yahweh's truth and any who try to live by it." Harman sat down again. "We will go down to London. I keep my money in a safe-deposit box in North London; it's near the Underground station at the end of the line. What I like about them is that they don't ask personal questions. You are completely in control of your safe, and they are open until eight o'clock on weekdays and five o'clock on Saturdays and Sundays—much better than any bank."

Desperate Dan couldn't believe his ears. This was the same conversation he had heard from Sammy Seal in London just a few months ago. It seemed surreal.

Harman continued. "I will personally authorise you and have keys to the safe deposit box and a security card issued to you. Then you will have access to the Harman gold. We Romanies don't trust money, only gold. When you have spare money, and only when the gold price is low, buy gold from a gold dealer I will introduce you to and put in the safe deposit box. When you need money or when the gold price is high, sell a little gold.

"I have to pick up money that has accumulated from the fish market in Mallaig, added to a fair sum from wild horses we tamed over the winter and sold in the spring; they got a really good price this year. We will also put the secret list of three hundred in the safe-deposit box.

"We need to be up early with a small backpack for a couple of nights away. If we catch the twenty past seven bus at the Acharacle Shop, it gets us into Fort William with five minutes to spare before the Mallaig bus leaves at five to nine. We will need to walk into Acharacle because we don't want to draw attention to bikes being found and causing people to ask questions about missing tourists and possibly call out the emergency services. We need to leave here at six o'clock."

They sat in the warm sunlight for a while. Then Harman said with a laugh, "Enough for today. Let's go back to camp; we both need an early night to prepare for our early rise in the morning—that's if my young wife will let me sleep, she is so demanding."

After the evening meal, instead of singing and dancing, Harman addressed the camp's extended family members. He shocked most of the audience, apart from Mirela, his wife; Esmeralda, his mother; and Kizzy and Desperate Dan who knew already. "I have cancer of the oesophagus. Unfortunately, the disease is terminal, aggressive, and very advanced. However, it is not about the past. You are all young, and you must procreate the new future for this family."

The rest of family was stunned, and Harman's wife, Mirela, began to cry again. Harman lifted her up and carried her to the edge of the trees, where he hugged her for several minutes and said to her, "You must find a new man when I am gone and have more children by him." That made her cry more.

They returned to the group, and Harman said, "Most of you are too young yet to take on the responsibility of leading this ancient Romany family. We have been blessed with the inclusion of Desperate Dan and Kizzy and their baby into our family, and they have agreed to my request: with the help of Esmeralda and Mirela, they will lead our family into the future. I now place on his finger the ring of authority to lead this ancient Romany family. On pain of death, let no person hinder his rule."

He removed a leather thong necklace that he wore round his neck, which had a finger ring threaded to it. After undoing the knot and separating the ring from the necklace, he tried to place the ring on Desperate Dan's finger, but the ring had been made for Harman, who had huge hands. The ring was far too big to stay on Dan's finger. Harman threaded it back on the leather thong necklace, retied the knot, and hung it round Desperate Dan's neck instead. "Now, I will tie it round his neck, where his big head will stop it from falling off."

As Harman performed this ritual, Desperate Dan looked at the ring with amazement: the two skull-and-crossbones motifs engraved in the bright stainless-steel metal were identical to the ring given him by Carroty Charlie, the news vendor at Queen Street railway station. All the family members took it in turn to acknowledge him with a kiss on each cheek, blessing him in his new responsibilities.

The installation of Desperate Dan as head of the family was formalised and accepted. Harman said, "Desperate Dan and I are travelling to London for a few days to secure the family's finances. The job for the rest of the family is to pack up camp and be ready to move out in the evening in two days' time. I have bought two good second-hand, long-wheel-base, high-top vans from this dealer in Glasgow." He handed over a piece of paper with the dealer information and continued speaking. "Two drivers will travel to the dealer by bus and drive two vans in convoy back here. Take your driving licences and passports with you, and the dealer will process the insurance cover before you drive them away. Bring back all the paperwork with you. When you get back here, remove the blockages to the track and drive them into camp. Load up quickly and drive to this farm on the outskirts of Blairgowrie, where we will be working on the berry picking for a few weeks, then the potato harvest. Esmeralda has made a deal. The farmer has supplied caravans with water and gas; the toilets are plumbed into a septic tank. She will negotiate with the farmer any further deals. Until Desperate Dan and I return, she will be in charge."

That final piece of information produced a cheer and a few witty comments about flushing toilets. The gypsy families retired to their bender tents, laughing.

Chapter Thirty-nine

Familiar Territory

The following morning, Desperate Dan and Harman were up at five o'clock. Esmeralda had the porridge and tea ready for them at half past five, and they walked out of the camp at five minutes to six. They were in plenty of time to catch the bus at the Acharacle Shop, which took them to Fort William bus station, and they quickly transferred to the Mallaig bus, which was waiting for them. They arrived at Mallaig at half past ten.

Harman had several loose ends to tie up with several different people, all involving money owed to him for services and goods supplied through the spring period. They made the rounds on foot, stopping midway at the Fishermen's Mission for lunch. Harman was careful not to go close to the police station at the pier. He coached Desperate Dan on all the key details as they progressed.

By 3.15 he had completed his last receipt of cash, and by this time he had accumulated and secreted about his clothing several thousand pounds. They stopped in at the Fishermen's Mission for another cup of tea and then made their way to the railway station, where they bought two second-class returns to London without booking seats and caught the five past four train to Glasgow Queen Street Station.

As the train pulled away from the station, Harman was in familiar territory and said enthusiastically, "This is recognised as the best rail journey in Britain. To the left, you'll see the white sands of Morar and the Atlantic waves rolling in."

Desperate Dan was captivated with the views, and his face was almost glued to the train window as he listened to Harman commentating in the background.

"As we pass Arisaig, look over Loch nan Ceall and see the islands of Rum and Eigg. With its distinctive flat top, Eigg reminds me of a giant aircraft carrier."

They passed beautiful Loch Ailort, Beasdale, tunnels, Loch Dubh on the right, a viaduct, spellbinding Loch nan Uamh, and more tunnels. Beyond Glenfinnan station, Loch Eil was studded with tiny islands bearing tall silver trees. Once again, they were down by the water.

Harman's voice became louder. "Look at the breath-taking curve of the Glenfinnan Viaduct as it sweeps us past the head of Loch Shiel and look to see the monument to Bonnie Prince Charlie."

At Banavie Harman said, "Look at the canal locks. That is Neptune's Staircase. And look over to the left and see if you can spot Ben Nevis, although you will be lucky to get a break in the cloud."

They were coming to a stop at Fort William station. Soon after leaving, Harman dozed off, making loud snoring noises, which Desperate Dan found a relief compared to the rapid and incessant commentary.

Harman woke as the train came to a stop at Queen Street Station in Glasgow at one-minute past ten. He looked at his watch and said, "We have plenty of time; the London Euston train does not leave until 11.40 from Glasgow Central station."

They put on their backpacks and walked the half mile or so towards

Glasgow Central station. As they approached, Harman entered a side street and said, "Let's go into the Horseshoe Bar. I know the staff here."

On entering the bar, Desperate Dan was impressed with the rich, old-world decorative scheme. The lighting, beautiful timber fittings, and mirrors combined to give the room a warm golden glow. The design of the spaces and decorative features were themed on horseshoes, with lots of other equestrian features.

Harman was well-known by the staff and engaged in prolonged hugs and handshakes. A space at the bar became available as three customers left, and Harman quickly filled the space, spreading himself wide as though defying anyone to take his place. The island bar top itself was enormous and provided lots of bar space, although almost every linear metre had a patron leaning on or against it with a territorial attitude

Without asking, he ordered two pints of beer and two pies, and then he said to Desperate Dan, "What do you think of this place? I always come in here for a pint when I come to Glasgow. I think it must be the horsy theme that appeals to the gypsy in me."

Desperate Dan replied, "I am very impressed, although I don't know much about bars."

The pints were served and then a few minutes later the pies. Both men were hungry and ate in silence until the pies were finished. Harman gave Desperate Dan instructions on how to keep the Shabbat and the annual festivals, and he gave him a concise book of instructions explaining them until the clock showed ten to eleven. Then Harman said, "Come on. Let's go find our London train."

Desperate Dan saw the familiar uniformed steward with a big moustache swaggering along the train towards him. As he approached, Desperate Dan said in a low voice to Harman, "That's Sleepy Stuart."

Harman responded by stepping forward with his huge hand outstretched and said, "Ah! My good friend Sleepy Stuart."

When Sleepy Stuart finally extracted his hand from Harman's

giant paw, he turned with his hand out, saying, "Ah! My good friend Desperate Dan. The Scotch mist must have done a good job." He added in a whisper, "I take it you have heard the shocking news about our friend Carroty Charlie."

Desperate Dan responded with a deep frown, and his head went down.

Sleepy Stuart quickly pushed his chin up with his finger. "No, it was not your fault. The entire world is against us, and many suffer, but some always survive." Then with a laugh he said, "That's why Romanies make many children."

Harman pushed back between them as a train inspector approached, saying loudly, "Here are our tickets, straight through from Mallaig."

The train inspector approached them and said, "Is everything all right, steward?"

Sleepy Stuart immediately replied, "Yes, yes, I am just dealing with these passengers' special needs."

The train inspector perked up and said encouragingly as he quickly walked on, "Good man. Look after your customers. That's the company mantra."

Sleepy Stuart said with a laugh, "Follow me. I have several empty sleeper cabins, and I will give you one each because you are a very big man, Harman."

They went straight to their cabins after asking Sleepy Stuart to wake them with tea at quarter to six in the morning.

Sleepy Stewart arrived at their cabin doors at quarter to six, as arranged, with steaming mugs of tea. Clean and refreshed, Harman and Desperate Dan stepped off the train at half past seven with their small backpacks on their backs and walked up to the main concourse of Euston station, knowing that they were trespassing near the wolf's lair.

Chapter Forty

Back into the Wolf's Lair

Harman said, "Let's find a breakfast bar to set ourselves up for the day."

They crossed over Euston Road and walked down Southampton Row, and as they passed Russell Square, they spotted Russell Square Café. They ordered kosher beef sausage, fried eggs, rolls, and tea. After taking off their small backpacks, they sat outside at one of the sets of tables and chairs.

Harman said, "This is a delightful place to sit. It's peaceful for the centre of London, and it is near Hatton Garden, where my gold dealer is based."

When the waitress brought the order, Harman ordered another two teas. He said to Desperate Dan, "With the cancer, I have trouble swallowing food. That's why I need two teas and can only eat little and often." Desperate Dan suddenly felt embarrassed and blushed. Harman noticed and said, "No, it's nothing for you to be concerned about. I have accepted it, and I know my time is short. But I am glad that I have found someone like you to lead the family on into the future. It won't be easy, but I think you have the mettle."

Harman coughed for a few minutes, bringing up mucus and spitting it into paper table napkins. This action reminded Desperate Dan of his father, with his miner's lungs.

They sat in silence for a while watching grey squirrels run back and forth to some sunflower seeds that someone had laid out on the grass for them, while at the same time apparently playing a game with a small terrier dog as it frantically ran back and forth, trying to catch them.

Harman slowly recovered his composure and said with a smile, "It's funny. The dog nearly gets his prey each time, but if you watch carefully, the squirrels are working to a plan. While one squirrel lures the dog away from the food, and the other nips in and steals a bit of food. Notice that the squirrel being pursued runs fast enough to not get caught and climbs the tree just ahead of the snapping jaws of the dog, which in its mistaken enthusiasm jumps up the tree trunk before crashing back down head over tail. It's so funny."

In order to squander time, they sat watching and laughing at the antics of the dog for a while longer. Then Harman said, "It's half past nine. The gold dealer must be open for business by now."

After putting on their small backpacks, they walked slowly to Hatton Garden, occasionally stopping to let Harman clear his lungs. Eventually he led them up a side street to the gold dealers. The receptionist greeted Harman and Desperate Dan warmly and led them to a small interview room with no windows.

Harman asked, "Is Zachariah available? Tell him his good friend Harman is here to see him."

They sat at one side of a desk. A door on the other side of the room opened, and a small, stooped man entered without looking at them. He sat on the other side of the desk, facing them. When he looked up, he switched to a big smile and asked with a strange accent, "Is my good friend Harman buying or selling today?"

Harman replied, "Buying."

The gold dealer rubbed his hands together and cackled a laughing but well-practiced sales pitch. "Ah! My good friend is in luck. I was working late into the night melting and casting good, quality scrap jewellery into three-nines-fine kilo bars. That is one thousand grammes of twenty-four carats. It's the very best quality, and it's a steal at fifteen thousand pounds a kilo. You are very lucky to come today—tomorrow will be too late."

Harmon looked worried and shook his head said bleakly. "Oh! I don't quite have fifteen thousand. Let me see how much I have got." He began slowly emptying his many pockets onto the desk, with the gold dealer watching like a bird of prey. Harman slowly counted the money into thousand-pound stacks. He got to nine thousand five hundred pounds before frantically searching all his pockets again.

The gold dealer asked, "Can you not find any more?"

Harmon replied in a defeated tone of voice, "No, that's the entire year's profits; there is no more to come this year."

The gold dealer looked at the money, shaking his head and wailing an audible indication of a strange kind of pain.

Harman sighed deeply and loudly. He slowly stretched out his huge hand, covered one of the piles of banknotes, and said despairingly, "Ah, well. It's a pity after the long journey to get here, but we will just need to come back next year after we have earned some more money."

The gold dealer quickly laid his small hand on top of Harman's giant hand and cackled, "Perhaps I could make a three-quarter kilo bar."

Harman began to slowly pull the pile of banknotes towards him, saying, "No, no. I started with small gold bars of one hundred grammes, and I have worked up to one-kilo bars. I am not going back down the way. No, I will come back next year when I can afford a lovely one-kilo bar."

The gold dealer now had two hands on top of Harman's hand and was crying out as if in pain, "How can I run a business, dealing with people like you? Just give me the money. I will suffer for my friendship—that's the kind of friend I am."

The gold dealer took the drawer out of the desk, placed the piles of banknotes in it, and carried the filled drawer out of the interview room, closing the door behind him.

Harman held his finger up to his lips as a silent way of indicating to Desperate Dan to not talk.

The gold dealer came back to the room mournfully carrying a one-kilo gold bar in its presentation pouch; he hesitatingly held it out to Harman. Harman snatched it out of the miserly gold dealer's hand as if it was about to escape, and he took the gold bar out of its presentation pouch. Harmon held the shining gold bar up at various positions to reflect all the available light, with the gold dealer moaning a kind of singing lament. "What a cruel, cruel world. Everyone expects me to work for nothing, nothing, nothing."

Finally, Harman said with a satisfied smile, "That's okay."

The gold dealer immediately perked up and looked directly at Desperate Dan. "You haven't introduced your friend. Perhaps he will be interested in investing in some gold. Does he know gold is the only haven in these turbulent times?"

Harman replied, "He is taking over this side of the family business, and his dealings will be strictly cash—no names and no paperwork. By the way, he is studying to be a lawyer, so you had better not try to cheat him."

Zachariah the gold dealer physically recoiled at that shocking revelation. He abruptly stood up, shook both customers' hands, and retreated through the door, moaning away to himself as though it was the end of the world. "Lawyers, lawyers. Are there no honest people left in this world?"

The receptionist came back to the room and led them out. They walked in silence, but when they were far enough away, Harman said, "Let's get over to the safe-deposit centre."

Chapter Forty-one

Feeling the Heat of the Wolf's Breath

Desperate Dan began to head back the way they had come and said, "Are you okay to walk?"

Harman interjected, "No, this way. I have done enough walking for now. Farringdon Tube station is just a few minutes away. It's on the Circle line, and we can change onto the Northern line at Moorgate."

Harman led Desperate Dan to Cowcross Street and then to Farringdon Tube station, where they bought a day ticket each and followed the signs to the Moorgate trains. They changed to a northbound Northern line train. They came out of their destination station onto a main road, turned left, and walked along to the street. Harman led, obviously knowing the way. Desperate Dan remembered one or two buildings from his visit with Sammy Seal.

As they approached the safe depository, a man hobbled out on crutches. He looked towards them, and then turned and started hobbling in the other direction. Desperate Dan shouted, "That's Sammy Seal!

Let's catch up with him." They soon caught the limping Sammy Seal, but he was panicking.

Desperate Dan stood in front of him and said, "Sammy Seal, calm down. You are all right. It's Desperate Dan."

Sammy Seal wailed, "I know, I know. I thought you would be dead by now. I wish I was dead. Look what they done to my knee. They smashed it with a heavy hammer. They are so cruel!"

Desperate Dan asked him, "Who did?"

Sammy Seal howled like a dog in pain, "The Boss and Samson. Go away and leave me alone. I don't want to know anything more about you. If they find out I have seen you, they will smash my other knee. What have I done to deserve this?"

Harman gripped Desperate Dan's shoulder with his giant hand and said, "Let him go. He is an emotional mess. Don't make it any worse for him."

Sammy Seal hobbled off as fast as he could towards the tube station, frequently stopping and looking back over his shoulder.

Harman said, "Come on. Let's get you registered as a user of my safe-deposit box. Let me do all the speaking. Have you got your proofs of identity with you?"

Desperate Dan nodded and added, "Remember, my proofs are in my real name, Douglas Hamilton."

Harman inserted his security card and keyed in his PIN code, and the door lock opened with a solid clunk. They entered the reception area, and Harman was greeted warmly by a security guard, who asked them, "Please let me frisk-search you, and take your backpacks off and open them for me to check the contents." He did not bat an eyelid at the gold. Satisfied, he let them put on their backpacks and pass through another set of doors to the main reception.

They were greeted by a smiling receptionist, who said, "Mr Harman, you are looking very well. Do I know your friend?"

He replied by introducing Douglas. "This is Douglas Hamilton, my business partner, and he will need access to our safe-deposit box."

The receptionist asked Douglas, "Do you have proof of identification?"

Douglas nodded and produced his small briefcase. He took out his passport and last utility bill, although somewhat dated, which he had picked up when he had vacated the flat. The receptionist photocopied them and handed the originals back to him, which he inserted in an envelope and put away. She invited him to sit in a chair facing a camera and took four photographs of his face.

Smiling, she said, "Come with me, and I will give you a tour of the depository while the Polaroid photographs are developing." She showed Douglas round the safe-deposit centre, carefully explaining the security and access procedures.

They returned to her reception desk. Harman gave her his key to his safe-deposit safe, and she mounted it in a key-cutting machine and cut a duplicate key. She handed both keys back to Harman.

The receptionist handed Douglas a plastic security card with his photographs, full face, and profile embedded in it. "Now. if you give me it back, I will let you change your PIN number to one of your choice." She inserted the card in an electronic terminal with a display screen and keyed in a code. "I will leave you for a few minutes to change your PIN number."

Harman assisted Douglas to change the PIN number to the same one that he used.

When all the procedures were completed, the receptionist led Harman and Douglas to a very impressive, secure vault room with rows of safe-deposit boxes. She left the two of them alone in the solid silence of the vault.

Desperate Dan said, "They could teach the banks a lesson in security procedures."

Harman laughed and replied, "When you see their clients. you will understand why. You bump into celebrities, high-ranking police officers, politicians, businessmen, and gangsters in these vaults. Be careful not to try to speak to anyone—people are usually heavily disguised and very furtive."

He quickly opened his safe-deposit box with his key and checked the contents. Then he showed Douglas what the contents were. Including the new gold bar, there were a total of sixty-nine one-kilo gold bars.

Harman beamed and said with obvious pride, "That lot is worth about a million pounds. It's the result of squirreling away the family's surplus earnings over the last twenty-five years. You probably thought I was hard on Zachariah, the gold dealer, but he virtually steals the gold from customers who trade in their jewellery. They probably get less than one-fifth of its true value. His business is not completely legitimate, and he is obsessed with untraceable cash.

"You need to remember that when you trade with him in future, check the market price of gold on the morning you do any deal with him. If you are buying, only offer two-thirds of that price. If you are selling, look to make the market price or only slightly less, or walk away because there are other dealers. Remember that he is a ruthless predator who smiles a lot. He could have made it big as a politician at Westminster."

After allowing Douglas five minutes to examine and feel the gold bars, Harman said, "Put them back and check your key in the lock."

When Douglas had satisfied himself that his key fitted, a phone on the wall of the vault rang. Harman picked up a phone at the side of the door and put it to his ear. He heard the receptionist say calmly, "The CCTV cameras show two cars that have just parked across the road from the main door. The occupants are talking with the gentleman on crutches I saw you talking to before you came in. Sir; if you wish, I can let you out through a fire exit, which leads to the back of the building."

Harman replied, "Yes, please." He quickly returned to the safe-deposit box. He took off his backpack, unzipped the top flap pocket, removed the clothing and toiletries, and said, "Hold the backpack open for me. We are in danger, we have to run, and we are taking the gold with us."

With Douglas holding the backpack just below the safe-deposit box, Harman scooped half of the gold bars into his backpack and zipped up the flap. Then he said, "Now your backpack." They repeated the actions with the second backpack.

He stuffed the redundant clothing and toiletries into the empty safe-deposit box, locked the empty box, and said, "Put your backpack on and follow me fast. There is a pack of snarling wolves close behind us."

Chapter Forty-two

Close Call

The receptionist let them out of the vault and led them down a short corridor to a fire escape. She activated a switch and said, "Okay, the alarm on this door is now switched off. You can push the panic bar to open the door. Go quickly. The East End gang will soon be in the building."

Harman quickly opened the door and walked out, closely followed by Douglas. He said with a laugh, "Your name now reverts back to Desperate Dan."

The fire escape quickly closed, leaving them alone in a backyard. They ran to the vehicle entrance to the yard and cautiously peeked out. It led to a side road running at right angles to the high street and along the gable end of the safe-depository building, and it was clear of people. Harman pointed away from the high street, and the two of them walked quickly along the side street and away from the danger.

They emerged onto another main road. Harman looked up at the position of the sun in the sky and said, "There are bus stops. I think the buses going in that direction are going towards the centre of London. Look—there is one coming now."

They ran across the road in front of the bus and boarded it, with the driver shouting, "Are you trying to commit suicide?"

Desperate Dan said, "Two singles to Central London, please." He paid with some coins and received two tickets, and the two of them sat in the nearest empty double seat, with Harman trying to control a coughing fit caused by the exertion of running for the bus. The two men sat in silence, looking out of the windows as Harman tried to recover his composure.

After a while, Harman said, "That's Regent's Park. We are not far from Euston station. Let's get off at the next stop." They alighted at the bus stop and started walking. "Are you hungry?"

Desperate Dan nodded and then said, "Look, there is a restaurant called The Canteen. Come on. With a name like that, it sounds okay. We will try it."

Harman spotted an empty table and walked over to claim it. Desperate Dan ordered two chicken and tarragon pies and three teas. They devoured them with a hungry intensity, although Harman struggled with each swallow and washed the food down with two of the teas. They sat for a while until the restaurant began to get busy.

Harman suggested. "Let's use the toilets; one can stand guard, then the other. We need to be ultra-careful of what we are carrying in our backpacks. Then we can go back and sit in Regent's Park and enjoy the sunshine. We have plenty of time to spare and are unlikely to see our pursuers in Regent Park."

The two men walked slowly to the park in silence. They found a quiet spot and sat on the grass, facing the sun.

Harman said quietly, "Desperate Dan, I am worried about these men who arrived unexpectedly at the safe depository. Although we don't know for certain, from what we do know, we have to assume that they are the East End gangsters and found out that we were there."

The two men sat in silence for a couple of minutes. Then Desperate

Dan said quietly, "If they know about us, they must have good information, probably from Sammy Seal, who is so scared he wants to stay in their good books. Could it be that they have taken over the network that Carroty Charlie, Sammy Seal, and Sleepy Stuart were previously a part of?"

Harman replied, "It is clear from the state Sammy Seal is in that they gave him a hard time to make him talk. We must assume the worst, and we can't trust anyone. It is also reasonable to think that they will be expecting us to travel back to Glasgow Central by overnight sleeper train, like we did on the way down."

Desperate Dan thought for a moment, smiled, and then responded. "Let's take the lesson about diversion from the squirrels. You go to Victoria bus station and book two tickets on the twenty-three hundred, London to Edinburgh, on one of the overnight buses. I am a good runner, and I will go to Euston station. I will make sure I am seen by Samson, Pat, or the Boss. I can easily dodge and outrun them with my rugby skills. That's assuming you can take my backpack, which now has thirty-five extra kilos of gold in it, as well as your own."

Harman grinned. "I may be having difficulty eating, but I am still a big, strong man."

Desperate Dan replied, "That's good. Just in case I have difficulty shaking them off, I will use the Underground to change lines and completely confuse our enemies. I'll join you at the Victoria bus station just before eleven o'clock. It's just coming up to nine o'clock. We have just enough time. Let's go now."

They went to Regent's Park tube station and caught a tube train to Oxford Circus. Desperate Dan saw Harman on to a southbound Victoria line train with the two backpacks. Then Dan changed platforms and caught a northbound tube train to Euston station.

As he passed a shop, he took the opportunity to buy a postcard, a pen, and a postage stamp. He wrote a quick postcard to his mother.

We are okay. Don't believe anything you read. Dad was right about the corruption of money and those who run the world.

Love you.

Douglas

He posted the card before carefully entering the main station concourse, where he stood facing the giant departures board. A shop was undergoing renovation for a change of use. Desperate Dan noticed that the interior of the shop was in darkness, and it caused the shop window to become like a giant mirror. Investigating the shop, he also noticed that there were two doorways, at this time loosely blocked with Heras temporary construction site fencing at each side of the window, as if it was intended to have a one-way system customer queue through the front of the shop. He squeezed past the Heras fence and waited for a minute to allow his eyes to adjust to the relative darkness. After scouting out the inside of the shop, which was badly littered with building materials, he discovered a relatively clear passage between the two doors.

Emerging from the shop, Desperate Dan stood in front of the shop window, using the reflected view of the station concourse to observe approaching people. It didn't take long. After about five minutes, he saw Samson approaching, flanked by Pat and the Boss.

He couldn't help smiling. Muscle-bound Samson was trying to tiptoe in a most comical manner towards him.

Desperate Dan waited until his enemies were close and then moved quickly to the side, lifting the Heras fencing out of the gap. He quickly went into the shop and, using all his body weight, jammed the fencing tightly back into the gap behind him.

The three gangsters recovered their surprise and tried to release the blockage firmly stuck in the doorway. With his previously acquired knowledge of the shop interior, Desperate Dan quickly moved through the shop and escaped out the other doorway, again jamming the Heras fencing tightly in place. After emerging from the opposite doorway, he sprinted across the station concourse.

He looked back and was relieved to see that the three gangsters had not yet managed to escape the debris-strewn shop.

After sprinting out of the main entrance of Euston station and along the road, he knew exactly what he was doing from the time he'd explored the Underground rail systems during the days when he'd worked nights at the scrap dealers. Desperate Dan stopped running and walked quickly south along Upper Woburn Place. He entered Russell Square tube station from Bernard Street, boarded a southbound tube train on the Piccadilly line, and got off again at Hyde Park Corner tube station.

While walking past Belgrave Square Gardens, he cut down Eaton Square and onto Elizabeth Street, which he followed all the way to the very impressive Victoria bus station. It was now quarter past ten, and Desperate Dan started a systematic search of the bus station to find Harman.

After fifteen minutes looking everywhere, he could think of, he was worried. Then he heard a low whistle like a birdcall. Again, it sounded.

He followed the sound to discover Harman with a big grin on his face, hiding behind a pile of old bus tyres stacked neatly in a corner. Harman asked, "Any sign of the enemy?"

Desperate Dan replied with a smile. "Yes, I saw all three of them, but I gave them the slip and lured them into a trap. I came here by a convoluted route, making it impossible for them to follow me. They will still be searching Euston station and will still be banking on us leaving on the Caledonian Sleeper at 11.50, because that was the train we travelled down on. By the time it leaves, we will be fifty minutes on the road north of London."

Harman smiled. "Great work. Learning from the squirrels shows me that there is a bit of a gypsy in you already. Anyway, it's twenty minutes to eleven. Let's go and get the bus. Here—you can carry your own heavy backpack."

Desperate Dan smiled at receiving the compliment; it was good to have a trusted companion after the loneliness of the past months.

Harman continued. "I bought a couple of books and magazines to read. Take one of each. One of us must keep awake if the other sleeps to keep an eye on the backpacks. If possible, try to give the impression that we do not know each other. Here is your ticket, bottle of water, and sandwiches; we are on opposite sides of the passageway."

They boarded the bus separately and found their seats without even looking at each other. It was midweek, and the bus was only about one-third full. No one tried to sit beside them, giving each of them a double seat, which was the minimum that big Harman required.

The bus pulled away at exactly eleven o'clock. They took out a bottle of water and a packet of sandwiches, which Harman had bought at the Victoria bus station, and then carefully installed their backpacks full of gold in the overhead lockers.

They were vigilant to take turns sleeping to keep an eye on the backpacks.

The journey was uneventful, and they approached Edinburgh at 7.40 in the morning. Harman stood up and slowly stretched his giant body. He dropped his book, stooped close to Desperate Dan to pick it up, and whispered, "Do you know Edinburgh?"

Desperate Dan nodded.

Harman continued in a whisper. "It's very unlikely that they know where we are, but you get off first, turn right down Elder Street, and walk slowly. I will follow you to check no one is following you. Go to Edinburgh Waverley station and buy a ticket for Perth for the first train after half past nine."

Harman made a show of cleaning his book and sat down.

Desperate Dan hoisted his backpack on and disembarked from the bus. Harman fiddled with his backpack, carefully watching all the passengers.

Desperate Dan walked so slowly out of the bus station that the last of the passengers passed him. Harman eventually seemed to sort out his backpack, hoisted it onto his back, and followed Desperate Dan at a distance.

Facing the famous castle on the skyline felt familiar as Desperate Dan made his way down to Waverley train station and bought a ticket to Perth. He looked at the timetable displayed on the wall and noticed that there was a train to Perth at 9.35 a.m. which meant waiting for an hour and twenty minutes. After sauntering over to a sandwich bar, he bought a coffee and a cheese roll. Then he found a concrete block in a quiet corner, which he assumed was a vehicle prevention measure and sat on it to eat his roll.

Harman arrive about five minutes later and walked slowly past but stopped and placed his foot on the concrete block to retie his boot lace. Desperate Dan whispered at him, "Train to Perth is at 9.35."

Harman continued walking into the travel centre and bought a ticket to Perth. Then he made his way to the sandwich bar and bought an egg roll and two cups of tea. Harman found a row of bench seats and sat down to slowly eat his roll and drink his two teas.

By watching the departures board, eventually the 9.35 a.m. train to Perth came up, and after a further wait, the platform number came up. Desperate Dan slowly made his way to the waiting train, followed at some distance by Harman.

As the train began crossing of the mighty Forth Rail Bridge, Desperate Dan looked out of the window at the massive steel cantilever structure, and then he looked at the huge frame of Harman. The strange comparison between this confident human giant and the robust steel icon seemed to give him a new sense of hope and a feeling of confidence about the possibility of a new future based on the old Hebrew values and anonymity of a travelling gypsy family.

The train arrived in Perth just before eleven o'clock. Harman got up, and as he passed, he whispered to Desperate Dan, "Follow me."

Harman led the way out of the train station and about half a mile or so to Mill Street bus station. He checked the timetables and found that the next bus to Blairgowrie was at 12.55 p.m. Right now, it was 11.20 a.m.

He backtracked to a café they had passed, went in, and ordered two teas and a plate of soup.

Desperate Dan followed about five minutes later, ordered a cheese omelette and a coffee, and sat at a separate table, where he ate his food and drank his coffee. He then went to the toilet in the café.

Harman struggled to swallow his food, but he eventually managed to wash it down with the two teas. He got up and visited the toilet, and then he left the café at 12.40 p.m. Desperate Dan waited another three minutes and then followed. They boarded the bus, taking separate seats, and the bus left at 12.52 p.m.

They arrived in Blairgowrie at 1.45 p.m. Harman spotted a taxi that one of Ferka's sons was driving as an extra part-time job, and he walked over to it. He beckoned with his hand to Desperate Dan, who walked over to him.

Harman said, "Get in."

Ferka's son drove them to a farm, explaining on the way that he had picked up this part-time evening job. Harman paid him with a big smile. Then the two men walked along a farm track towards a field in which they could see people working. They walked into the field, took off their heavy backpacks, and greeted each of the Romany family members.

Desperate Dan gave Kizzy an especially strong hug and long kisses. He said with a worried frown, "How are you, and how is baby Harman?"

Kizzy beamed her biggest grin and said, "Absolutely fine, but your beard and hair has grown long and prickly over the last few weeks. I think I will prefer to kiss my baby's smooth, wee bum."

Esmeralda said to Harman, "It's good here. The farmer cannot get enough workers this year, and we have agreed to pick strawberries, raspberries, broccoli, and potatoes because they come into season through July to November. In the winter, the farmer wants us to stay and do infrastructure work until the spring, when we can start planting for the new season. The caravans with full plumbing and heating are great. There is also a big communal kitchen, showers, and washing machines. He is paying top dollar to keep us."

Harman hugged his mother and said, "Well done. That makes my heart light. I think a more settled life with hot running water and proper toilets suits you better. I think we should try to make ourselves useful to the farmer and consolidate our position here. I have all our gold accumulated over my lifetime. Desperate Dan and I will hide it here at the camp, but later we will hide it in a more secure and secret place. There is so much that it should last the family for several generations. I feel I have done my duty as leader of the family. My dear mother, my sixth sense tells me that I may not see you again in this life. The cancer has a good grip now, and I can hardly eat anything."

Esmeralda hugged him hard, and tears streamed down her face.

Harman broke away and walked slowly towards Mirela, who ran towards him. He lifted her up like a little child and hugged and kissed her hard. An obviously emotional Harman broke away and shouted, "Come on. Let's get to work! The farmer is not paying us to stand and blether."

After working until eight o'clock, they stayed overnight with their wives in their nice new caravans, and after breakfast early the next morning, Harman rested.

Desperate Dan spent the next month with Kizzy and working on the farm. Esmeralda had developed a good relationship with the farmer, where payment for work was in kind, not money, thereby avoiding tax complications. She had a written and signed contract of their tenancy at the caravan site, and it was permanent so long as the Romanies were available for work on the farm and the standards of caravan installations were to the Romanies' approval. She also had access to an acre of ploughed land for her own cultivation.

At the first Shabbat Friday evening meal, Desperate Dan addressed the family following Harman's instruction book. "May the peace of Yahweh be on and through this family. This observance is not done for salvation, as Yeshua has won that for us, but out of love and respect for our Creator, Yahweh, and His Yeshuaic covenant with us. Revelations 14:12 says, 'Here is the patience of the set apart believers who keep the commandments of Elohim and the faith of Yeshua.' Through Yeshua, who is one with Yahweh, we invite Him to dine with us and share our family meal."

Desperate Dan hesitated and looked over to Harman, who gave him a thumbs-up and a big smile. Dan carried on speaking.

"In Revelations 3:20, Yeshua said, 'Behold I stand at the door, and knock; if any man hears my voice, and open the door, I will come in to him and dine with him.' Curiously, Yeshua did not say He will come in to discuss what you think about doctrine. He expects us to try to live by Torah, like a husband and wife expect faithfulness, and so he too expects faithfulness.

"If you are keeping the commandments, your family and community standards, your manners, your habits, and your table, fellowship will do all the theological talk for you. Let us enjoy our blessings in the presence of Yahweh."

Later, Harman said quietly to Desperate Dan, "You did well, and as you keep the Sabbath and read out the Ten Commandments each week, Yahweh's Spirit of holiness will add to your knowledge and confidence— and more so if you study the Bible a little each day."

On Sunday, Desperate Dan borrowed the van from Ferka and took Kizzy for lunch and an afternoon at Scone Palace near Perth, leaving baby Harman sleeping in Esmeralda's care. After lunch, they walked in the grounds and came upon a replica of the Stone of Scone, which was now located in Edinburgh Castle.

Kizzy knew all about the history and said with a smile, "The question is, was it the real stone that was returned? There have been doubts over the stone's authenticity ever since the Hammer of the Scots carried it off as war booty. Some historians claim that by a cunning sleight-of-hand, the Scots actually handed Edward the cesspit cover from Scone Castle rather than the real stone, which if true means that a long succession of English and British monarchs have been crowned while atop a medieval toilet seat lid."

They both fell about the grass laughing at the thought.

Eventually Desperate Dan sat up and said, "You have just given me an idea."

Kizzy asked, "What is it? Tell me."

He replied, "No, it is not fully formed yet. It is based on illusion, like you have just described, but it's only an inkling that has potential. Trust me."

Chapter Forty-three

The Showdown

Over the next few weeks, Desperate Dan made his plans, knowing that he was pitting his wits against not just Mr Smith and Mr James but the best in MI5.

One morning when they woke, he said to Kelly. "I am going to make a trip today, but I will be back tonight. I have to bring this nightmare of constantly looking over our shoulders to an end."

He found Ferka and said to him, "Please run me to Perth railway station, where I need to catch a train. I also need you to park in Cadogan Street near Central Station in Glasgow tonight at about nine o'clock, after all the car parking spaces have freed up. I will meet you between ten and twelve if everything goes well. Take this Glasgow street map."

Ferka immediately agreed and said, "Come on."

On arriving at Perth railway station, Dan bought a return ticket to Darlington and waited on the 9.56 a.m. train, which required no train changes. He was determined to make it difficult for the enemy to know where he was.

As the train crossed the Forth Rail Bridge, it reminded Desperate Dan of the mighty Harman, and he felt the responsibility of leadership steel his resolve. He enjoyed the journey down the east coast and was especially struck by the imposing Durham Cathedral dominating the skyline. Even in this modern age, it spoke of the power wielded in those medieval days by the Church that had built it.

He disembarked from the train at Darlington at 1.30 p.m. and checked a rail map in the station, carefully comparing it to the train departure information. He chose Thoranby on Tees to take him away from the main line stations.

The Darlington to Thoranby train was due at 1.53 p.m., and the journey was only about twenty minutes, just enough to confuse the enemy. He disembarked from this train at 2.14 p.m. Desperate Dan made his way out of the station, where he happened upon a nice pub not far from the station, and he realised he was hungry. After entering the pub, he approached the bar and asked if they did bar meals. The barmaid confirmed that they did and handed him a menu. He chose ale and steak pie with a pot of tea and took a seat at an empty table.

When the waitress brought his meal, he asked her, "Do you have a public telephone?"

She answered, "Yes, just around the corner."

He finished the meal and looked at the clock: 2.30 p.m. *They should be back from lunch now.* Then he went to the phone booth. He took out Ian Campbell's business card from his wallet, selected several coins, and carefully phoned the number. The secretary answered, and he quickly inserted several coins. He said, "Hello, is Mr Ian Campbell in the office?"

There was a slight hesitation, as if she was trying to recall his voice, and then the secretary replied, "Who is speaking, please?"

He replied, "Douglas Hamilton."

The voice on the phone said, "Just one moment please."

A few moments passed, and then Ian Campbell's voice said, "Douglas, good to hear from you again, my old friend."

Desperate Dan cut him off very sharply. "Cut the bullshit and listen.

I have the secret list you want, but there are conditions. My father, Sandy Hamilton, was murdered by your Mr Smith and Mr James of MI5. I have a written statement by a witness, and half a dozen people have seen the statement. My wife, Kelly, is alive and well. I know you are tracing this phone call, and I will contact you again, but if you want the list rather than my arranging to have my friends pass it to a newspaper, then don't even think about double dealing." He hung up the phone.

Dan left the pub and ran back to the railway station, looking quickly at the information monitors. He saw that a train for Leeds was just due, and he made his way to the platform indicated and got there just as the train arrived. He disembarked from the train in Leeds and saw that he had about forty minutes until the train for Preston left. He went to the station cafe, ate a sandwich, and drank a cup of coffee.

He caught the Preston train. He quickly left the train and rushed over the bridge to platform three, where the Glasgow train was due at 7.41 p.m.

The train was full, and he decided to not bother trying to find a seat. Instead, he went to the buffet car, where he ordered a lager and a hauf of Glenmorangie. He stood at the buffet counter and savoured the refreshments, glad that he had caught this train and satisfied with his effort to confuse the enemy. He ordered another hauf of whisky and slowly sipped it.

A large group of hikers got off the train at Oxenholme railway station, the gateway to the Lake District. Desperate Dan inherited a double seat and immediately dozed off with the aftertaste of the Glenmorangie still in his mouth. The train arrived at Glasgow Central station at 11 p.m.

He made his way to Cadogan Street and found Ferka parked in the now empty parking bays. Ferka drove him back to the farm, and they arrived at 12.50 a.m. The priority was to recover the original secret list buried under the paving slab in the church graveyard.

During the day, he decided to retrieve the secret list. Even though it was a wet evening, he and Ferka drove to the church near his mother's home and retrieved the original secret list buried by his father. They brought it back to the farm.

The following day, Desperate Dan walked to a nearby wood and sat on a fallen tree trunk at the side of a small pond. He sat and watched dragonflies laying eggs in the water, and then he began breathing slowly and deeply, clearing his brain of all stress and concentrating on his breathing.

After half an hour, he got up and walked back to the caravan, knowing what he was going to do. He said to Kizzy, "I am going to London for a few days, but I will be back."

He packed a rucksack with essential clothing and toiletries, including a pair of trainers, finally zipping the original secret list of the committee of three hundred for which his father had died. He put on his usual hiking clothing and boots and went out to find Ferka to ask him to give him a lift to Perth. Ferka dropped him at Perth bus station, and he caught a bus to Glasgow.

Dan walked to the underground station at Buchannan Street and bought a return ticket to Partick station, making a detour to confuse the enemy if they were tracing his calls. He came out to street level, found a public telephone box, and phoned Ian Campbell's secretary. When she answered, he said simply, "Douglas Hamilton speaking."

She replied quickly, "Just one moment. I will put you right through."

Ian Campbell's voice came on. "Douglas, I have been worried sick waiting to hear from you. You really should have phoned sooner."

Desperate Dan ignored the scolding and replied. "I have been chased by gangsters from the London, who first tried to drown me and then chased me all over the country. They are brothers, ex-professional boxers who run a scrap business, a gymnasium, and a trackside bookies business in the East End. They murdered four rivals and dumped their bodies encased in a concrete-filled skip in the English Channel, about a mile off Brighton."

"Terrible, terrible. But what about the list."

"Deal with these three brothers first. You have a record of my last phone call, and you know that I have evidence that Mr Smith and Mr James were responsible for the murder of my father, Sandy Hamilton. What you are going to do about them? May I suggest a posting to a precarious assignment in Bulgaria for both?

I have the secret list you want, but there are conditions. My father was murdered by your Mr Smith and Mr James of MI5 during their interrogation about that secret list."

Ian Hamilton tried to change the conversation back to his priority and asked tentatively, "Douglas, tell me, is there another list?"

Desperate Dan had a flashback to Carroty Charlie and Sammy Seal, and he said, "It's a terrible thing, but you can't trust anyone these days. I certainly don't trust you. I will meet you in the Chapter House in Westminster Abbey beside the Houses of Parliament at noon tomorrow. If you give me satisfactory proof that the gangsters are being rounded up, the sunken skip is being searched for, and Mr Smith and Mr James are being transferred to Bulgaria, then I will give you access to the secret list my father died protecting from you. You will need good evidence to obtain the list, but if anything happens to me, a copy of that list will go public."

He heard Ian Campbell begin to interject, but Desperate Dan hung up the phone. He went back to the underground station and made his way back to Buchanan Street bus station, where he bought a ticket to London on the overnight bus. He arrived at London Victoria bus station at 8 a.m., made his way to the underground, and caught a train to Embankment, where he changed to a northern line train.

Upon coming out of the, station he made his way to the safe depository centre. After being identified, frisked, and admitted entry, the receptionist said, "Good morning, Mr Hamilton. I am glad to see you looking well. Is your friend Harman not with you today?"

He hesitated, surprised by her memory for names. "Unfortunately, my good friend Harman is not very well, so may I have access to his safe-deposit box, as he arranged at our last visit?"

"Of course; I remember. We have your inclusion on our records."

When all the procedures were completed, the receptionist led Desperate Dan to the secure vault room with rows of safe-deposit boxes. She left him alone in the solid silence of the vault. Using his key, he opened the now empty safe-deposit box, placed the secret list in it, and locked it closed. A smile spread across his face as he thought, *that's like staking a hen out as bait to attract the wolves.*

He picked up the communication phone at the door, and when the receptionist answered, he said, "That's me finished." He heard the lock release and returned to reception. He said, "I have left important papers in my box, and I will give my key to a Mr Ian Campbell, who will pick them up personally."

She smiled and said, "Yes, so long as he provides identification. And can you supply a password that he will give before gaining access?"

Desperate Dan thought for a minute and replied, "The password is Conspiracy of Wolves."

He left the safe depository centre, returned to the tube station, and caught a train back to the city centre, this time getting off at Tottenham Court Road station. Upon emerging to street level, he walked the short distance to Oxford Circus underground station and made for the newspaper vendor pitch. He approached Sammy Seal.

When Sammy saw him, an expression of shock appeared on his face, but Desperate Dan quickly said, "Don't panic, Sammy. I don't mean you any harm. In fact, I have information that your friends might be interested in."

Sammy immediately perked up his ears. "A very important gentleman will visit your safe depository centre this afternoon and pick up a secret list of the three hundred people who rule the world. That list could be worth a fortune just to keep it secret."

Sammy immediately asked, "Who is he?"

Desperate Dan replied, "I think your friends will know him when they see him."

"A lot of people use the centre. Can you not give me his name? My friends will not be happy if I can't give them a name. Please, I can't go to them without a name."

"Tell them that your source says he thinks that they already know him."

Desperate Dan about-turned and walked down Regent Street towards the river. When Big Ben came into view. As he entered the Abbey, he counted Big Ben chiming twelve times.

Ian Campbell was already standing in the middle of the Chapter House. As Dan approached him, Ian Campbell said, "What a fantastic place. I always feel at home here."

Desperate Dan replied "Yes, this was where England's first medieval parliament sat in power. Maybe this is where your committee of Olympians should meet."

"Yes, yes. To the point: I came to get the secret list. Where is it?"

"I asked you for conditions first: you give me satisfactory proof that the gangsters are being rounded up, the sunken skip is being searched for, and Mr Smith and Mr James are being transferred to Bulgaria."

"Yes, they are in progress. The police cannot arrest people without evidence, and a Royal Navy minesweeper with divers is working to locate the sunken skip. Mr Smith and Mr James are to be relocated to Bulgaria as soon as false identities and local jobs can be arranged for them. Here are several e-mail conversations instructing the decisions."

Desperate Dan read the numerous e-mail printouts referring to these matters, which left no doubt they were being enacted. He carefully held out the key to the safe-deposit box. "This is the key to a safe-deposit box. The number of the box and the address of the establishment is printed on the key fob. You need proof of identity and a password."

Ian Hamilton displayed his impatience by grabbing the key and saying, "What is the password? Come on, give it to me."

"Conspiracy of Wolves."

Ian turned on his heel and walked away, leaving Desperate Dan alone in the ancient chamber.

***

Ian Campbell walked to Embankment underground station and caught a northern line train. He arrived at the safe depository centre and inserted his own card; the lock clunked open, and he entered. He was frisked by the security guard and then approached the reception. The receptionist greeted him by name, but he was impatient and said, "I have papers to pick up from this box." He held out the key."

The receptionist said with a smile, "Your proofs of identity, please, sir."

He exploded, "You know me! I have my own box here!"

"It's the procedure, sir."

"OK, OK. What do you want? I have my passport, my driving licence, credit cards, business card, and a utility bill."

"The passport and utility bill will be perfect, sir. One more thing, sir: a password is required to access that box."

"'Conspiracy of Wolves. Is that OK?"

The receptionist gave him access to the vault and pointed to the row. Then she shut the door behind him. He opened the box and retrieved the package. After removing the outer layers, he studied the list. He could see from the names that it was an old list from the early eighties, which the coal miner's union had somehow got hold of. Still, he had done his job and retrieved it.

He locked the now-empty box, picked up the phone, and said, "I am finished." When he returned to reception, he asked, "Do you have a large brown envelope I can put these two laminated sheets in?"

"Yes, sir." She opened a filing cabinet, extracted an envelope, and handed it to him.

Ian Campbell left the safe depository centre and walked along the pavement. Mr James and Mr Smith came from behind, and as they came alongside, one said, "Ah, Mr Campbell, what do you have there?"

Suddenly, there was the deafening sound of automatic gunfire, and the bodies of the three men suddenly fell amidst of a spray of blood.

***

Desperate Dan left Westminster Cathedral. He entered the underground and changed trains at various stations until he was sure he was not being followed. He bought a newspaper, checked the price of gold, and made his way to Hatton Garden with his one-kilo nugget in his anorak pocket. It would more than provide his gypsy family's financial reserves over the winter and beyond. After selling the gold nugget for a reasonable price, Desperate Dan slowly made his way back to the farm by a convoluted route, checking continually that he was not being followed.

Harman met him with a hug and said, "Welcome back. Tomorrow we will hide the sixty kilos of gold. We need to do it before I get any weaker."

Chapter Forty-four

Sacrifice

Harman shouted, "Ferka!" Ferka came running over, and Harman said to him, "Son, give me the keys to your van. I have an important assignment to carry out. But before I go, I want to tell you I am very proud of you. I know you will look after my mother and help my wife find a new husband."

His son's eyes filled with tears. He embarrassingly dipped into his pocket, retrieved a set of vehicle keys, handed them to Harman, and said, "Don't give me all that mushy stuff. It's the van nearest to us, and its tank is full of diesel. You will be back."

Harman took the keys and threw them to Desperate Dan. "Come with me."

The two men hitched on their heavy backpacks and walked over to the van. They took their valuable loads off and locked them securely in the back. Harman asked Desperate Dan to drive. Then he turned and waved to his mother and Mirela in the distance. They raised her arms and waved back. He quickly opened the passenger door and climbed in. Desperate Dan started the engine and drove back down the farm track. The last sight Harman had of his wife and his mother was of them standing together and waving at the receding van.

They drove slowly into Blairgowrie. Then Harman said, "It's a risk, but I want to pick up a copy of my will at the solicitors near Queen Street station in Glasgow. Head back down the road to Perth and then to Glasgow."

When they got to Glasgow, Harman said, "Let's see if we can find a parking space at Queen Street station." Desperate Dan swung into the car park at Queen Street station, and they managed to find a space for the van. Then Harman said, "Wait here until I get a copy of my will. I should only be about half an hour."

After Harman left, Desperate Dan got out the van and went into the station to use the toilets. After he came out, he bought a cup of coffee and sat at a table to drink it. He thought Harman would be back soon, and he began to walk back towards the car park. Harman came out of the station and began walking towards him.

Desperate Dan walked over to the payment machine, inserted his parking ticket, and paid the fee displayed. He collected the paid-up ticket, returned to the van, and climbed into the driver's seat. Harman reached the van and got in. Desperate Dan drove to the ticket barrier and inserted his ticket. The barrier swung up, and he slowly drove towards the exit.

As they drove out, they passed another white transit van coming in at high speed. In that moment, he recognised Samson, the Boss, and Pat sitting in driver's cab of the van. He accelerated out of the exit and turned sharp left up the hill. He managed to catch the green light to cross Bath Street and then moved along North Hanover Street, along Baird Street, right into Castle Street, and left onto the M8 motorway slip road towards Perth.

However, Pat recognised them and quickly skidded round the taxis, closely following Desperate Dan and even jumping the traffic lights as they changed to red. The motorway traffic was congested, and Desperate Dan could only drive as fast as the traffic. He carefully watched the following van in his mirrors as they drove out of Glasgow in the backed-up traffic.

They got past Cumbernauld, where the traffic congestion eased, and Dan got his average speed up a bit. As they slowed at a big roundabout at Dunblane, he caught sight of the white transit van right behind them and said to Harman, "They are right behind us."

Harman, who was studying the map, replied sharply, "Take the Perth road."

Desperate Dan accelerated away from the roundabout and managed to put some daylight between the vehicles. They bombed on past Auchterarder, and as they climbed the long, steep hill past the Cairnie Braes, the chasing white transit van slowly fell behind.

When they approached the Broxden Roundabout, Harman said, "Take the first left on to the A9, towards Dunkfield." They drove on in silence until Harman said, "After Dunkfield, head north for about eight miles, and then we turn left onto the A827 just as we reach Ballinluig. We then follow the River Tay to Aberfeldy, then along Loch Tay to Killen." They drove on steadily, looking occasionally at the beautiful views of Loch Tay.

Desperate Dan noticed the white transit van behind them kept coming up close as if to overtake, but it would then fall away and then come up close again, as if trying to intimidate them. He intently watched in his mirrors, and as the transit van came up close with the sun illuminating its cab, he recognised the stocky, bull-like head and torso of Samson sitting in the middle, his eyes staring intently at the back of their van as if the chase had become personal.

Harman said, "A few miles past Killen, we turn right onto the A85 to Crianlarich."

After passing Killen, they turned right onto the better A85 road. Desperate Dan accelerated hard to nip in front of a tractor with a trailer load of hay. The gangster's transit van tried to follow, but it was too slow and was now blocked by the tractor.

Desperate Dan shouted, "They are stuck behind a tractor!"

Harman said, "Now's your chance. Go for it."

Dan accelerated the van, reaching ninety miles per hour on the good straights. Harman had bought well when he'd picked his two vans, and Desperate Dan was confident that they were leaving the London gangsters well behind.

As they approached Crianlarich, Harman said, "Careful as you leave the village." Desperate Dan responded by dropping to third gear and slowing down as they went under the railway bridge, a blind double bend just in front of an articulated lorry that was coming the other way too fast. It braked hard, jack-knifing across the road and blocking the bridge to traffic.

Harman shouted, "Now's our chance. Go straight on to Tyndrum and stay right on the A82. We head for Bridge of Orchy as we leave Tyndrum. Keep the pace up because we need enough time to hide the gold."

Desperate Dan was still watching for the van in his mirror, but they had gotten well ahead of them due to the blocked road.

They passed the Kingshouse Hotel on the right, and Harman said, "Not far now, we will park just below the Devil's Staircase. We are going to traverse the dreaded Aonach Eagach ridge."

They parked the van, crossed the road, and started up the zigzag hillside path. They took it slowly, stopping occasionally to allow Harmon time to recover his breathing. The long, steady climb took them towards a ridge. Before reaching it, Harman suddenly said, "I am sure it is over there off to the side." They walked about a quarter of a mile and then across the hillside and into a natural depression, where they were out of sight of walkers on the West Highland Way.

The hollow formed a little concave basin strewn with lots of boulders and scree. Harman took off his backpack and with Herculean strength rolled six large boulders together to form a ring. He collapsed, exhausted, onto the hillside to recover from the effort. He gasped to Desperate Dan, "Take a one-kilo bar of gold and zip it into your anorak pocket as the family reserve. Then place all the gold in the centre of the circle of boulders. Place the list of the Committee of Three Hundred on top of the gold. That may come in handy in the future. It is unlikely, but you never know. You will notice I have had it laminated in plastic, and then I wrapped it in more plastic to waterproof it. Carefully cover it with a deep layer of stones."

Desperate Dan opened both backpacks and retrieved the entire sixty-nine kilos of gold. He transferred them deep into the centre of the ring of boulders and then carefully placed the laminated list on top. He covered them with small stones first, then larger stones, and then even larger stones. Harman joined him and placed even bigger stones on top until the whole central space between the six boulders was filled.

Harman finally stood back. Although heaving for breath, he said with a laugh, "'A good man leaveth an inheritance to his children's children: and the wealth of the sinner is laid up for the just.' Proverbs 13:22. Even if I say it myself, it looks completely natural. If anyone wants to find the gold, they will need a mechanical digger. Now, Desperate Dan, you must remember where this is, just below the ridge. See that large boulder on that side and that large boulder on the other side? These are your markers. If you are unsure, stand on the top of the ring. When you look down, you will see it has six points, just like the Star of David. You must bring Esmeralda and Kizzy and show them where the gold is hidden, in case anything happens to you. Now, back to the Devil's Staircase. I want the gangsters to see us."

Although it was wet, they lay on their backs for five minutes, with Harman trying to recover his strength. He gave Desperate Dan a document tube wrapped in a plastic bag. "Zip that into the spacious inside pocket of your anorak. It is a copy of my will, which is why we went to Glasgow. If it wasn't for me wanting my will, they wouldn't have seen us. However, maybe it was meant to be. It's better to conclude it here once and for all."

As they lay there, the driving cloud and rain cleared for a few moments, and below them they saw the white transit van appear, slow down, and turn into the car park and stop beside their van. One of them was busy scanning the hillside with binoculars.

Harman seemed to have a new lease of life. He got up and waved with both arms to the three figures getting out of the van. Then he said to Desperate Dan, "Good, good. They've seen us. Onwards and upwards to the summit of Am Bodach. We are going to traverse the dreaded Aonach Eagach ridge."

Desperate Dan looked back before they disappeared over the top, and he saw the three small figures climbing up the winding path.

They topped the mountain and waited until the gangsters could see them. As they began the descent from the summit; Harman said with a laugh, "I forgot to ask you if you had a head for heights."

Desperate Dan returned the laugh. "I have two choices: scramble onwards with you, clinging to the rock with my fingernails, or retreat and enjoy a loving embrace from Samson."

Harman laughed again and shouted, "Then enjoy our first scramble of the day!"

Desperate Dan surveyed the route ahead, which looked to be a steep descent of around twenty metres. The prospect seemed tricky and a bit daunting, but completing it gave him the confidence he needed.

Harman seemed on a high and shouted, "Onwards! Farther on, you might just see Ben Nevis to the north if the cloud clears!"

But Desperate Dan was more concerned with the view to the west, where he was to go, and that was much more foreboding. The worst part, without doubt, was halfway across the second pinnacle, where a there was short slab around two metres long by one metre wide, with enormous drops on either side. That was immediately followed by a steep climb. This initially involved having to step around the cliff to access the admittedly good foothold, the only problem being the potential for making one small step into oblivion.

Harman helped Desperate Dan negotiate to the end of this very difficult section. "It is called the Pinnacles. That's the worst bit over for you. There is still another difficult bit, but when you get to Stob Coire Leith, the ridge continues relatively easily with a broad path to Sgorr nam Fiannaidh, the highest part of the ridge. I am going back to meet the enemy on the slab. When the odds are stacked against you, pick the battleground wisely.

"Your job is to follow the ridge right to the end. Do not leave the ridge path. Then make your way safely back to the van and go back to the family. You are their leader, their future. That's your destiny." Harman shook Desperate Dan's hand with his giant hand and said with a smile, "Be happy for me. The gangsters will not follow you past the slab, and I will go out like a warrior instead of withering away like a spent flower."

Desperate Dan tried to object, but Harman had already turned and was disappearing back into the swirling mist. The frequent showers that were now arriving at the most inopportune moments did not help matters for Desperate Dan, but they suited Harman's purpose admirably.

***

Harman made his way to the middle of the slab and waited.

Samson came out of the mist first, and the two big men impacted chest to chest, with Samson locking Harman's waist in a tight bear hug. Pat arrived seconds later and leapt onto Harman's back, wrapping his arms around his head. The Boss quickly followed out of the mist and punched Harman hard in a kidney.

Although winded by the expert blow, Harman twisted round,

grabbed the Boss's wrist in his giant left hand and with a loud roar bent his knees, thrusting with all the strength in his great thighs. Harman launched himself off the slab, taking the three gangsters locked on to him and slowly whirling down into the mist-shrouded abyss below like a surreal swimming octopus, their legs looking like eight short tentacles trying to get traction on the white mist as though it was water.

***

Desperate Dan continued his perilous way, sometimes stopping and clearing his eyes when the cloud, rain, and his tears became too thick to see anything. He was wet, cold, and exhausted, but he kept driving on for the sake of Kizzy, wee Harmon, and his new extended family. The die was cast, and he was ready for whatever the future held.

Chapter Forty-five

Two Popes Appear on Earth

Desperate Dan, Kizzy, and Young Harmon had lived happily on the farm as part of an extended gypsy family for eighteen years as unpaid workers in exchange for caravans and two heated toilets and shower blocks, one female and one male.

The farmer supplied work clothing, footwear and work gloves, and now a couple of acres of land for family use.

Esmeralda, the family matriarch, managed her two-acre agricultural plot with the children working as her labourers. She rotated the cultivation in the old ways, always refreshing the soil with different crops, hens, geese, ducks, and goats.

A stream ran off the hillside next to her plot, and she got her grandson Ferka to hire a mini digger. After digging three exploratory holes, they hit thick, sticky clay in each just one meter down.

Freka dug her three fish trenches two metres wide, two metres deep, and twenty metres long. He lined them with the clay spoil, supported on the inside with a layer of woven hessian by splitting old hessian potato sacks and pegging them with thin bamboo canes which would not rot because they were totally submerged. He knew the sacks were well washed from years of use and would provide a secure network for aquatic plants to attach themselves, thereby, building a natural supporting plant network and keeping the clay secure for years to come.

Esmeralda managed the fish trenches by subdividing them with plastic sheets sliding in plastic frames. This way she managed each section by age and each trench by species, and she regulated the supply of fresh water to each to a trickle.

She collected the run-off in a catch pit that Ferka dug, and she hand-pumped the nutrient-rich waste water to her drip irrigation system head tank. It was the children's job to hand-pump the pit twice a day, especially in rainy weather; the fish manure was a rich plant nutrient.

She produced so much fish and vegetables that the extended family always had fish, and she pickled and dried many vegetables for use out of season, to the extent that apart from flour and oatmeal, the family was self-sufficient in food.

Ferka and Pesha ran a taxi van twenty-four hours per day between them, using a hands-free mobile phone fitted to the taxi. If not immediately answered, it would forward to a personal mobile that the duty driver held when he was on call.

Esmeralda was an avid studier of the book of Revelation, and she saw the present time as the beginning of the "End of the Age". She thought that the family had built up a good reputation with hotels in the area, that they got plenty of taxi work day and night.

Everything was good until, as prophesied in Revelation chapter 13, something unexpected happened that shook Esmeralda to the core:

Two popes appeared on earth.

Chapter Forty-six

Against Church Law

E smeralda knew: "Church Cannon Law says a Pope's resignation is valid only if he takes the decision in full freedom and without pressure from others."

So surprised was she with this news that she asked Desperate Dan to give a sermon on the end times and two popes at the next weekly Sabbath.

Desperate Dan paused, took a drink of water, and looked at the congregation.

He started. "Let me try to summarise. Pope Benedict's announcement that he was stepping down for health reasons shocked the Roman Catholic Church and much of the world. It also loosed conspiracy theorists who believe Benedict was forced to resign by Jesuit influences, especially given the fact that his resignation came not long after the Vatileaks scandal.

The release of internal Vatican memos revealed how Benedict's efforts to reform the Church, for example; to provide transparency on the global sex abuse scandal and the management of the Vatican bank, were undercut by internal politics."

Desperate Dan took a long pause and a drink of water. He was concentrating and almost in a trance.

"Revelation chapter 13 prophesies of a time when two leaders will come to power and authority to deceive the world and enslave them into worshipping a world god.

He will come acting like he is God, full of charisma and attractive to all who see or hear him. A powerful political leader will declare the him to be God and force the world to worship the world religious leader.

We have been waiting for the prophesied pair of the ages to arrive. And it looks like their arrival is much closer than most bible students suspected.

The Bible reveals that in the last days, two very powerful figures will arise to power and work together to deceive and destroy mankind:

Desperate Dan again paused, his eyes far away.

"In Revelation 13:11–18, This world religious leader will perform wonders and will deceive many people.

He will demand membership of his church to buy and sell."

He took another sip of water. "The Bible describes a man of Jewish or Israelite lineage rising 'out of the earth' which signifies the Jewish people. They are the natives of the earth, the Israelites. So that is his lineage bloodline of some degree. I am not saying he rises out of present-day Israel. Hitler himself had Jewish blood. It simply details that he will have Jewish or Israelite blood."

Desperate Dan paused, sweat forming on his brow.

"He exercises all the power the religious ruler has, and he takes over the global government. And he not only takes over the global government, but he takes over an enforced global religion. At this point, he has control of the entire world in both religious and political areas. He rules overall and gets this authority to do so by the world religious leader.

He deceives the world by being able to produce great miracles."

Desperate Dan pauses, labouring for breath.

"Verse 14 says he deceives those that dwell on the earth by the means of those miracles, which he had power to do; saying to them that dwell on the earth, that they should make an image of the religious leader, which had the wound by a sword, and did live.

The world political leader makes this statue look and act like it's a live, living thing.

The penalty for refusing to worship or bow down before it and pay it homage is death. This is where the armies of the world power act in unison. They will help the world religious leader to enforce the worship of this statue around the world."

Desperate Dan pauses to take a drink, clearly struggling to breathe.

"And that no man might buy or sell, save he that had the mark, or the name of the beast, or the number of his name.

The Star of David was never a national symbol of the Jews until the 1800s, when the Illuminati made it one. The codes indicate this mark could also be in the form of a crucifix or cross, like the swastika was a form of a cross.

You cannot buy or sell or run a business without this mark, name, or beast number on or in your right hand or forehead.

My brothers and sisters; stay away from putting anything on or in your right hand or forehead, and you will be OK. Because if you get this in your right hand or forehead, or on your right hand or forehead, you become owned by Lucifer as one of his.

When you join this enforced economy, which is really enforced by Satan himself, then you become a slave to him. Satan owns you from that point on, body and soul. For those who refuse, they will be killed. Believers in the real and true Most High God will choose to die rather than become owned by Satan.

They will understand the significance of what it really means to join this global economy and world government.

At this point in the prophetic time clock, America has been destroyed. Yes, America is going to be brought low.

The ancient pagans will be running rampant, and the beast and false prophet will be ruling probably from Jerusalem.

We know they are in Jerusalem to gather the world's armies there for Armageddon. So how will the world be warned to not accept this mark and chip, if most of the Nazarenes have already been killed from martial law?

The Bible reveals that in the last days, two beasts would arise to power and work together to deceive and destroy mankind."

Desperate Dan sat down and slumped into the chair, exhausted by the intellectual effort.

Chapter Forty-seven

The Antichrist and the False Prophet

On the weekly seventh-day Sabbath, Desperate Dan covered Revelation 13.

"Brothers and sisters, I am trying to simplify the greatest threat to your Bible promised eternity—namely, **world religion.**"

He paused and took a drink of water.

Along with John's vision of the beast, which is the Antichrist, John saw another beast (Revelation 13:11) who is later identified as the False Prophet (Revelation 19:20).

- During the worldwide chaos, the false prophet will use his authority and power to perform unusual signs, deceiving people into false hope and into worshiping an image of the Antichrist (Revelation 13:12–14).
- Those who refuse to worship the Antichrist will be killed (Revelation 13:15).
- The world's economy will crash.

- The False Prophet and the Antichrist will stabilise it with strict control over who can buy and sell.
- Every man, woman, and child will receive a mark, without which one cannot participate. This will lead to great suffering for those who refuse it.

From Revelation 13:11–12 and 19:20, we know a few things about the False Prophet.

- Many scholars believe he will be Jewish because John says he comes up out of the earth rather than the sea. In the Bible, the sea is used to refer to the gentile people and nations, whereas the earth (also figs, fig trees, and trees) is used to refer to the Jews and the nation of Israel.
- The False Prophet's arrival on the earth will look like a lamb with two horns. Lambs do not have horns, which are symbols of authority. Lambs are meek and mild animals. Yeshua said in the Sermon on the Mount, "Watch out for false prophets" (Matthew 7:15). The False Prophet will come to Israel in sheep's clothing, but Yahweh terms him a beast.
- This False Prophet will then deceive people by acting like a lamb, but he will really speak the words of Satan. Satan is not against religion. Therefore, the False Prophet will most likely be one of the chief spokesmen in the Holy Land for the ecumenical power described in Revelation 17.
- The False Prophet will be given power from the Antichrist.
- The False Prophet made the earth and all its inhabitants worship the first beast. His basic purpose and operation (with power from the Antichrist and the power of speech from Satan) will be to drive people to worship the Antichrist.
- No false teacher from past to present has possessed the supernatural powers that the False Prophet will have.

- During the Tribulation period, the Antichrist and the False Prophet will have the power to perform "counterfeit miracles, signs and wonders (2 Thessalonians 2:9).
- It does not come as any surprise that the False Prophet will be able to reproduce everything that the two witnesses sent by Yahweh (described in Revelation 11) will be able to do.

The Mark of the Beast

- The apostle John foretold that the Antichrist (the Beast) will be assassinated with a wound to the head or neck and then satanically resurrected at the midpoint of the seven-year long Tribulation period.
- During the first three and a half years of the tribulation period, the Antichrist will present himself to the world as a messiah figure who is an economic, political, and military genius.
- However, after this resurrection, he will claim to be God. The False Prophet will then demand that everyone on earth worship the resurrected Antichrist as God by taking his mark.

Revelation 13:12

- During the time of Great Tribulation, people will still need to buy and sell in order to earn a living for their families and themselves.
- The Antichrist and the False Prophet will strike their most severe and horrific blow at the level of necessities.
- The False Prophet will institute the Mark of the Beast, which will be a system associated with the number 666.
- If you do not take the mark of the beast, you will be killed.

- The book of Revelation describes a cashless society in the last days. To buy or sell, it will be necessary to possess a certain number (666), which is the mark and number of the Beast (the Antichrist).

Revelation 13:16–18

- No one can buy or sell unless he had the mark, which is the name of the beast or the number of his name.

This was an astonishing and improbable prophecy when John proclaimed it in the first century.

Think that's still not possible?

The governments in World War Two used a rationing system for food and other items. It was not enough to have money enough to pay for an item. It did not matter how much money you had—if you didn't have the stamps, you couldn't purchase the item.

How could one number be the key to allow a person to transact business, to obtain commodities, or to complete any financial transactions?

Today, not only is it possible, but it's easy to implement, and the technology is already in use. Already, people live in a cashless society. Less than 3 per cent of the money in our economy exists as either paper currency or coin.

John, in the book of Revelation, prophesies that the number 666 will be placed beneath the skin of people on the right hand or on the forehead to enforce people's allegiance to the Antichrist as their God and to control people throughout the Antichrist's world empire.

The new VeriChip, a beneath-the-skin radio frequency chip, can be implanted beneath the skin and contain comprehensive information about an individual. This chip, together with a GPS locator system, will allow any interested party or institution to not only locate an individual but also identify a person with his financial, medical, and even criminal records.

If you find yourself at this time, you must not take this mark. All who take this mark will be lost to Yahweh forever. This point cannot be stressed enough!

Life to the Image

- Part of the deception perpetrated by the False Prophet will be his power to give life to the "image of the beast" (Revelation 13:15).
- The Bible uses the word *eikon* (icon) for *image*. It means a representation derived from a prototype or a "perfect likeness". It looks like the real thing, but it isn't.
- Sometime after the midway point of Tribulation, after the Antichrist has been slain and resurrected, the False Prophet will have an image of the Antichrist created and demand that it be worshiped. If you do not, you will be killed (Revelation 20:4).
- By some mysterious means unknown in the previous history of the world, he will give life to the image.
- What characteristics it will have, we are not told.
- Possibly the characteristic it will manifest is the ability to speak and interact.
- With the robotic technology of today, that is certainly possible and even easy to do.
- Mix in with that closed-circuit video monitoring and GPS tracking via the mark of the beast, and authorities will certainly know if you are or aren't worshiping these images.

You must not take this mark, or worship the beast or its image, or keep the beast's Sunday law.

THIS IS REALLY THE RESURRECTION
OF THE HOLY ROMAN EMPIRE

The Holy Roman Empire was a multi-ethnic complex of territories in central Europe that developed during the Early Middle Ages and continued until its dissolution in 1806 during the Napoleonic Wars.

The present-day German coat of arms is a single headed version of the Two Headed Eagle Symbol representing the might, discipline, and authority of the original Holy Roman Empire, and German nationals still await the birth of an empire that will be even greater.

Chapter Forty-eight

EU Referendum Announced

Freka was on taxi duty when news of David Cameron's decision to hold an EU referendum came over the late-night news bulletins on his taxi radio on 19 February 2016. There were press reports on 20 February 2016, and for the next few weeks, he listened and read as much as he could about the developments.

> David Cameron told Britain he had "negotiated a deal to give the UK special status in EU".

> Theresa May, Sajid Javid, and Michael Fallon backed the final deal and vowed to join PM's campaign.

> But Michael Gove led a group of six cabinet ministers directly to a Vote Leave rally after historic cabinet meeting. Chris Grayling said the deal failed to win power over borders, trade deals, or control of the "national interest".

Cameron confirmed the referendum date as Thursday, June 23.

Boris Johnstone, Cameron's old public-school Etonian friend, they've been friends and rivals since they were at Eton, and both said they wanted to be prime minister one day. Boris seizes his chance and reverses his original intention and leads the campaign to leave Europe. (this is the vote winner)

Brexit: Wave of hate crime and racial abuse reported following EU referendum.

Hate crime surged in England, Wales, and Northern Ireland in the second half of July—nearly a month after the EU referendum vote—and remains at significantly higher levels than a year ago.

The latest set of figures quietly released by the National Police Chiefs' Council show a 49 per cent rise in incidents to 1,863 in the last week in July when compared with the previous year. The week after saw a record 58 per cent increase in recorded incidents to 1,787.

Michael Gove has been accused of "desperate" and "hypocritical" scaremongering after he claimed five million more migrants could come to Britain if the public votes to stay in the European Union.

Despite Boris Johnson once saying he was pro-immigration, his campaign focused its message on immigration, creating unrealistic and unachievable expectations of what migration figures could be. Not only did it falsely claim that Turkey was about to join the EU, but it also claimed that Turks were in some way a threat to our national security, highlighting its proximity to Iraq and Syria on a poster.

Nigel Farage, UKIP's leader sponsors a vile anti-migrant "breaking point" poster, which was even reported to the police for allegedly inciting racial hatred.

This deliberate hatred inducing propaganda causes long-term damage to communities"—a prediction that is unfortunately being proved correct in daily incidents of racial hatred.

This scaremongering is not new. Prime Minister David Cameron talked about the "swarm" of migrants in Europe and has failed time and time again to stop the spread of such anti-immigrant feeling.

Nor did he support the next stage of the Leveson inquiry, whose recommendations are yet to be implemented on ensuring the press is more responsible in its treatment of minorities. Furthermore, he failed to take any meaningful action to tackle the alarming rise in Islamophobia.

The Crown Prosecution Service review allegations that Nigel Farage incited racial and religious hatred during the EU referendum campaign.

Freka thought to himself, *"Yes, Nigel Farage, Michael Gove, David Cameron, and Boris Johnstone are the main race hate instigators, but there are millions affected by their dishonest propaganda".*

As the weeks progressed, Freka noticed signs of resentment towards himself, especially from locals.

One evening about 6 p.m., he got a call on the taxi mobile requesting a pick-up from a Rangers supporters pub to pick up Carroty, Blue Nose, and Hegarty and take them to the local Chinese restaurant.

Chapter Forty-nine

Racial Hate Attack

Freka arrived at the pub, parked the taxi van, and went inside, where he spotted Carroty, Blue Nose, and Hegarty holding court amidst a crowd of other Rangers supporters. He approached and said, "Taxi for Hegarty."

The fat football supporter reacted aggressively. "I don't want an immigrant, greaseball, gypsy driving me. Come on, boys. Let's do this immigrant in."

Even though Freka, like his brother Pesha, was a cage-fighting champion of his weight, he could see that he faced about a dozen foes with hatred written all over their faces and body language. He backed quickly to the door and ran out of the pub, followed closely by a now howling mob.

His taxi was parked in the car park with no escape route, and so he ignored the taxi and sprinted along the pavement. The mob of drunk overweight supporters had no hope of catching Freka, and so they turned their attention to his taxi van. Within minutes it was in flames.

Freka saw the flames rise above the hedge and guessed that it was his taxi on fire. He took out his mobile, phoned 999, and asked for the police. After the usual process of collecting his details, he reported the incident, naming Carroty, Blue Nose, Hegarty, and his fellow supporters, including the racist insults and the torching of his taxi.

The call handler told him that due to the St Johnstone home game with Rangers, the police were heavily committed to trying to get the losing Rangers support away from the city of Perth, but someone would attend as soon as possible. Due to disturbances, it may be tomorrow or later.

Freka then phoned Pesha. "I had a call from Carroty, Blue Nose, and Hegarty requesting a taxi, but when I entered the pub, he and about a dozen friends chased me out. I couldn't go to the taxi because it was parked in a trapped area, so I sprinted away. The supporters all have beer bellies and gave up, but they turned on the taxi and torched it. I have phoned the police, but they may be some time, and not likely today."

"Go to the gym, and I will meet you there," said a curt Pesha.

Ferka made his way to the gym, which was in darkness, and waited until Pesha turned up. Persha used his membership key to open the door, and they both entered the gym.

They went into the male changing room, and Pesha said, "Take off your light-coloured clothing and put on your black martial arts uniform."

They both stripped down to their underpants and quickly put on their martial arts uniforms. They also put on black socks and trainers. Finally, they took out black balaclavas but carried them in their hands.

By the time they emerged from the gym, it was dark. Pasha locked the door, and they made their way back to the pub.

The publican had installed a bus shelter at the rear of the pub so that smokers could smoke in the fresh air without causing undisciplined gatherings, embarrassing passers-by in this upper-middle-class district.

Ferka led Pesha silently to the rear of the pub, and they donned their balaclavas, which combined with their black outfits made them almost invisible in the darkness. Pesha whispered to Ferka, "Punch or hit their solar plexus hard and deep, and we won't have marks on our fists. As they go down, strike them with the heel of your hand hard on the temple, and we won't break our knuckles."

Ferka and Pesha were cage-fighting champions of their respective weights, and they practiced specialist punches every day on a big rubber, heavily weighted, life-sized punch dummy at the gym. The punch dummy was located on a raised steel mezzanine floor, and their punches were so powerful that the vibrations could be felt through the whole steel-framed building.

There was no one using the smoking shelter, and so Pesha led Ferka to shadows in the corner of the shelter, where some tables and parasols had been stacked.

They waited, and two football supporters appeared in the doorway. They hesitated as the supporters responded drunkenly to some banter coming from within. "No, we'll not set anything on fire. One fire a night is enough. Ha!"

As they moved farther out into the darkness and lit their cigarettes, Ferka and Pesha silently struck with lightning speed. First blows to the solar plexus followed with a heel of hand blow to the right temple. The two football supporters went down. Ferka and Pesha dragged them behind the tables, turning them onto their fronts to prevent them from choking on vomit.

They had hardly finished hiding the unconscious bodies when another two football supporters came out laughing hysterically, Pesha and Ferka did not hesitate. They dispatched and hid them in the same way.

Again, another two came out and received the same treatment. Pesha whispered to Ferka, "Now the odds are more even—only six against two."

Carroty, Blue Nose, and Hegarty came out shouting, *"What's keeping you guys? I still have to eat, and I am ravenous.*" Pesha grabbed Hegarty's arm in a throwing grip and propelled his overweight body towards Ferka, who met him with a perfect left-hand punch to the solar plexus followed with a hard palm blow to the right temple.

Hegarty was already vomiting when they turned him on to his front.

Pesha whispered, *"That's enough. Let the others find them and care for them. Let's go."*

They took their balaclavas off and jogged back to the gym, where they stripped, showered, and dressed in their normal clothing. They locked the gym and made their way to a well-known Celtic supporter's club. The club had an area of dining tables and served pub food, which suited Pesha and Ferka because they did not drink alcohol.

There was a good atmosphere in the club, with couples dancing to a small band of an accordion, double bass, and fiddle.

However, the atmosphere changed when six police officers marched in. They spotted Pesha and Ferka and came over to their table. The police sergeant shouted, "Get up! Raise your hands and put them on the bar." Two police constables thoroughly frisked them, and then the sergeant said, "Let me see the backs of your hands … It's not them. It's definitely not them."

One or two of the club members had become incensed by the police intrusion and were angrily confronting the six officers. The situation got out of hand, and the police retreated before a now large hostile crowd.

Ferka and Pesha slipped out quietly into the night by a back door.

Chapter Fifty

Recovering Some of the Hidden Gold

D esperate Dan, Kizzy, and their son, young Harmon, lived happily in their caravan. There were two other gypsy families. Pesha, one of the young Romani gypsy men; Pesha his wife, Donca; and their daughters, Deka (thirteen) and Drinka (fifteen), lived in another caravan.

Ferka, one of the young Romani gypsy men and Ferka's wife, Jaelle; and their sons Danior (twelve) and Beval (fourteen) lived in another caravan.

Esmeralda, the gypsy family's matriarch, now used a rough terrain wheelchair and lived in another caravan. Mirela, the deceased Harman's young and sexually driven Romani gypsy widow, lived in another caravan, giving her freedom and privacy.

Young Harmon had grown up and had just accepted a place in Glasgow University studying law.

On Friday night as it approached sunset, it was a warm, calm summer evening. The men of the family produced tables, chairs, and tablecloths and began laying cutlery. The women produced bowls of delicious and strongly smelling food covered with cling film.

Esmeralda placed two large candles on two plates on a small table. The candles had been used before, and the wicks were well down in the hollow, giving them good protection from the light breeze. She lit the candles using a long match and said, "These represent shamor (keep or guard) and zakhor (remember or observe), the words of the commandments regarding the Sabbath."

As sunset approached on the Friday evening, eighteen minutes before sunset she called loudly for silence and said, "'And Yahweh blessed the seventh day' (Genesis 2:3). With what did He bless it? Light. Blessed are you, Yahweh our Elohim, ruler of the universe, who has sanctified us with commandments, and commanded us to light Shabbat candles."

Desperate Dan then said the Shema very loudly. "Hear, O Israel! Yahweh, our creator Elohim, is one and is the only Elohim. Blessed are you, Yahweh, for giving us the Torah and Yeshua, the Messiah who suffered and died to pay for our sins with his spilt blood.

"Shabbat shalom. Great Father Yahweh, we invite you to be with us as we eat our Shabbat meal and celebrate your creation allowing our existence. All together: Shabbat shalom and Hallelu Yah, Hallelu Yah, Hallelu Yah."

The extended family helped themselves to the delicious food, and a loud noise of cheerful conversations filled the now dark evening lit only with carefully placed big candles.

As the bowls of food, plates, and cutlery were cleared away, washed and dried, and replaced with steaming mugs of tea, Desperate Dan called for attention. He waited until the women were again seated at the table then he said loudly, "As you all know, young Harmon is going away to study law at Glasgow. Deka and Drinka and Danior and Beval are growing up fast. I wish to ask Yahweh's blessing on them. Will you young people come together in a circle around me? Place a hand on your neighbours' heads to each side of you. forming a complete joined circle."

Desperate Dan asked Yahweh to bless all the family. They sat again at the table, and Desperate Dan said, "We are living in troubled times. This Tory government and its corrupt press have caused division amongst the people of this once great country, to the extent that middle England has voted to commit economic suicide to get rid of ethnic minorities like us, whom they have always looked down on.

"This is the same as what happened in Germany before the last World War. Christians joined the Nazi party and engaged in a frenzy of satanic cleansing of Jews, trade unionists, communists, homosexuals, and disabled to establish their own human vision of a master race of blond, white Caucasians.

A heinous marriage between church and state resulted in the murder of six million Jews, now carefully covered up and receding into the mists of time. The Vatican even signed the Reichskonkordat (concordat between the Holy See and the German Reich), a treaty negotiated between the Vatican and the emergent Nazi Germany. By their complicit support, they propelled Hitler into power. Such is the power of religion and propaganda.

"If you can understand the Bible Book of Revelations, a similar marriage of the religious beast and the political beast come together to rule Europe and threaten the entire world at the end of this age.

Many of the English people who voted for this selfish decision are not aware that many of the best people working in our research and caring industries come from all parts of the world. Such is the evil and power of prejudice and propaganda."

Desperate Dan looked around at the now gloomy faces.

Ferka suddenly said, "Yes, you are right. Pesha and I have several times had to fight off aggression from locals when we have been going and coming from the local gym. However, these locals are fat beer drinkers, and so far, they have not presented serious risks, although a couple have pulled out knives. We are national champions at cage fighting, but yes, there is a sea change in attitude since all this referendum about the EU started. The locals even torched our taxi van, and the police don't seem to care much about our loss."

Desperate Dan shouted, "Thank you, Ferca. I appreciate your confirmation. To make the family more financially secure, I propose we recover a little of the gold and turn it into smaller coin that can more easily be exchanged. I fancy gold and silver are going to shoot up in value.

"What we must face is our farmer, with whom we have worked well with for years. He is one of the Rangers supporters who torched Freka's and Pesha's taxi, and he has informed me this morning that he won't need our work services anymore. He has served us a month's notice. We have finished the season's berry picking for the farmer, and the weather forecast is good tomorrow. I propose we all get up early on Sunday and go to the Devil's Staircase. We can park our two vans at Altnafeadh on the A82, directly across from Buachaille Etive Mor, which is at the beginning of the footpath. We will all go; the young people can easily help push Esmeralda's wheelchair up the path. and the men can lift it where required."

Esmeralda shouted: "Goody, goody!" Everyone laughed.

On Sunday, they all got up at around 5 a.m., showered in the separate male and female shower blocks, and then each ate a plateful of Esmeralda's special porridge. She said, "Made with just a little honey, sultanas, bananas, and cinnamon." Several expressions of "Scrumptious" were heard, some with involuntary adjectives added.

The group dressed and loaded Esmeralda's rough terrain wheelchair, along with leather gloves, a couple of spades, crowbars, backpacks, a crate of bottled water, and a basket of food. The two vans were soon loaded with the adults in the front and the young people lying on mattresses placed in the back of the two vans.

The journey from Blairgowrie wasn't too long across Scotland via Perth, Crieff, Crianlarich, and finally the entrance to the famous Glen Coe. They parked the car, got out of the vans, and looked up at the huge mountains. They were not surprised to see several people climbing the rough path, as it is one of the most popular walking challenges: The West Highland Way.

They apprehensively anticipated the climb up the pass from the road at a point on the map called Altnafeadh.

Desperate Dan laughed and said, "It's not nearly as bad as it looks, and although the path is a bit rocky, with strong, young men pulling we will manage to push Granny's wheelchair up."

He continued. "The trail switchbacks up the south face of the pass, gaining 250 metres. Known as the Devil's Staircase, this is the most famous section of the West Highland Way. It is up there on the Aonach Eagach Ridge that Big Harmon sacrificed himself taking three deadly gangsters with him to protect our family."

In silence and thinking about Big Harmon for more than a few moments, the family looked up to the mountain side disappearing into the distance.

Desperate Dan produced two ropes from one of the vans; gave them to Danior and Beval, Ferka's two boys; and said, "Now, tie your ropes to Granny's wheelchair and pull her up the path. Take your time and rest when you are tired."

Esmeralda's rough terrain wheelchair was a remarkable construction made by Ferka and Pesha from two mountain bikes that they had cut up and rebuilt into a three-wheeled pushed vehicle, with a chair made from an old aluminium chair with a low, single tubular frame and fixed foot rests. It could become vertical and joined to a conventional sprung steerable front fork and wheel, without the handlebars.

The only disadvantage was it needed to be pushed and, for this extreme climb up the Devil's Staircase. Pulled.

A couple of weeks earlier, Desperate Dan had noticed a distinct change in the farmer's body language. He had asked Ferka and Pesha to replace the old aluminium chair on the wheelchair with a new tubular aluminium chair made from a platform of six aluminium tubes cut from scrap bicycles and fitted with welded end plates; one end of each tube was presently open. The Alumweld fused at a lower temperature than the bike tubes, enabling the end caps to be removed.

The inside of the tubes was just the right diameter, 33 millimetres, to take American Buffalo gold coins.

With the men carrying the tools and backpacks, some with food and some with water, and with the women attending Esmeralda's precarious assent, the party set off up the rough path.

Following desperate Dan's directions, the family left the well-worn path and made across rough ground and over the top of a ridge before descending into a shallow hollow.

Desperate Dan said, "Halt and rest. Look at that pile of stones. See the six slightly larger stones that are like the six points of the Star of David."

Drinka (Pesha's and Donca's daughter) suddenly spotted the shape and ran over, pointing out the six stones in a star shape. The others smiled as they saw the significance.

Esmeralda suddenly shouted, "The Jewish Star of David. This six-sided figure symbolises that Yahweh rules over the universe and protects us, even in death, from all six directions: north, south, east, west, up, and down, with the middle, the hexagram, providing the spiritual dimension.

Remember now the more than fifty million killed since the third century BC, mainly by Christians, for keeping Yahweh's seventh day Shabbat. There will be yet many more martyrs to come before the end of this pagan age of Christianity."

They stood silently for about a minute.

Then Desperate Dan said, "Deka and Drinka, would you go up to the edge of the ridge and keep lookout while we dig? We don't want anyone seeing what we are doing—or more important, where we are digging."

Under Desperate Dan's instruction, the men and boys soon uncovered the first package of gold and carefully unwrapped it. The gold shimmered brightly in the sunlight. Desperate Dan let them feast their eyes for a few minutes and then said, "Boys, go up and relieve the girls to let them see the gold."

The two girls came down and were fascinated by the shimmering sight, lightly touching it to see if it was real.

Desperate Dan remembered Big Harmon saying, "That's sixty-nine one-kilo gold bars worth about one million, if you deal through Zachariah." Desperate Dan worked that out to be about fourteen thousand pounds per kilo.

Desperate Dan knew the gold price had gone up to over twenty-five thousand pounds per kilo. Allowing for Zachariah's commission, especially if he was converting it to smaller value gold coin, he reckoned each kilo bar would be still be worth £17,500–20,000.

He decided that because there were three couples, two with two children and two single adults, he would give each couple with children two one-kilo gold bars each. He and Kizzy would take one and a half kilos, and Esmeralda and Mirela would have one kilo, with half a kilo leftover as a family slush fund. That made a total of eight kilos.

He took eight one-kilo bars, wrapped them in individual cloths, and carefully placed them in an empty backpack. He pushed more cloths into the bag, preventing the gold from moving about.

They rewrapped the remaining gold, placed it back in the hole, and covered the hole with many stones.

Everyone inspected the site, and everyone was happy that it was indiscernible from the rest of the landscape unless one recognised the symbol and meaning of the six large stones.

Highly satisfied with their day's work, the extended family slowly made their way back to the path and down the hillside to the vans, with Pesha carrying the backpack containing the gold bars.

On the journey back, Esmeralda returned to Matthew 24:6. "You will hear of wars and rumours of wars but see to it that you are not alarmed. Such things must happen, but the end is still to come."

She looked at the state of the world and saw that Bible prophecy was coming true before her very eyes.

Chapter Fifty-one

Gold Bars to Smaller Currency

O n Monday morning, Desperate Dan walked the three miles to the farm track road's end, where it joined the main road from Braemar. He caught a passing bus going to Perth.

As he walked along, he thought about the peaceful years they had spent on the remote farm. He knew it was coming to an end, and although he put on a big smile, his bad attitude showed in so many other ways.

Dan was making this journey to Perth to make a phone call to Zachariah, the gold dealer in Hatton Garden, London. He was sure all phone calls were monitored, so phoning from Perth made their job a little more difficult, and that gave him pleasure.

He got through to Zachariah's secretary and after some resistance was put through to the familiar voice of the miserable London gold dealer. "Is that Harmon?" asked the gold dealer.

"No, this is his lawyer," replied Desperate Dan.

"Oh! No, no, no!" whined Zachariah. "Not you! Dealing with you will cost me money! Why did I answer this phone call?"

Desperate Dan waited until this familiar performance died down.

Then he said brightly, "I see gold prices have rocketed, and I want to take advantage of the high market. I will bring eight kilos of gold bars down to convert into much smaller golden currency that can be carried about easily. Prepare me suitable coin: only one-ounce American Buffalo. Weight 31.1 grammes. Pure gold content: 31.1035 grammes. Fineness: 999.9. Dimensions: 32.7 by 2.95 millimetres. This diameter is important."

Zachariah started to whine. "There are heavy overheads in this business …"

Desperate Dan cut him off. "I will be down in two days' time with two colleagues. We will be looking for £160,000 in American Buffalo coins. That is 160 gold coins. Incidentally, my two colleagues are cage-fighting champions."

Zachariah let out a high-pitched, prolonged whine, and Desperate Dan put down the phone before the wailing finished.

Two days later, Desperate Dan, Ferka, and Pasha walked to the road's end, where the farm track met the main road. They boarded the bus, travelled to Perth, and then caught the London train.

They didn't waste any time. Desperate Dan had calculated on yesterday's gold prices, but unknown to him, it had suddenly gone up while they were travelling by train. Zachariah was only too keen to deal on Desperate Dan's out-of-date terms.

When they got back to the farm, Ferka and Pasha inserted the gold coins into the tubes of Esmeralda's wheelchair seat. Using the Alumiweld, which fused at a lower temperature than the bike tubes welded, the end caps completely closed the aluminium tubes.

In addition to the gold coin hidden in Esmeralda's wheelchair, the family members all had spare British currency on them.

Chapter Fifty-two

Evicted

It was four o'clock in the morning, and Desperate Dan and Kizzy lay naked on top of the bed after waking and making love. Douglas said, "Come on, lazy bones. We need to get up and take the bull to the cattle market."

Kizzy slid her hand evocatively up the inside of his thigh to his now limp member and said, "Try one more time."

"No, we have a job to do."

She held his dick tight as he tried to roll away, and then slowly she let him go. He leapt out of bed, shouting with a laugh. "You are a nymphomaniac! Come on. Let's get to work".

As he made towards the shower, there was a loud bang followed by a splintering sound as the caravan door crashed inward. Then there were loud shouts of, "Armed police, armed police!"

Half a dozen black-suited police with body armour and guns burst into the caravan. "Lie down on the floor, face down. Lie down on the floor!"

Desperate Dan immediately lay down, and one of the policemen pulled a screaming Kizzy off the bed and pushed her down beside

Desperate Dan. The police were hyperactive and full of adrenalin, pointing automatic guns at the couple.

One of the policemen kicked the inside of their legs and shouted, "Spread your legs, spread your legs!" He carefully checked their backsides all over and then shouted, "Turn over on your backs." Kizzy and Desperate Dan, now in a stake of shock, complied. Again, the policeman kicked the inside of their legs and shouted, "Spread your legs, spread your legs." He looked them over carefully, spending a little more time on Kizzy.

Apparently satisfied, he shouted at the other officers, "OK, just three of us in this small caravan is enough. The rest of you stand by outside the door and get a woman police constable in here."

A WPC entered, and three of the four male constables left to make room for her.

The policeman in charge shouted, "Pick clothing for travelling, and pack a small bag each of essentials. Let the WPC check every item before you put it on or put it in your bags."

Desperate Dan asked, "What's this all about?"

The officer said, "All I can tell you is your whole family is being arrested and, if necessary, forcibly taken to Dungavel Immigration Removal Centre. It is an immigration detention facility in South Lanarkshire, Scotland, near the town of Strathaven, also known as Dungavel Castle.

The centre is operated by the American private prison firm GEO Group, under contract with the law-enforcement command Border Force, for its detention of immigrants for the Home Office."

Desperate Dan asked, "Why?"

The police officer answered, "We have been given information that your large, extended family of gypsies working on this farm are all illegal immigrants. Now, that is all I am permitted to tell you. Do not ask any more questions, or we will tape your mouths, and that will make the journey very uncomfortable."

Kizzy took the threat of the police officer seriously, especially the powerful-looking guns pointed at her and Desperate Dan. She bit her tongue and kept quiet. She was well informed about human rights and knew that the authorities had all the physical power and control of most of the evidence.

Many past cases involving minorities found vital evidence had gone missing. She kept her thoughts to herself. *"The hatred of foreigners or people who are different is fanned by the Tory Party and their media to manipulate public opinion—the age-old Tory tactic of divide and conquer".* In the cauldron of hatred, people could do the most heinous cruelties (including murder) when enflamed by crowd hysteria.

Eventually the WPC was satisfied that they did not have weapons, and she let them dress in clothes she had carefully checked. They packed what they could into two medium bags.

Kizzy and Desperate Dan were escorted out of their caravan and led over to where the rest of the gypsy family was gathered.

Desperate Dan mentally accounted for the extended family.

> Esmeralda, Harman's mother and the queen of the Romani gypsy community
>
> Mirela, Harman's young Romani gypsy widow
>
> Pesha, one of the young Romani gypsy men
>
> Pesha's wife, Donca, and her daughters, Deka and Drinka
>
> Ferka, one of the young Romani gypsy men.
>
> Ferka's wife, Jaelle, and her sons, Danior and Beval

Desperate Dan noted that Ferka's nose was bleeding and that everyone had a bag.

The policeman in charge shouted at them and pointed to a giant prisoner transport van. "Get into that van."

The gypsy family slowly climbed into the van, and the rear doors were closed and locked—but not before Desperate Dan saw the farmer watching from just inside one of his barns. Desperate Dan suspected that the van was wired to record any conversations and used gypsy sign language to convey a message. "Stick together and face the unknown together."

They were processed into the Immigration Removal Centre by gender, stripping (again), showering, having invasive health and hygiene checks, redressing, getting mug shot photographs, and registering.

Kizzy noted to herself that most of the nurses were very matter-of-fact, almost aloof, as if they considered the refugees inferior and did not protect their human dignities as a normal, civilised society would. Then she answered the question in her own head. *"Of course, this incarceration centre was Tory policy in action, run by American contractors who were in it for profit. No wonder human rights are secondary".*

They were allocated beds in several rooms with strangers also occupying them, making the family feel insecure. Esmeralda suggested that Desperate Dan request two rooms for the extended family only.

Desperate Dan asked the men and boys to join him in prayer, and he called on Yahweh by name to bless and protect them and their women. Then he gave thanks for the idea to speak to the officer in charge tomorrow, and to help the decisions to favour the family.

He finally stripped down to his underpants, lay down on his bed, and thought, *I wonder what tomorrow will bring?* Desperate Dan drifted into a light sleep, his ears cocked for any threat.

Kizzy calmed the women and girls by asking for Yahweh's blessing and protection. Her brassier was uncomfortable, so, she removed it. She kept her knickers on for security, lay on her bed, and pulled the duvet over herself. The thought came into her head that Desperate Dan had jokingly called her a nymphomaniac. Perhaps she was.

She also remembered an occasion during primary school holidays when she was fed up with the three boys, who were neighbours and classmates, constantly playing cowboys and Indians or football.

She grimaced at the memory of when she went out to play football with them—intentionally with no knickers on.

Looking back, she now realised that the boys were still pre-puberty and did not know what it was all about, or how her early sexualised behaviour was attention seeking and the only young female amongst a bunch of immature boys.

Kizzy also remembered often lying naked on top of her giant teddy bear and pretending to have sex. She still cringed at the memory of being caught by her father.

He had then taken the teddy and, once out of her sight, hid it in the garden shed. One happy day, she found Teddy behind some deckchairs and sneaked it back up to her room, where she immediately stripped off her clothes, and cuddled and kissed it as though it was her boyfriend.

Through her adolescence, she also had two or three girlfriends, and they stripped naked and experimented with each other when privacy allowed—even after her relationship with Desperate Dan had become a committed relationship.

What did all this mean? She was a proven unfaithful deceiver. Was she really a nymphomaniac, or was she lesbian, or was she just a normal female driven by her hormonal cycles?

She drifted into a troubled sleep still pondering the question.

Chapter Fifty-three

Settling into the Detention Centre

D esperate Dan rose at 5 a.m. still wearing his underpants, and he immediately kneeled in prayer as he faced the unknown. He called on the name of Yahweh, his Elohim (God), and asked for protection and blessing on his whole family.

He quickly wrapped a towel round his waist and made his way to the shower block, where he brushed his teeth, shaved, shampooed, and showered. The place was deserted; even the guards were dozing.

Desperate Dan made his way back to the room where he had slept. He made his way round the rooms and wakened each of the male members of his family, saying, "We are incarcerated in Dungavel Immigration Removal Centre. Take care not to upset the guards but protect the women and girls. I will try to get a meeting with the person in charge to make sure we can keep the seventh day Sabbath."

Desperate Dan made his way to the main office and asked to see the officer in charge. After a time, he was introduced to a middle-aged woman, Helen Cassidy, who was constantly interrupted by officers asking what to do about this or that problem. She was American and obviously at the end of her tether.

While waiting for a gap in the relentless pressure, Desperate Dan had an idea. When she eventually was able to give him some attention, she faced him and with a look of exasperation said, "You can see things are not working very well. The morale of the detainees is very low, and the morale of staff is also very low. Sorry—I should not say these kinds of things to you. Perhaps my morale has also sunk very low."

Desperate Dan reverted to his best well-educated voice and said, "Perhaps I can be of help?"

Helen's eyes locked onto his as though she had received an electric shock.

"My extended family of twelve could be accommodated in two gender-specific rooms with six single beds in each. This way we can keep the family together and relatively secure. If you also allow my extended family to keep the seventh day Sabbath as commanded by Yahweh and recorded so many times in the Bible, we will extend a welcome to all who wish to keep the Bible Sabbath with us. All we will require is your cooperation and assistance to cook up and prepare some food for the Sabbath on Friday, and for you to print an invitation notice for your notice boards.

"Of course, we will need to use your big hall all day on the Saturday starting on the Friday evening. I assure you your staff will have their easiest day of their week, and detainee moral will greatly improve from the hopeful sermons I will deliver. Many of these immigrants are very familiar with the Old Testament and will find my sermons compatible with most of their own beliefs. You will know from working with immigrants that they are very religious and very family centred. They have been deeply missing what I will give them."

Helen Cassidy's eyes looked straight into Desperate Dan's as she considered silently. *"What was there to lose"*? There had already been serious disturbances over the last few weeks, and these disturbances were drawing attention to the reported draconian regime and the hopelessness of some long-term detainees. Dan had promised hopeful sermons, and she could get a couple of officers to monitor his sermons and call in reinforcements if they prove to be radical, violent Islam.

She finally said, "Yes, I think it may do a lot for the morale of the immigrants. I will instruct my officers accordingly, but you must be very careful not to incite or radicalise others."

For the first time since getting up this morning, Desperate Dan felt he had possibly influenced the welfare of his family.

Chapter Fifty-four

Keeping the Seventh Day Sabbath

Word about the open invitation went around the detention centre very quickly. If nothing else, this was a diversion from the usual numbing boredom.

Esmeralda, the matriarch of the gypsy family, took charge of the food preparations for the Sabbath, which had to be prepared on Friday. Some of the women who previously had been strangers came together under Esmeralda to prepare favourite dishes from their home countries.

Helen Cassidy had allocated sixty pounds of chicken breast and as many vegetables and fruits as they needed, plus access to all the cooking herbs and spices.

With these ingredients, the women came into their own genius, they were used to making the best out of vegetables and fruit. They finely chopped and curried the chicken, and they used it in dozens of varieties of strong-tasting and strong-smelling dishes, along with the huge quantities of naan bread they made from British flour. There was more than enough to feed the two hundred and fifty immigrants for

Friday night Sabbath supper, the Saturday Sabbath meals, breakfast, lunch, dinner, and supper again on Saturday night.

The women stored the various dishes in polythene bags keeping the cooked, cold food, fresh for each of the five meals.

It was remarkable to see what women from ethnic backgrounds could do if given respect, opportunity, and even the cheapest of ingredients.

Esmeralda, although wheelchair bound, was in her element and constantly encouraged the women as they worked.

Almost everyone came to the Sabbath services even if only to share in the scrumptious food, which they could smell all Friday afternoon and Saturday. The group was not allowed Sabbath candles because of fire risk.

Esmeralda took two dark green bottles and shaped silver paper around the tops to look like candles. She shouted out to the assembled immigrants, "We are not allowed to light candles. These represent shamor (keep or guard) and zakhor (remember or observe), the words of the commandments regarding Yahweh's Sabbath."

As sunset approached on Friday evening, eighteen minutes before sunset, she called loudly for silence and said, "'And Yahweh blessed the seventh day' (Genesis 2:3). With what did He bless it? Light. Blessed are you, Yahweh, our Elohim, ruler of the universe, who has sanctified us with commandments and commanded us to light Shabbat candles."

Chapter Fifty-five

Baal, the Sun God, versus Yahweh, God of Abraham

Desperate Dan delivered one half-hour sermon on Friday evening, two half-hour sermons on Saturday morning, and two half-hour sermons on Saturday afternoon.

He said, "The early human families and tribes were so dependent on the cycles of the sun that they began to erect stones to mark the length of days through the seasons; these took the form of stone circles. Some of these stone circles grew more stones dedicated to predicting phases of the moon."

He stopped looking out at the sea of faces, but they were silently engrossed in what he was saying because they recognised the circular stone solar calendar he was talking about. He continued.

"The shortest day of the year is 21 December, and time seems to hesitate for a few days before the lengthening day is discernible on 25 December. That is why all the early religions celebrate on 25 December every year: the returning sun and warmer weather.

"The sun understandably became their god and was named Ba'al or Baalzebub

"Baal was a fertility god who was believed to enable the earth to produce crops and the people to produce children. The Canaanites worshiped Baal as the sun god and as the storm god—he is usually depicted holding a lightning bolt—who defeated enemies and produced crops. They also worshiped him as a fertility god who provided children.

Baal worship was rooted in sensuality and involved ritualistic prostitution in the temples. At times, appeasing Baal required human sacrifice, usually the firstborn of the one making the sacrifice.

"Ahab, also spelled Achab, flourished in the ninth century BC and was the seventh king of the northern kingdom of Israel (reigned c. 874–c. 853 BC), according to the Old Testament. He was the son of King Omri. Ahab, king of Northern Israel, was captivated by Jezebel, took her as a wife, and served and worshipped Baal. All the other sins of Ahab were light compared with his marriage with Jezebel and the serving of Baal that followed (1 Kings 16:31:32). He not only considered it trivial to commit the sins of Jeroboam, son of Nebat, but he also married Jezebel, daughter of Ethbaal, king of the Sidonians, and he began to serve Baal and worship him. See also Micah 6:16.

For over sixty years, idolatry had made terrible inroads upon the life and ways of the Hebrews, and it meant more to them than the breaking of the first two commandments of the law. It produced spiritual and moral disintegration, which was accentuated by Jezebel's determined effort to destroy the worship of Yahweh (Jeremiah 19:5)."

Desperate Dan hesitated to scan the crowed room. He was aware these truths were not easy to take for some of the audience, who were brought up in Christian communities. However, he also realised that most adults knew Sunday was not the seventh day and Christmas was the celebration of the retuning sun.

Desperate Dan finished this gloomy description of the sins of

Northern Israel some 2,850 years ago. "I find myself compelled to warn you all that deportation from what once Great Britain may well be preferable to what is about to happen to this Commonwealth of idolatrous nations when the prophecies of Mica 6:16 may well be repeated.

> You have observed the statutes of Omri
> and all the practices of Ahab's house;
> you have followed their traditions.
> Therefore I will give you over to ruin
> and your people to derision;
> you will bear the scorn of the nations
> Mica 6:16 NIV

Desperate Dan added, this is what is happening in Brexit".

***

"I also feel compelled to warn you that the use of the word *amen* is pagan.

"The Egyptians called their sun god Ra. You all know the strong Egyptian iconography of men dressed in high headdresses and shaped as birds, animals, and fish.

One of their other gods was Amen, a secret, hidden, mysterious god with derivatives of his name being Amun, Amon, Ammon, and Amounra. By 1500 BC he had been elevated to the national god of southern Egypt, and his name became Amen-Ra.

Hebrews settled in Egypt for four hundred years from 1847 to 1447 BC, and they were exposed to this worship of the idol god Amen-Ra. The word *amen* assimilated into their common Hebrew language. Unfortunately, Jews and Christians vehemently deny this truth and allowed *amen* to be inserted into their modern versions of the Bible. The New Testament itself was edited and compiled by largely pagan authorities of the Roman Empire under Emperor Constantine."

A voice from the audience called out, "Hallelu Yah," and other voices followed suit. Clearly some of these ethnic immigrants knew of this truth.

Dan shouted, **"Abraham!"** After pausing for a minute, he continued. "Abraham, the founding father of the nation of Israel, was a man of great faith and obedience to the will of Yahweh. His name in Hebrew means 'father of a multitude'. Originally called Abram, or 'exalted father', Yahweh changed his name to Abraham as a symbol of the covenant promise to multiply his descendants into a great nation that Yahweh would call his own. All Abraham had to do was obey Yahweh and do what Yahweh told him. Abraham demonstrated remarkable faith and trust, immediately leaving his home and his clan the moment Yahweh called him to the unknown territory of Canaan."

Desperate Dan announced, "Now I will give you a brief summary of the history of Israel, the main people of the ancient Bible before it was Hellenised, as well as the sacred names removed and replaced with pagan names and titles as we have just explained, including the mysterious and sneaky Egyptian god Amen."

Esmeralda, the family matriarch, let her mind wander to the time the Israelites were in the wilderness after their escape from Egypt and how Yahweh had provided manna for them to eat. She equated that with the modern-day plight of the refugees being blocked by selfish Europeans, with some starving to death. Matthew 24:7 came into her mind.

Chapter Fifty-six

Desperate Dan Gives a Brief History of Israel

D esperate Dan looked at the large assembly of immigrant detainees and shouted, "The Hebrews. The first person to be called a Hebrew was Abraham, and the name commonly refers to his descendants, known as the Jewish people, but this is modern misuse and ignorance of the history. They comprise much more than just the Jewish people. They comprise all the Hebrew people.

"The word for *Hebrew* used in the Bible is pronounced *Ivri*, meaning 'ever'. So, Hebrew means the one who is opposed, on the other side, and different from all others. The name Eber celebrates the wading through of the world's great waters—the Abas of Persia's beliefs, the Sea of Reeds of Egypt, and the Jordan of Canaan—and ultimately the arrival upon the dry land of truth (Genesis 1:9).

"Incidentally, in Scotland and Wales, one finds numerous names with the root *Aber*. This is another form of *Eber*. The exact meaning of this word root in these areas is not certain, but it appears to be linked with the meaning of crossing over. This is like the Hebrew meaning of the word root!

"Aberdeen, Arbroath, Aberdour, Aberfeldy, Abernethy, Aberfoyle, Hibernia—these are names for Ireland. Heber is an ancestral figure in Irish mythology. Iberni is in south-west Ireland. The Iberni Ocean is east of Ireland.

"Hebrides are islands off the north-west coast of Scotland, a Celtic region. They were once known as the Hebrew Isles. This root is said to connote river mouth, junction, or ford—that is, a place of or passing into, or crossing over. It is thus quite like the Hebrew root *ibr*, which also connotes 'pass over'.

Abraham was a solitary believer in a sea of idolatry. The people of the present nation of Israel (also called the Jewish People) trace their origin to Abraham, who established the belief that there is only one God, the creator of the universe. Abraham, his son Yitshak (Isaac), and his grandson Jacob (Israel) are referred to as the patriarchs of the Israelites. All three patriarchs lived in the land of Canaan, which later came to be known as the land of Israel. They and their wives are buried in the Ma'arat HaMachpela, the Tomb of the Patriarchs, in Hebron (Genesis 23). The name Israel derives from the name given to Jacob (Genesis 32:28–29).

His twelve sons were the fathers of twelve tribes that later developed into the Hebrew nation. The name Jew derives from Yehuda (Judah), one of the twelve sons of Jacob: Reuben, Shimon, Levi, Yehuda, Dan, Naphtali, Gad, Asher, Yisachar, Zevulun, Yosef, Binyamin (Exodus 1:1). So, the names Israel, Israeli, and Jewish refer to people of the same family origin."

Desperate Dan paused.

"The second person to be called a Hebrew is Joseph. An innocent Hebrew boy is abandoned by his brothers and ends up in Egypt, the decadent land of the Pharaohs, where people and their accomplishments were worshipped instead of Yahweh. A lone teenager with foreign Hebrew beliefs from abroad, in the strongest society of his day.

Joseph did not cave in to the pressures. He stood firm in the faith of his ancestors and ultimately rose to the top of Egyptian society until he was second to Pharaoh himself. In fact, it was after the wife of Potiphar had tried to tempt him into sinning, and he withstood the temptations, that he is first referred to as an Ivri—Hebrew. Then he showed that he was a faithful bearer of the contrary tradition of Adam, Noah, Shem, Eber, and Abraham. He was a commandment keeper of yet unwritten but known standards, which set him apart.

Even as slaves to the Egyptians, the Hebrews were sexually very productive and produced many children. The descendants of Abraham crystallised into a nation at about 1300 BCE after their Exodus from Egypt under the leadership of Moses (*Moshe* in Hebrew).

Soon after the Exodus, Moses transmitted to the people of this new and emerging nation the Torah and the Ten Commandments (Exodus 20).

After forty years in the Sinai desert, Moses led them to the land of Israel, which is cited in the Bible as the land promised by Yahweh to the descendants of the patriarchs Abraham, Isaac, and Jacob (Genesis 17:8).

The people of modern-day Israel share the same language and culture shaped by the Jewish heritage and religion passed through generations, starting with the founding father Abraham (ca. 1800 BCE). Thus, Jews have had a continuous presence in the land of Israel for the past 3,300 years.

The rule of Israelites in the land of Israel starts with the conquests of Joshua (ca. 1250 BCE). The period from 1000–587 BCE is known as the 'Period of the Kings'. The most noteworthy kings were King David (1010–970 BCE), who made Jerusalem the capital of Israel, and his son Solomon (Shlomo, 970–931 BCE), who built the first Temple in Jerusalem as prescribed in the Tanach (Old Testament).

Around 722 BC, the Assyrians invaded and destroyed the northern kingdom of Israel. In 568 BC, the Babylonians conquered Jerusalem and destroyed the first temple, which was replaced by a second temple in about 516 BC. It is not exactly clear who these Assyrians were. It is likely that they were Syrians from the north of Israel, who were powerful around this time. But there are also theories that they were Assyrians, now the modern nation of Germany.

For the next several centuries, the land of modern-day Israel was conquered and ruled by various groups, including the Persians, Greeks, Romans, Arabs, Fatimids, Seljuk Turks, Crusaders, Egyptians, Mamelukes, Islamists, and others.

In 587 BCE, Babylonian Nebuchadnezzar's army captured Jerusalem, destroyed the Temple, and exiled the Jews to Babylon (modern-day Iraq). The year 587 BCE marks a turning point in the history of the region. From this year onwards, the region was ruled or controlled by a succession of superpower empires of the time in the following order: Babylonian, Persian, Greek Hellenistic, Roman and Byzantine Empires, Islamic and Christian crusaders, Ottoman Empire, and the British Empire."

Chapter Fifty-seven

Long Prophesied Messiah

Desperate Dan read from his notes.

The Messiah will be the offspring (descendant) of the woman (Eve). (Genesis 3:15)

The Messiah will be a descendant of Abraham, through whom everyone on earth will be blessed. (Genesis 12:3; Genesis 18:18)

The Messiah will be a descendant of Judah. (Genesis 49:10)

The Messiah will be a prophet like Moses. (Deuteronomy 18:15–19)

The Messiah will be the Son of God. (Psalm 2:7)

The Messiah will be raised from the dead (resurrected). (Psalm 16:10–11)

The Messiah crucifixion experience. (Psalm 22 contains 11 prophecies; read them yourself)

The Messiah will be sneered at and mocked. (Psalm 22:7)

The Messiah will be pierced through hands and feet. (Psalm 22:16)

The Messiah's bones will not be broken (a person's legs were usually broken after being crucified to speed up their death). (Psalm 22:17; Psalm 34:20)

Men will gamble for the Messiah's clothing. (Psalm 22:18)

The Messiah will be accused by false witnesses. (Psalm 35:11)

The Messiah will be hated without a cause. (Psalm 35:19; Psalm 69:4)

The Messiah will be betrayed by a friend. (Psalm 41:9)

The Messiah will ascend to heaven (at the right hand of God). (Psalm 68:18)

The Messiah will be given vinegar and gall to drink. (Psalm 69:21)

Great kings will pay homage and tribute to the Messiah. (Psalm 72:10–11)

Freemasons are very familiar with Psalm 118:22–23 "The stone the builders rejected has become the cornerstone; Yahweh has done this, and it is marvellous in our eyes."

However, Isaiah 28:16 identifies this metaphoric stone or rock as "The Messiah is a 'stone the builders rejected' who will become the "head cornerstone".

Peter said, "Yeshua is 'The stone you builders rejected, which has become the cornerstone'."

The Messiah will be a descendant of David. (Psalm 132:11; Jeremiah 23:5–6; Jeremiah 33:15–16)

The Messiah will be a born of a virgin. (Isaiah 7:14)

The Messiah's first spiritual work will be in Galilee. (Isaiah 9:1–7)

The Messiah will make the blind see, the deaf hear, et cetera. (Isaiah 35:5–6)

The Messiah will be beaten, mocked, and spat upon. (Isaiah 50:6)

The "Gospel according to Isaiah". (Isaiah 52:13–53:12)

People will hear and not believe the "arm of the LORD" (Messiah). (Isaiah 53:1)

The Messiah will be rejected. (Isaiah 53:3)

The Messiah will be killed. (Isaiah 53:5–9)

The Messiah will be silent in front of his accusers. (Isaiah 53:7)

The Messiah will be buried with the rich. (Isaiah 53:9)

The Messiah will be crucified with criminals. (Isaiah 53:12)

The Messiah is part of the new and everlasting covenant. (Isaiah 55:3–4; Jeremiah 31:31–34)

The Messiah will be our intercessor (intervene for us and plead on our behalf). (Isaiah 59:16)

The Messiah has two missions. (Isaiah 61:1–3; the first mission ends at "year of Yahweh's favor")

The Messiah will come at a specific time. (Daniel 9:25–26)

The Messiah will be born in Bethlehem. (Micah 5:2)

The Messiah will enter Jerusalem riding a donkey. (Zechariah 9:9)

The Messiah will be sold for thirty pieces of silver. (Zechariah 11:12–13)

The Messiah will be forsaken by His disciples. (Zechariah 13:7)

Desperate Dan paused for a drink of water before he continued, "The fact that all of the Old Testament prophecy concerning the Messiah and his first coming has come true with such detail brings clarity to the issue of what is going to happen in the future. For there are prophecies concerning the Messiah that still await fulfilment.

"The biggest lesson for us to learn here is that Yahweh keeps his promises, and just as the prophecies concerning the coming Messiah have been fulfilled in Yeshua's first coming, so the rest of the messianic prophecies will be fulfilled in the second coming.

Yeshua himself brought our attention to that dual coming when he read from a prophecy found in Isaiah 61:1–2, also recorded in Luke 4:18–19. Yeshua left off his reading of this passage in the middle of Isaiah 61:2. The first half of the prophecy found in Isaiah 61:1–2 passage deals with the first coming of the Messiah and the presentation of his signs to Israel. However, the last half of that verse, 'and the day of vengeance of our Elohim, to comfort all who mourn', deals with his second coming.

In his first coming, the Messiah came as the suffering servant and offered his life a sacrifice to reconcile man to Yahweh. In the second coming, the Messiah will come as the triumphant king, and all his enemies will be made his footstool (Matthew 22:44).

From 1517 to 1917, Israel, along with much of the Middle East, was ruled by the Ottoman Empire. World War I dramatically altered the geopolitical landscape in the Middle East. In 1917, at the height of the war, British Foreign Secretary Arthur James Balfour submitted a letter of intent supporting the establishment of a Jewish homeland in Palestine. The British government hoped that the formal declaration—known thereafter as the Balfour Declaration—would encourage support for the Allies in World War I.

When World War I ended in 1918 with an Allied victory, the four-hundred-year Ottoman Empire rule ended, and Great Britain took control over what became known as Palestine (modern-day Israel, Palestine, and Jordan). In recent years, the Jews have started to return to the land, in partial fulfilment of the Old Testament prophecies.

The revival of the State of Israel is a sure sign that soon Yeshua the Messiah will return as King Yeshua to re-establish the kingdom of Israel as the kingdom of Yahweh."

Chapter Fifty-eight

What Does the Immediate Future Hold?

D esperate Dan tried to keep it simple. "The beginning of the end really started when Britain fought two very costly world wars against the old enemy Germany, but the end was really signalled when she turned her back on her Commonwealth blessings from Yahweh's promises to Abraham and finally entered the European Community in 1973.

"This left particularly New Zealand and Australia in the lurch, because Britain had to disadvantage imports from commonwealth countries in favour of imports from Common Market countries. This treachery began to take the gilt off the illusion of 'Great'.

"It is likely modern Assyrians ancestors of our captors in 734 BC and 722 BC will be found amongst the Semitic nations who migrated into Europe as Caucasians (having light white characteristics, blond hair, etc.). The Saxon branch of the Germanic tribes bore the name of Isaac upon them (in Asia it was Saka, Sacae, and Sacan, but the Romans rendered it as Saxon), and Isaac's name was placed on the Anglo

Saxon birth right tribes of Ephraim and Manasseh. 'The Angel who has delivered me from all harm—may he bless these boys. May they be called by my name and the names of my father's Abraham and Isaac, and may they increase greatly on the earth' (Genesis 48:16)."

Desperate Dan paused to take a drink of water and then continued.

"But the ending of an empire is rarely a tidy affair. On 29 October 1956, Israeli armed forces pushed into Egypt towards the Suez Canal after Egyptian President Gamal Abdel Nasser nationalised the canal in July of that same year, initiating the Suez Crisis. The Israelis soon were joined by French and British forces, which nearly brought the Soviet Union into the conflict, and it damaged their relationships with the United States. In the end, the British, French, and Israeli governments withdrew their troops in late 1956 and early 1957.

"The Rhodesian rebellion was to last until the late 1970s. Britain fought a war to retain the Falkland Islands in 1982, and Hong Kong continued with tacit Chinese agreement as a British dependency until 1997. Britain experienced a large inflow of migrants—a legacy of its imperial past. The British at home had to come to terms with an unforeseen legacy of their imperial past: the large inflow of migrants, mostly from South Asia.

"In the twenty-first century, old imperial links still survive, particularly those based on language and law, which may assume growing importance in a globalised world. Even the Commonwealth, bruised and battered in the 1960s and 1970s, has retained a surprising utility as a dense global network of informal connections, valued by its numerous small states. The experience of the empire recedes more deeply into Britain's own past when the UK joined the EEC in 1973, along with Ireland and Denmark. Despite a referendum in 1975 on whether to pull out, the UK stayed in the organisation.

"The European Union began in 1951 as the European Coal and Steel Community, an effort by six nations to heal the fissures of World

War II through duty-free trade. In 1957, the Treaty of Rome created the European Economic Community, or Common Market. Britain tried to join later, but President Charles de Gaulle of France vetoed its application in 1963 and in 1967. Britain finally joined in 1973. A referendum was held in 1975, two years after Britain joined the European Economic Community, on whether it should stay. More than 67 per cent of Britons voted in favour.

"With regard to Brexit, most economists favour remaining in the bloc and say an exit would cut growth, weaken the pound, and hurt the city of London, Britain's financial centre. Even economists who favour an exit say growth would be affected in the short and medium terms, though they also say Britain would be better off by 2030. But that's a long time to suffer deprivation if you are in most of the population.

"The negotiation will decide Britain's relationship with the bloc. The serious issues will surround trade. If Britain wants to remain in the European Union's Common Market—the world's largest trading bloc, with five hundred million people—Brussels is expected to exact a steep price to discourage other countries from leaving. So much for EU ministers stating that it is not their intention to punish Britain! Germany, France, and Ireland are rubbing their hands, scrambling openly to shift the big financial centres and highly skilled staff to their countries before the race officially begins."

Desperate Dan concluded, "Yes, as Bible prophecy predicts, this is the beginning of Jacob's troubles, and Brexit is the vehicle to demolish Britain's major businesses, academia, and economic institutions."

Chapter Fifty-nine

A Surprise Religious Leader Arises from Nowhere

Desperate Dan continued his sermons. "Benedict XVI shocked the world in February when he became the first pope to resign in almost six hundred years. But attention shifted quickly to the succession, and the election of the new Pope, Francis.

"Pope Benedict's official resignation statement offered his waning physical and mental powers as the explanation, but insiders know that there was far more to it. Father Federico Lombardi said, 'The Church needed someone with more physical and spiritual energy who would be able to overcome the problems and challenges of governing the church in this ever-changing modern world.' It's clear that the Church had become ungovernable and needed someone else at the helm to stop the rot. What it boils down to is that Benedict XVI was forced into abdicating, but this was done under the guise of a resignation to not split the long-established institution with controversy.

"Credible reports from 2015 indicate that Benedict XVI was coerced into stepping down, which was providentially foreshadowed in Pope

Benedict's inaugural speech of 24 April 2005 when he said, 'Pray for me, that I may not flee for fear of the wolves.' Who was He talking about? Was there some sort of Conspiracy of Wolves at the heart of the Vatican?" Perhaps, The Jesuits? Desperate Dan paused and then said, "Interesting, very interesting."

Again, he paused.

New World Order

"Pope Frances seems to have a completely new agenda for the whole Christian church. The new Pope surprised everyone when he said in New York on September 24, 2015":

"If at times our efforts and works seem to fail and produce no fruit, we need to remember that we are followers of Jesus… and his life, humanly speaking, ended in failure, in the failure of the cross."

"He again repeated and enlarged on this theme On November 27, 2015 while in Nairobi, Kenya, 'Pope Francis' said to a group of youth":

"I am going to tell you something private. In my pocket I always carry two things: a rosary to pray something which seems odd, this is here, is the history of God's failure, it's the way of the cross, a small way of the cross, as Jesus suffered and when they condemned him right up to where he was buried with these two things I do the best I can. And thanks to these two things, I never lose hope."

"One of Pope Frances first acts on 24th September 2015 was to address USA Congress in which he made this statement among many others":

"In Laudato Si', I call for a courageous and responsible effort to "redirect our steps" and to avert the most serious effects of the environmental deterioration caused by human activity".

"Following this on September 25, 2015 Pope Frances addressed the United Nations".

"Central to the new set of global goals, which extend to 2030, is the idea of caring for the planet and for the world's poorest citizens, which was also at the heart of the Pope's address — his first at the United Nations".

"Any harm done to the environment, therefore, is harm done to humanity," Francis said, later reprising his argument that the poor are the biggest victims of environmental destruction.

"A selfish and boundless thirst for power and material prosperity leads both to the misuse of available natural resources and to the exclusion of the weak and the disadvantaged,"

"He seems to have concluded that the 2,000 years of Christian teaching has largely been a failure in bringing the Kingdom of Heaven to earth".

"On the contrary, the rich have got richer and the poor have become more numerous, and the planet with its diverse ecosystems, has been pillaged and plundered close to the point of planetary death.

A time for strong clear leadership.

"He has concluded that under strong leadership the religions of this world need to urgently unite into a huge and as an unstoppable force to bring about a new world political and religious order, based on sound, human, environmental management and social justice.

This will first require the unification of world religions: The adjective ecumenical; refers to something universal, or something that has a wide, general application. .... The word catholic, meaning "universal.".

"Today it most often refers to bringing people of diverse Christian religions together; however, an ecumenical religion might also bring Christians, Jews, and Muslims together under one roof.

Finally becoming a Single World Religion working for the common good.

"To this end Pope Francis meets with Russian Orthodox Patriarch Kirill at Havana airport on February 12th, 2016. Where Pope Frances makes strenuous, but charismatic efforts to heal the ancient breaches of history and to begin to bring these ancient peoples of faith together.

"In so doing he signals that the ecumenical movement is his first and most important goal.

"Unity was always a principal aim of the Catholic Church.

"Before the Second Vatican Council, the Catholic Church defined ecumenism as a relation with other Christian groups to persuade these to return to a unity that they themselves had broken".

***

Desperate Dan diverted for a few moments to explain:

"Major branches. Christianity can be divided into five main groups: The Church of the East, Oriental Orthodoxy, Eastern Orthodoxy, Roman Catholicism, and Protestantism.

Major denominational families in Christianity:

Protestantism

Restoration Movement

Anabaptism

Calvinism

Anglicanism

Lutheranism

(Latin Church)

Catholic Church

(Eastern Catholic Churches)

Eastern Orthodox Church

Oriental Orthodoxy

Assyrian Church of the East

This Reunification of the Christian Churches has long seemed to be the right thing to do, in fact there is a new testament verse, Matthew 12:25 "A house divided against itself will not stand". This verse has been a long-standing agitation against the splintered Christian Churches".

"This New Unified World Church, although seemingly promoting socialist and environmental ideals, which in themselves are very commendable, is about power vested in a single dictator and the sign of its world authority will be the re-establishment and enforcement of the Sunday Law.

"This is not the first time, Emperor Constantine's laws enforced Sunday as sacred on March 7, 321 A.D.

"Sunday already dedicated to the Roman Sun God Sol Invictus (Baal) and so, Sunday was declared an official day of rest".

"In 1 Kings 18:21 the distinction between Baal and Yahweh is made very clear".

21 "Elijah went before the people and said, "How long will you waver between two opinions? If Yahweh is Elohim, follow him; but if Baal is Elohim, follow him."

But the people said nothing".

"This charge from 900B.C. is as true in these end times as it was in Elijah's days.

This scripture above is directed at you right now, are you also going to sit on the fence until it is too late?"

"New World Church

"Every individual will be accountable and whose status will be determined by their compliances to church and social laws and possibly their carbon footprint.

"Only by being registered with an identity number will individuals be able to buy or sell in the shops.

"Those outside the faith will at best be left to perish, although on past evidence, their demise will be accelerated by a zealous faithful.

"The new world order will be based on pure socialism monitored by a world church hierarchal structure, with informants reporting on friends and even family members not in the world church, reminiscent of the loveless East German communist regime of the 1950's, 60's 70's and 80's".

"Treachery and cruelty against outsiders justified in the name of the common good and common "One World Religion" and accompanying political "One World Government" intent on a sustainable planet will be an act of duty".

"Interestingly the Chinese working with the Vatican are beginning to embrace the principles of the new World Order. The Chinese hope to have everyone registered with a digital number by 2020.

"The great resistance is coming from Donald Trump who will not bow to any human authority and North America is very important to complete the New World Order.

"It is unlikely that the Vatican will allow Donald to stand in their way for very long.

"This final rejection of a benevolent God and the domination of capitalism which has resulted in most of the world's wealth being in the hands of the few, and at least a tenth of the world's human population facing starvation".

"Yes, this proposed New World Order seems to be the very thing to right the capitalist wrongs of the past and specially to try and reverse global warming.

"Most people will agree that social justice is a good thing and with weather disasters out of control even governments will submit to the New World Order."

"But such a radicle and rapid change needs a superstar and an extensive world organisation".

"Europe to reawaken its Nazi past.

"Germany is looking for a strong leader to lead a revival of a yet to be formed Holy Roman Empire, with recognition from the Pope and led by Germany.

"Now, at the end of 2018 as Britain prepares to leave the European Union, German Nationalism once again rears its ugly head.

"With Britain intent on Brexit and leaving the European Union, it will position Germany even more strongly at the centre of Europe and as Angela Merkel's approval rating has dropped to an all-time low amid the ongoing row over migration policy and a spate of violent far-right protests, nationalistic Germans are looking for a new leader.

"A male politician is emerging, or should I say re-emerging, a descendant of Otto Von Bismarck, 'The Iron Chancellor' who has the potential to become the "Strong German Leader" to restructure and reinvigorate the New European Union after Brexit.

"The leader of this end-time European power with his emergence and military capabilities will surprise the world.

"But, more, much more than that, he could be the man working with the World Church religious leader to completely dominate the New World Order".

"What Is Next for once Great Britain?

"Yahweh gave the promised birth right blessings to Joseph's modern descendants in Britain and America. He has made available the knowledge of what He expects of them spiritually. He has accurately preserved this knowledge in the Bible.

"If you understand that the British people are called Ephraim in Bible prophecy, you will discover that the same Bible that prophesied modern Ephraim's wealth and power also prophesies of its cataclysmic upheaval! Read Leviticus 26:14-16

"Yahweh (God) prophesied that after Ephraim and Manasseh received their promised wealth and power, if they did not turn to the Yahweh who blessed them, He would remove those blessings and punish these nations with war and captivity.

"Daniel 12:1 prophesy of "a time of trouble, such as never was since there was a nation even to that same time." The Bible called it a period of "great tribulation," that would annihilate mankind if He didn't intervene! (Matthew 24:21-22).

"Yahweh specifies that the U.S. and Britain will receive the worst of this punishment when He says: "Alas! for that day is great, so that none is like it: it is even the time of Jacob's trouble; but he shall be saved out of it"

(Jeremiah 30:7). "The name Jacob refers to Joseph's two sons, Ephraim and Manasseh, who were given Jacob's name. The next verse shows that the descendants of Ephraim and Manasseh will go into captivity!

"And who does the Bible prophesy will take them into captivity? The EU, the very people from whom the British are trying to free themselves politically. Those prophecies are tied directly to Brexit, going on between the United Kingdom and the EU! Yes, right now".

"Who will believe that once Great Britain will be taken captive by their old enemy Germany? (I can't make it plainer than that, but you probably didn't think you would see Brexit happen)".

Desperate Dan shouted. "But I remind you of a very important scripture: To come out of the great world church".

"Revelation 18:4 King James Version (KJV)"

4 "And I heard another voice from heaven, saying, come out of her, my people, that ye be not partakers of her sins, and that ye receive not of her plagues".

"King James Version (KJV)"

Desperate Dan grabbed hold of the lectern, emotionally spent with the shear concentration of trying to put together this complex sermon.

Chapter Sixty

David Cameron's Colossal Misjudgement

D esperate Dan explained the lead-up to Brexit.

"According to a 2015 survey by YouGov, the polling group, 75 per cent of people in the UK thought there had been too much immigration over the previous ten years.

"If the EU had not been wracked by crises. First was the eurozone crisis, which eroded trust in the institutions of the bloc. Since then, the southern countries—Italy, Spain, and Greece—have been wracked by economic problems and high youth unemployment.

"Then came the challenge of the Syrian civil war, with large numbers of refugees fleeing to the safety of Europe through the eastern Greek islands. Bickering amongst EU members over how best to address the migration crisis have once again damaged its reputation for competence.

"Mr Cameron promised the referendum in January 2013, at the time the Conservatives were about ten points behind Ed Miliband's Labour in the polls".

Desperate Dan finished this analysis by saying, "A colossal misjudgement."

"Immigration was the political Hot Potato in the Shires of England. England was progressively settled by Germanic groups Angles and Saxons from what is now the Danish/German border area and Jutes from the Jutland peninsula in Europe. The first shires were created by the Anglo-Saxons in central and southern England—long-standing English identity from beginning of formation of Britain after Roman era".

These cultural traits continue to present day.

Chapter Sixty-one

The Clowns Take Centre Stage

Desperate Dan took a break to regather his thoughts, and then he went on. "The threat of refugees swarming across the Mediterranean stoked selfish nationalistic fears. Cabinet ministers, including Michael Gove, pressed for a ceiling on EU migration to the UK. Cameron, in desperation, strongly suggested a discriminating policy of curb on In Work Benefits paid to EU immigrants.

"Coupled to this was Boris Johnstone joining the 'leave the EU' campaign with lies and propaganda. Boris says, 'So let us say knickers to the pessimists and the merchants of gloom and do a new deal that will be good for Britain and good for Europe.'

"If we hold our nerve, and we are not cowed, and we vote for freedom and democracy on June 23, then I believe that this country will continue to grow and thrive as never before, and June 24 will be Independence Day."

Desperate Dan continues. "An impossible aim printed on the Leave campaign bus reads, 'We send the EU £350 million a week. Let's fund our NHS instead. Vote Leave.' But the main theme of the leave campaign was immigration and foreigners flooding our country, taking our jobs, and keeping our wages low.

"Boris Johnson abandons ambitions of becoming PM after Michael Gove drops him and launches own campaign. Justice Secretary Gove says Johnson was not up to job and questions if his heart and soul were in pushing through Brexit. A Boris aide is said to have vented anger at Gove in expletive-laden text. accusing him of plotting to win the keys to Number 10. Furious Conservative MP Jake Berry says on Twitter that there is a 'very deep pit reserved in Hell' for Gove.

"Alliance between Leave campaigners ripped up as Treasury Minister Andrea Leadsom enters Tory contest. Home Secretary Theresa May installed as favourite after delivering bravura performance at her launch. Racism and hatred rapidly increase. David Cameron loses referendum and country—or more exactly, Middle England—vote to leave the European Union, the biggest single market in the world."

Desperate Dan finished in thankful prayer to Yahweh, the one and only self-sufficient Creator and Sustainer, Elohim.

The sun set on Saturday night, and the singing of psalms gave way to ethnic folk favourites. It had pleasantly surprised Desperate Dan as to how many immigrants knew the popular psalms they had sung.

Esmeralda came up to him and said, "You did very well, but your latter sermons made me realise that racist Britain is no place for us. Deportation, even to foreign refugee camps, will be better for the family."

Matthew 24:12 came into Desperate Dan's mind.

Esmeralda said, "Just like a forest fire, hatred is fanned by lies and propaganda."

Desperate Dan recalled the news over the last few months: "Fire fighters fighting more forest fires in Canada, in California, in Australia, in Portugal and in France." He thought, *what does Revelations 8:7 say?*

A third of the earth was burned up, a third of the trees were burned up, and all the green grass was burned up.

Desperate Dan shouted, "One-third of the grass and trees destroyed. Looking at the wild fires across the world, it's already started."

Chapter Sixty-two

Decision to Accept Immediate Deportation

Helen Cassidy, the officer in charge, approached Desperate Dan with a big smile. "You did really well, and for the first time in months, we had a weekend without trouble. What a blessing it was".

Desperate Dan replied, "Can you please tell me what the deportation options are for my complete family of twelve?"

She looked at him a little surprised. "For immediate deportation, I can probably get you all on a plane to Jordan within a fortnight. But you realise that you will be confined to a tented refugee camp where facilities are very basic."

Desperate Dan said, "Esmeralda, our family matriarch, has decided racist Britain is no place for us. Deportation, even to foreign refugee camps, will be better for the family. Can you start planning? I have to consult the family, but I am sure we will all accept because we have all felt the hatred."

Later, Desperate Dan called the family together. "Esmeralda has expressed her opinion that we would be better in a foreign refugee camp than staying here. I have brought the officer in charge to meet you, and she says she could get us on a plane to Jordan within two weeks, although we would be restricted to a tented refugee camp."

Mirela asked, "What will the camp be like?"

Helen answered, "When I visited recently, I observed that the refugee camp in Jordan, is big, very big, housing about 100,000 people in Aid Agency tents but it is fast evolving into a permanent settlement.

"The refugees have not been slow to develop the camp into an organised town with all sorts of services. Zaatari is a fast-growing economy with its own leaders making the best of a bad hand.

"Economic development is unstoppable, but their Syrian cultural identity is very strong, stronger now they have been displaced.

"Many of the older tents have been improved with a huge range of building materials and now have a feel of permanence.

"Extensive water storage and electricity distribution systems have been installed providing the most essential of life's necessities.

"Like many shanti towns, the camp has grown according to its own ad hoc, populist urban logic, which includes a degree of social mobility.

"Either way, it's a very dynamic place, unforeseen by the humanitarian actors running it, which is giving refugees a sense of ownership and dignity.

"This economic development is largely black market. Smugglers traffic in camp vouchers and goods, undermining legitimate Jordanian businesses, profiting criminal gangs pass freely in and out of the camp.

"Installing a permanent municipal water system there would cost what the United Nations now spends every year trucking water to the camp, and it would be an investment in long-term development."

Mirela asked with a smile, "Are there many men in the camp?"

Helen looked a little surprised, but she smiled and said, "Yes, but the ratio is 54 per cent women to 46 per cent men, so you will have a little competition. Sex is still one of the basic human needs, thank goodness."

Desperate Dan asked, "Well, what do you all think? Who wants to go to Zaatari Refugee Camp in Jordan?"

Everyone in the extended family silently put up a hand. They were reluctant to leave their place and memories on the farm, but that was now in the past, and as gypsies they must face life as it was forced upon them, in this case by strongly racist England.

Chapter Sixty-three

Final Sabbath Service in Britain

Helen Cassidy worked fast and arranged the deportation of the extended family. After all, that was what she was paid for: to get rid of as many people as possible.

Desperate Dan conducted one more round of seventh day Shabbat services on Friday evening and all-day Saturday.

He covered the personal commandments contained in Torah, the first five books of the Bible.

"The Ten Commandments, Short Form

1. You shall have no other Elohims (gods) before Me. (Desperate Dan said, "Christians ignore this, the first and most important commandment, reconstructing God as a mixture of God, human, and Spirit—a trinity, totally against Bible teaching.")
2. You shall not make idols. ("What are Christian churches full of? Yes, idols.")

3. You shall not take the name of YHWH your God in vain. ("Both Jews and Christians have removed both Yahweh's name and Messiah Yeshua's name from commonly available modern Bibles.")

4. Remember the Sabbath day, to keep it holy. ("What are the sneaky Christian churches doing slowly in front of your eyes? Yes, they have changed most diaries and calendars to run from Monday to Sunday. They will eventually claim Sunday as the seventh day; by that time, people will be used to Monday to Sunday.")

5. Honour your father and your mother.

6. You shall not murder. (Desperate Dan said, "Look at the record of the Christian churches, with over fifty million seventh day Sabbath keepers murdered over the centuries.")

7. You shall not commit adultery.

8. You shall not steal.

9. You shall not bear false witness against your neighbour.

10. You shall not covet".

"Range of Personal Commandments in Torah

Ex20: I am YHWH your Elohim. Honour YHWH above everything. Keep the Sabbath. Honour your parents. Don't do wrong to your neighbours.

Ex21: If you buy a Hebrew slave, he shall go free in the seventh year. Whoever kills shall be put to death. Whoever injures shall compensate.

Ex22: Whoever steals shall make restitution. If a man sleeps with a virgin, he shall marry her. You shall not oppress strangers or the poor.

Ex23: You shall not pervert justice. Each year you shall hold feasts. My angel will lead you and I will drive your enemies from the land.

Lev11: You may eat animals with cloven hooves that chew the cud, and fish with scales and fins. Anything that touches a carcass is unclean.

Lev12: A male child shall be circumcised on the eighth day. A woman who gives birth shall bring offerings after her days of purification.

Lev13: If anyone has leprosy the priest shall declare them unclean and they shall live outside the camp. A leprous garment shall be burned.

Lev14: If anyone is healed of leprosy, they shall shave their hair and bring offerings. If a house has mildew, the priest shall inspect it.

Lev15: When a man has a discharge, he is unclean. When he ejaculates, he is unclean until evening? When a woman has her period, she is unclean.

Lev18: Don't have sex with a relative, a woman on her period, your neighbour's wife, another man or an animal. These things defile the land.

Lev19: Be holy. Keep my Sabbaths. Don't turn to idols. Love your neighbour as yourself. Don't mix livestock. Do no injustice. I am YHWH.

Lev20: Anyone who worships Molech, curses their parents, commits adultery or has sex with a man shall be put to death. You shall be holy.

Lev23: Proclaim as feasts: Passover, Unleavened Bread, First fruits fifty days later, the Day of Trumpets, the Day of Atonement and The Feast of Booths.

Lev25: Every seventh year the land shall rest. Every fiftieth year shall be a jubilee, when property shall be restored, and slaves released.

Lev27: If anyone dedicates a person or land to YHWH you shall make a valuation. A tithe of everything from the land belongs to YHWH.

Num5: Anyone who sins shall make restitution and add a fifth. If a man suspects his wife of unfaithfulness, he shall take her to the priest.

Num6: Anyone who makes a Nazirite vow shall not drink wine or cut their hair. Aaron's blessing shall be: "YHWH bless you and keep you."

Num9: In the first month of the second year the Israelites kept the Passover. Whenever the cloud lifted from the tabernacle they journeyed.

Num15: There is one law for you and for strangers. Make an offering if you sin unintentionally. Anyone who sins defiantly shall be cut off.

Num28: Bring offerings each morning and evening, on the Sabbath and on the first of the month. Celebrate Passover and the Feast of Weeks.

Num29: In the seventh month on first day sound the trumpets; on the tenth day make atonement; on the fifteenth day celebrate for seven days.

Num30: When a man makes a vow, he must not break his word. When a woman makes a vow, it shall stand unless her father or husband forbids it.

Num36: The clan of Gilead asked about Zelophehad's daughters. Moses said, "Daughters who inherit land must marry within their own tribe."

Dt4: Now, Israel, hear the commandments and obey them. You heard YHWH speak from the fire. Take care not to make idols. YHWH is Elohim.

Dt5: YHWH made his covenant with us: Have no other YHWHs; Keep the Sabbath; Honour your parents. You shall do all that he has commanded.

Dt6: Hear, O Israel: YHWH our God is one. Love YHWH with all your heart, soul and strength. Teach your children these commandments.

Dt7: Make no treaty with the nations of the land. You are a holy people, YHWH has chosen you.

Dt14: You may eat animals with cloven hooves that chew the cud. Bring a tithe from your fields to eat before YHWH and for the Levites.

Dt15: Every seven years you shall cancel debts. Hebrew slaves shall go free in the seventh year. Set apart every firstborn male animal.

Dt16: Celebrate the Passover in the month of Abib. Celebrate the Feast of Weeks and the Feast of Booths. Appoint judges in all your towns.

Dt19: Set aside three cities so that anyone who kills accidently may flee there. A matter must be established by two or three witnesses.

Dt22: If you find your neighbour's ox you shall return it. If a man falsely claims that his new wife was not a virgin, he shall be punished.

Dt24: If a man divorces his wife, he must not remarry her. Do not withhold wages. Leave the gleanings of your harvest for widows and orphans.

Dt27: Write the law on large stones. The Levites will say, "Cursed is anyone who does not keep the law."

Dt28: If you obey YHWH he will bless you above all nations; if not, you will be cursed, and YHWH will send a nation to destroy you.

Dt29: You have seen all that YHWH has done so keep this covenant. If you break it the land will be cursed, and YHWH will uproot you.

Dt30: When you return to YHWH he will have compassion; he will circumcise your heart. I have set before you life and death. Choose life.

Dt32: Ascribe greatness to our YHWH! YHWH's portion is his people; They turned away, so he spurned them; But he will provide atonement."

Desperate Dan shouted, "Take note of a prophecy: But He will provide atonement in Messiah Yeshua, whose name means Yahweh's salvation."

Chapter Sixty-four

Deportation and Time to Hold Fast

Helen Cassidy, the officer in charge, approached Desperate Dan with a big smile. He thought to himself, "*Yes, big outward smile to me covering your own delight at increasing your deportations target*".

She said, "I have managed to get you all on the same plane, leaving at 12 a.m. tomorrow. Immigrant transfer van for airport will leave at 8 a.m. sharp. Try to keep tight together. Be careful that you don't get split up when they transfer you to busses to take you to the camp—the guards do not care about splitting families. they just want people on the busses. I know because I have served there, and I have seen some sad sights."

Desperate Dan thanked her. At least she had given him adequate time to prepare the family. He called a meeting that night and repeated the main points. "We are allowed one hold bag each and one small cabin bag. Here are leaflets with the size and weight limits. Be careful to be under these limits; if they are overweight, the guards will open them and throw some stuff out."

The morning came, and the extended family gathered to meet the big prisoner transfer bus. Keeping their bags with them, they stayed close together and shuffled towards the back doors. Ferka and Pesha quickly pushed Esmeralda in the wheelchair on to the tail lift and up into the bus. Then they loaded their bags, followed by the rest of the family.

The bus ran them to Glasgow Airport. After security checks, the bus could drive right up to the plane, like a flock of starlings holding close together. The extended family boarded the plane with little interference from the guards.

The plane was an old, propeller-driven, nineteen-seat, charter flight which was ideal for the extended family of twelve and two armed guards. The plane did not cruise very fast, and so the flight took over seven hours.

Glad to get out, they piled out on to the runway and were immediately hit by the searing heat. They got Esmeralda into her wheelchair.

A bus, obviously late, came careening and bouncing across the rough land between the runways. Three gun-toting soldiers jumped out and began shouting and gesturing to the extended family to get into the bus, however no ramp was available for Esmeralda's wheelchair. Pesha and Farka immediately lifted Esmeralda and her wheelchair into the bus as if it weighed little. The soldiers came on to the bus and searched through their bags, leaving each family member to repack them.

After a long run in the scorching heat they arrived at the camp. They were met and processed by some United Nations personnel, who were also withering in the heat.

Desperate Dan asked, "What tenting or housing options are possible for my extended family? I wish to keep then together."

One of the United Nations officers pointed to a table displaying a sign: "Real Estate".

Dismissed from the reception process, the extended family approached the real estate table, and Desperate Dan asked the man,

"What housing options do you have to keep my extended family safe and compliant with Bible incest laws?"

The man smiled broadly. "That's what I like to hear—a Torah-compliant family. How many units together do you need?"

Desperate Dan answered, "Ideally five."

The man looked carefully at him and said, "Do you have money"?

Desperate Dan nodded.

Lots of money?

Desperate Dan nodded.

The real estate man said, "I have what you may like. The previous owner imported a hotel from China made from shipping containers. It is beautifully designed and appointed with a total of thirty bedrooms. The only mistake the man made was refusing to share his good luck with the quite reasonable protection arrangements. Take my advice: this business will immediately take off again. Demand for rooms is very high. Just don't resist the protection insurance. This is an immediate money-making opportunity, and it will keep your family together."

Desperate Dan said, "Can we see it, please"?

The real estate man said, "Let's talk about the price options first. If you can't meet these, it's not worth the trouble looking. By the way, can you guess what my name is?"

Drinka shouted, "Mohammad! I bet it is Mohammad."

"Yes, it is. You are a clever young woman. How did you ever guess?" Mohammad replied with a lot of laughter.

Then he took off his smile. "OK, let's talk about money. Although it is made from shipping containers, it will still bring you immediate revenue. Because it is made from shipping containers, I estimate its value at $160,000 US, but I am prepared to sell to you for $130,000 because it is unlikely that many poor immigrants will have that kind of money. Most of them are already in debt and certainly out of money or valuables, which they have had to pay to the people traffickers. "Assuming you use twelve rooms for yourselves, you will have up to eighteen to let. The clever thing the previous owner did was install a giant African thorn hedge round his ten-acre property with a micro drip irrigation system feeding the plant roots. He was here at the beginning, before the big influx of refugees, and so he secured his ten acres.

"Aqaba is becoming a linchpin in Jordan's grand water strategy. Jordan's first seawater desalination plant, providing ten to fifteen million cubic meters of water per year, matches Aqaba's current usage. The reverse-osmosis treatment plant is the first step in an ambitious plan to build a canal to send water from the Red Sea to the shrinking Dead Sea, generate hydropower on the canal, and install another desalination facility along the way.

"The previous hotel owner had a secure yard around his hotel, and so he was given possession of three road water tankers and a contract to run water supplies from the big desalination plant to parts of the now-expanding refugee camp near his hotel. It's a long run of more than one hundred miles each way, but each night he does one extra run with one of the lorries, filling up his hotel water tanks. He gets paid by the United Nations.

"He installed tanks, piping, and pumps supplying chlorinated water to his hotel bathrooms. The high ambient temperatures average thirty-two degrees Celsius and heat the water held for extended periods in his container tanks. It is a bit cool in the winter months, but in Jordan, where water is very scarce, the constant supply of water is valued highly. All drinking and cooking water is bought in bottled water.

"The showers are fed through a coin-operated water meter, and each coin gives you one minute of very fine spray. Most of the rooms are taken by United Nations personnel, and they put two or three coins in showering morning and night. So, eighteen times an average of two dollars twice a day gives an income of up to $72 per day, or $25,000 per annum, just from the showers. United Nations Staff will fall over themselves to get rooms at $30 per night or even more. So, you see, the hotel could bring in a gross sum of more than $190,000 per year."

Desperate Dan said, "Yes, we are very interested. Can we inspect the hotel"?

Mohammad said, "Yes, let me see if I can get a bus to pick us up."

After a wait of about one hour, an old bus arrived, and the extended family got on board after lifting Esmeralda's wheelchair with her on it.

Mohammad showed them round the hotel. Ferka spotted a workshop on the ground floor and a box of miniature propane welding torches and spare gas cylinders. He asked, "Can I use the workshop tools to adjust Granny's wheelchair?"

Mohammad led the rest of the family on to inspect the rest of the hotel, leaving Esmeralda and Ferka in the workshop. Ferka helped Esmeralda out of the wheelchair, and he removed the seat cushion. He quickly lit one of the propane welding torches and heated the end of four of the aluminium tubes, removing the end caps. He tipped up the wheelchair and emptied gold coins out of the four open tubes. He estimated that it was worth $106,000, and he wrapped it in a towel that he found at the workshop sink. He tied the towel tightly with string and then welded the end caps back in place on the end of the tubes. He positioned the seat cushion and helped Esmeralda into the wheelchair, giving her the gold coins wrapped tightly in the towel. Freka then pushed Esmeralda in the wheelchair until they caught up with the rest of the family.

Mohammad was saying, "You need to resume the emergency water supplies, or you will lose the contract and the water tankers."

Esmeralda interjected. "How much do you want, and what Jordanian legal deeds do we get as proof of our purchase?"

Mohammad replied quickly, "The price is $130,000, plus $10,000 insurance money, which also gives you security protection."

Esmeralda said, "Get your lawyer here. I will offer you no more than $106,000 including insurance money and it's a deal. I want to move in here tonight. You will have to get men to show our men the water tanker runs over the next two days."

Mohammad was surprised by the suddenness of the absolute offer, but he was a realist and said. "A bird in the hand is worth more than two in the bush!" He smiled and shook Esmeralda's hand, then immediately dialled a number on his mobile phone. "Can you bring a contract to the hotel? I have a buyer, we need to complete tonight."

The lawyer came with two witnesses, and they signed the documents.

Esmeralda produced the towel and handed it to Mohammad, who opened it and took out a couple of the gold coins, handing one to the lawyer. They carefully examined them, and then Mohammad phoned a number. "Bring my gold scales over to the hotel right away."

After Mohammad weighed a couple of gold coins, he beamed a big smile and said, "Yes, good American thousand-dollar coin. The best."

Chapter Sixty-five

Occupying the Hotel

Mohammad left them to occupy the hotel after promising to keep in close touch and help them with any difficulties. He also promised to send three men to show them the runs and routines of the water tankers. He added that he would put the word out the hotel was reopening.

The extended family held a meeting to decide on room allocation. Then it was agreed that the three men would drive the three water tankers and assess the men supplied by Mohammad as possible drivers.

Esmeralda; Pesha's wife, Donca, and her daughters, Deka and Drinka; and Ferka's wife, Jaelle, would head up the domestic workforce, but they would hire in cleaning, kitchen, and waitress staff.

Desperate Dan said, "Esmeralda, I think you handled the purchase very well. You saved us a lot of money. I think we will split it into ten lots and hide them well in the grounds."

Within two hours of Mohammad leaving, two women arrived at the hotel asking to see "the domestic boss". Esmeralda met them and asked them to sit at a table.

One of the women spoke hesitatingly. "Pleased to meet you, thank you. We have four children still alive between us. No husbands or blood brothers, all killed. We need to feed the children. This is my sister, and we both worked here before the hotel was shut. Now we have no jobs and no money. We are very good workers and were both lead hands, I in the kitchen and my sister in bedrooms and cleaning. Thank you, for hearing us." She finished speaking with a little bow, replicated by her sister.

Esmeralda smiled warmly and said, "Here is ten American dollars. Go buy some basic food, go home, and feed your children. It is getting late tonight. Come back at 6 a.m., and we will talk about your new jobs." Both women laughed hysterically and then began to cry. Esmeralda, pulling on tables with her arms, worked the wheelchair out of the room, leaving the women to compose themselves and go to their children.

Ferka and Pesha waited until 2 a.m. in the morning and then donned their black martial arts uniforms along with black socks, black trainers, and black balaclavas. They were invisible under the overcast night sky.

Ferka quickly melted the solder holding the remaining two endplates on the filled tubes of Esmeralda's wheelchair, extracted the fifty-four gold coins, and re-soldered the endplates. They split them into nine bundles of nine coins and a tenth bundle containing the savings Esmeralda had negotiated for the sale. They cut up a few bath towels and went to the perimeter thorn hedge.

Pesha had previously inspected the African boxthorn perimeter hedge. It was impenetrable, a spiny thicket that inhibited the movement of stock animals. He had picked out the nine tallest bushes in the hedge, and he could just see them on the clearing sky. They worked quickly, with one watching while the other dug holes two metres deep precisely two metres from the base of each bush.

They buried one gold bundle in each and filled in the holes, and then they smoothed the dry, sandy ground with the rake. The two men silently lay on the ground for about fifteen minutes, watching and listening for any movement or sound. Satisfied, they retired to their beds after putting away their outfits.

The following morning at 5:30 a.m., when it was still dark, Ferka opened the front doors for the water tanker squad to go to the lorries. The three men supplied by Mohammad were carrying Kalashnikov AK-47s wrapped in blankets. Esmeralda's two women workers were also sitting outside the front door. The empty water tankers drove out of the hotel yard.

Esmeralda came to the door and invited the two women in and gestured to a table. She put on the kettle and took down three mugs. The kettle boiled, and using a very fine tea strainer, she poured three mugs of black tea. One of the women stood up, stepped forward, and took the three mugs to the table.

Esmeralda propelled her wheelchair to the table where the two women were seated. She took a sip of her hot tea, looked up, and smiled as she introduced herself. "I am Esmeralda, the granny of the family. Unfortunately, as you can see my legs have stopped working, but I am still very much alive. My wheelchair is an amazing vehicle, and its big wheels can deal with the rough ground, but it needs someone to push because the bike frames prevent hand-driven wheels being fitted to the wheels."

One of the women gave a little bow. "I am Miriam, and I worked in the kitchen of the hotel until the previous proprietor stopped paying his insurance money. I believe he rented the hotel from Mohammad. I was lead hand in the kitchen, but my children have gone hungry since he lost the hotel." She looked towards the other woman.

The other woman gave a little bow and said, "Mistress, I am Rebecca. I too worked in the hotel as lead hand for cleaning and bed changing, and I waitressed at mealtimes." She finished by giving another little bow.

Esmeralda said, "Good. Yes, it is good for me to have two experienced hotel workers. Here is how we will work. Make a list of the workers and their jobs before the hotel closed. You will manage your old areas of responsibility, but you will keep the number of employees to the minimum appropriate for times of day and night. You can pay slightly above the local wages for minimum staff efficiencies and incentives. Making a job in this hotel something to be sought after. Make it clear when you start an employee that if people do not turn up for their shifts without permission or do not keep their work areas clean, they will be dropped off the work force.

"Make a list of minimum staff numbers you need for all hours of day and night. For instance, during the night you will only need a security man and a room servant. Remember my family are using twelve of the rooms, which cuts down profits. If you manage the efficiencies well, you can pay yourselves a monthly bonus.

"You can use a corner of the ten-acre grounds for family tents, which the hotel will buy, if you feed and look after a flock of geese I intend to buy as security guards for our ten-acre grounds. Their wings will need to be clipped every year to stop them from flying."

Miriam and Rebecca grinned and gave repeated bows towards Esmeralda, getting family tents in a secure place was beyond their wildest dreams..

During the rest of the morning, a constant stream of previous hotel guests arrived seeking to reoccupy their long-term occupancies. Esmeralda took the opportunity to increase the rate to forty dollars per night for long-term occupancy and sixty dollars per night for short-term occupancy. This made up the shortfall caused by family occupancy of twelve rooms.

Esmeralda was warming to running a hotel.

Chapter Sixty-six

Keep the Sabbath While Running a Hotel

L ate in the evening of the first day, even though the extended family was exhausted, Desperate Dan held a meeting.

He started by saying, "We now have a hotel, but the hotel runs seven days a week. How do we keep the seventh day Sabbath while running a seven-day-a-week business?"

Everyone was silent for a few minutes, and then Esmeralda smiled and said, "I know. We prepare all the food as usual on the Friday, and everyone is invited to join our Sabbath service and meals. They can come and go as they wish. We will still be keeping Yahweh's Sabbath, which we will share as open hospitality with others, if they wish. We will also include staff members and their families, even if we need to put up some tents in the grounds."

Desperate Dan smiled. "Yes, that's a perfect solution. Thank you, Esmeralda."

Friday, the day of preparation for the Sabbath came around, and the kitchen staff had to do double work preparing the Sabbath food, which was a sumptuous feast. However, the staff felt included and equal, especially because their children were included, and they worked with a joyous countenance.

Mohammad came around first thing on Friday morning flashing his big smile, and he said, "Just popped in to see how you are getting on."

Desperate Dan said, "Fine, thanks, Mohammad. We are preparing for the Sabbath, and we expect big numbers. What we need is some overflow tents in the grounds, and I can hold the services outside."

Mohammad said, "No problem. I have hundreds of United Nations tents left over in my warehouse."

Desperate Dan frowned. "I can't take them, if it is stealing. You know that is one of the Ten Commandments."

Mohammad said, "What a difficult man you are to work with. OK, you have a huge, ten-acre yard that you will never fully use. I will erect ten tents in the west corner and run it as a foot clinic for the United Nations six days a week. You can use it for Sabbath services on Saturdays. That way I will make even more money. Many of the refugees have serious foot injuries and fungus infections from their long walks. My men will erect the tents before sunset."

The temperature also went down as the sun set. The women had rows of tables, and at the last minute they brought out dozens of big, covered bowls of food.

Desperate Dan had prepared a short sermon on Creation for Friday night. The west corner of hotel yard, where the tents were erected, was full of people, hotel guests, staff, and their families. Everyone, no matter how poor, had tried to wear clean, bright Sabbath clothing, even if it was only a thin, printed cotton sheet pinned at strategic places and a head scarf. Even Mirela respected the Sabbath by tying her ribbons tightly on her sari, showing no sensual flesh.

The smell of the food wafted across the yard, and the children sat patiently in anticipation. As sunset approached on Friday evening, eighteen minutes before sunset, Esmeralda shouted out to the assembled immigrants, "Let us light Shabbat candles. These represent shamor and zakhor, the words of the commandments regarding the Sabbath. 'And Yahweh blessed the seventh day' (Genesis 2:3). With what did he bless it? Light. Blessed are you, Yahweh, our Elohim, ruler of the universe, who has sanctified us with commandments and commanded us to light Shabbat candles."

Desperate Dan stood and started the short Friday sermon by saying the Shema. "Hear, O Israel! Yahweh, our Elohim, is one and is the only Elohim. Blessed are you, Yahweh, for giving us your Torah and brother Yeshua, the Messiah who died for our sins with his spilt blood. Shabbat shalom, great Yahweh."

He paused to gather himself.

"My friends, the Bible is probably one of the most read books, yet it's the most misunderstood books in the world. Under the severe pressure of Hellenisation, The Jews allowed their scriptures, now known as the Old Testament, to be corrupted by removing the sacred name Yahweh and replacing it with Ba'al or Lord, the name of the pagan sun god. The Christian Church developed under Emperor Constantine took the writings of the early Church of Messiah Yeshua. The name Yeshua was changed to Iesous Horus Krishna to encompass three major pagan gods of the Roman Empire. He, a simple rabbi, was embellished with stories of supernatural powers and elevated to a man-god. Centuries later, this name morphed to Jesus Christ."

Chapter Sixty-seven

The Sacred Name

Desperate Dan continued from his notes.

The most important and most often written name of God in the Hebrew Bible is יהוה (YHWH, or YHVH), the four-letter name of God, also known as Tetragrammaton, which derives from the prefix *tetra-* ("four") and *gramma* ("letter").

In the Hebrew Bible and Judaism, "He Who Is", "I Am that I Am", "I will be what I will be", or "I will be who I will be" and the tetragrammaton YHWH (Hebrew: יהוה, which means: "I am who I am", "He Who Exists") are used as names of God, whereas Yahweh is sometimes used in Christianity as vocalisations of YHWH.

Another common name of God in the Hebrew Bible is Elohim (אלהים).

Elohim then would mean "the all-powerful One", based on the usage of the word "el" in certain verses to denote power or might (Genesis 31:29; Nehemiah 5:5).

In the Hebrew Bible, אל (El) appears very occasionally alone (e.g., Genesis 33:20, ישׂראל אלהי אל, "El the god of Israel"; Genesis 46:3, אביך אלהי האל, "El the god of your father").

(i) ישׂראל אלה (Elah Yisrael), God of Israel (Ezra 5:1)

(ii) ירושלם אלה (Elah Yerushelem), God of Jerusalem (Ezra 7:19)

(iii) שׁמיא אלה (Elah Shemaya), God of Heaven (Ezra 7:23)

(iv) אבהתי אלה (Elah-avahati), God of my fathers, (Daniel 2:23)

(v) אלהין אלה (Elah Elahin), God of gods (Daniel 2:47).

Desperate Dan became visibly angry and shouted, "Unfortunately, in modern Bibles this sacred name has been translated as Lord, which in English means Ba'al. Baal was a god worshipped in many ancient Middle Eastern communities, especially among the Canaanites, who apparently considered him a fertility deity and one of the most important gods in the pantheon. Baal, Bel, and Babylon are all interrelated words pertaining to chief sun deities of pagan sun worship. Baal means "to shine", and it's also used for Lord/husband."

Desperate Dan paused for a couple of minutes, regaining his calm. The fact of such a huge deception upset him.

Chapter Sixty-eight

Metaphoric Nature of Parts of the Bible

D esperate Dan continued his sermon.

"Bible creationists have long contested the order and time frame of our existence with evolutionary scientists in often bitter disputes.

Let us compare the two positions.

The sun created after the world (Genesis 1:1–2). Scientists say sun first, then planets.

Grass, plants, and trees (Genesis 1:11–18). Scientists say sun first, then grass, plants, and trees.

Land plants first (Genesis 1:11). Scientists say marine organisms first.

Birds first, then animals (Genesis 1:20–21). Scientists say land animals first, then birds.

Fruit trees created before fish (Genesis 1:11–12, 20). Scientists say fish before fruit trees.

I could give more examples of how the creation timeline is a little out of sequence, but I don't wish to bore you.

However, most will know that many stories in the Bible are metaphoric, a figure of speech in which a word or phrase that ordinarily designates one thing is used to designate another, thus making an implicit comparison, as in "a sea of troubles" or "All the world's a stage" (Shakespeare).

"The point proved by these chronological errors is not that the Bible Creation story is wrong; remember that it was subject to much copying and translating. It is metaphoric or representative of much bigger and longer processes. We should approach it and our world with more than a degree of thankfulness.

- Look up at the stars and wonder about the Creator, Elohim, God. He, although equally encompassing female characteristics is unity and perfection in a single entity.
- Appreciate the plants and trees and thank Yahweh for all our blessings.
- Compare other life forms and observe all our similarities.
- These common features, from the simple to the complex, can't be denied.
- Did He fill the great void with electrons and quarks the building blocks of atoms?
- Did these energy particles become numerous beyond imagination over time?
- Did this energy become so vast that its equilibrium became critical, resulting in the big bang?
- Did the big bang form atoms and scatter them in all directions?
- Did mainly hydrogen gas form into distinct and receding clouds?
- Under the attraction of gravity, were stars like our sun born?
- Was that when Yahweh said, "Let there be light"?
- On earth, when humans finally emerged as a distinct species, Yahweh set standards for his now searching family.

- Long before our miraculous escape from Egypt, he revealed himself to our early biblical father figures.
- His name was Yahweh, and he revealed to Moses, "I AM WHO I AM, and my name is YHWH-Elohim. The only self-existent one, the Creator of the physical universe. You shall not have any other Elohims (Gods) before me. Do not let any idols rule you or any person, thing, or false concept, including suns, the wonders of the universe, thunderstorms, and disasters.
- Misuse of my name, Yahweh, will be accounted for. Remember my seventh day Sabbath by keeping it holy and resting in my presence.
- Yahweh blessed the seventh day Sabbath and made it holy".

Almost all the people enjoyed the Sabbath and came and went as they pleased. The hotel staff and their children felt valued and were treated as brothers and sisters.

Esmeralda had a great sense of comfort from Desperate Dan's explanation of how the Bible's Creation story of Genesis fit with scientific knowledge.

Chapter Sixty-nine

A Fight Challenge

Mohammad came to the hotel on Sunday morning smiling warmly. He walked over to Desperate Dan and said, "I have had many good reports about your Sabbath meals. Some of the children have never tasted such a variety of food, and they have as much as they want. Yes, Desperate Dan, your name is misleading. There is a lot more to you than meets the eye."

Desperate Dan didn't reply.

Mohammad continued. "I didn't come to engage in idle chat. Your two sons, Ferka and Pesha, come as silent servants, but on the Internet my people have found them as cage-fighting champions."

Again, Desperate Dan remained silent.

Mohammad looked a little annoyed because he wasn't used to getting the silent treatment. He stepped up close to Desperate Dan, stared into his eyes, and said, "I need the two boys to represent me in a power play for this territory. The war, with participants from regional powers, is mostly divided between Sunni powers generally supporting the rebels and Shias generally supporting Assad. As part of Iran's long-term strategy, Assad's Shias are trying to push into Jordon and are trying to use the immigrant influx to gain footholds. They have a couple of crack fighters in their ranks, and they have challenged the local warlords to put up a couple of challengers, with the winners taking power in the district.

"This custom of having champions fight goes way back to David and Goliath. If your boys can handle this high-profile fighting, my heavily armed men will reinforce who really runs the immigration camps and stamp our authority here."

Desperate Dan approached a woman who was cleaning the floor and said, "Find Pesha and Ferka, and ask them to come here."

Pesha and Ferca arrived shortly, and Desperate Dan said, "There is a serious power play for control of the refugee camps. Assad's Shias want to take control and have two crack fighters who are challenging the local warlords to put up two challengers. This will be hand fighting, but it could be to the death, and their fighters are known for dirty tricks.

Ferca said, "If these are Assad's men, then I will take them on myself for all the children they killed with chlorine gas." Pesha nodded his agreement with a steely expression.

Mohammad's face broke into a big grin. "I can accept the challenge."

Mohammad supplied two drivers to drive the water tankers, in order to let Ferca and Pesha train full time. The big fight was scheduled two months ahead. It became the main topic of the refugee camp.

The hotel filled and settled into a routine, and the Sabbath services became a popular feature.

Ferka and Pesha watched several videos of the opposition fighters. They were big, powerful men with seven attack techniques: straight boxing punches to the head with either hand, big hooks to side of head with either hands, uppercut to chin with either hand, or a kung fu mule kick to the head always with right foot. Several of Assad's champions fights had reportedly resulted in the death of their opponents, but these reports were unconfirmed.

One month from the fight, their opponents publicly announced that the fight would be two against two, causing the betting to narrow in favour of Assad's heavier champions.

Eventually the fight day arrived, and one would never guess this was a refugee camp. It was more like cup final day at a national football stadium.

A very tall boxing ring had been constructed so that spectators standing on flat ground could see the fighters on their elevated platform.

Ferka and Pesha were very experienced and knew that the heavier men would grapple with one of them, trying to hold them in a position for the other to land heavy blows. They knew their only chance was to keep moving and use speed.

As they were paraded through the crowds, Ferka and Pasha noticed that there were a lot of armed men in the crowds. When they approached the boxing ring, fanfares of trumpets rang out, and large sections of the audience cheered and shouted.

They climbed up to the high platform by means of a ladder and occupied one corner of the very large boxing ring.

President Assad's two fighting champions made their entrance by climbing over their corner post and jumping into the ring.

Mohammad appeared briefly in Ferka's and Pesha's corner and shouted, "You two boys can determine the course of history and Assad's penetration into Jordon today, but you will need to watch out for your opponent's dirty tricks."

Chapter Seventy

The Big Fight

The master of ceremonies, resplendent in a black diner suit and bowtie, held a microphone and boomed out through powerful amplifiers and loudspeakers, "Fight of unlimited number of four-minute rounds. Only unconsciousness or death reaching a conclusion by order of President Bashar Hafez al-Assad. The fight is between brothers Samid and Samir, free unarmed combat champions of Syria, and brothers Ferka and Pesha, champion cage fighters of the Romany Tribe."

The starting bell was struck, and the four men warily came out of their corners circling the centre of the big ring. Samid and Samir were bigger and strutted confidently. Samid rushed Ferka, who neatly sidestepped and delivered a powerful blow to Samid's heart.

Pesha saw Samid's knee's momentary give way as if he was going down, and he stepped in and delivered a right fist to his solar plexus. This time Samid went down. Samir rushed to protect his partner with big, swinging hook punches.

One of the seconds in the Assad corner threw a bucket of soapy water under Ferka's feet, causing him to slip.

The bell rung loudly, signalling end of round one, but the crowd went wild following these exchanges, especially after the bucket of soapy water. It was difficult to hear anything.

Ferka quickly took off his shoes and stepped away from the soapy water. He returned to his corner, where his seconds cleaned his training shoes before fitting them back on.

The surface of the ring was mopped dry, and the bell rang for round two. This time, Samir led the exchanges using his mule kick. Ferka and Pesha kept moving out of range of his mighty kicks, but Pesha had noticed a little shuffle before each kick.

Round two ended with no actual physical contact. It was obvious that each of the fighters could deliver telling blows, and the contest was falling into a cautious pattern. Assad's fighters were huge but quickly exhausted their energy in big attacks, whereas the Romany fighters were lighter, fast, and very fit.

Round three sounded, and Pesha saw the second slip: a cylindrical lead weight into Samid's right hand. He whispered to Ferka, "Samid's carrying a weight in his right hand."

Samid led the attack on Pesha, clearly trying to land a right hook to the head. So intent was he on his right hand that he threw seven mighty right hooks. Ferca getting used to the single attack strategy stepped inside the next great hook and hit Samid with a straight right in the centre of the solar plexus. The blow, correctly delivered, irritated a nerve in the diaphragm, causing it to spasm. Samid was unable to breath. Ferca followed up with a hard palm blow to Samid's right temple, and he went down.

Samir panicked and began his little shuffle. Pesha read it perfectly, ducked under the mule kick, and stamped hard on the inside of Samir's lower leg, breaking Samir's fibula.

Assad's champion fighters were taken out of the ring by men, using ropes to lower the heavy fighters onto stretchers. The master of ceremonies made the announcements, milking the situation for all it was worth.

Mohammad eventually came into the ring, took the microphone, and loudly said, "History could have changed today in favour of Assad and his Shias, but our Romany brothers have kept the power in Sunni hands." The crowd erupted at this announcement with many shootings into the air.

Desperate Dan looked on and thought, *Yes, but for how long? With the Russians working with the Iranians, power in this part of the world can be very unstable.*

Chapter Seventy-one

Mirela

After the fight, life settled back into the everyday work routines. Mirela, Big Harmon's widow, had found her niche as the hotel receptionist. It was a job that allowed her to dress up and display her trim body to men coming and going at the hotel. It was a big glamour illusion because she knew she would never find a replacement for Big Harmon, and she did not want to. But since recovering from her initial grief, which had taken about three years, she had taken up Latin American dancing, and wearing very revealing clothes gave her a thrill.

Her favourite dresses were saris, which fastened down the right side with a shoulder strap above her right shoulder, a ribbon tie just below her right armpit, a ribbon tie at her right waist, and a ribbon tie halfway down her right thigh. All were tied reasonably tightly, but just a little slack still allowed flesh to be glimpsed through the join to the extent people could see up the sides of her thigh, hip, and breast and note that she was not wearing knickers or a brassier. The double take it caused gave her a thrill.

The ribbons could be tied loosely, which allowed a greater amount of flesh to show, to extreme looseness on occasions when she was "hot", which was decidedly pornographic.

On Saturday nights after sunset, when the Sabbath was past, she would go outside to where a patio had been laid around a little wooden dance floor. The patio accommodated about thirty people seated, and Mirela would appear with a guitarist and singer whose guitar and microphone were connected to an amplifier. The guitarist would play a few low-key tunes, and then Mirela would explode onto the dance floor with her sari ties loosened to their maximum extension. She would dance a series of fast Latin American dances with a spotlight highlighting her every move. The resulting vision was a blur of bright green silk sari and naked body parts—just glimpses of tits, nipples, thighs, and crotch. The glimpses of her body were so fleeting that the audience were unsure of what they saw, but both males and females were aware of sexual arousal and wanted more. Mirela was an expert tease and only performed a maximum of four dances, and then she ran off into the hotel and her room.

Kizzy was very much aroused as they watched Mirela's performances, but she tried to disguise her intense interest around Desperate Dan, who seemed mildly entertained and politely applauded. Desperate Dan worked about fourteen hours every day and about twelve hours on the seventh day Sabbath and Kizzy and he did not now have time for sex.

The following morning, Mirela rose at 4.30 a.m. and began her ablutions and glamour applications. At 6 a.m. she took up her position at her reception desk just inside the main doors and checked e-mails on her computer.

"Good morning, Mirela," said the night shift security guard as he was about to go off shift.

"Good morning, Ishtar. Is there anything worth looking at on the overnight CCTV?"

"There was a bit of corridor nakedness, do you want me to find it on the CCTV for you?"

"Yes, please."

Ishtar pushed in beside her. She loosened the bottom tie on her sari, opened her legs, and said, "Stand between my legs. There is enough room for the two of us."

He got flustered, but he turned to look at the television monitor and started reversing the CCTV recording. He changed to play and said, "There he is."

Mirela watched the video of the naked man as he sneaked along the corridor, looking this way and that.

Ishtar was getting excited while standing in front of her so close, and she occasionally rubbed her hand up the inside of his thigh, lightly touching his genitals.

"I am eighteen today. I am a man."

She said, "Turn around and face me and let me see your body".

He nodded with an embarrassed smile, then he pulled the lose gown up over his head.

She looked at him now completely naked, and she said with a smile, "I see you are not circumcised."

Mirela looked at him intently, appreciating his thin, boyish, nubile, body, especially his taught stomach muscles and his thin, strong thighs. She looked up at his expectant and nervous face.

It wasn't really about his nakedness—it was the risk she was taking that excited her. She said with a breaking smile and an extended hand, "Come closer it's your birthday. Remember that this is just your birthday treat. You only get this on your birthday."

***

However, Esmeralda had witnessed the exhibition from the serving hatch to the kitchen, and as Mirela returned to her desk, Esmeralda pulled her wheelchair up to her and said, "When I was sixteen, our family had no money coming in, so I took a job as a stripper, which included sexual favours. I know all about seduction and how easily led men are, especially about sexual attraction. "However, after a couple of years, the work situation got better. With difficulty, I was able to break free and go back to cleaning as a means of earning a living. I said with difficulty because once you get used to taking your knickers off for easy money, it is hard to stop and go back to cleaning all day long".

"But I must tell you that Ferka and his wife, Jaelle, and her sons Danior and Beval, are being affected by your open-sided saris. Jaelle caught her oldest son, Beval, masturbating. She asked him, 'What do you think about that brings an erection on?

"Beval told her, Seeing Mirela's naughty parts.

"Jaelle told me she didn't scold him. Instead she bent over and kissed him on the forehead."

Esmeralda waited to let what she had heard sink in, and for Mirela to realise that she was deadly serious.

"Mirela, as matriarch of the family, I have to tell you that I understand your deep loss and continuing grief for your late husband. I know that your 'glamour puss' image is just a cover for your loneliness, but you need to be more careful around family.

"You are aware of our incest laws. As you know, the laws take precedent over individuals, and incest is one of the most serious. Men are weak creatures and can be easily led by a skillful woman. I have seen Ferka looking at the naked flashes you give him, but he is married to Jaelle, and marriage is sacred in this family." With that, she manoeuvred away, freewheeling from one piece of furniture to the next.

Mirela knew that she had been given a stern warning about family and incest. She had been teasing Freka with flashes of her nakedness, and at times she had him aroused to the extent that he had briefly exposed his dick in front of her as though it was accidental.

This must have been noticed by Esmeralda or possibly Jaelle. Yes, that would account for the black looks coming from Jaelle.

It wasn't about the Arab night security boy; he was not family, and Esmeralda was not concerned about her flirting or even fornicating with outsiders.

The sight and feel of the boy's genitals meant little more than an entertaining diversion to Mirela. She longed for someone like her dead husband, Big Harmon, who knew how to make love to a woman. She lovingly remembered his touch as he played her almost like a musical instrument.

The difference with Big Harmon was he had patience and was focused on her and the slowness of her arousal; he was willing to be patient and hold his gratification until much later. Because he was so big and heavy, he would let her sit on him and bounce up and down. Mirela smiled at the many memories.

Chapter Seventy-two

Bible Prophecy

D esperate Dan decided to set up a Bible prophecy and world affairs study group. He announced it at the next Sabbath service and got a good response. He held the first study the next Wednesday evening.

He read the summary handout to the congregation.

According to Bible Prophecy about the End of the Age:

The Tribulation begins. (Time of Jacob's troubles).

Triggered by Brexit, the world economy will crash.

Weather disaster, especially wild fires, caused by global warming will continue to get worse.

These wild fires in grain producing regions will result in food prices escalating.

Three and a half years after the beginning of the start of the Great Tribulation, King Yeshua will return.

A soon coming Russian-Arab invasion of Israel will be World War 111.

But Yahweh, her Elohim, although she chases after pagan idols, will come to her rescue.

This invasion will be thwarted, and the attacking armies will turn on each other.

A false religious leader will arise.

This false leader will encourage an ecumenical faith producing a single world religion.

Most of humankind will accept this improper, idol-based faith.

A false religious leader will perform signs and lying wonders. His charisma will be hard to resist.

Nearly all humankind will be deceived by signs and lying wonders.

In the power vacuum left by the surprise Russian defeat the World Religious Leader will promote the final "King of the North" A Strong German Leader, that the Bible warns against.

The German led "King of the North" that the World Religious Leader supports, will destroy the Anglo-descended nations. (English speaking).

The "King of the North" will eventually destroy an Arabic confederation.

A few years after the start of the Great Tribulation, Rome will be destroyed.

Messiah Yeshua, now King Yeshua ben David, will come after Rome is destroyed.

***

The Jewish state has not been able to "dwell safely". The present threatening situation compels Israel to spend more of its budget on defense than any other country in the world.

It is only a question of timing.

Desperate Dan shouted, "Keep watch for an unholy alliance between Russia, Syria, Iran, Libya, and others. And keep watch for the rise of the German strong man."

Chapter Seventy-three

The Touchstones of Desperate Dan

Friday came, and everyone prepared for the Sabbath. As they gathered on Friday evening, Desperate Dan handed out a single page of paper, which contained the content of his short sermon. He read it.

"My Touchstones

"In Hebrew, the word *brit* means "covenant", coming from the word meaning "to cut", i.e., "to cut a covenant".

"Furthermore, the word *ish*—that is, as in Brit-ish—means "man".

"Therefore, the "Brit-ish" are the descendants of the "covenant man", Abraham, Isaac, and Jacob, with whom Yahweh made a special covenant.

"So, the "Brit-ish" are the covenant people.

"The Saxons were originally known as the Sacae, or the people of Sac, and Sac is merely an abbreviation of the name Isaac, or Itzak, with the initial vowel sound being dropped off.

"Thus, the Saxons are literally the sons of Isaac.

"The name of Hebrides Islands was the Isles of the Hebrews.

"The Stone of Destiny, Jacobs Pillow, was brought in 569 BC by an elderly, white-haired patriarch sometimes referred to as a "saint", when he came to Ireland with the Scots.

"With him was the princess daughter of an Eastern king and a companion called Simon Brach.

"The princess had a Hebrew name, Tephi—a pet name. Her full name was Tea-Tephi.

"This royal party included the son of the king of Ireland, who had been in Jerusalem at the time of the siege.

"There he had become acquainted with Tea-Tephi.

"He married her shortly after 585—when the city fell.

"Their young son, now about twelve years of age, accompanied them to Ireland.

"Besides the royal family, Jeremiah brought with them some remarkable things, including a harp, an ark, and a wonderful stone called lia-fail, or stone of destiny.

"A peculiar coincidence is that Hebrew reads from right to left, whereas English reads from left to right.

"Read this name either way, and it still is lia-fail".

Desperate Dan concluded, "Despite all their blessings and evidences of Yahweh favours, Israel still chases and whores after idols and false gods, always reverting back to Ba'al, the sun god, and his major festival on 25 December, with trees decked with symbols and ornaments."

A couple of psalms were sung, and blessings were attributed to all sections of the congregation. After the short service, delicious food choices were shared with various dilute fruit juices, and the congregation broke into many joyous groups.

On Saturday, Desperate Dan reviewed world affairs. "There is little doubt that the world is careering towards the end of the age, precisely as described in the book of Revelation. Unstable governments and dictators abound all over the world, and 99 per cent of the world's wealth is in the hands of 1 per cent of its people. Although there is plenty of land, most of it is owned by the few, who also own multiple homes, so there is nowhere for displaced or poor people to live.

"The Middle East remains a powder keg ready to explode at any time. Far East and South China Sea disputes over islands threaten major warfare. There's North Korea and its relentless military threat. There are hostile military actions along the Pakistan-Indian border. Russia and some Arab nations continue to threaten Israel.

"The most sinister of all is being caused by Brexit: the restructuring towards the east of the European Union and a possible rebirth of the Hapsburg or Austro-Hungarian Empire, only this time including the huge powerhouse Germany".

Chapter Seventy-four

Donald Trump Effect

Desperate Dan dedicated his afternoon sermon to the Donald Trump effect on world politics and economies. He climbed up on to the small speaker's platform, looked at the crowded hotel yard, and began.

"Donald John Trump is the forty-fifth president of the United States, in office since 20m January 2017.

Before entering politics, he was a failed businessman and television personality.

"Win or lose, the Trump effect will be felt long after his election.

Trump and his followers are in many ways a rebuke to the elites, who are perceived as controlling popular culture.

Just like the Anglo Saxon English prior to Brexit, the previously dominant American people who feel left out—the white, power-wielding minority—now have a champion.

Admire him or loathe him, most Americans are fascinated by Trump, and that fascination is most felt in white previously working-class communities whose great coal and steel industries have collapsed."

Desperate Dan paused and looked at his silent but engrossed audience.

"White supremacy, white nationalism, anti-immigration, support for patriot veterans, and 'America First' are the core values Trump promotes to his supporters. His alpha male persona also attracts many deprived Americans amongst the millions of Afro-American blacks and more recent immigrants from Central and Latin America.

"However, the biggest effect of 'America First' is driving the world to restructure its economic activity into new trading blocks. China is the one major power still talking about increased integration. China is the only major country in the world projecting the idea that globalisation brings benefits. There is an old-fashioned, adding-up constraint: one country's surplus is another's deficit, and if Asia is running a large surplus collectively, it mathematically must be selling its goods to the rest of the world. Asia's collective surplus in goods trade is now very large."

Desperate Dan continued. "Let me try to make it clearer. America has, for a century or so, provided a market buying other countries' surpluses, largely enabled by her huge agricultural capacity and surpluses. Americans, however poor, have generally been able to gather, beg, and hunt enough food. If President Trump imposes protectionist policies and reduces America's debt, a cold economic wind will blow around the world. He is playing to past nostalgia; the old, coal-based industries employing millions are long gone. Climate change is affecting everything in the natural world, yet Trump is in climate change denial. However, his 'America First' mantra includes Britain making this fatal mistake, Brexit".

"Britain's real national debt, factoring in all liabilities including state and public-sector pensions, is close to £12 trillion, or some £179,000 for every person in the UK. Where on earth is Britain going to find the money to pay that back, especially if America cuts British imports?"

Chapter Seventy-five

The Flight of Refugees

Desperate Dan opened his next Sabbath with a sermon named "The Flight of the Refugees".

Seven Trumpets of Revelations:

The Rohingya Muslims, escaping ethnic unrest in Myanmar, have overwhelmed Bangladesh's Cox's Bazar in under a month.

The UN made an emergency appeal for $78 million on September 9, but UN resident coordinator in Bangladesh, Robert Watkins, said much more would be needed as the exodus grows.

"Our best estimate at this point is $200 million. We are putting together a plan right now that will be ready in about four or five days," Watkins told AFP.

He said aid workers were already struggling to get food, medicine and drinking water to the refugees, many of whom were limited to one meal a day.

The Doctors Without Borders (MSF) group has warned that refugee camps are on the brink of a "public health disaster", saying filthy water and faeces flow through shanties now bursting with Rohingya.

"The fact that there are 430,000 refugees here is in fact a catastrophic event. There is no question about that. We are coping the best we can," Watkins said.

"We are working very hard with the government to get out assistance to all the people, to make sure that everyone is covered with shelter, getting food and getting access to healthcare and pure water and sanitation. This is our priority right now."

He described the government allocation of new land for a massive new refugee camp as a "big breakthrough".

The 2,000 acres of land between two existing camps is already being developed.

"People have been supplied with building materials, so they can build their own shelters in the short term. In the medium term they can build something more resilient.

He also offered UN help in government attempts to register refugees.

"The government has started doing that. We have been offering the government to assist with our biometric registration technology and staff and that is still being negotiated with the government."

The registration could play an important role in any future accord to send Rohingya back to Myanmar, where the Buddhist-dominated army has been accused of killing Rohingya and burning their villages.

A huge relief operation has started with truck convoys carrying aid to some of the remotest border areas.

Some one hundred tonnes of food, tents, sleeping mats and blankets sent by Saudi Arabia have started arriving in Cox's Bazar. The United States has also pledged $32 million to help Bangladesh cope with the influx.

The International Organization for Migration said the Saudi aid would be distributed to some of the thousands of people who have arrived from Myanmar with nothing and are now camped out and living rough on the side of the road or in muddy fields.

"We urgently need more supplies like food, water, medicine and shelter. We can, and we must do more," Save the Children International chief executive Helle Thorning-Schmidt said at the United Nations in New York.

Desperate Dan said, "It is like the run-up to the last World War. People turn against minorities and do terrible things in perceived self-interest."

Chapter Seventy-six

The First Trumpet Warning

Desperate Dan continued his Revelations sermon series.

"'First Trumpet: Hail and fire mingled with blood will cause all the grass on earth and a third of the trees to be burned up' (Revelation 8:7)."

He looked out over the congregation. Upon seeing that they were engrossed, he continued.

> "Wildfires are started by lightning or accidentally by people, and people use controlled fires to manage farmland and pasture and clear natural vegetation for farmland.
>
> Fires can generate large amounts of smoke pollution, release greenhouse gases, and unintentionally degrade ecosystems.
>
> But fires can also clear away dead and dying underbrush, which can help restore an ecosystem to good health.

In many ecosystems, including boreal forests and grasslands, plants have co-evolved with fire and require periodic burning to reproduce.

For example, naturally occurring fires are common in the forests of Canada in the summer.

For example, the intense burning in the heart of South America from August-October is a result of human-triggered fires, both intentional and accidental, in the Amazon Rainforest and the Cerrado (a grassland/savanna ecosystem) to the south.

Across Africa, a band of widespread agricultural burning sweeps north to south over the continent as the dry season progresses each year.

Agricultural burning occurs in late winter and early spring each year across Southeast Asia.

Unusually large wildfires ravaged Alaska and Indonesia in 2015.

The following year, Canada, California and Spain were devastated by uncontrolled flames.

In 2017, massive fires devastated regions of Chile - and now, a deadly blaze in Portugal has claimed dozens of lives.

Science suggests that over the past few decades, the number of wildfires has indeed increased, especially in the western United States.

According to the Union of Concerned Scientists (UCS), every state in the western US has experienced an increase in the average annual number of large wildfires over past decades.

Extensive studies have found that large forest fires in the western US have been occurring nearly five times more often since the 1970s and 80s. Such fires are burning more than six times the land area as before and lasting almost five times longer.

"2015 was a record-breaking year in the US, with more than 10 million acres burned," he told DW in an interview. "That's about 4 million hectares, or an area of the size of the Netherlands or Switzerland."

"It's a scale we haven't seen in recent history and it's very concerning."

"In recent years, there have been big fires in Siberia and various other places around the world where we typically don't see large-scale wildfires," he said.

Projections by the UCS suggest that wildfires could get four, five and even six times as bad as they currently are within this century".

Desperate Dan paused and took a drink of water. Then he shouted, "Revelations says that a third of all trees and all grass will be burned up, and still we as a supposedly intelligent species won't act."

Chapter Seventy-seven

The Second Trumpet Warning

Desperate Dan continued his Revelations sermon series.

"Second Trumpet: A great mountainous burning object will be thrown into the earth's oceans, causing one third of them to become blood, one third of sea life to die and one third of the ships to be destroyed (verses 8–9).

"The second angel sounded his shofar, and something like a huge mountain, all ablaze, was thrown into the sea.

"John is trying to describe events that he has never seen before. It wasn't a mountain but something like a mountain.

"A giant meteorite will probably be hurled towards the earth, surrounded by combustible gasses that will catch fire as they enter the atmosphere. Although its actual collision with the sea will only impact one location, the whole earth will get the message.

"People will track it from space as it enters the earth's gravitational pull and inevitably be pulled toward the sea itself. The entire world will be watching on a continual, twenty-four-hour news cycle and see the whole thing.

"The powerful explosion will dwarf that of any hydrogen bomb and be frightening beyond belief.

"One-third of the sea will be turned into blood. (This could mean blood coloured.)

"Here we are reminded of the first Egyptian plague, where the Nile was turned into blood, killing the fish and making the water undrinkable.

"The Nile was turned into blood when Moses struck the Nile with his rod, and one-third of the sea will be turned into blood when struck by what seems to be a giant meteorite.

"And like all the plagues of Egypt, the sea turning to blood defies any natural phenomena.

"One-third of the living creatures in the sea died because the blood poisoned it.

"It is not surprising that a third of the fish and other marine life will die, thus adding to the poisoning, stench and horror of it all.

"Though no mention is made of the land animals, there can be no doubt that they will also be affected.

"The grass was scorched because of the first trumpet judgement, and a third of the marine organisms died when the second trumpet sounded.

"These are the lowest and most basic components of many of the world's food chains, so their destruction must produce a domino effect on many higher life forms. There is no doubt that the physical effects will be devastating.

"The psychological effects, however, will be even greater because of Yahweh's two witnesses.

"They had already called for a worldwide drought that will still be in effect, and then they prayed for the waters to become blood.

"These men have the power to shut up the sky so that it will not rain during the time they are prophesying, and they have the power to turn the waters into blood (11:6a).

"And one-third of the ships were destroyed. How could that happen?

"More than likely the same meteor impact that poisoned the sea would also generate a monstrous tsunami, which would batter the great number of ships anchored on shore to pieces and capsize huge vessels in the ocean.

"The loss of human life will still be minimal despite the vast destruction in the biosphere and hydrosphere.

"The resulting disruption of commerce and transportation will cause worldwide economic chaos.

Chapter Seventy-eight

Mirela and Kizzy Serve in the Foot Clinic

One morning, there was a queue of people outside the foot clinic. After getting permission from Esmeralda, Mirela and Kizzy volunteered to help.

They were met and welcomed by a very overworked doctor, who gave them a quick induction training. It involved watching a video made by International Red Cross and Red Crescent Movement, and they read a printed booklet of photographs and treatments for various skin conditions.

The two women were given disposable paper suits with hoods, paper knickers, antiseptic socks, and light slip-on plimsoll shoes. They were given a simple plastic carrier bag for their own clothing.

The doctor said, "Please change outside the treatment tent to avoid contaminating your own clothing. It is not very private, but there is a screen. You don't want to carry these infections home with you. When you finish your shift, remove all your disposable clothing, bag it, and then shower before dressing in your own clothes. The shower is not exactly hot, but it is reasonably warm, and there is a screen around the shower. You will get used to nakedness; as you can see, we must remove everyone's clothing and footwear and incinerate it all before they enter the treatment tents. It is the only way to control these persistent infections and funguses."

The doctor then informed them, "Refugees coming in were suffering from trench foot from wearing wellington boots supplied by a well-meaning charity, not realising that they did not take their boots off for fear of losing them.

Growing numbers of children and adults were being diagnosed with the condition, with new cases emerging every day and the severity reaching levels worse than they have ever seen.

"With no means of cleaning their clothes except in dirty water, and not enough socks to go around in the charity donations, refugees are routinely wearing damp clothing, causing trench foot and other conditions to worsen. Any attempts to provide treatment for skin infestations such as scabies are not working because upon returning to the squalor, people are re-infected within days or weeks.

"An estimated seven hundred refugees, including more than 120 unaccompanied children, were currently sleeping rough outside the official camp, where refugees were sleeping in bare scrubland and often exposed to damp, insanitary, and cold conditions for long periods of time. A mobile water tank with merely ten taps was installed, which is open for five hours a day, and ten portable toilets were placed at a common gathering point for women, but with no hygiene items were provided. Two showers had also been installed but were limited to the use of women, children, and those with recognised health conditions. They were hopelessly inadequate for the numbers wishing to use them.

"Spending prolonged periods of time outside also means refugees were suffering from scabies and pressure sores from sleeping on hard ground. A lot of refugees, including kids, have pressure sores around their groin area and on their bottoms from where they've been sleeping on hard ground and bushes.

"There's also a lot of Leishmaniasis, a tropical skin infection that gives them angry-looking ulcers that will leave lifelong scars.

"Coupled with their rapidly declining physical health, the mental well-being of refugees is said to be at an all-time low, with self-harm becoming increasingly common amongst both adults and children. People frequently have self-inflicted razor cuts and cigarette burns on their skin. Unaccompanied minors are a concern, with the number displaying destructive behaviours rising at an alarming rate. Self-harm is really common. Most of kids display destructive behaviours towards themselves, whether it's smoking, drinking, or the more serious cases of serious self-harm. We're seeing kids who very obviously have signs of depression and very low moods. The longer that kids are here, the more these behaviours become predominant. They begin to show a slow deterioration of spirit and positivity as they become increasingly tired and worn down, leading them to turn to escapist behaviours. Looking for control often leads to the self-harm. They're in control of nothing here.

"Refugees soon heard about the foot clinic in the grounds of the Hotel of Desperate Dan, the name used by locals for the container hotel. The potential for complications of gangrene and surgical debridement as the cases become more severe is highly likely, and it's likely to happen at some point, especially with winter and colder wetter nights in sight.

"Back home, I've known of cases of trench foot cropping up here and there in the recent decades, often amongst homeless populations, but nowhere near on the scale that is being seeing amongst refugees, particularly with the torrential rain this year."

The Doctor rushed off towards one of the treatment tents.

Mirela and Kizzy looked at each other, and Mirela said, "Let's go for it." She began to untie the lacing ribbons on her sari and lifted the shoulder strap over her head, leaving her naked except for her shoes.

Kizzy felt a tingle in her groin and stomach as she looked at now naked Mirela, and then she quickly removed her blouse, brassier, skirt, and knickers. She looked at Mirela, who was standing there and looking at her with a look of smouldering desire. Kizzy felt an excitement and a strong attraction towards her, however she shook it off and pulled on her paper knickers and her paper protective suit. She sat on a lorry tire and pulled on her socks and plimsolls.

Mirela and Kizzy worked as a team, first showering and then bathing in water and disinfectant the naked men, women, and children, but mostly women and children. Then they treated their various skin conditions with the appropriate treatments, as specified in the instruction booklet.

It was unpleasant work, but their noses quickly desensitised to the smell despite the hot temperature. It soon became immaterial whether it was male or female genitalia they were washing or treating.

They worked for six hours without food or drink for infection control reasons, but they felt symptoms of dehydration, especially thirst. Now taking nakedness for granted, they collected their carrier bags with their clothing and walked over to the external shower, unconcerned about the small boys following them at a distance.

Mirela said, "Yes, I suppose you could call this a screen, but it won't stop the men and boys looking if they really want to."

Kizzy surprised herself by saying, "Lets shower together. We can ensure that we don't miss any bits."

The water was reasonably warm, and the two women soaped each other with strong carbolic disinfectant soap. Mirela said with a sly smile, "Use plenty, and give my groin a good rub to get the soap into all my crevasses."

Kizzy gently and slowly washed Mirela's genitalia, and Mirela began to pant. Kizzy suddenly put her arms round Mirela and kissed her.

Mirela responded by hugging her tightly and forcing her mouth open with her tongue.

They broke their embrace when they realised that three small boys had come inside the screens and were looking intently at them. They shooed the boys, but they didn't go away, so they away and dressed in their normal clothes.

As they went towards the hotel, Mirela said, "Is this not the night that Desperate Dan does the extra water run?"

Kizzy quietly answered, "Yes. He won't be home until about midnight."

Chapter Seventy-nine

Kizzy and Mirela Make Love

Mirela said, "Then come to my room, and we can wash off this smelly carbolic."

Kizzy was very apprehensive, but the two women entered the hotel and made their way to Mirela's room, where they stripped again and went into the shower together.

After showering, they nervously dried each other and helped each other fit towel turbans on their wet hair. Kizzy said, "I am not sure about this." She paused, laughed, and added, "It's good to wash that carbolic off, but I can still smell it."

Mirela put her arms around Kizzy, putting her thigh between Kizzy's legs, and they locked tightly together. Kizzy had a memory flashback of lying naked and cuddling her giant teddy bear.

Kizzy involuntarily kissed Mirela. They fell on top of Mirela's bed and began kissing and massaging each other's breasts. After their passions were spent, Mirela became completely relaxed and fell asleep after what had been a gruelling day.

Kizzy began to think. What was this that was happening? She was married to Desperate Dan.

Kizzy was disturbed and confused. She didn't feel for Desperate Dan as she used to, but that was just normal aging, was it not? Or was it that Desperate Dan had become obsessed with his hotel work and his ministry?"

She lay there naked and troubled beside a sleeping Mirela. She looked at the other woman and felt a strong attraction to her, much stronger than she felt for her husband. This realisation shocked and disturbed her. Kizzy was exhausted, and she fell asleep.

She showered again upon waking. Mirela dried her and then blow-dried and brushed her hair with more than tenderness.

Kizzy dressed, left Mirela's flat, and returned to her own at 10 p.m.

Kizzy expected Desperate Dan to come in after midnight. He arrived about 12.45, exhausted and sweaty. Kizzy helped him out of his clothes and started running the shower. He was almost sleeping standing up, and she quickly took off her clothes and helped him into the shower. She soaped him all over, rinsed him, dried him, and then helped him to the bed. He collapsed on to it face down and immediately fell asleep. Kizzy lay beside him with her left hand fondling his neck and hair.

She thought to herself, *what has happened to our love? Is it because of your love of the Bible? Or is it me? Have I always had this nymphomaniac inside me? Not only that, but one with a lesbian aspect to it. Where did my weakness and obsession for sex begin?*

Kizzy thought back to the school summer holidays where three of her female classmates would go to a little wood behind their houses. They would strip naked, pair off, and kiss each other. The kissing would lead to fondling and fingering. It was slow and progressive and sometimes lasted an hour or so. These were the best times she could remember.

Desperate Dan woke at 5 a.m. as usual, got up, did his toilet routines, dressed, and let Kizzy sleep on. He went out for breakfast and to his day's driving.

Kizzy woke after seven and wondered what had happened to Desperate Dan until she looked at the clock, she had slept in. The fact that they hadn't spoken this morning made her feel worse. She felt like a despicable trollop.

Chapter Eighty

Fresh Water Polluted

Desperate Dan began his sermon on the Third Trumpet of Revelations.

"Third Trumpet: John saw a burning star fall from heaven on sources of fresh water, causing the water to become bitter and kill many (verses 10–11).

> And the third angel sounded, and there fell a great star from heaven, burning as it were a lamp, and it fell upon the third part of the rivers, and upon the fountains of waters; And the name of the star is called Wormwood: and the third part of the waters became wormwood; and many men died of the waters, because they were made bitter. (Revelation 8:10–11)

"The world's worst ever nuclear meltdown occurred in 1986 at Chernobyl in Ukraine, at that time one of the states of the Soviet Union.

"Incredibly, Chernobyl is the Russian word for wormwood!

"The prophecy of the third trumpet emphasises that the star called Wormwood made the waters bitter.

Desperate Dan shouted, "Could the third trumpet of Revelations have been sounded in 1986?" He paused. "It is an awesome thing to contemplate the possibility that the third trumpet of Revelation 8 was sounded in 1986.

"Yet the evidence that this is true seems undeniable. What are the odds that the world's greatest ever nuclear accident would occur at a power plant named Wormwood—the exact name prophesied two thousand years ago in the Bible? The prophecy says that it was because of the waters that were made bitter that many men died. The conveyance of nuclear radiation by the water was the thing that caused so many to die.

"Some have thought that the events of the seals, trumpets, and vials of Revelation must all occur during the Great Tribulation, but scripture does not say this.

Chapter Eighty-one

Darkness

Desperate Dan stepped up and started his sermon.

"Fourth Trumpet: The light of the sun, moon and stars upon the earth will be diminished by a third. (Revelation 8:12–13)

"Like the previous trumpet judgements, the fourth affects natural objects—in this case the sun, moon, and stars, resulting in diminished light on the earth. The final three trumpet judgements, which we will begin to address in the next lesson, affect men's lives with pain, death, and hell.

"In this judgement, John notes that "a third of the sun was struck, a third of the moon, and a third of the stars, so that a third of them were darkened". He then reports seeing an eagle fly in mid-heaven, pronouncing woes on the earth's inhabitants, who are about to experience more severe judgement when the fifth, sixth, and seventh trumpets are sounded.

"How can a third of the sun, moon and stars be stricken? Are a third of the stars destroyed, or is the brightness of these celestial bodies dimmed? What's so bad about this judgement? What's the significance of an eagle who speaks? Where is mid-heaven? And why does the eagle give advance warning of the coming woes?

"Let's take a closer look.

"The fourth angel blew his trumpet. As we noted previously, the "trumpet" each angel blows in this series of judgements is the shofar, or ram's horn, and has special significance for Israel. In the case of the trumpet judgements, the sound of the shofar alerts us that Yahweh is moving righteously in judgement, extending His mercy a little while longer for those who will repent, destroying the wicked, rewarding his people, and preparing the created order for new heavens and a new earth.

"It's also important to keep in mind that Yahweh's judgement falls only after his calls to repentance go unheeded.

"The flood in Noah's day comes 120 years after Noah begins building the ark and warning the earth's wicked about God's coming wrath. The idolatrous residents of Canaan are destroyed to make room for the Israelites only after their measure of sin is full; Yahweh waits patiently for nearly half a millennium for them to set aside their idolatry until it is clear to all that they will not.

"And Yeshua graciously delays His return so that people have ample opportunity to turn to him in faith (2 Peter 3:8–9). Unbelievers who stand before the him in final judgement will not be able to say they didn't have time to repent—or to offer up any other excuses (Romans 1:20).

"John writes that "a third of the sun was struck, a third of the moon, and a third of the stars, so that a third of them were darkened. A third of the day was without light, and the night as well".

"There are some similarities between the fourth trumpet judgement and the sixth seal judgement in Revelation 6:12–14. In both cases, the sun, moon, and stars are affected. But in the sixth seal judgement, it appears the darkening of the entire sun is due to an earthquake that perhaps is connected to a volcano, which in turn spews ash far into the atmosphere. The moon appears to turn blood red, perhaps for the same reason.

"And the stars of heaven fall to earth as a fig tree drops its unripe figs when shaken by a high wind. This could be a description of meteors. But as we read about the fourth trumpet judgement, it seems Yahweh touches these celestial objects directly, reducing light in the daytime and the night by one-third.

"Some commentators take this judgement literally, likening it to the plague of darkness that falls upon Egypt in the days of Moses. Others understand these words symbolically. Regardless of whether John's words are to be taken literally or figuratively, darkness in scripture often is a sign of Yahweh's judgement.

"In Exodus 10, God sends "thick darkness" throughout Egypt for three days in the ninth plague. In Isaiah 13, Yahweh tells of a day when he will bring disaster on the world: "Indeed, the stars of the sky and its constellations will not give their light. The sun will be dark when it rises, and the moon will not shine" (Isaiah 13:10).

"In Isaiah 34, at the judgement of the nations, "All the heavenly bodies will dissolve. The skies will roll up like a scroll, and their stars will all wither as leaves wither on the vine, and foliage on the fig tree" (Isaiah 34:4).

"In Ezekiel 32, Yahweh tells the king of Egypt, "When I snuff you out, I will cover the heavens and darken their stars. I will cover the sun with a cloud, and the moon will not give its light" (Ezekiel 32:7).

"In Joel 2, we are told that the day of the Lord is coming: "A day of darkness and gloom, a day of clouds and dense overcast … The sun and moon grow dark, and the stars cease their shining … The sun will be turned to darkness and the moon to blood before the great and awe-inspiring Day of the Lord comes" (Joel 2:2, 10, 31).

"In Amos 5, we read that the Day of the Lord "will be darkness and not light … Won't the Day of the Lord be darkness rather than light, even gloom without any brightness in it" (Amos 5:18, 20).

"And in Mark 13:24–25, Yeshua warns us that just before His return,

"The sun will be darkened, and the moon will not shed its light; the stars will be falling from the sky, and the celestial powers will be shaken."

"The first three trumpet judgements impact a third of the land and waters, but the fourth judgement affects the entire world. Why? Because it gets to the very source of the earth's life and energy, the sun. With one-third less sunlight on the earth, there will be one-third less energy available to support the life systems of man and nature. Think of the vast changes in temperatures that will occur and how these will affect human health and food growth. It is possible that this judgement is temporary, for the fourth bowl judgement will reverse it, and the sun's power will be intensified (Revelation 16:8–9).

"Even more, under the cloak of darkness, human depravity no doubt will thrive. As Yeshua reminds us, "For everyone who practices wicked things hates the light and avoids it, so that his deeds may not be exposed" (John 3:20). It will take the blinding light of Messiah Yeshua's return to finally drive out all darkness.

"One additional thought: the precise impact of this judgement on the sun, moon, and stars isn't clear. The text says that a third of the day was without light, and the night as well. If the days are made shorter, the nights should be longer, but that does not appear to be what is happening. Likely, the celestial bodies are smitten in such a way as to diminish their light-giving (or in the case of the moon, light-reflecting) qualities.

Chapter Eighty-two

Wind and Rain

Desperate Dan dedicated a sermon on hurricanes and typhoons. Hurricanes, typhoons and cyclones are huge storms, they are basically the same, but In the Atlantic and Northeast Pacific, the term "hurricane" is used. The same type of disturbance in the Northwest Pacific is called a "typhoon" and "cyclones" occur in the South Pacific and Indian Ocean.

In recent decades these have been getting more sever, now they can be up to 600 miles across and have strong winds spiralling inward and upward at speeds of 75 to 200 mph.

Each hurricane usually lasts for over a week, moving 10–20 miles per hour over the open ocean.

Hurricanes gather heat and energy through contact with warm ocean waters.

Evaporation from the seawater increases their power.

Hurricanes rotate in a counter-clockwise direction around an "eye" in the Northern Hemisphere and clockwise direction in the Southern Hemisphere.

The centre of the storm or "eye" is the calmest part.

It has only light winds and fair weather.

When they come onto land, the heavy rain, strong winds and large waves can damage buildings, trees and cars.

He went on: "How do hurricanes form?

Storm surges are frequently the most devastating element of a hurricane and can be up to tens of meters high.

As a hurricane's winds spiral around and around the storm, they push water into a mound at the storm's centre. This mound of water becomes dangerous when the storm reaches land because it causes flooding along the coast. The water piles up, unable to escape anywhere but on land as the storm carries it landward. A hurricane will cause more storm surge in areas where the ocean floor slopes gradually. This causes major flooding.

When does hurricane season start?

The Atlantic hurricane season is from June 1 to November 30, but most hurricanes occur during the fall months.

The Eastern Pacific hurricane season is from May 15 to November 30.

The increasing severity of hurricanes is due to global warming, and they will get worse.

Chapter Eighty-three

Hurricanes, Earthquakes, and Volcanoes

N ext Sabbath, Desperate Dan stepped up to the lectern and started his new sermon.

Donald Trump denies climate change yet witnesses the most devastating effects of Hurricane Irma: property damage, lives lost, and severe flooding.

Hurricane Irma's recent rampage across the Caribbean and southeastern United States has been blamed as a backlash of global warming driven by humanity's polluting activities, but no one seems to take real action to reverse it.

While a warmer world will not necessarily mean more hurricanes, it will see a rise in the frequency of the most powerful, and therefore more destructive, variety. As the Atlantic continues to heat up, the trend is widely expected to be towards more powerful and wetter storms. An additional feature is that mid-latitude storms may become clustered, bringing the prospect of one after another event of damaging and disruptive winds.

Tornadoes, typhoons, hurricanes and mid-latitude storms, along with heat waves and floods, are widely regarded as climate change's weather effects; they are forecast to accelerate the destruction, loss of life, and financial pain as planet earth continues to heat up.

Here is something that you don't hear on the news.

An earthquake that is ready to go is like a coiled spring; all that is needed is a trigger.

Reduced atmospheric pressure that characterises these powerful hurricanes and typhoons is enough to allow earthquake faults deep within the crust to move more easily and release accumulated strain. An earthquake fault that is primed and ready to go is like a coiled spring.

It also seems that the huge volume of rain dumped by tropical cyclones, leading to severe flooding, may also be linked to earthquakes.

In some parts of the tropics, large earthquakes tend to follow exceptionally wet hurricanes or typhoons, most notably the devastating quake that took up to 220,000 lives in Haiti in 2010.

It is possible that floodwaters are lubricating fault planes. The 2015 Nepal earthquake took close to 9,000 lives. During the summer monsoon season, rain soak into the lowlands of the Indo-Gangetic plain, immediately to the south of the mountain range, which then slowly drains away over the next few months.

This annual rainwater loading and unloading of the crust is mirrored by the level of earthquake activity, which is significantly lower during the summer months than during the winter.

And it isn't only earthquake faults that today's storms and torrential rains are able to trigger.

Volcanoes seem to be susceptible too.

On the Caribbean island of Montserrat, heavy rains have been implicated in triggering eruptions of the active la Soufrière Hills volcano.

Alaska's Pavlof volcano appears to respond not to wind or rain, but to tiny seasonal changes in sea level.

The volcano seems to prefer to erupt in the late autumn and winter, when weather patterns are such that water levels adjacent to this coastal volcano climb by a few tens of centimetres.

If today's weather can bring forth earthquakes and magma from the Earth's crust, it doesn't take much to imagine how the solid Earth is likely to respond to the large-scale environmental adjustments that accompany rapid climate change.

Now, global average temperatures are shooting up again and are already more than one degree centigrade higher than during preindustrial times. It should come as no surprise that the solid Earth is starting to respond once more.

In southern Alaska, which has in places lost a vertical kilometre of ice cover, the reduced load on the crust is already increasing the level of seismic activity.

In high mountain ranges across the world from the Caucasus in the north to New Zealand's southern Alps, longer and more intense heat waves are melting the ice and thawing the permafrost that keeps mountain faces intact, leading to a rise in major landslides.

Does this all mean that we are in for a more geologically active future as well as a hotter and meteorologically more violent one?

Where an earthquake fault or volcano is primed and ready to go, climate change may provide that trigger that brings forward the timing of a quake or eruption that would eventually have happened anyway.

As the world continues to heat up, any geological response is likely to be most obvious where climate change is driving the biggest environmental changes. For example, in areas where ice and permafrost are vanishing fast, or in coastal regions where rising sea levels will play an increasing role.

Iceland is rapidly rising due to hydraulic pressure. Whether this will cause more, or bigger, eruptions remain uncertain.

Climate change is melting of ice on many volcanoes worldwide.

The potential for more landslides is also likely to be a problem in high mountain ranges as the ice cover that hold rock faces together vanishes.

Looking ahead, one of the key places to watch will be Greenland, where large masses of ice have been lost recently. More earthquakes in Greenland seem certain. The submerged margins of Greenland are currently not very well mapped, so the likelihood of a future earthquake triggering a landslide capable of generating a major tsunami in the North Atlantic is unknown.

One of the world's largest lava domes has been discovered in an underwater volcano south of Japan, suggesting an enormous build-up of magma may exist underneath it. The bulge of molten rock beneath underwater structure could be capable of triggering super-eruption like one that took place 7300 years ago.

Desperate Dan shouted, "The bottom line in all of this is; that as climate change progresses, we should certainly contemplate more and bigger hurricanes with loss of life and property damage, flooding, droughts, famines, tribal conflicts, earthquakes, volcanoes, and war."

Chapter Eighty-four

Where Are We on the Revelation Timeline?

D esperate Dan climbed on to his platform and began to speak.

This is where we are at on the Revelation timeline. The Jesuits are gathering the major religions against each other by pitting the Muslim kings of the East (Syria, Jordan, Iraq, Saudi Arabia, Kuwait, Iran, etc.), against Israel. This will lead to World War III, where Muslim countries and Israel will war against each other. World War III will cause the world to cry out for peace and safety, and the World Religious Leader may offer unity and peace in its One World Government, promising that it will prevent any future religious wars.

Before the Jesuits push the world into their One World Government, I believe that they will want every country to have a Jesuit-Rothschild central bank, so that they can control the money supply (**to determine who can buy and sell**). The countries that do not have a Jesuit-Rothschild central bank yet are Syria, Iran, and North Korea, which is why they are being demonised as the enemy, to justify military action against them.

Before or after World War III, there will most likely be a worldwide financial collapse, which will shut down commerce, preventing people from buying and selling food and goods. The World Religious leader may proclaim that they have been preparing for this inevitable event, saying that they have planned out a solution which will allow people to buy and sell in their One World financial system.

In Revelation 16:15, Messiah Yeshua is warning his followers that he is coming soon. This tells us that he will not have come until after the sixth bowl. I believe that he will allow the One World Government to form, and the mark of the beast to be enforced, before he returns. "Behold, I am coming as a thief. Blessed is he who watches, and keeps his garments, lest he walk naked and they see his shame."

Messiah Yeshua's return will be like a thief to believers who do not know prophecy fulfilment, but to those who know where we are at on the prophecy fulfilment timeline, they will be watching and not be caught by surprise.

The proper context of Messiah Yeshua's return is the fall Feast of Trumpets. Elohim's seven holy feast days are divine appointments which Messiah Yeshua is still fulfilling to redeem his set-apart ones.

He fulfilled the spring feast days of Passover (representing his death), Unleavened Bread (representing his sinlessness) and First Fruits (representing his resurrection). He poured out his Father's Spirit on the summer Feast of Pentecost.

Messiah will return at the "last trump", on the fall Feast of Trumpets, which represents the harvest.

We don't know the year that he will return, but we know the proper context, so we must wait for World War III and the formation of the One World Government. I don't believe that he will return until those things happen.

World War III will lead to the formation of the One World Government of the seventh bowl.

Earthquakes in prophecy represent government upheaval, so this mighty and great earthquake in Revelation 16:18 symbolises the formation of the New World Order, which is split into three parts.

It will be the greatest political upheaval in history!

"The cities of the nation's fell" and "every island fled away, and the mountains were not found" speak of the time when the great countries and cities will lose their independent powers and be subservient to the New World Order. It's telling us that the Roman beast, called the great city, will control the world via their three city-state corporations, which are already in place.

The religion part is the city-state corporation of Vatican City, which is used to control the world's religious and political leaders.

The financial part is the city-state corporation of London, which is used to control the world's financial and trade organisations.

But Brexit may cause the re-location of the London financial centres to Frankfurt in an increasingly powerful Germany.

And the military part is the city-state corporation of the District of Columbia, which is used to control the world's intelligence and military powers.

The antichrist beast religious leader and the false prophet Jesuit general will most likely rule their One World Government from Jerusalem, because it is the place that connects all the major religions. And no doubt they want to rule from there because it was the central place of the people of Elohim.

Who you revere during the One World Government will determine whose mark you have.

Chapter Eighty-five

Iran Builds Road across Syria

Desperate Dan opened his sermon.

Danger! Danger! Danger!

Iran has changed the course of a land corridor to the Mediterranean coast.

It has now swung down through Isis-occupied town of Mayadin as a hub in eastern Syria, avoiding the Kurdish north-east.

The changes have been ordered by Maj Gen Qassem Suleimani, commander of the Shia-dominated Quds force, and Haidar al-Ameri, the leader of the Popular Mobilisation Front in Iraq.

As the project has taken shape, the evolving Syrian conflict has added new difficulties.

The US build-up in north-eastern Syria has alarmed officials in Baghdad and Tehran.

Iran's game plan emerges: a road to the Mediterranean

Militias controlled by Tehran are poised to complete a land corridor that would give Iran huge power in the region

Observers said Isis was fighting fiercely to defend the town, which has remained a hotbed of Salafi jihadi fighters since the US-led invasion of Iraq fourteen years ago.

The fall of Ba'aj will be devastating to Isis's shrinking presence in Iraq, leaving parts of Anbar province as the its last remaining stronghold in the place where it all began for the terror group more than a decade ago.

As Isis has rapidly lost ground in Iraq, attention has been diverting to the next—and possibly final—phase of the war, the push to take its last strongholds in Syria, which include Raqqa and Deir Azzour.

The political jostling has made the battlefield in Syria even more complex, forcing Iran to change course on one of its most important long-term goals, just as its progress had seemed assured.

Iraqi officials say that the newly chosen route is from Deir Azzour to Sukhna to Palmyra, then Damascus, and towards the Lebanese border, where the central goal of emboldening Hezbollah could partially be achieved through demographic swaps.

From there, a path to Latakia and the Mediterranean Sea has also been envisaged, giving Iran a supply line that avoids the heavily patrolled Persian Gulf waters.

This new road will allow Iran to transport troops, weapons and supplies to its intended attack on Israel.

Chapter Eighty-six

Russia Prepares to Lead Attack on Israel

Desperate Dan and Esmeralda watched the news. It was coming to the end of 2018, and Iran had nearly established a road across Syria to the Mediterranean.

Dan said, "It is time to do a warning sermon on Russia, Iran, and Libya."

Esmeralda sat upright in her wheelchair. "Yes, you must blow the warning Shofar. Israel is in great danger."

The next Sabbath, Desperate Dan blew long and hard on a Shofar, then and he delivered his message with confidence.

Yahweh foretold that Israel would arise miraculously from the graveyard of the nations, where she was buried with the ruins of Jerusalem in AD 70 by the Roman army led by Titus.

Incredibly, Yahweh promised 2,600 years ago, through Ezekiel, that the Jews, after almost two thousand years of exile, would return to the Promised Land.

The ancient prophets also foretold that the Jewish exiles would become "a mighty army" in her ancient homeland.

More than twenty-five hundred years ago, Ezekiel prophesied about an invasion by Russia (called "Magog") and her allies that would occur during the last days, "after many days."

He said that after Israel was reborn as a nation, Russia and her allies would attack her in a violent attempt to annihilate the Jewish state.

Naturally, Ezekiel did not describe the present nations of Russia, Syria, and Iraq by their modern names.

Rather, he referred to them by the names of the ancient tribes that occupied the geographical territories of the present nations at the time of his writing.

The Nations of Ezekiel 38: 1 6	
The Ancient Nations	**The Modern Nations**
The land of Magog - Meshech and Tubal - Persia – Ethiopi – Libya – Ashkenaz – Gomer - Togarmah - "Many peoples with thee"	Russia - Somewhere in Russia – Iran - Iraq - Afghanistan - Ethiopia and Sudan - Libya - Austria and Germany - Eastern Europe - Southeastern - Europe – Turkey - Various other nations allied to Russia

The first war, as described by Ezekiel, is the War of Gog and Magog (a Russian-Arab invasion against Israel), the subject of this chapter.

The second war, known as the Battle of Armageddon, will occur a minimum of seven years later. Armageddon is described in the prophecies of Joel, Zechariah, and especially the book of Revelation (16:16). This cataclysmic conflict will involve nations across the entire world as the significant armies of the East battle against the armies of the West under the Antichrist.

The Coming Russian-Arab Invasion of Israel

Bible prophecy also provides some insight into the ongoing peace negotiations between Israel and its Arab neighbours. Thousands of years ago, the prophet Ezekiel (chapters 38–39) predicted that a huge confederacy of Arab nations under Russian leadership would join to attack Israel in the generation after the Jewish exiles returned to their homeland. Despite massive changes in Russia, the hard-liners in the KGB, the army, and the military-industrial complex maintain their solid grip on the levers of power.

But the aggressors will not prevail.

After three and one-half years, the Antichrist will betray Israel and break the treaty. He will enter Jerusalem and claim to be Yahweh.

When he demands, that Israel worships him, most of the Jews will rebel against him. The book of Revelation describes the righteous Jews fleeing into the wilderness for 1260 days (three and one-half years) after this betrayal.

When the "Gog and Magog" invasion occurs, it appears that the only response from the Western democracies will be a diplomatic protest. (what's new?)

Ezekiel 38:13 says that "Sheba and Dedan and the merchants of Tarshish" and "the young lions thereof, (probably the United Kingdom, the United States, and the British Commonwealth nations) shall say unto thee, "Art thou come to take a spoil?"

Tarshish, Sheba, and Dedan were ancient trading nations and are believed by many Bible scholars to refer to Spain or Britain and their former colonies ("the young lions thereof"). It will not be the Western democracies that respond to this attack.

The superpower who intervenes to save Israel in its greatest hour of need will be their great defender, the Elohim Yahweh of Abraham.

The prophecy recorded in Ezekiel 38:21 and 39:21 ¬ 22 indicates that Yahweh's purpose in this extraordinary intervention in history is to glorify and sanctify His Holy Name in the sight of Israel and the Gentile nations".

Desperate Dan began to shout:

"The awesome destruction associated with this victory over the Russian-Arab armies will not be confined solely to the invading armies.

Yahweh declared, "And I will send a fire on Magog, and among them that dwell carelessly in the isles: and they shall know that I am the Lord" (Ezekiel 39:6). Russia (Magog) will be devastated by the wrath of Yahweh, as well as those nations "dwelling carelessly in the isles" which may refer to Britain and Her Commonwealth of nations including America and western coastal European nations (the Celtic nations).

We need to wake up this sounds like nuclear and includes the English-speaking nations".

Desperate Dan took time to calm down:

"Although Scripture does not indicate the year in which this future invasion and defeat of Russia will occur, the prophet Haggai gives us a strong indication of what the actual day may be.

Haggai reveals that on the twenty-fourth day of the ninth month (Chisleu) of the Jewish calendar, the day before Hanukkah, God will deliver Israel as He did twice before on this day:

(1) the defeat of the Syrian army and recapture of the Temple in 165 BC and

(2) the British capture of Jerusalem from the Turks in 1917 during the closing battles of WWI.

The prophet Haggai declares: "The Word of the Lord came unto Haggai in the four and twentieth day of the month (Chisleu), saying, Speak to Zerubbabel, governor of Judah, saying, I will shake the heavens and the earth; and I will overthrow the throne of kingdoms and I will destroy the strength of the kingdoms of the heathen; and I will overthrow the chariots, and those that ride in them; and the horses and their riders shall come down, everyone by the sword of his brother" (Haggai 2:20¬22).

This description by Haggai, and the exact language of his prophecy, is like the language of Ezekiel 38 and 39 that describes Russia's defeat.

The interesting point is that Haggai names the exact day of the year 18th December Gregorian calendar, on which this will occur.

Since so many other prophecies have been so precisely fulfilled to the day, there is a strong probability that this prophetic event will also occur on its appointed anniversary date of the biblical calendar. "Behold, it is come, and it is done, saith the Lord God; this is the day whereof I have spoken" (Ezekiel 39:8). God's appointment with Russia is set; it will not be postponed.

Russia has prepositioned enormous military supplies in Lebanon, Iraq, Syria, Libya, and Egypt in preparation for the coming Russian-Arab invasion of Israel.

Ezekiel 38 and 39 that describe an oral tradition recorded from the Vilna Gaon that advises Jews to observe carefully when the Russian fleet (Magog) passes from the Black Sea through the Bosporus to the Mediterranean. "It is now the time to put on your Sabbath clothes because the Messiah is coming." For the first time in history, the Russian Navy has surpassed all other navies in the world in size.

> Behold, it is come, and it is done, saith the Lord Yahweh;
> this is the day whereof I have spoken. (Ezekiel 39:8)

Desperate Dan finished. "Well, my good friends, hunker down. We may be as safe here in Jordon as anywhere but get ready to rock and roll. You are certainly going to feel the earth shake. Yahweh's appointment with Russia is set; it will not be postponed.

All together: Shabbat shalom and Hallelu Yah, Hallelu Yah, Hallelu Yah."

About the Author

Ernie Hasler began working for the Ministry of Defence at Royal Ordnance in Bishopton, Scotland, when he was sixteen. From his beginnings as an apprentice engineer, he retired fifty-one years later as a health and safety advisor. He was the first advisor in Scotland to earn the NEBOSH diploma in environmental management and as a result of this knowledge presently funds the planting of 20,000 tree seeds each year.

For years, Hasler funded the Plant Tree Save Planet charity, mainly with support from his two sisters, although his work colleagues also gave donations on his birthday. The financial donations helped women in poor nations start their own tree nurseries. The charity closed when age and poor health prevented him from properly vetting recipients. He continues funding tree planting through Trees for the Future.

Hasler has been a voluntary trustee with Emmaus Glasgow for two decades, helping the organisation transform from a concept into a thriving community of twenty-seven previously homeless people.

Emmaus Glasgow now matches Hasler's giving to Trees for the Future.

Hasler steering a friend's boat past the lair of the nuclear monsters on the River Clyde.

Printed in Great
Britain
by Amazon

31382140R00244